Divergent Deaths

Deborah Rine

Divergent Death is a work of fiction. The characters, incidents, and dialogue are drawn from the author's imagination and are not to be construed as real. Any resemblance to actual events or persons, living or dead, is entirely coincidental.

Divergent Deaths: Copyright © November 2015 by Deborah Rine. All rights reserved. No part of this book may be used or reproduced in any manner whatsoever without written permission except in the case of brief quotations embodied in critical articles and reviews.

ISBN-13: 978-1519392572

ISBN-10: 1519392575

For

Larry Rine

My consultant and helpmate.

Books by Deborah Rine

Banner Bluff Mystery Series:

THE LAKE

FACE BLIND

Contemporary Novel:

RAW GUILT

Deborah Rine can be contacted at:

> www.deborah-rine-author.com
>
> http://dcrine.blogspot.com/
>
> Face book and Twitter

Acknowledgements

Thank you to Diane Piron-Gelman, my editor, who continues to instruct me in the art of writing.

Thanks to Meg Dolan, my superb book cover artist.

Thanks to Patrol Sergeant Kevin Zelk of the Lake Forest Illinois Police Department for taking the time to discuss crime scene techniques.

Thanks to Lia Reich of the PrecisionHawk Company.

Thanks for the inspiration of the wonderful Chicago Botanic Gardens.

An Ancient Prayer of the Woods

I am the heat of your hearth on the cold winter nights,
the friendly shade screening you from the summer sun,
and my fruits are refreshing droughts,
quenching your thirst as you journey on.
I am the beam that holds your house,
the board of your table,
the bed on which you lie,
and the timber that builds your boat.
I am the handle of your hoe,
the door of your homestead,
the wood of your cradle,
and the shell of your coffin.
I am the bread of kindness and the flower of beauty.
'Ye, who pass by, listen to my prayer: Harm me not.'

(A prayer used in Portuguese forest preservation for more than 1,000 years)

Chapter 1
Tuesday morning

E8494E96299882E9679E016.1

Tom stood in the kitchen peering at his iPhone. Francesca was emptying the dishwasher and humming to herself.

"Hey. Check this out." He frowned at the phone screen.

Francesca glanced at it. "It must be a secret code. Lots of E's and 9's. The Department of Homeland Security is going to wonder what you're up to." She raised her eyebrows. "Maybe communicating with a terrorist?"

"I got the same thing last night, but I deleted it."

"Who's texting you?"

"It comes up *unknown*. I'm going to save it this time and have Coyote Blackfoot check it out." He was still frowning and pondering the small screen. Francesca looked up at him. Tom was Banner Bluff's Chief of Police. Tall and solid, he presented a commanding figure. Normally quiet and watchful, he was rarely the life of the party. This morning he was in uniform, his dark blond hair still damp, his full lips pursed.

Francesca reached up, wrapped her arms around his neck and kissed him. He put his free arm around her waist and pulled her close. They stood that way, pressed together.

"Hmm, that was nice," Tom murmured. "Maybe I'll stay home today." He nuzzled her neck.

Francesca gave him another brief kiss and then pulled away. "Unfortunately I won't be here this morning. I'm off to the Banner

Botanic Gardens. I've got an in-service training for volunteers. That's why I'm rushing around. I've got to write one article before I head over to the Gardens."

"Well, okay. I guess I'll go to work after all. What else are you doing today?"

"After the training session, I'm having lunch with Delia Banner. Then I'm going to the office to meet with Vicki. She's back from college and wants to work for me part-time this summer. We're going to discuss her job."

"Okay, then." He turned to leave.

"Let me copy down that secret code. Maybe I can figure it out."

He handed her his phone. She took it and a light blue pad of paper, carefully copied down the series of numbers and letters, and gave the phone back.

"I'll be home about six. Nothing earth-shaking is happening today," Tom said.

"Me, too. Let's grill tonight…maybe some steaks. Sound good?"

"Superb!" Tom kissed her again lightly on the lips and patted her rump. Then he went into the hall to the closet safe. He tapped in the code, took out his gun and placed it in its holster. Francesca didn't know the code and didn't want to. She'd marched in several rallies against Illinois' new concealed weapon law. It was ironic that she'd fallen madly in love with a gun-carrying policeman.

Francesca heard the front door bang shut. Tom was gone. She always felt a moment of regret when he left. She sighed and went into her study at the back of the house. The windows faced south onto a wide green lawn bordered with a mad array of flowers and bushes…*mad* being the operative word. Tom's deceased wife had been a master gardener and maintained a beautiful yard.

Initially, Francesca told Tom she was volunteering at the Botanic Gardens in order to write a series of articles. She was editor-in-chief of the *Banner Bee*, an online newspaper that served the town of Banner Bluff and surrounding communities. The *Bee* covered local events and provided a forum where citizens could voice their views. She'd begun the *Bee* on a small scale and it had grown considerably since its inception. She now had a large raft of advertisers and an ever-growing number of readers.

The truth was Francesca was volunteering so she could return the backyard to its former glory. When she finally admitted her plan to Tom late one night after they'd shared a bottle of pinot noir, Tom hadn't been too pleased.

"I don't want you to feel you're competing with Candy. She was one person, you're another. You're perfect the way you are."

She nestled closer to him on the sofa. "I don't feel like I'm competing. I just want to figure out how to rein in the jungle out there."

Tom sighed. "Sometimes I think we should have started our married life in a new house."

"I don't feel Candy's shadow here. If anything, she's like a sister who loved you like I do." Francesca reached for his hand, warm on her thigh.

Tom groaned. "This is beginning to sound like polygamy."

Francesca laughed. "Anyway, I want the yard to look nice when we have our party, don't you?" Francesca and Tom had married quickly and quietly in March, with the thought of having a reception for family and friends in the summer when the weather was nice. They'd chosen August 19th as the date.

The kitchen clock read eight. Francesca went upstairs for a shower. The master bedroom was at the end of the hall. She passed another bedroom on the right, a guest room containing the bedroom furniture from her condo. On the left was a laundry room, a full bath and a third bedroom right next to the master. The door was shut, as always. Francesca opened it.

Sunlight poured in from two windows that overlooked the backyard. The room was painted yellow and white. A border of yellow duckies, interspersed with pink and blue flowers, marched around the top of the wall. The only furniture was a brand new white crib and a changing table, intended for Tom and Candy's unborn child. Not long after Candy got pregnant, they'd discovered she had a virulent form of cancer. She, and the unborn baby, died within a few months.

Tom kept the door shut. He didn't want to see this room. He didn't want to talk about having a baby someday. He refused to discuss it whenever she brought it up.

Francesca let out a breath, left the door open and went into the master bedroom.

#

Tom whistled as he backed out of the driveway. He felt happy, wonderfully happy. Five years ago, when Candy died, he had thought his life was over. Then a few years later he'd met Francesca and his life had taken on a new rhythm.

On the whole, Tom prided himself on being logical and clearheaded. He kept his feelings in check and responded to things by thinking first, then acting. These qualities made him a good policeman and had earned him advancement to Chief of Police in Banner Bluff.

Heading down the street, he waved to Kate Marshall, who was pushing a stroller on her way to the farmers' market. She raised her arm and smiled. The Marshalls had three children and lived a block away. Rosie, the eldest, was a handful.

Tom drove past the farmers' market that was already in full swing. The colorful canopy-tents sheltered fruit, vegetable and flower stands. He could hear a guitar and flute along with chattering voices and laughter. Everyone in town made it a point to buy their produce locally. He saw Officer Romano talking to Lorinda Landers. In Tom's memory, there had never been an incident at the market. But citizens liked to see a friendly policeman on patrol. When you got right down to it, it was good PR.

He swung into the parking lot behind the police station. As he got out of the car, Detective Sergeant Ron Puchalski came out of the building. Puchalski was a tall man with Nordic features, sandy blond hair and clear blue eyes. His uniform was impeccable, his shoes polished to a shine, his hair perfectly trimmed.

"Hey, Chief, I'm on my way to the lake. Doc Stoddard called last night. He asked me to come down and take a look at a piece of wreckage he dragged up. You want to come?"

"Let me go in and check with Arlyne. I don't know what's on my calendar this morning."

"Okay, I'll be out here."

Inside, Tom walked down the hall to his office. Several pink message slips were aligned neatly on his desk. Nothing looked pressing. He could drive down to Lake Michigan with Puchalski. He called down to Arlyne, said he'd be back in thirty minutes, then went outside and got into Puchalski's patrol car.

"So what's this about? What wreckage?" Tom attached his seat belt and opened the window part way. It was about seventy degrees, a perfect spring day.

Puchalski pulled out of the lot. "Doc claims he found part of a boat. He wouldn't say any more; just that we should take a look at it."

"Hm. Sounds mysterious," Tom said.

Doc Stoddard managed the marina in the summertime. Banner Bluff had a small harbor and dock, where local youngsters took sailing and kayaking lessons. Stoddard owned an ancient wooden fishing boat, and went out on fishing expeditions with other old codgers whenever Lake Michigan was calm. Tom was sure these excursions included a case of beer. Stories floated around that Doc had been a physician, until he was hit be a malpractice suit that held him responsible for a baby's death. The suit dragged on and on, and at the end of it all, Doc left medicine and became a handyman, fisherman and boat aficionado. Whatever the truth of it, Tom knew one thing—Doc was a lot smarter than he let on.

"Yeah. He sounded worried." Puchalski looked over at Tom. "That's why I thought we'd check it out."

They reached the bluffs above Lake Michigan. Puchalski put the car in park and got out to open the gate at the head of the service road. The steep ramp beyond led down to the beach. He rummaged in his pocket for the key, walked around to the front of the car, and bent over to unlock the gate. A moment later he straightened, turned to Tom and shook his head. He pushed on the metal crossbar, and the gate swung open with a loud screech.

Puchalski got back in the car. "Somebody left that gate open again."

"It's hard to know who's responsible. So many people have a key to the padlock these days, between the park district staff, the guys working at the pumping station and everyone who borrows a key for a picnic and forgets to turn it in," Tom said.

They drove down the ramp to the lake. To the north stretched a wide sandy beach with a children's play area and a beach shelter complete with stone fireplace. Straight ahead, a low wall of boulders formed a breakwater. To the south, another beach formed a bay. The marina lay beyond.

Tom looked out at the sparkling water. Today it was a deep blue. Seagulls sailed through the sky, looping down to the surf. "It's beautiful down here."

"Yeah, heaven on earth…in the summer, anyway. In the winter it's the next best thing to Antarctica." Puchalski turned right, taking the road around the beach up against the bluff.

As they approached the marina, Tom looked along the shoreline and noted deep ruts in the sand. "Looks like some kids drove down to the water's edge in a truck."

"Yeah, and then they dragged something back to the road." Puchalski gestured. "See, there's a smooth path leading the other way."

Tom shook his head. "That's probably who left the gate open."

They continued around the beach to the marina and dock. The road ended at a parking area next to a weathered wooden shack with a small porch. This was Doc Stoddard's kingdom. Most days in the summer he sat outside in an old rocking chair, puffing away. He was about the only person Tom knew who still smoked a pipe. Today, the porch was empty.

Puchalski parked next to Doc's Volvo station wagon. They got out and walked together towards the shack. No one was around. It was early in the season and Lake Michigan was still frigid. After the winter ice and snow melt, it took a long time for the water to warm up, and few people ventured out on the lake.

They walked up the porch steps and Tom knocked on the door. They waited. He knocked again. "Are you sure he said he'd be down here at this hour?"

"Yep. He said he'd be here all morning." Puchalski stepped over to one of the windows that flanked the door. The blinds were drawn on both. "What's bothering me is he sounded upset on the phone last night. Not like his normal laid-back self."

Tom tried the doorknob. It didn't turn. He gestured with his thumb. "What's around back?"

"I think there's another entrance."

They went down the stairs and around the small building. Tom tried the back door, but it was locked as well. They continued around the shack. A rowboat leaned against the side wall, one oar balanced next to it. Another oar lay some distance away, as if flung into the sand.

They continued around to the front again and went back up on the porch.

"Let me call him," Puchalski said. He pulled out his cell and tapped the screen. An instant later they heard a phone ringing inside the shack. It rang several times but no one picked up.

Tom frowned. "I think we should break in. Doc's an old guy. For all we know, he had a heart attack or something."

Puchalski stepped back, then plowed shoulder first into the door. It flew open and he nearly fell forward. Tom came up behind him and they both peered inside.

The light from the open doorway spilled across the room. Doc Stoddard's body lay face down on the wooden floor in a pool of blood. His head was smashed to a bloody pulp; his hands were splayed to either side of his head; his pipe hacked to bits.

Chapter 2
Tuesday morning

Francesca found a seat halfway down on the aisle. She looked around the auditorium. There were about fifty people all spread out in different rows. It made her smile. People wanted to keep their distance and nobody except one eager beaver dared sit in the front row. It was just like her lecture courses in college.

Two seats over to her left was a woman in a worn black pantsuit with a crumpled white shirt. Her legs were crossed and Francesca could see scuffed low-heeled black shoes. Her short brown hair could do with a trim. She looked harried and barely put together, or maybe she didn't give a damn how she dressed.

Sensing Francesca's appraising scrutiny; the woman turned and met her gaze. A pretty face, in a way. She was about thirty-five, Francesca's age, and her grey eyes were sharp and calculating. Francesca found herself drawing back under the aggressive stare. Then the woman's face broke into a broad smile and she stuck out her hand. "Hi, Melinda Jordan."

Francesca smiled in return and shook the woman's hand. It was rough and callused. "Hi. I'm Francesca Barnett. What brought you here today?"

"I'm a nut about plants and gardening. I moved here recently and I'm in an apartment, all I have is a window box to grow a few geraniums. I decided this would be a good way to help out in the community and get my hands dirty. What about you?"

The casual chatter didn't match the woman's sharp-eyed gaze, Francesca thought. "I've got a two-fold agenda. I'm the editor of the *Banner Bee*, an online newspaper for the local area, and I thought it would be fun to do some stories about what goes on in the Banner Botanic Gardens."

Melinda frowned. "I haven't heard about the *Banner Bee*. I'll have to check it out."

"It's great for learning about what's going on in town. My second reason for being here is that I recently got married. The house we live in has a big garden and I want to learn how to take care of the plants and flowers. I'm somewhat clueless about gardening." *Why am I telling this woman my life story?*

Melinda laughed and then asked, "Have you lived here a long time?"

"About ten years." Francesca noted that Melinda wore no rings. Never married? Divorced?

"So you must know a lot of people in town."

"Well, yes. I suppose I do. Partly because of my job…lots of hobnobbing."

"Do you know the people who work here at the Gardens?"

Francesca felt bombarded with questions. "Actually, I don't. Or, I take that back. I know one young man who just got back from college, who'll be working here this summer."

"What's his name?"

It seemed an odd question, but Francesca answered anyway. "Colman Canfield. He's an exceptional young man. He's attending Stanford."

Melinda's gaze sharpened. "Stanford in California?"

"Right." *What other Stanford was there?*

"And he just got back here?"

"Yes, for summer vacation." Why so interested, Francesca wondered.

"What was his name again? Maybe I'll run into him."

Francesca hesitated. "Colman Canfield."

Melinda looked thoughtful, as if considering her next question. Just then a woman stepped up to the podium. "Good morning. I'm Taylor Emerson, CEO of the Banner Botanic Gardens." Her voice was smooth and well-modulated. She was elegantly dressed in a tailored navy-blue suit, a brilliant crimson patterned scarf looped around her neck. Her blond hair, pulled back into a low ponytail, revealed burnished gold earrings. She looked like M-O-N-E-Y.

Francesca felt kind of scummy in her jeans, tee-shirt and dark blue hoodie. She'd dressed for gardening. Maybe she would be out pulling weeds before the morning was over.

"Welcome, everyone. This morning I will tell you a little about the Banner Botanic Gardens, what it means to be a volunteer, and then some of our specialists will inform you of the various ways you can be of service." From there, Taylor Emerson expounded on the motto of the gardens, which was: *to nurture the power of plants and to sustain and enhance life.* Francesca was struck by the word *power* used for slow-growing vegetation. Up until now she had thought of plants and trees as just being there. But they covered ninety-five percent of the earth's surface and they kept on growing, come what may.

Francesca listened, fascinated by all the activities that went on at the Gardens. There were nearly three hundred volunteers and the department was run like an army. Each volunteer chose an area to work in, and was trained by a garden specialist. Each volunteer was also required to choose a four-hour shift. Three tardies and you were out. Volunteers also had to turn off their phones when working; absolutely no talking or texting. Probably because you should be communing with nature, not with your sister-in-law, Francesca figured. She looked over at Melinda, who was scanning the crowd and hardly seemed to be listening.

"There is a process to be accepted as a volunteer at the BBG," Taylor Emerson continued. "First you must fill out an application. Then you must attend a volunteer orientation session, followed by an interview with a staff supervisor. We will also run a criminal background check before your training begins."

That made sense. Background checks were becoming the norm everywhere, and they certainly didn't want a serial rapist or worse running around the Gardens.

"Now I would like you to meet our area specialists, who will tell you about volunteer opportunities available here at the BBG." As Taylor said this, a door opened to the left of the stage, and several people walked in and lined up. Taylor introduced each one and they each talked about their area of expertise.

Poppy Jorgenson, athletic-looking and exuberant, talked about the Welcome Committee. Greeters stood at the gates to the BBG, handing out maps and helping new guests. Next to her, a sweet and dithering woman discussed opportunities in the garden's library. Lillian Roth, exuding efficiency in a swinging blond bob, khakis and a tailored pink shirt, extolled the joys of working with school groups. Francesca had met her once at a school board meeting.

Next to Lillian was a tall, thin, nerdy-looking man with a full head of grey hair. He wore round steel-rimmed glasses and enunciated each word as though he were speaking to the intellectually challenged. Introducing himself as Dr. Holmes, manager of the science center, he explained that they were evaluating the best plants and soils for growing produce on roof-gardens in the city. He also oversaw the freeze drying of seeds from local prairie plants, to be saved for further generations. Dr. Holmes barely smiled. He was all business.

Next to him stood a large-boned, full-breasted woman who looked like Francesca's idea of a pioneer woman. She wore a calf-length jeans skirt, a flowered blouse, and a red apron. Her hair was in a messy grey bun. "Hi all, I'm Irma and I run the Vegetable and Kitchen garden center. We help people with the planting and care of vegetables and herbs. We also run a series of cooking classes in our outdoor kitchen. We're particularly in need of people who can man our specialty carts that educate visitors about the cultivation and cooking of produce such as peppers, tomatoes and herbs."

Francesca would enjoy the cooking classes, but she didn't know anything about how to grow vegetables. She glanced over at Melinda, who had leaned forward in her seat and was studying each individual at the front of the auditorium. She seemed unaware of Francesca's gaze.

The next man to talk was small and slight. He gave his name as Dr. Miyamoto, manager of the Japanese Gardens and the bonsai exhibit. He spoke with an accent and was deferential in manner. When Taylor Emerson interrupted him, he bowed. "Dr. Miyamoto is a world renowned specialist in Japanese garden design. Through his efforts, beginning tomorrow, we will be hosting an international bonsai conference and exhibit. The famous bonsai specialist, Dr. Kaito Takahashi, will be arriving this afternoon for this fabulous event." She turned back to Dr. Miyamoto, but he seemed reluctant to say anything more.

Next to him stood a tall, heavy-set man with a shock of pitch black hair falling across his brow. Something about his smile was as odd as his name, Maelog Gruffydd. "It's Welsh and not much heard in this country." He sounded slow and ponderous, his lips moving out of sync with the muscles in his cheeks. He shrugged. "I'm the guy that manages planting and weeding for several areas of the garden; maybe not the most exciting activity, but the most basic…and necessary. I'll teach you to love and appreciate plants." He looked up at Taylor Emerson. "That's it."

Francesca thought planting and weeding might be the right spot for her. It sounded as though you didn't need much experience. She looked over at Melinda, but the woman had quietly disappeared. Francesca hadn't even noticed her leaving.

Chapter 3
Tuesday morning

Tom looked down at Edmond Hollister's bald head. A neat circle of greying brown hair encircled the smooth pate. The medical examiner was a short, compact man. He had been wearing cargo shorts and a plaid short-sleeved shirt when he arrived. Now he was covered head to toe in protective gear. His feet were shod in white booties.

"Doc's head was bashed in with a dull, wooden object. I can see wood splinters imbedded in the indented grooves." He stood up and looked around the room for a possible weapon. A trail of blood led towards the door; they had all carefully stepped around it when entering the room.

Puchalski moved to the door. "I bet I know what we're looking for." He ducked outside, and Tom heard him clattering down the wooden steps.

"What brought you guys down here, anyway?" Hollister asked.

"Doc called Ron last night and said he wanted to show him something. Ron said he sounded worried. Things have been slow lately, so I decided to come along."

They heard Puchalski coming back up the steps. In one gloved hand he carried the wooden oar he and Tom had seen earlier, apparently thrown in the sand. He held it up by the handle. The other end was caked with sand that adhered to a dark brown substance.

"Hey, you know what the captain said. 'Get in the boat, oar else.'" Hollister chuckled.

Tom and Puchalski groaned. They were used to Hollister's corny jokes. He was an excellent ME and a renowned pathologist, whose flippancy enabled him to handle his gruesome job.

"Bag it," Tom said. "It looks like our murder weapon. Let's hope our killer was in too much of a hurry to wipe off his prints." He looked around the room. Several wooden captain's chairs were grouped on each side of a small table littered with sailing magazines. Sailing charts were pinned on the wall. An antique pop machine stood in another corner. It was throbbing loudly. Blood spatters speckled the room like chicken pox gone viral.

Tom frowned. His gaze darted around the room. "I wonder if he called anyone else. Where's his phone?"

Puchalski stepped over to the body, carefully avoiding the spatters of blood. He reached into the pockets of Doc's old tweed jacket. From one pocket he pulled out a bunch of keys and a blue Bic lighter, from the other a cell phone. "Here we go." Puchalski opened the phone and tapped his fingers across it. "Here's my number. And guess who he called next? Harry O'Connell."

Tom rubbed his chin. "Harry O'Connell?"

"Yep. It looks like Harry picked up, too. Let's see what time." Puchalski tapped again. "Eight-thirty. He called Harry five minutes after calling me."

"Let's try calling Harry now," Tom said, and then shook his head. "No, let's go over to the Banner estate. I'd like to see Harry's face when we talk to him."

Hollister looked up from his examination of the body. "As a preliminary finding, I'd guess Doc was probably killed between eight-thirty and ten-thirty last night. I'll know more later."

"Between eight-thirty and ten-thirty? Hmm…. Well, we know he was alive at eight-thirty." Tom turned to the ME. "We'll leave you to it. The technicians from the homicide task force should be here momentarily. Let's talk later."

Hollister nodded. Then he said, "Here's another one: There was a huge paddle sale yesterday." He grinned. "It was quite an oar-deal."

Tom groaned. "Enough. We're out of here."

Chapter 4
Tuesday morning

Francesca walked up to the front of the auditorium and presented herself to Mr. Gruffydd. "I'd like to begin my internship with you." She held out her hand. "Francesca."

Gruffydd's handshake was powerful, his skin rough. "Please call me Maelog." His smile was slow but genuine, his eyes friendly but watchful.

"I know zilch about gardening so you'll have to start at the very beginning."

His laughter rumbled out of his chest. "We'll start with weeding. How's that?"

"Sounds good. I'll see you Thursday."

Francesca left the parking lot and took the inner roadway that meandered through the Botanic Gardens. It led to the Banner family mansion, where she had a luncheon date with Delia Banner. As she drove, she looked out at the new young leaves on the burgeoning plants and trees. In her mind spring green was an innocent color. As summer arrived it would give way to a deeper, more mature hue.

The Banner Family Trust had donated hundreds of acres of land for the Banner Botanic Gardens. The family still maintained a narrow road through the Gardens to a private entrance to their property. Few people knew about this back way in. Francesca stopped to lift the gate, drove through and closed it behind her. The drive wound its way through impenetrable woods and brush. It was dark under the trees after the bright open gardens of flowers and shimmering blue ponds. The forest spread across many acres and housed deer, raccoons and coyotes. On the far side it bordered the Deer Way Golf Course.

Just as she was thinking she might have driven too far, she came upon a heavy wrought-iron gate. High metal fencing stretched both ways through the woods. Francesca got out of the car and approached the gate. She had been told there was a buzzer under a clear plastic protective screen. She spotted it, pushed the button, and almost instantly she heard a voice she recognized. "I see it's you, Miss Francesca. I'll open the gates. Please step back and get in your car."

"Hi, Harry." She looked to the right and left and then above. There was a camera on each side of the gate. Harry must be checking her out. She gave a wave and stepped back into her car. A minute later both gates swung open and Francesca drove through. She looked in the rearview mirror and watched them close behind her.

She drove down a red brick drive that meandered through some dense woods and then suddenly opened up to a wide spread of luscious green grass. Stately trees lined the drive. Before her loomed an impressive Georgian mansion. The original grey stone house bore a graceful white portico. It was flanked by two wings added some fifty years later. A gurgling marble fountain enhanced the central courtyard. Francesca loved the statues of dancing children frolicking in the cascading water.

The courtyard held enough parking places for a fleet of cars. Francesca pulled up to the right of the front door and got out.

"Hello there."

She looked over and saw Harry O'Connell coming around the left wing of the house. He was a slight man with a shock of reddish-grey hair atop a face full of freckles and deep wrinkles. He'd worked as a chauffeur for Delia's parents and grandparents for fifty years, and he maintained the ten antique cars in the heated garages as well as Jack's Jaguar, his truck, and Delia's BMW. Delia, at least, considered him a part of the family.

"Were you spying on me a few minutes ago?" Francesca asked with a laugh.

"It can't be helped. A man's drawn to the sight of a beautiful woman like a bee to honey." Harry stretched out both of his hands and took Francesca's in his warm grip. "You are a lovely sight to behold."

Francesca blushed. "How are you, Harry?" She looked into his washed-out blue eyes.

"Can't complain…just a little arthritis but I keep on moving." Then he frowned and glanced around. He dropped her hands, leaned toward her and spoke more quietly, almost a whisper. "Things are not exactly copacetic around here, my dear. Miss Delia is unhappy and I worry about her. Young Jack is meaner than a rattlesnake. First there was the loss of the mister and missus, and then Delia's accident. You know how they say trouble comes in threes? Well, I'm waiting for the third calamity." He shook his head, gazing down the driveway. "I'm not a suspicious guy, but I have bad feelings."

Francesca felt unsettled. She knew it had been a difficult year for Delia. Last fall her parents had drowned while out for a late afternoon sail on Lake Michigan. The Banners were experienced sailors and the weather had been perfect. Neither their bodies nor the boat had ever been found.

Then in February Delia and her fiancé were in a horrendous car accident on the North-South Highway at the curve near Lakeland Road. Delia was driving and suffered a concussion, a broken arm and two broken legs. Lincoln Caldwell, her fiancé, was killed outright. Since the accident, Harry had driven Delia in the family limo. Francesca had seen them from the windows of her office.

"Third calamity? Like what?" She wanted to laugh it off, it seemed so over the top, but Harry was dead serious.

His voice dropped even further. "Listen, Francesca. There's been some funny business going on…"

The heavy oak front door of the house swung open. Francesca glanced up. Jack Banner stood in the doorway. Of medium height, with jet black hair and a powerful build, he looked as impatient and arrogant as ever.

"Harry, didn't I ring you ten minutes ago? Where's my car? I told you to bring it around. I don't have all day."

"Yes sir, Mr. Jack. I'm on my way. Just welcoming Miss Francesca." Harry spoke respectfully, nodded to Francesca and then headed for the garages.

Jack turned toward Francesca and said, loudly enough for Harry to hear, "He's getting old and forgetful. I've told Delia we ought to put him out to pasture. Get some young techy engineer that really knows cars."

Francesca mounted the stone steps to the front door. Jack remained in the doorway, forcing her to brush by him. He smelled of sweat and a strong, unfamiliar men's cologne.

"How are you, Francesca?" he murmured, and caressed the small of her back. She slipped quickly past him and started down the hallway, but he reached out and grabbed her arm. "Not so fast." He spun her around. "So tell me, are you happy with your cop? Any regrets?"

"Very happy, thank you." She could smell his slightly sour breath.

"You ever change your mind, I'm available—and soon I'll have a lot more money than you can even imagine." He squeezed her arm. His eyes bored into hers.

Francesca yanked her arm away. "You need to find another girl. I'm taken." She started down the hall again. He followed her. She did her best to ignore him. At the end of the corridor she turned left into a bright sunny room that looked out on a spacious green lawn. This solarium was Delia's favorite spot. She was there, seated on a chaise lounge under a potted ficus tree, typing on her laptop and oblivious to Francesca's entrance.

Francesca took in the beauty of the view. To the right was a gazebo with tennis courts beyond, to the left a well-tended rose garden. A grassy path meandered through the flowers. Lattice work and white wrought-iron benches provided cozy nooks to sit and chat. The expanse of lawn ended with a low, white marble wall that marked the edge of the bluff. Below and beyond, Lake Michigan sparkled cerulean blue.

Jack came in, just a few steps behind her. "Hey, gimp, you've got a visitor. Upsy-daisy, on your feet." His voice was snide.

Delia moved her laptop to a side table, grabbed her cane and used it to leverage herself to a standing position. Francesca rushed over and took her arm. "Don't bother to get up." It shocked her, how little Delia weighed. Since the accident, she'd become a ghost of her former self.

Delia was as fair as her brother was dark. Straight silver-blond hair fell to her shoulders. Striking violet-blue eyes looked up at Francesca. There was pain there, and something else…fear?

"I certainly do need to get up to welcome a dear friend." Delia stood straight and smiled warmly, giving Francesca a careful hug. "It's lovely to see you, Francesca. I thought we'd have lunch out here." She gestured to a round table surrounded by pots of geraniums.

Jack swaggered further into the room. "How about a little male company for lunch?"

Delia glanced warily at him. "If you really want to stay and talk girl-talk, you're certainly welcome."

"No, just pulling your leg…and I don't mean the deformed one, either." He laughed. "Just joking. I'm outta here. Places to go, people to see…" With that he turned and left.

Francesca looked at Delia. The woman's tense face began to relax. To Francesca, it felt as though the entire room gave a sigh of relief. A malevolent spirit had just decamped. "Why do you let him talk to you that way, Delia? He's vicious."

"I'm sorry you had to witness that. Jack's angry at me today. He wanted an advance on his allowance." She sighed, gazing out at the lake. "I've got him on a tight budget. He's gambled away so much money." She shook her head.

Francesca wasn't privy to the Banner family finances but she'd figured out that when Jack Senior died, he left everything in Delia's hands. She was to deal with her brother as she saw fit. The younger Jack Banner—named Horatio James like his father—was nothing like him or their mutual namesake, the sea-captain forebear who'd come here from England back in the 1830s.

Delia limped slowly over to the table and hooked her cane onto the back of a chair. She picked up a silver bell and rang it. Immediately, Jorge the butler came into the room. A tall imposing Spaniard, he had the elegant presence of a bull-fighter. Like Harry O'Connell, he had been with the family for many years. He helped Delia sit and pushed in her chair. Then he came around behind Francesca and did the same. She smiled up at him. "How have you been, Jorge?"

"Very well, thank you, Miss Francesca." He turned to Delia. "Shall I ask Luisa to bring the luncheon?"

"Yes, please. Thank you, Jorge."

Jorge left, then came back with a pitcher of water garnished with bright red strawberries. He poured them each a glass. A short, plump woman came bustling into the room. She wore a pink maid's dress with a white apron, her hair in a shiny, black bun at the nape of her neck. She smiled at Francesca as she set down a basket of warm rolls and a silver dish with pats of butter shaped like flowers.

"Hello, Luisa," Francesca said.

"Good day, Missus. I am happy see you." Luisa's smile was genuine.

"How are the children?" Francesca asked.

Luisa chuckled. "Happy school soon to be over."

She bustled out of the room and returned a minute later with a large tray bearing several dishes. A shallow bowl held curried chicken salad on a bed of baby greens. Another platter displayed a selection of roasted mini-vegetables. She set the tray down and placed small bowls of mango chutney beside their plates.

"This looks delicious," Francesca said.

Luisa smiled and turned to Delia. "Is good, Miss Cordelia?"

"Yes, thank you, Luisa. We're all set." Delia opened her napkin and Francesca did likewise. They served themselves from the platters.

Not one to mince words, Francesca asked, "How are you really feeling, Delia?"

"I think I'm better. I've got therapy three days a week and they tell me I'm getting stronger. I'll be having another short operation to remove the pins from my left leg but I'll probably always have a limp."

"I admire your willpower with everything you've been through."

Delia shrugged. "I don't sleep so well. Pain, nightmares. I still see that night in my mind…the car sliding, not being able to brake." Her fork rattled against her plate as her hand shook.

Francesca reached out and took Delia's slim hand in hers. "You're strong. You'll make it through. I just know it. That's why your dad left you in charge of things."

"Yes, but he had no clue what this would do to Jack." She shook her head and eased away from Francesca's grasp, then picked up her water glass, her hand still shaking. The delicate crystal goblet slipped from her hand and crashed to the stone floor, breaking into a thousand shards.

Chapter 5
Tuesday afternoon

Tom and Puchalski decided to stop off at Churchill's for a quick lunch on the way to the Banner mansion. Churchill's was a favorite breakfast and lunch spot. London street signs and pictures of Winston Churchill, Queen Elizabeth II, and King Edward VIII covered the walls. A bright red phone booth stood in a corner.

Tom ordered the Cajun chicken sandwich with spicy hot giardiniera peppers. Puchalski went for an Italian sub piled high with salami, capocollo and picante provolone cheese. The place was jammed. They took a table in the back corner facing the door so they could talk.

Puchalski carefully tucked a napkin under his chin and laid another on his lap. The other detectives always kidded him about his fastidious behaviors. In the office his desk was meticulous. Papers and file folders were organized, pencils sharpened and his computer dust free.

His home, on the other hand was total chaos, with kids running wild, babies crying and dogs barking. Tom knew Puchalski was happily married to Bonnie, a Rubenesque blond with an infectious laugh. She was the yin to his yang.

Puchalski sipped his iced tea. "We know for sure Doc was murdered but we don't know why. He found something on the beach that he needed to show the police."

"Then he calls Harry O'Connell, either because Harry's a buddy or because Harry would benefit by knowing the information." Tom took a bite of his sandwich.

"Damn. I wish I'd quizzed him last night. I was anxious to get off the phone because Bonnie was at a parent-teacher meeting and I had to get the kids to bed. Nicolas is having trouble at school. His teacher says he's distracted. This has been going on all year." Puchalski sliced his pickle with a fork and knife and took a tentative bite.

"What grade is Nicolas in now?"

"He's in fifth and he can never sit still. He's got more energy than you can imagine. His teacher says we should put him on Ritalin."

"Just be patient. Don't drug him up. I was like that in school. He'll settle down." Tom spoke with authority. Then he realized he didn't have a clue about raising kids and he ought to just shut up.

"I hope so. Bonnie is in a real state." Puchalski took a bite of his sandwich and wiped his mouth.

Tom moved the conversation back to the crime. "So when we get over to the Banners', let's not begin with Doc's death. Let's find out what Harry was doing last night when that call came through and what happened next."

"You've got to be kidding. He's going to know Doc's been killed. Around here, information travels faster than the speed of light." Puchalski glanced around the café. "I'm surprised we haven't been accosted here by some eager beaver who wants the gory details."

When they arrived at the Banner mansion, they turned to the left, avoiding the circle driveway, and pulled up in front of the garage. An elegant dark wood building with a gabled roof, it had once served as stables for a herd of horses. Now it housed a fleet of cars. Harry O'Connell lived upstairs in a roomy apartment. Tom had been up there several years before when Harry's wife died of a heart attack. He remembered that night. He had responded to the call with the paramedics. Now here he was again because of an untimely death.

They got out of the patrol car and Tom stepped up to the heavy oak door. He pulled a rope and they heard a carillon ringing. "This building doesn't look it, but it's as secure as Fort Knox. This door is reinforced with steel rods," Tom said.

Puchalski was inspecting the façade. "What's inside?"

"Cars worth thousands of dollars." Tom turned as the door swung open.

Harry O'Connell stood there, his eyes and nose red from crying. He was wearing jeans and a dark green shirt with the Banner logo on the pocket. "I just heard." He choked up as he stepped back and let them in. "Doc was about the best friend I ever had."

Tom nodded. "This must be a difficult time for you, Harry. Can we come in and talk?"

Harry nodded, gesturing toward the stairs up to his apartment

They moved into the dim entryway. To the right Tom saw a polished roll-top desk next to a dark steel door. To the left, a sofa and chair upholstered in burgundy and gold stripes made a small seating area. British paintings of horses and hunting dogs adorned the walls.

Harry switched on a light and led the way, trudging heavily up the staircase. At the landing a door stood open. They entered a large living room that spanned the width of the building. Through the windows, Tom could see the entrance to the Banner mansion on the right and the formal gardens on the left. The furniture in the apartment looked old and tired but comfortable. A kitchen was visible through an archway at the back.

"Can I make you fellows some coffee?" Harry asked.

"Make some for yourself, we don't need anything," Tom said.

"Right. Okay." Harry made no move toward the kitchen. He shuffled around the room, looking briefly outside and then continuing his meanderings.

"Come sit down for a moment," Tom said. "We won't bother you for long."

Harry looked at him as though he'd just realized Tom was there.

"Please sit down," Tom said again.

"Right. Okay." Harry sank into an old rocking chair. He dug a handkerchief from his pants pocket and wiped his eyes.

Tom wondered how old Harry was. He seemed fragile and in shock.

"Can we get you a glass of water?" Puchalski asked.

"No thanks. I'm alright. You can ask your questions." Harry sighed.

Puchalski sat on the red plaid sofa and Tom sat on a matching chair.

"What were you doing yesterday evening at eight-thirty?" Tom said.

"Eight-thirty?" Harry looked like he was trying to focus on the question. He frowned. "I don't remember."

"Did you receive a phone call last night about that time?"

"A phone call? I don't think so." He pulled out his cell phone and tapped the screen. Then he looked up. "I didn't talk to anyone last night."

"Doc called you at about eight-thirty. We have a record of the call."

Harry shook his head, looking fully alert now. "Wait a minute. You don't mean my phone. You mean the garage phone. That's the number Doc usually called. I'm always down there."

"Where's that phone?"

"Downstairs in the entryway." Harry sat up, more alert. "Last night I was bushed. I had a beer and a frozen pizza. Funny thing, I fell asleep on the sofa. It had been a long day and I was fed up with Jack Junior."

"How's that?" Tom asked, keeping his tone casual. He always gleaned as much information as possible even if it didn't seem relevant to a case.

"Oh, nothing. Jack can be a real jerk." Harry rubbed both sides of his head with his palms.

Tom waited for more and then asked, "Is there an answering machine attached to the garage phone?"

"Yes. But why would Doc call me there so late?"

"That's what we want to find out. Let's go down and check out the answering machine."

They all clomped downstairs. Harry walked over to the roll-top desk and showed them the answering machine attached to a black desk phone. A light on the machine was flashing. He pushed the play button. They all listened to the single message, about some motor oil to be delivered the next day. There was nothing from Doc.

"But we know he talked to someone at this number last night. It was a one-minute call," Puchalski said.

Harry shook his head.

Puchalski studied the answering machine. "Could someone else have answered this phone?"

"If they did, I would have heard them."

"Is there another extension?" Tom asked.

"Yes, out where the cars are. But no one would have been in there at night," Harry said.

"Please show us the extension."

Harry walked over to a keypad to the right of the steel door and punched some numbers. After a series of beeps and flashing lights the door rolled open. Harry led the way into the garage and flipped on the lights. Tom drew in a breath, and Puchalski whistled softly. Lined up in the enormous open space was a fleet of exquisite cars.

Harry led them down the line of automobiles. Each vehicle was in mint condition, shiny and breathtaking. Tom recognized a 1931 Bugatti. There were Bentleys, Ferraris and a 1937 Mercedes roadster. Together they represented a fortune.

"Man oh man, this is unbelievable." Puchalski's eyes shone in wonderment.

Harry smiled and gestured for them to follow him. In the middle of the garage was an alcove outfitted like a library with oak wood paneling. Leather-bound books filled the shelves, and a bar lined one wall. A sofa and two dark brown leather chairs were separated by heavy mahogany tables. On one table sat another old desk phone.

"This is the extension," Harry said to Tom. Puchalski was still walking slowly down the line of cars, inspecting each one.

"Who can get in here and answer this phone?"

"Only Miss Cordelia and Jack Junior. They're the only ones with the code."

"Do you know if either one was in here last night?" Tom walked over to the bar. It contained an impressive line-up of bourbons and single-malt scotches. Two crystal tumblers sat on the counter.

"No. Miss Cordelia goes to bed early and Jack was out." Harry walked over to a red Ferrari and blew invisible dust off it. "They were in here earlier in the day. I heard them arguing. I was over there working on the Shelby Cobra."

"What about?"

Harry looked uneasy. "Well, I don't know how much I should say. I mean, this has nothing to do with Doc."

Tom waited. In his experience, people tended to fill silence, and usually ended up revealing useful information.

"Well. You see. Jack Senior left everything in Delia's hands. He knew Jack Junior couldn't be trusted to make wise decisions. So…" More silence.

"So…" Tom repeated.

"Well. What I heard is, Jack wants to sell his half of the cars. He had some buyers in here last week. He wants the money for his share right now. Delia wants to wait for a year until after their parents' will goes through probate. Since everything is in her name, Jack can't do squat."

"That sounds like a recipe for disaster," Puchalski said as he joined them. "I'm familiar with Jack Banner. I've stopped him for speeding a couple of times. He can be a real jackass."

Harry was looking edgy. "Jack was always a difficult kid."

"Kid? Give me a break. He's an irresponsible adult." Puchalski walked over to one of the leather chairs and sat down. "So what is this little library doing here?" He smoothed his hand over the chair's leather arm.

"Jack Senior liked to come down here sometimes after dinner. He would read Shakespeare and drink bourbon. He liked to be surrounded by his cars." Harry's eyes filled with tears.

"Man. Wouldn't that be the life?" Puchalski shook his head in amazement.

Tom stayed standing, his hands clasped behind his back. "You're sure neither Jack nor Delia could have answered the phone?"

Harry rubbed his eyes. "I know Miss Cordelia was probably asleep. She goes to bed about eight o'clock. I saw the light go off in her bedroom window while I was fixing my pizza. I can see her bedroom across the courtyard."

"What about Jack?"

"I heard him tell Delia he wouldn't be around for dinner. He was meeting someone at the casino down on the river. At six-thirty I heard his car peel out of here."

"What about the house staff, do they have access to the garage?" Puchalski asked.

"No, like I said, only me, Delia and Jack." Harry stood in the middle of the garage, shaking his head. "I knew something bad would happen. Bad luck comes in threes."

Chapter 6
Tuesday afternoon

Francesca walked briskly up the short flight of stairs to Hero's Café and Market. The weather had turned grey. Angry little clouds scuttled across the sky. That morning spring had seemed a sure thing. Now a nasty wind blew off the lake. The change in weather matched her mood after the luncheon with Delia.

She pushed open the door and entered the shop. The dusky smell of freshly brewed coffee and sweet cookies filled the air. Hero had recently acquired a pizzelli press. Ladies came in for coffee and a fresh pizzelli in the afternoon, as did the kids on their way home from school.

Hero Papadopoulos was Francesca's landlord and dear friend. Her office was located above the market. The shop served as a convenience store for locals to pick up a gallon of milk, a can of soup or a bunch of bananas. Hero also carried homemade Greek specialties that made for a delicious lunch or supper item.

"There you are, Francesca." Hero was wiping off the dark oak counter in front of the espresso machine. He was a short, sturdy man in his fifties, with thick grey hair combed back from a deeply lined face. Kind brown eyes questioned Francesca's frown.

"Hi. It's already been a long day and I've got to go upstairs and write a couple of stories for tomorrow's edition." Her voice didn't carry its usual lilt.

"Problems?"

"Oh, I had lunch with Delia Banner. She isn't doing well and her brother is a real jerk. I just got this weird feeling while I was there."

"It will take a long time for her to get over the death of her parents and the loss of her fiancé. I know about that." He nodded at Francesca and clasped his hands together on the counter. He had lost his wife and children back in Greece in a freak accident. Only his granddaughter Vicki remained.

"You're right, Hero. But there was something else…bad vibes." She shuddered and headed for the alcove and the staircase up to her office. "I better get to work."

Francesca's office was to the left at the top of the stairs. To the right was Hero's apartment where he lived with Vicki when she was home from college. Francesca unlocked the door. Her mood changed as she stepped into her office. She loved this light, airy workspace. Three windows faced south framing the tops of leafy trees. She had a view across the Banner Bluff green and could look down at her friends and neighbors out doing errands.

Spring-green walls, white moldings and shiny wooden floors made the room cheerful. When she was working here she felt energetic and optimistic. Her large wooden desk stood under the windows. To the right, a colorful Chinese screen marked off a mini-kitchen area with fridge, electric kettle and a microwave. In the center of the room was a round oak table and chairs. A counter along the long wall contained printers, PCs and some photography equipment. Colorful prints of Catalina Island hung above.

Sometimes Frank Penfield, her friend and advisor, came here to work. He was retired from the *Chicago Tribune* but still wanted to keep his finger in the business. Frank enjoyed doing research and wrote an article now and then.

Francesca sat down, opened her laptop, and began scrolling through her email. Better to get that out of the way before she started her article on Dutch elm disease. She had learned that initially the disease is spread by the elm bark beetle but eventually it travels through connecting root systems underground. Several streets in town were lined with elms that would soon be decimated. People in Banner Bluff were sick about losing those trees. There was a lively debate about whether they should be replaced by black oaks, red maples or blue ash.

Loud talking and exuberant laughter floated up from below. Then Francesca heard footsteps charging up the stairs, followed by someone knocking at her door. She never used to lock it, until she'd been kidnapped by members of the Russian mafia a year ago. After that, she felt safer behind locked doors.

When she answered the knocking, Vicki was there with Colman, both of them beaming at her, their faces young and vibrant. She gave each of them a hug. "Welcome home, you two." How was school this semester?"

"I got straight As," Vicki said. She was small with long, lustrous black hair and shining dark eyes. Vicki had arrived in the US when she was twelve years old. Back then she didn't speak a word of English and Francesca had tutored her for a couple of years. They became fast friends and Francesca had often served as a surrogate mother. Vicki had worked hard and graduated from Banner Bluff High School as valedictorian. Francesca was proud of her.

Vicki and Colman were holding hands. "I did pretty well, too," Colman said. "Straight As, and I've got my scholarship again for next year."

"You two are amazing! How about we celebrate with a cup of tea? I've got some toffee crunch cookies."

"I've been dreaming about your cookies, Francesca. Thanks for the care packages by the way," Colman said. A lanky young man, he had longish brown hair, brilliant blue eyes and a likeable grin. He and Vicki had become friends when he was a senior in high school and she was a sophomore. Francesca had wondered if their relationship would continue when they were separated this past year. Colman was a junior at Stanford in pre-med and Vicki was down at the University of Illinois. It looked as though they still were an item, though.

"Sit down and I'll put on the kettle."

It took hardly any time for the water to boil. Francesca assembled the tea things in the kitchenette. "What are your plans for the summer?"

"I'm working at the hospital when I'm not helping my grandpa with the shop," Vicki said

"Hospital?" Francesca said, surprised, as she came out from behind the Chinese screen and set the teapot, three mugs and the antique cookie jar on the table.

"Pappou thinks I should be looking into a career in the medical field. Then I will always find a job. He says journalism isn't a sure bet."

Francesca sat down. 'Well, he's right in a way. The world of journalism is changing. There are fewer print newspapers and what's online is often poorly written. I mean, anybody can write a blog. I really don't know how many jobs are out there." She poured them each a cup of tea and passed the cookie jar.

"I'll be working at the hospital for six hours a day, filling in as receptionist in various departments. Then I can come home and do some writing for you, Francesca." Vicki poured milk in her tea and added a spoonful of sugar.

"That would be great." Francesca turned to Colman. "I heard you've got a job at the Banner Botanic Gardens? You should be working in a hospital, too."

"I can't afford to volunteer there. I need to make money. I found the job at the Gardens listed online and I like the idea of being outside all summer. I've been buried inside studying this past year."

"What are you doing exactly?" Francesca asked.

"I'm just working maintenance...I guess I'll be doing some of the heavy lifting, planting trees. I don't really know yet. I went there yesterday for the first time. I think I partially got the job because Luis Gonzales put in a good word for me. He's head of the full-time gardening staff."

This was news to Francesca. She thought he was still employed by the Banner Bluff Park District. "Good for Luis. He'll do a great job there." She passed the cookie jar to Colman. "So, I'll see you sometimes. I'm going to volunteer a couple of days a week at the Gardens. I was there today for a training session. I'm hoping to learn a lot about planting and cultivating flowers. Then I can do something with the over-grown forest in our back yard." She sipped her tea. "Today we met the people in charge of the various areas. I think I'll be working with a big guy named…May-log, I think it is."

"Right, the guy with the Welsh name. It's Maelog Gruffydd. I had him spell it out for me. He seemed pretty friendly." Colman wrapped both hands around his mug.

"I'd like to work in the kitchen garden area, too…learn how to grow vegetables and herbs. I think the woman in charge is named Irma," Francesca said.

"Yeah, I met her too. She looks like my idea of a farmer's wife."

Francesca smiled. "I know what you mean."

Colman's face turned somber. "Something weird happened yesterday afternoon, though. I wandered around to get my bearings, figure out where everything was, you know? I walked into the Plant Science Center and went into a lab. It felt like a biology lab at school. I was checking out some petri dishes with seeds growing in some gunky liquid, and all of a sudden, somebody grabbed my arm. I yelled and pulled away. Knocked down a couple of petri dishes. It was that guy, Dr. Holmes. Man, I was scared. He was yelling at me, 'Who are you? Who let you in here?' I showed him my brand new badge and told him I was just looking around. I tried to apologize.

But he didn't calm down. He pointed to the door and told me to get the hell out of there."

Chapter 7
Tuesday afternoon

It was four o'clock when Tom and Puchalski left the Banner garage. Tom looked at his watch. "The task force meeting is in an hour and a half. Let's take a chance and see if Jack and Delia Banner are in. I'd like to verify where they were last night."

"Sounds good to me." Puchalski inspected the mansion's façade. "It's amazing that people still live in places like this."

"Maybe one percent of the top one percent." Tom rang the doorbell and stepped back.

A minute later the door was opened by a tall, stately, gentleman in a dark suit. "Chief Barnett, good afternoon."

"Jorge. It's good to see you. We're here to speak to Delia and Jack."

"Miss Cordelia's in the library, sir. Come this way." He stepped back to usher them into the circular entryway. A crystal chandelier hung from the domed ceiling over a Florentine marquetry table, its gleaming veneer graced by a large bouquet of fresh flowers in a porcelain vase.

Jorge continued down the wide hallway. Puchalski glanced left and right at the ornately framed paintings depicting the town of Banner Bluff and the Banner family.

"This way, gentlemen." Jorge stopped halfway down the hall at a closed door and knocked. They heard Delia's voice: "Come in."

Jorge opened the door and waved them inside. The library was an enormous room, two stories high. Books covered the walls from floor to ceiling. A ladder led up to a gallery that circled the room. At one end, four matching chairs flanked a marble fireplace. A vast Aubusson carpet covered the floor. Heavy dark rose-colored curtains framed three sets of French doors that opened on to a walled garden.

Delia sat at a mahogany desk, her laptop open. Her leg was propped up on a footstool. She turned as Jorge ushered them in. "Tom, what are you doing here?" She grabbed her cane and tried to stand.

"Delia, please don't get up." He walked toward her, holding out his hand.

"I'm not some invalid." She took his hand and smiled up at him. "Did you know Francesca was here for lunch? We had a lovely time."

"I knew she was planning on coming here after her orientation at the Gardens." He smiled back, then turned serious. "But I'm here on another matter." He gestured to Puchalski, who stepped forward. "This is Detective Sergeant Puchalski. We've come to ask you a couple of questions."

"Oh?" Delia's blue eyes were wide and questioning, like a child's. She gestured to the leather armchairs. "Why don't we sit down?"

Jorge hovered at the door. "Miss Cordelia, would you like some refreshment, tea or soft drinks?"

"Yes, please bring coffee and tea with some of the chocolate cake." She turned to Tom and Puchalski. "This cake is to die for."

Following Delia's lead, they sat down in two armchairs. "Is Jack around? We'd like to talk to him as well," Tom said.

Delia looked mystified. "What is this about? Did Jack get into trouble again?"

Tom glanced over at his sergeant. "We're here about Doc Stoddard. He was murdered last night down at the marina shack."

Delia blanched. "Oh, my God. Doc? Murdered?"

"Yes. He was bludgeoned to death."

Delia brought her hand to her throat and tears filled her eyes. "He was such a kind man."

Tom gave her a moment to absorb the shock, then continued. "Before he was killed, he made a phone call to Detective Puchalski."

Puchalski nodded. "He asked me to come down to the beach and look at something."

"Then he made a call to your garage phone," Tom said.

She twisted the cane in her lap. "Why would he have called here?"

"We think it was to talk to Harry. They're buddies. But Harry didn't pick up the phone last night. He was upstairs and didn't hear it ring."

"Daddy used to sit among his cars for hours reading and sipping bourbon. But no one goes into the garage at night these days."

"We think someone else answered the phone. We know Doc talked to someone for about a minute."

Delia frowned. "What time was this?"

"About eight-thirty," Tom said.

"I was asleep by then. I've been taking a sleeping pill and I go to bed early." She turned to gaze out at the garden. "I find the day is just too long."

There was a knock and Jorge entered the room, pushing a rolling table set with two silver pots and delicate china cups, hand-painted plates, and silver forks and spoons. A crystal cake stand displayed a three-layer chocolate cake.

Puchalski grinned. "This is like being on the set of *Downton Abbey*."

Delia smiled.

Jorge served each of the men coffee and a generous piece of cake. "Thank you, Jorge. This looks delicious," Tom said.

Delia accepted a plain cup of tea. "Jorge, is Jack around?"

"I think he's upstairs, Miss Cordelia."

"Could you please ask him to come down here?"

When Jorge had left the room, they continued their conversation between frequent bites of the delicious cake. "Would anyone else have the code to get into the garage?" Puchalski asked.

"Isn't there an old answering machine out there? Did you check it?" Delia asked.

"We did. There was no message from Doc recorded," Tom said.

"What about the code to allow access to the garage?" Puchalski said again.

"Only Harry, Jack and I have the code. It's changed monthly." Delia sipped her tea.

Then the door flew open and Jack Banner strode into the room. He stopped, clearly surprised. "My, oh my. We're serving tea to the local cops. We should take some selfies. Officer Puchalski stuffing himself with chocolate cake would make a great picture." Jack laughed. "By the way, you've got some frosting on your cheek."

Puchalski turned red, from embarrassment or anger. Tom wasn't sure which. Puchalski and Jack Banner had a history of run-ins, but the sergeant could be trusted to keep his cool.

"Jack, please sit down and talk with us," Delia said, her voice soft and coaxing.

"I've only got a minute. What do you guys want? Make it snappy." Jack stood in the middle of the room, his legs spread in an imposing stance. He was dressed in black jeans and a tight black tee-shirt that showed off his chiseled body, the result of many hours of strenuous work-outs.

"Jack, what were you doing last night at about eight-thirty?" Tom asked.

"Why do you want to know?" He leaned against the wooden ladder that led up to the upper gallery and crossed his arms.

"Because Doc Stoddard called here about that time."

"Why?"

"That's what we're trying to find out," Puchalski said.

"Doc was murdered last night. We have to help the police," Delia said, her tone pleading.

"I know he was killed. I heard about it. But I never talked to him." Jack eyed his thumb, bit an errant piece of skin and then spit it on the carpet. "I never liked that guy. He was always butting into other people's business."

"So where were you at eight-thirty?" Tom repeated.

"I was at the casino on the river."

"Can someone vouch for your presence?"

"I'm sure they've got me on videotape."

"We'll look into it." Puchalski stood and walked around behind his chair to join Jack. At six foot four, he loomed over the other man. "Are you sure you weren't in the garage at eight-thirty last night?"

"What garage?"

"Your family's garage, where all the luxury cars are kept."

"I told you, I wasn't here. I was at the casino." He jabbed his finger into Puchalski's chest.

Puchalski reached down and shoved Jack's hand away with a hard squeeze. "Somebody answered the garage phone last night. I think it was you."

Chapter 8
Tuesday afternoon

After Colman and Vicki left, Francesca cleaned up the tea mugs and put away the cookie jar. Now that Colman was home she would have to make sure the jar was full. When he was around, he often came over to talk. Her heart went out to him. He was making his way alone in the world. His father was in prison for running a Ponzi scheme with two other Banner Bluff residents. They had fleeced senior citizens of their life savings. After the indictment, Colman's mother had left town with his sister. They were living in Grand Haven, Michigan, with Colman's grandmother. He rarely saw them.

Colman had remained in Banner Bluff, living in a room over Churchill's Café, doing odd jobs and putting himself through Lake County Junior College. Then he'd applied to Stanford as a junior and received a scholarship. He was a hard-working kid.

Francesca's purse was on the desk where she'd thrown it. She dug through it and retrieved her phone. She'd turned it off before the in-service at the gardens. There were a bunch of emails and a couple of texts from Tom. She scrolled to the first text, read it and sank into her desk chair.

Doc Stoddard murdered at beach. Francesca's eyes filled with tears and her breath came in gasps. *Oh my God.* A terrible memory surfaced of three years ago when she'd discovered a little girl floating face down in Lake Michigan. She closed her eyes, willing her mind to dwell on calming images. After a few minutes she got hold of herself, feeling mentally drained.

Tom's second text read; *Don't know when I'll be home, ongoing investigation.* That figured. He'd be working twenty-four hours a day until they caught the killer. Francesca punched in Frank Penfield's number. As she waited for him to answer she stood up and walked over to the window. In the late afternoon sun, the village green looked idyllic. A ray of sunlight came through the clouds. Majestic trees, bright green lawns and flowered borders surrounded the pristine gazebo. Her heart ached for this village she had come to love. Again Banner Bluff had suffered a horrendous crime. She knew what came next…fear seeping into psyches, a black cloud of distrust hovering like a malevolent spirit. She shivered and placed her left palm against the glass.

"Francesca, I thought you might call. It's about Doc. Right?" Frank's voice throbbed with emotion. Doc had been an old friend.

"Hey, Frank. Yes. I just found out. This is terrible. Are you all right?"

"Unfortunately this isn't the first friend I've lost. At my age, friends move away or they die. But Doc was a special person. We'd known each other for nearly fifty years." She heard him take a deep breath. "Can you imagine…fifty years?"

"Do you want to write the obituary? Or would that be too difficult?" Below her Francesca saw a throng of men and women coming from the train station, headed home after a long day of work in Chicago.

"I would very much like to tell the people of Banner Bluff about their dear, lost friend. I've already been working on it. I'll probably have it for you tonight." He fell silent and then she heard a sob. She waited. After a moment, Frank continued. "Doc was really a medical doctor, you know. He was an obstetrician."

Francesca sat back down. "I guess I never thought about it. When did he stop practicing?"

"Years ago when he was a relatively young man…about forty-five, I guess. There was a lawsuit. A newborn baby died, and the family sued Doc and they won. Doc told me the baby wouldn't have lived anyway. But it was the Raleigh family and they had big bucks. They lawyered up and won the case. After that Doc's malpractice insurance went through the roof, and people questioned his ability. He was engaged to Molly Lawson but she broke off the engagement and married Simon Bergsten. For a while Doc became a recluse. Then he started working at the hospice center. He used to say it was a good place for him. No one would question his patients dying." He gave a shaky chuckle. "After he retired, he started fishing and ended up running the sailing classes and the marina."

Francesca ran her fingers through her dark, wavy hair. "What about the Raleigh family? I don't remember anyone by that name in town."

"They moved away shortly after the lawsuit. As I remember, they went out East. Maybe Connecticut?"

"Hmm. If you could write the obit, I'd be most grateful."

"Okay." Frank's voice was tentative. "So, Francesca…how are you doing? When I heard they found Doc down at the beach, it made me think of you. How are you handling this?"

"It was a shocker at first. Now I've calmed down. I've got an over-active imagination."

"With just cause."

"I know. But I'm still fighting that old enemy…fear." As she said the words, Francesca felt the cold hand of terror clutching at her heart.

Chapter 9
Tuesday, late afternoon

Tom had alerted the county's Homicide Task Force, a group of detectives and technicians from different localities who came together to work homicide investigations. The task force enabled small towns to share cost and expertise. Each village chipped in resources and specialized manpower. As Chief of Police, Tom oversaw the operation in Banner Bluff.

By five-thirty the task force had assembled in the spacious, well-lit downstairs meeting room at the Banner Bluff police station. The walls were covered with white boards, one of which held blown-up pictures of the crime scene attached with magnets. Several long tables were pushed together to form a U. A Keurig coffee pot sat in a corner. After everyone had gotten their coffee, the meeting began.

Tom looked around the room as he spoke a few words of welcome and thanks. "Detective Sergeant Ron Puchalski will describe what we know thus far about the murder of Dr. Robert Stoddard." He nodded to Puchalski, who stood up to address the group.

Puchalski smiled briefly and then looked down at his notes. "Last night I received a phone call from Dr. Stoddard. He asked me to come down to the beach to look at some wreckage he'd found. He said it looked like part of a boat. I couldn't go, because…I was babysitting." He glanced up with an apologetic smile as laughter rippled around the room. "Anyway, I told him I'd meet him down at the marina shack in the morning. Chief Barnett came in as I was about to head down to the beach, so we went down there together."

He paused for a sip of coffee. "At the top of the service road, the metal gate was unlocked. We attributed this to some irresponsible park district employee. We drove along the south beach and walked up to the marina shack. No one responded when we knocked, so we walked around the shack. Doc's car was there, and something just didn't feel right. I gave Doc a call. We heard his phone ring inside the shack, but he didn't pick up. At that point we decided to break in. We found Doc sprawled on the floor in a pool of blood. His head was bashed in with an oar."

Tom watched everyone's faces. Puchalski was holding their attention. Cindy Murray was taking notes. A short, slight redhead with a perky face and a ready smile, she wore her usual jeans, cowboy boots and tee-shirt. She was an ace detective and came from Lake Woods, the community right next door.

The other redhead in the group was Brendan O'Connor, a burly, broad-shouldered detective with bright blue eyes. He was on loan from Somerset, a village to the west. He and Cindy had worked together on a drug-related murder in Banner Bluff. At first they'd been like oil and water, fighting about everything. Eventually they meshed and learned to play off each other's talents, and now they made a great team.

"It must have happened fast. The guy probably burst into the sailing shack and surprised him." Brendan suggested.

"What time did this happen?" Cindy asked.

"The ME gave a preliminary time slot of eight-thirty to ten-thirty last night," Puchalski said.

Cindy made a note of it. "What time did the victim call you?"

Puchalski shook his head. "Whoa there. Let me finish up."

Cindy sat back, crossing her arms. She sometimes forgot proper protocol when she was hell-bent on an idea.

Puchalski went on. "Detective José Ramirez is investigating the crime scene. He's currently down at the beach with his evidence technicians. We'll know a lot more tomorrow when they've finished." He looked down at his notes. "We did find an oar with blood residue on it. Hollister thought it could be the murder weapon. We bagged it and it's being tested."

He turned to Cindy. "Doc called me at eight-twenty-five. But he called over to the Banner estate a few minutes later." Puchalski glanced at Tom, who smoothly took over.

"Doc tried to call Harry O'Connell, longtime chauffeur for the Banners. Doc and Harry have been buddies forever. We interviewed Harry this afternoon. He claims he never answered the phone. But we know from Doc's phone that someone picked up and talked to him for about a minute. The number he called is a landline and there are two extensions in the family's garage—one in the entryway and one located in the garage space itself."

The task force looked mystified. "Harry runs the garage and takes care of the cars," Tom said.

Puchalski chimed in. "We're talking eight or ten fabulous vintage cars; a Bugatti, Ferraris, Bentleys and a 1937 Mercedes roadster. Together they must be worth thousands of dollars. Anyway, there's a phone in the middle of the garage, in a sitting area that looks like a library from some old French château. It is something else."

Mark Sanders, a balding detective from Lindenville, spoke up. "Doc called his friend Harry, who manages the garage? Why?" As he talked, his hand, inadvertently, spread over the large port-wine birthmark on his right cheek. His gaze was steady and shrewd. Like Tom he was a thinker; often quiet but always listening.

"We don't know yet. Harry lives upstairs over the garage. Like we said, he claims he didn't answer the phone. But somebody did, and within the hour Doc was dead," Tom said.

Cindy frowned. "Could someone else have entered the garage?"

"Not easily. The place is like Fort Knox, with steel doors and all sorts of security. The only people with the entrance codes are Harry O'Connell and Jack and Delia Banner."

"Jack Banner? I know him. He was putting the moves on me at a country music bar over in Lindenville. That guy has one hell of an ego."

The men around the table all smiled, trying to imagine someone cozying up to Cindy. She was a spitfire, especially when it came to unbidden advances.

She looked around the room, her eyes flashing. "Jack Banner told me he was going to be very rich and that I'd better be nice."

"When was this?" Tom asked.

"Last January or February. I remember it was snowing outside."

Tom thought about what they'd learned from Harry that afternoon. Maybe Jack was counting on selling those cars. "I think we need to do a full investigation of Jack Banner. Cindy and Brendan, tomorrow morning go back over to the Banner estate and interview Jack, Delia and Harry again. Verify everyone's whereabouts yesterday. Find out if they had any visitors recently. Ron, you and I will go out to the casino." He shifted his gaze toward the back of the room. "Coyote?"

"Yeah, Chief?" Coyote Blackfoot looked up from his laptop. Native American, with thick black hair, black eyes and a chiseled face, Blackfoot was a digital forensic researcher, an essential specialty in modern investigations.

"Get everything you can on Jack Banner."

"I'm already on it," he said.

There was a knock on the door. Arlyne, the dispatcher from upstairs, poked her head in. "Chief, there's an army of television and newspaper people upstairs. It's a zoo. Your press conference is scheduled to start in ten minutes. The mayor is waiting in your office." She sounded out of breath.

"I'll be up in a minute. Thanks, Arlyne." Tom turned back to the task force. "Doc mentioned some wreckage, but Ron and I didn't see anything. We did see evidence of a truck being driven down to the shore and something being dragged from the water's edge. We'll have forensic information about that when Ramirez finishes his analysis of the crime scene."

Chapter 10
Tuesday evening

It was six-thirty when Francesca left her office. Frank had sent Doc's obituary. In a computer file she'd found several pictures of Doc surrounded by kids. In one, he was in a rowboat supervising a sailing class. The picture made her think of a mother duck and her ducklings. After posting the obituary, the pictures, and her article on Dutch elm disease, she was ready to leave for the press conference.

Hero was downstairs with Vicki, having supper at a small table in the front of the shop. Francesca took a look at the Greek salad they were eating with grilled lamb chops. "Yum, that looks good!" She realized Tom wouldn't be home for steaks tonight after all. She would need to get something he could eat whenever he arrived. "Is it okay if I help myself to a salad?"

Hero nodded. "Sure, go ahead."

Francesca took a prepared Greek salad out of the display case.

"We've been talking about Doctor Stoddard," Hero said, shaking his head. "He was a kind and gentle man. I do not understand that someone would kill him."

"Everybody liked him, all the kids," Vicki said. "And he was funny, always telling jokes."

"Have you talked to the chief?" Hero asked.

"No, he texted me this morning, so I don't know any more than you do. There's a press conference at seven. I'm going to attend it and get the lowdown with the rest of the media hounds."

Francesca laid money on the counter and said goodbye. Outside she turned to the right. Next door was the Bistro Mexicana, a restaurant run by her friend Yahaira Gonzales. Yari had opened the restaurant a year ago and it was terrifically successful. The ingredients were fresh and each dish was hand-prepared. Francesca decided to go in and get some chicken enchiladas.

"Hola!" Francesca said as Yari rushed over to give her a hug. Yari was an attractive woman with velvety brown eyes, shiny black hair and a small compact figure.

"Hola, Francesca. Are you here for dinner?"

"Just thought I'd get some enchiladas to take home. I don't know when Tom will be back."

Yari's face turned grim. "We heard about poor Doc. He used to eat here often. He loved my fish tacos."

"I'm going to the press conference in a few minutes. Hopefully I'll learn more about what happened."

"Will there be something in the *Banner Bee* tomorrow morning?" Yari asked.

"Yes. Frank wrote an obituary…they were good friends, you know."

"Yes. They often came here together." Tears filled Yari's eyes. "Let me place your order. I'll be right back."

Francesca looked around the bright, cheerful restaurant. Terracotta Spanish tiles covered the floor, and the walls were painted a Tuscan red. Paintings of Mexican towns were set off in bright green and yellow frames. The tablecloths picked up the color scheme. Francesca saw Yari's boys, Roberto and Raul, sitting at a back booth doing their homework. She waved just as Yari came back with a paper sack. She paid and left the restaurant. As she walked through the village green to the press conference, she could feel the wind whipping up. It would probably start to rain before long.

It was chaotic outside the Village Hall. Trucks from the local TV stations disgorged reporters, and photographers from the major newspapers had turned out in force. Spotlights illuminated the open door to the building. As she approached, she saw Tom come out with Mayor Criche. Several reporters started shouting questions before the mayor could open his mouth. Criche looked annoyed.

Francesca stood at the back of the crowd. With all the lights focused on him, Tom wouldn't be able to see her. The mayor said a few words and introduced Chief Barnett. Tom gave a bare bones accounting of the murder. The Lake County Homicide Task Force would be working the case, he said. They were still collecting evidence from the crime scene. Doctor Robert Stoddard had been bludgeoned to death with an oar from a rowboat at around nine o'clock the previous evening. There were no suspects identified at this time. He ended by asking the public to come forward if they had seen or heard anything the previous evening that would be helpful to the investigation.

It had begun to rain and the wind circled down in mini tornados. Some people ran for cover but many reporters kept pelting Tom with questions, oblivious to the driving raindrops. Francesca ran for her car. She slammed the door just as the heavens opened up.

When she arrived home, the house seemed dark and forbidding. She switched on the lights in the kitchen. The dogs greeted her as though she'd been on a year-long cruise. She opened the side door to let them out, but they didn't stay out long. Francesca scooped out a mug of kibble for each dog and filled their water bowl. While they were eating, she made the rounds of the first floor doors and windows, checking that they were locked. Doc's mysterious murder filled her with apprehension.

Upstairs, she took off her wet clothes and stepped into a hot shower. Then she wrapped herself in a flannel robe, slipped on some warm socks and padded downstairs. She poured herself a glass of pinot noir and carried it into the den. The room was dark and she flicked on several lamps. It was still raining to beat the band and it felt cool in the house. She decided to light the gas logs in the fireplace to take off the chill.

Seated on the sofa wrapped in a throw, Francesca thought about the day. Thursday she was supposed to start at the Botanic Gardens, working under the tutelage of Maelog Gruffydd. He'd said to meet him at the tool shed at eight sharp. From there they would head out to the waterfall garden to do some weeding. She smiled to herself. So far, she was at the bottom of the pile in terms of her gardening skills.

She took a sip of wine. It tasted rich and smooth.

Lunch today had been delicious but the tension she felt in the Banner house was palpable. After an espresso served with mini chocolate tarts, Delia had suggested a walk outside around the house. She was supposed to exercise her legs every day and hadn't been out that morning. They followed the meandering path around the property. Behind the extensive garages, the path wound its way among trees and bushes that hid her and Delia from view. Several garage doors were open, and inside Francesca could see Delia's BMW and Jack's Jaguar. Next to an empty bay was a full professional carwash, where Jack was washing a black pickup truck.

They stopped and watched. Jack was absorbed in rubbing down the wet vehicle. Delia rolled her eyes at Francesca and laughed. "This is the first time I've ever seen Jack washing his own car. He always leaves it to Harry. And I'll tell you…sometimes that truck is filthy. He drives it purposely into mud puddles."

Now, looking out at the rain beating down, Francesca had to smile. Jack's truck would need another wash after tonight's storm.

Chapter 11
Tuesday night

Delia lay on the chaise lounge in her sitting room, listening to the rain pelting the windows and the waves crashing on the beach below. She'd been trying to read for the last half hour, to no avail. She couldn't concentrate. Sleep and oblivion were calling her.

It was in the evening that she most missed Lincoln. Theirs had been a perfect relationship. They'd loved theatre, sailing, picnics and reading. After her parents' disappearance, Lincoln had moved in to be with her. In the evenings they'd sat together in her sitting room, while the winter storms buffeted the house, and talked for hours. He'd helped her get through the worst of it. If he'd lived, they would be married now.

In search of distraction, she glanced around the sitting room. She'd chosen the color scheme, yellow with blue accents, after visiting Monet's house in Giverny. The kitchen of the French master had seemed so upbeat with its yellow and blue tiles. Delia's sitting room faced Lake Michigan and was bright and sunny in the morning. Usually she breakfasted up here in her cozy hideaway. Tonight, it felt more claustrophobic than cozy.

A knock came at the door and Anka walked in, carrying a silver tray. On it was a blue patterned Chinese mug with a porcelain lid. As the older woman drew nearer, Delia caught the fragrance of chamomile.

"Here's your tea, Delia." Anka placed the mug on the low table. "Would you like some help getting into bed?"

Delia sat up obediently. She was exhausted and her leg ached. "Thank you, I think I would." She smiled up at Anka, who took her outstretched hand. Together they made their way into the adjacent bedroom. Anka pulled back the covers, fluffed the pillows and helped Delia into bed. Then she brought the tea.

"You'd better go home, Anka. This has been a long day for you."

"Have you got everything you need?" Anka folded the robe and placed it on a satin flowered chair. Delia watched her with affection. She'd moved to America from Poland with her brother when she was eighteen. Years ago, Delia's mother had hired her to help with Delia and Jack. Anka had since become a beloved member of the family.

"Yes. I'll just drink this tea and then I'll drift off to sleep."

Anka headed for the door, then stopped and turned around. Her eyes were moist. "I worry about you. Remember, you can call me any time."

"I know. I've got my phone right here."

After Anka left, Delia reached into the bedside table drawer and took out her bottle of sleeping pills. She swallowed one with a sip of tea. After a few more sips, she placed the mug on the bedside table and reached over to turn off the light. She was exhausted.

Such a long day. The confrontation with Jack, then lunch with Francesca, followed by the visit of Chief Barnett and his detective. Why had Jack been so aggressive with the police? They were just doing their job. But that was Jack, always picking a fight.

She thought back to their childhood. Jack was a mean kid. When she was six and he was ten, they'd wandered into the woods and found a clearing that had once been the site of a homesteader's cabin. She remembered a giant oak that stood in the middle of the glade. Under some bushes they found a wooden trapdoor that led to an underground cellar. Jack had convinced her to go down the rickety wooden ladder. Then he'd slammed down the cover. She'd been stuck in there for hours before he let her out. She remembered with fear the darkness and the feeling of spiders running over her skin. Afterwards, Jack warned her she would never be safe if she didn't do what he said.

Jack had always been jealous of her. He'd done poorly in school. He started fights and skipped classes. Often he was grounded and spent weeks grousing around the house.

Shortly before Jack's eighteenth birthday, a phone call came in the middle of the night. Her father left the house. He came back an hour later with Jack in tow. Delia snuck out of her room and crouched at the top of the stairs. Her mother and father were down in the entryway with Jack. Her father was yelling, "What in the hell were you doing? That girl said you raped her! What kind of monster are you?"

Delia's mother was crying. Jack stood looking at his father, hatred burning in his eyes. "You never would have known about this if it wasn't for that old coot, Doc. What an asshole."

"He was there to save that poor girl. Thank God he called me instead of the police!"

"Come on, Dad. I wasn't raping her. She wanted it."

Her father slapped Jack across the face. "Get out of here. Go up to your room. I can't stand to look at you."

Later, Delia learned that her father had hired a lawyer and paid off the girl's family. Nothing was ever said again, but Delia always thought they might have paid off Doc as well.

Two months later, Jack had joined the Marines. Her parents had tried to get him to go to college but he didn't want to fill out the applications or write the essays. One day he came home and said he'd signed up and was on his way to boot camp. For several years, there was no contact. Then he sent intermittent emails. He served two tours in Iraq, then was stationed in Japan for three years. Two years ago, he was discharged and came home little changed. Before his death, their father had tried unsuccessfully to interest his son in various jobs. By pulling strings, Jack Junior could have been gainfully employed. Now he just hung around, partied, gambled and waited for Delia to hand him a big chunk of money.

As she thought about all this she could feel the tension building. How long could she put up with Jack without giving in? Her father had put everything in her hands because he thought she could handle it. She could handle the finances, but could she handle Jack?

She had to think about something else or she would go nuts. She switched on the light and retrieved the little plastic bottle from the bedside table. Another sip of tea, another pill, and she lay back down on the pillows. Soon the drug would send her into oblivion.

She thought about Lincoln and how it felt to lie beside him, his body warm and demanding. Her mind was beginning to let go. Her thoughts grew less clear as sleep pulled its gauzy veil. She turned over on her side as a fuzzy memory bobbed into her consciousness. Had she heard Jack's truck last night when she was falling asleep? Had it rumbled down the driveway?

Chapter 12
Wednesday morning

Francesca crept out of the bedroom. She looked back at Tom, who was sleeping like a baby; arms above his head, his hands curled open and his face turned towards her. In sleep, his expression was serene. The tension she had witnessed at the press conference last night was smoothed from his face. She hadn't heard him come in but it had probably been late.

    Downstairs she made a small espresso to give herself a kick-start. From the kitchen window she could see blossoms on the apple tree and a big, fat robin hopping from branch to branch. Spring was definitely back in the picture.

    She pulled on her jogging clothes. The dogs danced around. They knew they were going for a run. She attached their leashes and quietly opened the side door. Just as she'd shut it, Bailey saw a squirrel and started to bark. She hushed the big Lab. Hopefully, Tom hadn't heard the racket.

    Francesca headed down the street toward Lake Michigan. The world had been scrubbed clean and smelled dewy fresh. She decided to do her usual three-mile run. She saw other joggers out enjoying the early morning air. When she arrived on Lake Avenue, which ran along the bluff, she could see a patrol car at the head of the service road down to the beach. There was a TV truck and a couple of media guys milling around. They must think there was some hot new info to be gleaned. She waved to Officer Romano, who was standing guard by a patrol car. He was a rookie with a fresh, baby face. Tom said he was eager to please and got a lot of ribbing from the older guys.

"Hey, Mrs. Barnett. Great morning for a run."

"What's this 'Mrs. Barnett'…please call me Francesca." She stopped for a minute and ran in place. "Is there still a lot of action down at the crime scene?"

"No, but Ramirez went down there this morning with a couple guys." Romano glared at two journalists who had moved over to listen to their conversation.

"I bet the rain last night didn't help," Francesca said.

"Yeah, you're probably right." He looked over at the two men. "Move back behind the yellow tape," he yelled. Then back to Francesca: "I don't know why they don't just go home. There's nothing happening around here now."

Francesca smiled. "Stand strong," she said, smiling, and then took off with a wave.

She continued down the street and then ran up through the village that was just waking up. The lights were on in Churchill's Café and Hero's Market. She kept running and made it home in good time. As she came through the door, she saw Tom in the kitchen leaning against the sink, a cup of coffee in hand. He was looking out at the apple tree.

"Do you see our resident robin?" Francesca asked.

"Yep. It looks like she's making a nest up in the higher branches." Tom turned to smile at her. He moved forward to give her a kiss but she held up a hand.

"I'm hot and sweaty. Wait till I've taken a shower."

"I don't think I can wait that long. I'm actually on my way out the door." He leaned over and kissed her lips. "I love you hot and sweaty."

"So when will we see each other again?" Francesca asked.

"No idea. But don't expect me home early tonight. We've got a lot going on. Criche wants action."

"God, what does he expect? Miracles?"

"Yes, miracles and right away." Tom went into the front hall to get his gun from the safe.

Francesca followed him. "Is there any progress since the press conference last night? Any secrets you want to share with your in-house reporter?"

"Not really. Today Cindy Murray and Brendan O'Connor are going back to talk with the Banners, Harry, and the staff. We didn't learn anything yesterday when I was there with Ron. Jack Banner was a real jerk. Ron would like to pin Doc's murder on him, but we have no motive and no proof." He snapped the gun in the holster.

"I know what you mean. He was vicious to Delia while I was there. I don't like him and I don't trust him. And then he kind of came on to me."

Tom's eyes blazed. "What do you mean?"

Francesca laid her hand on his chest. "It was nothing. He was just flirting."

"He better not touch you."

"No, Tom, it was nothing like that." She remembered Jack's hand at the small of her back and changed the subject. "Why did you guys go over to talk to the Banners?"

Tom explained about the mystery telephone call from Doc's phone to the Banner garage. Francesca thought about this piece of information. "Where did Jack say he was at the time of the call?"

"He claimed to be out at the River Casino. Ron and I are going out there to check his alibi. They have video cameras watching every corner of the place." Tom still looked upset. He stared out the window as he smacked a fist into his palm.

Francesca reached up and rested her hand against his cheek. "Tom, look at me."

He stared into her eyes.

"It was nothing. Jack was just being a jerk. Okay?"

"Yeah, okay." He held out his arms and she slipped into his embrace. They stood that way, feeling each other's hearts beating in perfect rhythm. They kissed long and hard. Then Francesca pulled away.

"Why don't you text me if you see a break in the action today? I could bring over a sandwich or a cup of good coffee from Hero's."

"We'll see." He was distracted, fingering his gun.

They kissed again. Tom walked out the door and slammed it with force.

Chapter 13
Wednesday morning

After Tom left, Francesca went upstairs. She paused in front of the nursery door and then opened it. Sunshine was pouring through the window. She walked over and lifted the sash. Moist spring air wafted into the room. Below she could see the back garden with clumps of purple iris here and there. Daffodils and tulips were long gone, but several tangled rose bushes were in bloom. She stepped over to the white and yellow changing table and pulled open the top drawer. Mini tee-shirts were neatly stacked inside. Francesca fingered the soft cotton. Then she slammed the drawer. Why was she acting this way? Did she really have time for a baby? She had Tom and they were everything to each other. Wasn't that enough for now? Why did she feel vaguely discontented? Probably hormones. Wasn't that what ruled women?

After a shower Francesca decided to dress for spring. She put on a blue patterned swinging skirt and a white chambray shirt. She left her dark, wavy hair free. With a swipe of red lipstick she was ready to go.

As she started her walk to the office, she saw her new neighbors coming out of their house. She crossed the street to say hi. Rosemary looked uncomfortable, and her little girl stared at the ground. The little boy was balancing on crutches. He had a black eye.

"What happened?" Francesca asked.

George, the father, came around from the back of the minivan.

"We're in a hurry. Rosemary can't talk now," he said. His smile didn't connect to his Aryan blue eyes.

Rosemary didn't say a word, but helped her son into the back of the van and pulled the sliding door shut. She waved at Francesca as she got into the passenger seat, keeping her hand low and close to her chest.

"Let's go, Rosemary. Into the car. Now." George slammed the driver's side door.

A minute later, they were gone. Francesca watched the van recede down the road, remembering when they'd moved in a month earlier. Two days after their arrival Francesca had gone over with a plate of chocolate chip cookies. She'd waited until three-thirty in the afternoon, when the children came home from Banner Elementary. When Rosemary came to the door, she'd smiled shyly and welcomed Francesca into the house.

The living room already looked organized, with pictures on the walls and no boxes in sight. Rosemary led the way into the kitchen where the children were seated, each eating a banana. When Francesca introduced herself, the children had smiled shyly like their mother.

"This is Peter." Rosemary introduced her son, a slim boy with deep brown eyes. He glanced at Francesca and then at the floor. After Rosemary prompted him, he got up and came over to solemnly shake her hand. His palm felt cool and moist. He wore pressed navy pants and a short-sleeved button-down shirt, nothing like the tee-shirts and loose pants that other kids wore around town.

"Hi, Peter," she said. "How was school today?"

"Fine," he mumbled, his voice soft and uncertain.

"And this is Jane. Peter is nine and Jane is seven," Rosemary said.

Jane also got up and came over to shake Francesca's hand. Her grey-blue eyes were sunk in her little face. A navy blue dress hung on her small shoulders. On her feet were brown oxfords and white socks. To Francesca, these kids looked like they came right out of the nineteen-fifties. Where could you get brown oxfords these days? Even Rosemary, in a grey wool skirt and twin set, was dressed like a woman from another era.

"I brought you some chocolate chip cookies." Francesca set the plate on the table. The children's eyes lit up. They looked from the cookies to their mom, their eyes silently pleading.

Rosemary looked at the kitchen clock. It was almost four. "Okay, you can have a couple of cookies, this once." She went to the refrigerator and got out the milk, poured them each a glass, and put two cookies on napkins. "This is a special treat," she said. "Say thank you."

They said "thank you" in unison, their voices subdued.

Rosemary made a cup of tea for Francesca and they talked as the children nibbled their cookies. Francesca got the feeling they were trying to make them last as long as possible. Rosemary said the family had moved from out east. Rosemary's husband, George, had a new job with Aftat Labs. He hadn't wanted to move to Banner Bluff because he'd lived here as a child and something terrible had happened. But they got a great deal on the house. As she talked, she kept looking at the clock. The children cleaned up their places, put their glasses in the sink and got homework out of their book bags. They didn't say a word.

"Have you made new friends at school?" Francesca asked. Both children shook their heads.

"Have you been to Banner Park on the lake?"

They looked at their mother, then shook their heads again.

Francesca turned to Rosemary. "You should take the kids over. It's really a special place, with all sorts of equipment to climb on."

Rosemary nodded. She was twisting her fingers, looking uncomfortable. Francesca talked about the *Banner Bee*, and kept on babbling to fill the silent room. "I'm kind of new to this neighborhood myself, though not to Banner Bluff. I moved here when I got married in March."

Rosemary gave her a strained smile. "I hope you'll be very happy…you know sometimes marriage isn't what you think…" She glanced out the side window, then at the clock again.

Wow, thanks for the vote of encouragement, Francesca thought.

"I'd better get going," she said, just as a car came up the driveway. As she stood, she felt the tension in the room jump. Rosemary shot up and quickly brushed crumbs off the table into her palm, scurried over and dumped them into the garbage can under the sink. As though on cue, the children each picked up a pencil. Then the side door flew open and a tall, blond man came into the room.

"George, this is our new neighbor, Francesca. She came over to say hello." Rosemary was gripping the counter as she spoke.

George strode over and stuck out his hand. "Francesca, how nice of you to come by." He had perfect features and flashed a hundred-watt smile. He reminded Francesca of the TV version of a state senator.

He scanned the room, and his gaze landed on the cookies. "I bet you brought these over." He gave her that smile again. "That was a kind gesture, but we don't eat cookies at this house. Right, kids?"

They nodded, not looking up. "No one ate any cookies, right Rosemary?" He looked at her with that smile on his face and steel in his voice.

"No, we didn't eat any cookies. I was just telling Francesca she would have to take them home." Rosemary rushed over, picked up the plate, and handed it to Francesca. Luckily, Francesca had piled a bunch of cookies on it, and it looked as though none had been eaten. Francesca glanced at the children. They were all in collusion, lying to this master sergeant.

Thinking about it today, Francesca remembered fleeing the house as though she were escaping prison. She wondered what the family's last name was. She couldn't remember Rosemary mentioning it.

After the mini-van turned the corner, she looked up and down the street. Then she opened the neighbors' mailbox. She was in luck. Yesterday's mail was still there. She glanced around again, then pulled out several letters. They were addressed to George Raleigh.

Later, as she walked into the village, she mulled over the name. George Raleigh. Rosemary had said he lived in Banner Bluff as a child. Could he be related to the Raleighs that moved out of town after their baby died? The Raleighs who'd sued Doc Stoddard thirty or more years ago? When she got to work she would google the name and see what came up.

Chapter 14
Wednesday morning

Tom and Puchalski got out of the patrol car in the River Casino parking lot. The building resembled a beached Mississippi riverboat, painted white with blue trim. To the left behind the faux paddle wheel they could see the muddy river swollen from spring rains. A mock gangplank led up to a veranda along the front. In the bright morning light, the casino looked tired. The paint was peeling and the wrought iron railing had rust spots. Two tourist busses were parked by the entrance ramp. A blue clad worker was picking up debris from the parking lot.

    They headed up the gangplank and into the dark interior of the casino. It took a moment for their eyes to become accustomed to the dimness. The décor was burgundy and gold with flickering mock gaslights. Velvet-covered sofas and easy chairs reflected the 19th century riverboat theme. Off to the right was the entrance into the slot machine gallery. To the left through an archway, the game tables beckoned. Tom stepped over and looked in, spotting a nearby craps table and a roulette wheel. In the subdued light, the room seemed limitless. A scantily clad hostess glanced up from the craps table, noticed him, and smiled.

    "Welcome to Wilder's River Casino." A woman appeared from behind a curtain, startling Tom. In her tight-fitting, low-cut red gown, sparkling gold jewelry and black hair swept up on top of her head, she looked like a real-life Scarlett O'Hara. She stood with one hand on her hip, her full, red lips curved in a practiced smile. "You don't look like you're here for fun."

Tom identified himself and Puchalski. "We're here to verify the whereabouts of a person of interest in an investigation. We understand this individual was here on Monday night. We'd like a look at your security camera footage."

She looked briefly at the badge he held out toward her. "I think you'd better talk to Mr. Wilder. He just came in a few minutes ago. What was your name again?"

"Barnett."

She nodded. "I'll be right back."

Puchalski sat on the nearest velvet sofa and pulled out his phone, probably texting Bonnie. Tom watched Scarlett walk toward a set of doors, her hips swaying rhythmically. He turned and ambled through a wide doorway into the slot machine gallery. In the low light, the machines flashed and beeped, a distracting counterpoint to the pounding music. At this hour, a gaggle of senior citizens populated the room. A pudgy, white-haired woman dressed in pink sweats was giggling hysterically as she drew handfuls of coins from the machine in front of her. More money was falling to the floor. When Tom walked over to help her, she looked up at him, daggers in her eyes.

"This is my money. Don't you touch," she growled.

"Just wanted to help, ma'am." Tom backed away, shaking his head. He turned away and almost bumped into one of the tallest men he'd ever seen. The guy must have been six foot eight at least. He towered over Tom. His blotchy face bore ancient acne scars, and heavy bags hung under his bloodshot eyes as if he never got enough sleep.

He held out his hand. "John Wilder." Scarlett O'Hara hovered at his elbow.

"Chief Barnett, Banner Bluff Police." Tom's own hand was engulfed in the other man's large paw. Puchalski walked up and Tom introduced him.

"What can I do for you, officers?" Wilder's smile was broad, his teeth large, yellowed and chipped.

"We'd like to view your security camera footage from the night before last to verify that a certain individual was here between eight and ten o'clock."

"Is this a frequent patron of the casino?" Wilder asked.

"Probably. Jack Banner. He's a regular, isn't he?"

"Yeah, he's here three or four times a week." Wilder looked to be mulling this over. "He's a good customer. I wouldn't want to offend him."

"Good customer? Meaning what? That he spends a lot of money and loses most of it?" Puchalski's smile was brief. More than once he'd told Tom gambling was the scourge of society.

Wilder didn't answer. He looked uncomfortable, as if thinking through his options and finding none he liked. "We can keep this quiet, can't we?" he said.

"Don't see why not," Tom said. *Unless this goes to court.*

Wilder turned to Scarlett O'Hara. "Jessica, take these gentlemen up to the control room. Ask Guido to roll the footage for Monday night."

Jessica nodded and gestured to Tom and Puchalski. "Follow me."

They went back across the foyer to a curtained doorway. Jessica entered a code into a keypad and a soft click sounded. She pulled open the heavy door. "Right this way, gentlemen." She stepped back so the men could move past her. Her jasmine perfume filled Tom's nostrils as he brushed by. After the door banged shut she took the lead again and proceeded up a flight of stairs, holding her dress above her ankles. She had a nice little twitch to her hips.

A glassed-in control room lay to the left at the top of the stairs. Jessica pulled open the door. Inside, two men in short-sleeved blue shirts with the casino logo were seated on rolling work chairs before a bank of screens that lined three walls. They looked up briefly and then back down at the screens. One man pointed at an image of a heavy-set guy at a blackjack table. "Hey, Rog. What's that guy doing? Are they in collusion?" He gestured at a middle-aged blond woman seated at the same table.

"Yeah, that's the third time he's pulled out that handkerchief."

"Right, the blond is watching his every move. Who the hell carries a big white handkerchief these days? She's been winning." The man talked into his headset. "Table ten, the blond and the big guy. Watch them."

Jessica spoke. "Guido, Rog. These are two detectives from Banner Bluff. They'd like to watch footage from Monday night. Wilder says it's okay."

"Got it, Jess. I'll set that up." Guido, taller than his co-worker and olive-skinned, stood and shook hands with Tom and Puchalski, and led them across the room to three dark screens. "Our system is digital, so you'll find it easy to run through the videos." He logged in and opened up the system, all the while explaining how to run through the footage. "Think you've got it?"

Tom nodded. "Piece of cake," Puchalski said.

Guido stood and glanced back at the screen that showed table ten. Tom followed his gaze. The big guy and his blond partner were standing now. Two black-suited men were talking to them.

Tom and Puchalski sat down. Puchalski opened a briefcase and took out a yellow legal tablet and a pencil. He drew several columns and then began running through the videos. The date and time appeared at the bottom corner of the screen. Seven o'clock Monday night and the camera was focused on the entrance to the casino. Jessica came over and stood behind Tom. "That's him." She pointed to a man wearing a red Cubs hat, jeans and a white polo shirt. The man—Jack Banner—looked up at the camera and waved as he headed for the roulette table.

"What an arrogant asshole," Puchalski muttered. The time-stamp read seven-ten. Ron flicked through images at rapid speed. There were no more views of Banner until eleven o'clock when he left the casino. His gait was unsteady; he was probably too drunk to drive.

"Looks like he was here all evening," Jessica said.

"We'll want to look at footage from all the camera angles before we come to that conclusion," Tom said

"I'll leave you to it." Jessica left the room. Her heavy perfume lingered.

They each took a computer so they could run through the videos faster. Tom went through several. He saw Banner playing roulette and then at one of the craps tables. As the evening wore on, the gaming rooms grew busy, with a lot of people milling around. Tom followed the white shirt and the Cubs hat. At eight o'clock he saw Banner go into Buster's Grill, one of three restaurants in the casino. He yelled over to Guido. "Hey, are there cameras in Buster's Grill?"

"No. We cover the entrance and the exit by the dumpsters."

Fast forwarding, Tom saw Banner exit Buster's at eight-fifty. Meanwhile, Puchalski watched a video taken from a camera above the entrance to the slot machine gallery. After getting a bunch of quarters from a machine, Jack Banner settled down in a corner, drinking a beer and slowly going through his coins. He won several times and stacked his winnings in neat piles. He talked to the woman next to him and she laughed. From the angle, Puchalski couldn't see Banner's face. He and the woman seemed to be flirting with each other. This went on for a while. At ten-eighteen Banner pulled out his phone and spoke briefly. He played another couple of rounds and then pocketed the few coins that remained. He got up, saluted the woman, and walked toward the casino's foyer.

On another video, Tom spotted Banner entering the restrooms at ten-twenty. Three minutes later he came out, looked at his phone, pocketed it and went back into the game room.

As they worked through the videos, they kept track of the time; where Jack was and what he was doing. If a case against Banner ever went to trial, they would need to come back, copy the video footage and do a closer examination. Jack Banner had moved around from the blackjack table, to craps, to the roulette wheel. He'd won some but lost a lot. Tom wondered about Banner's skill, or lack thereof, at gambling. If he consistently lost, where would the fun be?

When they'd finished, they thanked Guido and started for the door. "Just a minute, detectives," he said. "I'll get someone to escort you out."

"We know the way."

Guido shook his head. "Company policy. This place is like a prison. You need the code to get in and out." Guido pushed a button. A minute later, a black-suited security guard arrived. They followed him back down the hall and the stairs.

"I'm thinking we ought to check out Buster's Grill," Tom said to Puchalski.

"Right, and let's see if they have a credit card receipt for Banner's meal."

At the bottom of the staircase, the guard punched in the door code. "I'll take you over to Buster's," he said.

Tom nodded. "Great." Wilder probably wanted to keep track of them.

Following their guide, they wound their way through the casino to Buster's Grill. Tom asked to speak to the manager, who turned out to be a thin, handsome man with slicked-back dark hair and a diamond earring in one ear. He wore a river captain's outfit complete with epaulettes.

"These are the Banner Bluff police. Wilder wants you to help them out," the security guard said, as if giving an order.

The manager looked from Tom to Puchalski. "What can I help you with?"

Tom said, "We'd like to see the receipts from Monday night. We're looking for a credit card receipt for a Jack Banner."

"This might take a while."

"We need it right away."

The manager fluttered his hands. "I'll see what I can do. Can we get you something while you wait? Why don't you take a seat?"

"Sure. I'll have a cup of coffee," Tom said.

"A Coke would be great. Thank you," Puchalski said.

They sat down and looked around. It was early for lunch but in this place it was hard to know what time it was. The coffee and Coke arrived; they drank their beverages and looked over the yellow tablet, tracing the time sequence of Jack Banner's evening at the casino. There were few moments when he wasn't visible somewhere on the premises.

The manager returned a half an hour later, with a signed receipt for a hamburger, fries and two beers. The credit card was in the name of H. James Banner, the signature an unintelligible scrawl. At the bottom, the name *Rita* was typed. The waitress who'd served the order, Tom guessed.

"Is Rita around?" he asked.

"Rita? Yes, she's over there." The manager pointed to a skinny girl with a blond ponytail, delivering two steak platters to a booth in the back. "I'll get her. She can't talk long, though. I need her. The restaurant's filling up." He strode over to her and pointed to Puchalski and Tom. She followed him back to their table.

"Hi, Rita." Tom gave her a friendly smile. "Just want to ask you a couple of questions.

She nodded nervously, crossing her arms tightly across her chest. She was wearing a skimpy blue calico dress and a white apron. Her jaws worked on a piece of gum.

Puchalski showed her the receipt. "Do you remember this man from Monday night?"

She studied the receipt. "Hamburger…fries…beer." She looked up, bewildered. "Do you know how many hamburgers I serve here? Maybe like two hundred a week."

"This guy had on a Cubs cap, white shirt, jeans." Puchalski looked hopeful, until Rita eyed the receipt again.

"Sorry. If he'd given me a big tip or screwed me over, I might remember. But a five-dollar tip? That's like, average, like nothing special." She looked up at them and shook her head. "I'd never remember this guy."

Chapter 15
Wednesday morning

Francesca went up the steps to Hero's Market. Hero was nowhere in sight, so she guessed he was in the back kitchen. Four retired men were sitting around a table having coffee and arguing sports. Francesca went into the back to say hello before trudging upstairs to her office.

"Hi, just wanted to check in." She smiled. "That smells heavenly."

Hero looked up from a large pot. "This is lemon-rice soup, my secret recipe."

"What makes it so special?"

"It's the broth. I make my own broth just like my grandmother did back in Greece. Come down later for a cup."

"I'll do that." Francesca fingered the keys in her pocket. "How's Vicki doing at the hospital?"

"She likes it there. At first she did not want to work in a hospital. She thought I was crazy to push it. Now she is happy."

"Good. Grandpa knows best." Francesca smiled again and headed for the stairs.

Upstairs, she unlocked the door. The office smelled musty. She walked over to the window and opened it to let in some fresh air, then stood a moment and listened to the chirping outside and watched the leaves rustling in the breeze. Down below at the corner she could see some buildings and grounds workers with ropes, saws and other paraphernalia, getting ready to cut down another tree. An ash this time. Not only were they removing the elm trees in droves, but the ash trees as well.

She sat down and booted up her lap top, then typed in *ash tree* and started reading articles. She learned that the emerald ash borer was a bright green beetle that had come from Russia. It laid its eggs in tree bark. When the larvae hatched, they ate their way around the trees, disrupting the flow of nutrients and water. With their lifeline to moisture cut off, the afflicted trees dried out, raising the risk of branches or an entire tree falling on houses or people.

Francesca closed her browser, opened her word processor, and started typing.

The Banner Bee—June __, 20__
Are you feeling the pain as you watch the ash and elm trees disappear up and down our streets? We are all mourning the disappearance of our friends. They are the silent sentinels of our community; the underappreciated giants that populate our neighborhoods. Let's face it, we take them for granted.

For the tenth straight year the village of Banner Bluff has won the "City of Trees" award for the state of Illinois. This isn't an accident. It's because we've nurtured our urban forest.

Here are a few facts to set you thinking. According to the Arbor Day Foundation, a mature leafy tree produces as much oxygen in a season as ten people inhale in a year. The New York Times *tells us: "One acre of trees annually consumes the amount of carbon dioxide equivalent to that produced by driving an average car for 26,000 miles. That same acre of trees also produces enough oxygen for eighteen people to breathe for a year." To put it more simply two mature trees can provide oxygen for a family of four.* [Environment Canada, Canada's national environmental agency.]

Have you ever imagined Banner Bluff with no trees? There would be no protection from storms and wind. Our town would be a desert in summer, bitter cold in winter, drab and dreary in spring and fall.

> *Nurture the trees and shrubs around your house. Water them long and deep. Create a safe zone with mulch. Try not to disturb their roots. Give them the TLC they deserve. They are the silent partners to our daily life.*

She saved the article and went to her email. Along with several emails bewailing the deforestation of Banner Bluff, there were quite a few from people mourning Doc Stoddard's passing. Several contained touching stories, which she decided to run in the *Banner Bee* as a tribute to their lost friend.

That reminded her about George Raleigh, her new neighbor. She googled his name. His LinkedIn bio said he'd recently been hired by Aftat Labs, a multinational pharmaceutical company on the outskirts of town. On the Aftat Labs site, she found a full-blown article about the new CFO, George Raleigh. He had been born in Banner Bluff but moved to Connecticut as a small boy. Further down, the write-up quoted him as saying a family tragedy had greatly affected him as a child. He must be the brother of the baby who had died so many years ago, Francesca thought.

She sat back and stared at the words on the screen, while an uneasy feeling crawled through her mind. Could that death, so long ago, have caused George Raleigh to kill today?

Chapter 16
Wednesday afternoon

Tom and Puchalski arrived back at the station in the early afternoon. Tom felt like they'd wasted their morning. Puchalski went down the hall to type up their interview at the casino. Tom stepped into his office and took care of the most pressing calls from the pile of pink slips on his desk, then went down the hall to talk to Deputy Chief Conroy. A short, solid man with greying hair and a bulbous nose, Conroy had thin skin and had to be treated with kid gloves. Right now, he looked stressed. His face was flushed and he was perspiring heavily.

"We could use some more manpower, Chief. I've got people out canvassing the neighborhoods. Lots of loony-tune calls over the tip line, but I've got officers verifying each one."

"Let me see what I can do. I'll call over to the Lindenville police; see if they can spare another detective."

"That would help. But we could use twenty more guys." Conroy reached up and ran a finger around his collar.

"Why don't you take a breather? Go home for a couple of hours."

"No, I'm all right. Just feeling a bit frazzled, is all." The deputy chief turned away as he listened to a call on his headset.

Tom went back to his office and put in a call to the Lindenville police, thinking of Ricky Stiles. Ricky was a young officer who'd grown up in Banner Bluff. In college he'd studied Spanish and criminal justice, intent on joining the police force like his grandfather, a Chicago cop. He saw it as a calling, he'd said. Tom would have hired him, but there were no openings in Banner

Bluff, so Ricky had gotten a job in Lindenville and moved quickly up the ranks. With a few years under his belt and his intimate knowledge of Banner Bluff, Ricky would make a valuable addition to the investigation.

At three o'clock, the task force met in the basement war room. Tom cleared his throat, but couldn't be heard over the raised voices. He needed a gavel to bang on the table.

Ron Puchalski caught his eye and then gave an ear-splitting whistle. The noise level dropped to zero. Puchalski grinned. "The meeting's come to order."

"Thanks, Ron. You should patent that whistle." Tom looked around the room. "This afternoon we're going to run through the murder of Doc Stoddard. Detective Ramirez is here to start us off." He turned to José Ramirez, who was in charge of the crime scene investigation.

Ramirez stood up and moved to the front of the room. He opened his file folder and removed several papers. Dark circles outlined the bags under his eyes. Clearly he'd had little sleep in the last few days. "We completed our investigation of the crime scene. Dr. Stoddard was hit with an oar found lying on the beach. His blood was on the blade. There were many fingerprints on the shaft but also a series of bloody glove prints. We found bloody glove prints on the door of the marina shack as well."

Detective O'Connor glanced up from his notebook. "What sort of gloves?"

"The lab is analyzing the prints. They have little dots up the fingers and on the palm."

"Dots? Sounds like driving gloves. I've seen some like that at Macy's. They're very in," Cindy said.

Tom smiled. Thank God for Cindy. No one else in the room was into fashion.

Ramirez moved over to a series of pictures. Using a pointer, he indicated the blown-up crime scene photos. "From the blood spatter, we know Doc was hit first on the forehead. He fell forward and then was struck multiple times on the back of the head." Ramirez pointed to the autopsy photos. "The report from ME Hollister describes contusions indicating he was also kicked numerous times on the left side. There are no identifiable footprints. Whoever committed this murder took the time to wipe up his shoe treads before he left. Not very well, but well enough." He pointed to smeared blood on the floor by the door.

"Detective Puchalski said the door was locked when he and the Chief arrived. Doc had no keys on him, so we think the killer took the shack keys and locked up when he left. There are dried glove prints on the doorknob.

"There was no sign of a struggle in the room. From the angle of the body, we think Doc must have opened the door, stepped back, and then been attacked with the oar."

"So Doc knew his killer," Detective Sanders said. He was leaning forward in his seat; his elbows on the table, his hand covering the port-wine birthmark.

"That is our judgment," Ramirez said.

"So Doc calls over to the Banner estate, someone answers, and Doc's dead a half hour later. Only a member of the Banner family, or Harry O'Connell, can get into the garage to answer the phone. Seems like an open and shut case. Right?" Sanders looked around the room.

Everyone nodded.

"Let's get back to the crime scene," Tom said, and nodded at Ramirez.

They continued to discuss the scene in the shack and the surrounding area. Then they moved on to the beach shore and the tire tracks leading down to the water. "A truck drove down to the beach sometime on Monday night. There was a thunderstorm and funnel clouds in the afternoon. So we think the wreckage Doc found might have been tossed up on the beach sometime late Monday afternoon. We can tell a heavy object was pulled from the water and loaded onto the truck."

Cindy looked over at Brendan and gestured to him. Brendan cleared his throat. "Cindy and I were over at the Banner estate today. We questioned everybody in the household. Didn't learn anything new, but we could tell Jack Banner is not well liked by the staff. Afterwards, Harry O'Connell took us around. We saw the antique car collection, and there's a secondary garage with the family's personal cars. Jack Banner owns a Dodge Ram Charger as well as a Jaguar."

"Did you check out the truck?" Conroy asked.

"Not thoroughly. But I can tell you it was spotless," Brendan said. "There was no sand on that baby."

Tom rubbed his chin. "Call over there later and find out if Harry washed the car in the last two days."

Brendan nodded. "Will do."

"Did you learn anything more about Jack's whereabouts on Monday night?" Cindy asked, directing her question to Tom.

Tom turned to Puchalski. "You tell them."

Puchalski stood up, cleared his throat and removed a piece of fluff from his sleeve. O'Connor poked Sanders, grinning.

If Puchalski spotted it, he gave no sign. "We went out to Wilder's Casino. We talked to the manager and checked out the video. Jack Banner is there on camera, as large as life, heading into the casino at seven-ten. He's visible from several cameras throughout the evening. We saw him entering Buster's Grill at eight. There is no camera in the restaurant. According to his receipt, he had a hamburger and a couple of beers, all paid for with a credit card. The time stamp on the credit transaction is eight-fifty. Not long after that, he shows up on-camera again, first in the slot machine gallery, then back at the craps table."

Silence fell as the task force digested this.

"So he was there all the time?" Cindy said.

"Until eleven o'clock. He gambled and he drank," Puchalski said.

Sanders scowled. "So we've hit a dead end."

"Apart from our inability to pin this on Jack Banner," Puchalski said, "what's his motive for killing Doc? We've zeroed in on him, but—"

Just then the door opened and Ricky Stiles walked in. His eyes searched the room looking for Tom. "Sorry I'm late. I had to bring a colleague up to speed on my case load."

Tom introduced Ricky to the group. Many of them already knew him.

"We're talking about the murder of Doc Stoddard. Our major suspect at the moment is Jack Banner but we have no proof and no motive. You're about Jack's age, if I remember right. Anything you can tell us about him?" Tom asked.

Ricky pulled out a chair. "Well, when I heard Doc had been murdered, Jack was the first person I thought of."

That comment got everyone's attention.

"Why?" Tom asked.

Ricky sat and leaned his elbows on the conference table. "We were in high school together. Jack was a senior when I was a sophomore. He'd always gotten in all kinds of trouble. His senior year, he raped a girl down at the beach, and Doc caught him. The gossip was that the Banners tried to hush it up and paid the girl's parents a bunch of money. Shortly after graduation, Jack left town and joined the Marines. I figure he must have had it in for Doc after that incident."

Cindy raised the question that had crossed Tom's mind, and likely everyone else's. "But if it's him, what would have triggered this murder now? There's a lot we're missing."

Chapter 17
Thursday morning

Colman arrived at the Banner Botanic Gardens at six-thirty AM. He rode his bike around the service buildings to the designated parking lot for employees. Across from the lot were the deep woods that separated the Botanic Gardens from the Banner property. As he attached his bike to the rack he breathed in the spring air. It smelled fresh and clean. This was going to be a great summer. He'd build some muscles and make some good money.

He removed his lunch box from the saddle bag on his bike and headed toward the building. As he came around behind a black mini-van he looked over at the woods and saw somebody coming through the trees. Curious, he stepped back and peered around the van's side mirror. As he watched, a man stepped from the tree line into the bright sunshine. It was impossible to see who it was in the glare. A couple of cars drove by and obstructed his view. When he looked again, the man was gone. Probably somebody taking a leak.

As Colman entered the Employee Center, Luis Gonzales spotted him and stretched out his hand. "Hola, amigo. Are you ready to work?"

"Si, Señor, ready and able." Colman smiled and shook Luis's hand. He and Luis went back a few years. When Colman was at his worst, Luis had tried to help him out. Back then Colman had been in a downward spiral induced by drugs and alcohol. Ultimately, he had found his way, with help from a lot of people including Luis, Hero and Francesca.

"Good, my friend. Today we're going to be loading flats of flowers and delivering them to several sites in the gardens. Then we're going to dig holes for the fruit trees down by the kitchen gardens. It will be a busy day."

"Sounds good." Colman walked over to his locker to put away his lunch. Maelog Gruffydd was standing there hanging up a sweatshirt. He smiled his slow smile at Colman.

"Baptism by fire," he drawled.

"Right." Colman turned as someone came through the door and cast a shadow across the floor. At first, with the low morning sun shining from behind, Colman couldn't see who it was. As the man approached, he saw it was Dr. Holmes. He felt like disappearing. Was he going to get yelled at again? "Listen, Dr. Holmes, I'm sorry about the other night. I wasn't trying to trespass or anything," Colman blurted out.

Holmes shook his head. "I wanted to apologize for my reactions. We're doing some radical new studies in plant growth and I'm quite jealous of our discoveries. There's a lot of competition these days in plant genetics; both in the gene-gun method as well as the agrobacterium method. You wouldn't know what I'm talking about, but it is an exciting field of study." He sounded condescending, as though he were talking to a small boy. Colman just nodded. He didn't know about the gene-gun method, let alone the agrobacterium method, but he would google them later.

Holmes continued, "So our little area is off-limits. Do you understand?" He wagged a finger at Colman.

Maelog interrupted him, his voice low and slow, with a pause between each word. "Listen, Holmes. Get off his back. You're not God."

Holmes glared at him. "You listen, half-wit. Mind your own business. I don't want you in my laboratories, either. James told me you were in there the other day. Stay out!" He turned on his heel and left, once again throwing a dark shadow across the floor.

**Chapter 18
Thursday morning**

Francesca walked into the volunteer center shortly before eight o'clock. The center was a cheerful open area with lockers to store valuables along one wall. She smelled coffee from the pot next to the fridge. On a counter nearby, an open box of doughnuts from Bonnie's Bakery was beckoning her. She would have to remain strong and resist. Plants were everywhere; on the window sills, on the counter, and on the two round tables in the middle of the room. There were copies of *Kitchen Garden*, *Fine Gardening* and *Country Garden Magazine* strewn on the tables and counters.

Already a large number of volunteers were there enjoying coffee and doughnuts. Laughter and chatter filled the air. Many of the volunteers were senior citizens, and they all seemed to know each other. Francesca recognized Emma Boucher across the room. She walked over to say hello.

"Francesca, how good to see you. I didn't know you were volunteering!" Short and energetic despite her age, Emma gave her a vibrant smile.

Francesca hugged her. "I'm hoping to learn something about gardening that I can apply at home. I hate to see Candice's garden going to pot. And of course I'm planning to do a series in the *Banner Bee*."

"That's great. The BBG needs all the publicity it can get. And Francesca, if you need help with your garden, I can come over and putter around."

Francesca laughed. "I might just take you up on that."

Emma introduced Francesca to her friends. They were talking about Doc's murder, and Francesca saw sorrow flickering in their eyes. As they chatted, she looked over Emma's head and spotted Melinda Jordan. The woman wore black sweats and a black headband, an outfit that definitely wouldn't show any dirt. Francesca caught her eye and waved. Melinda smiled and raised her hand, but then something caught her attention outside. She turned abruptly and headed for the door. *What an odd duck. She has the attention span of a mosquito.*

Taylor Emerson came into the room from the hallway. She was dressed impeccably in a black suit, white blouse and a yellow-and-black jacquard scarf. The suit enveloped her curves in just the right way. Her pumps were gleaming black leather.

"Welcome, ladies and gentlemen. Time to get to work. Our staff leaders are outside. Please find your leader and follow them to the appropriate work site. Let me thank you again for all of your wonderful help. The BBG couldn't do it without you." Her voice was strong and her smile engaging. What a class act, Francesca thought. She'd like to be as put-together as Taylor.

They all tromped outside after their leaders. From a cart, Maelog Gruffydd handed tools and a bright yellow recyclable bag to each volunteer. He led the way, stopping to point out a burgeoning plant or a budding flower. He spoke of each struggling seedling with love and respect. They stopped to look at flowering trees, and Francesca felt amazed by everything she saw. All around her, plants were waking after a long winter and vying for a place in the sun. The flora was in stiff competition for power and glory, just like mankind.

Maelog instructed his volunteers as they trooped along. The seasoned veterans seemed to know the tasks at hand. Today there would be a lot of weeding and planting. There was much talk about annuals, perennials and biennials. Francesca felt clueless. Clearly, she had a lot to learn.

After setting up several volunteers at their appointed tasks, Maelog led Francesca to the waterfall garden. It was one of her favorite places. A man-made hill had been constructed with a pond at the top. The water cascaded down the hill, falling into pools and then flowing down again. Two paths crisscrossed the slope, with miniature bridges and stepping stones across the gushing water. Trees shaded the area. A rock garden nestled among the ponds and flowing water.

Maelog showed her the weeds that she should be looking for. He demonstrated the characteristics of the buckwheat family plants that revealed alternate or whorled leaves along the stems. Then he knelt, pulled out a piece of skinny grass, and pointed out the ligule and collar of the grass plant. As he talked, Francesca studied his face. He looked Mediterranean, maybe Greek or Italian, with his dark eyes and swarthy complexion. Did the Welsh have similar characteristics? There was definitely something odd about his facial features but she couldn't put her finger on it… and his slow speech pattern, too.

He stopped and smiled up at her. "Are you listening to me?"

"Yes. I was just thinking you look Mediterranean."

"The Welsh are part of the Celtic race. We're often dark-haired, but usually with light eyes. I'm the anomaly." He gestured to the weeds. "Are you ready to go? You know what you're pulling up?"

She nodded. "I've got it."

"And make sure you get the roots." Saliva oozed from the corner of his mouth, and he wiped it away with a tissue. He stood, moving with strength and ease, his bulky clothes concealing the outlines of the body beneath.

#

Robbie was bugging her again. Mommy said not to pay attention. "Rosie, don't let him get your goat." But Mommy didn't have to put up with him every single day.

She felt a pebble hit her backpack. It bounced off and skipped across the stone path. Another one hit her leg. That one kind of hurt. She bent down and picked up a handful of pebbles. When she looked up, Mrs. DeBeers was frowning at her. Slowly she let the pebbles fall. Then she held up both hands, palms up. Mrs. DeBeers nodded and turned away. Why did she always get caught?

Rosie looked behind her again. Jenny was staring right at her. She was a skinny girl with long dark hair draped behind large ears. Her eyes were sharp and mean.

"What's the matter, four eyes?" Jenny held her hands up to her eyes like binoculars and wagged her head. "Ooo, I can't see." Then she started to laugh. Ever since Rosie got her glasses in March, Jenny teased her every day. Mommy said Jenny was probably jealous because Rosie looked so cute with the red frames. Mommy had no clue. No matter how terrible Rosie looked, Mommy would always say she looked cute.

Today the third grade class was visiting The Banner Botanic Gardens. Mrs. Roth, their guide, had led them by the water garden with the beautiful lily pads. Now they were in the rose garden and the roses were just beginning to bloom. In summer when Rosie came here with her family there were oodles of flowers and it smelled really good.

Ka-chunk. Ouch. Robbie had thrown another pebble. This one hit her arm. She turned to see a flash of red hair and an orange tee-shirt. Mrs. DeBeers was bent over a rose bush talking with the guide. Rosie picked up a pebble and pushed her way to the back of the group. She took a shot at Robbie but he skipped away giggling and headed toward the rocky stairs leading up the hill to the top of the waterfall garden.

Rosie knew she should stay with her class, but she had to get Robbie back. She picked up another pebble, a big one, and started up the stairs. It was a steep climb. At the top of the hill was a pond and from there the water cascaded down the hillock on the other side. She saw Robbie's orange tee-shirt as he headed down the path that zigzagged across the descending stream with a series of bridges and stepping stones. Rosie took off after him, careful not to slip on the wet rocky path. Halfway down she saw a woman crouching, partially blocking the way. The woman looked up and smiled at Rosie. It was her mom's friend Francesca.

"Where are you running so fast, Rosie? You better slow down or you'll hurt yourself. The path is slippery."

"Hi, Francesca. I've got to get this kid who keeps bothering me." She pointed to where she could see Robbie, down at the bottom of the hill on the road that went around the lake.

"Is your mom here?" Francesca squinted up at her. She had her hair up in a scarf and there were smudges of dirt on her face. Usually, Rosie thought Francesca was beautiful, but today she looked kind of scuzzy.

"No, I'm with my class. I've got to go. I've got to catch Robbie." She took off down the hill and was soon down on the lake road. She glimpsed the orange tee-shirt at the top of the arched bridge that led to the Japanese islands. She took off at a run and was soon at the top of the bridge. Robbie was nowhere in sight.

Rosie slowed down and walked along a sun-dappled gravel path. She took the steps up to the sand garden. There were large stepping stones across the sand that was usually carefully raked to form smooth, curvy lines. Today somebody had messed it up. Probably Robbie. She hopped across the stepping stones and entered a narrow path bordered by high trimmed bushes. It was shady here. She knew the path led to the Japanese tea house.

Rosie stopped to listen. There was only the sound of the breeze ruffling the leaves. She walked more slowly, following the path that turned twice before coming out onto the small front garden of the tea house. Usually the wooden panels were closed and you couldn't see inside. But today the walls were slid back and she could see right through to the funny trees cut in layers and the lake beyond.

A low table stood in the middle of the room. Usually there were cushions surrounding it. Rosie had always thought it would be fun to have a tea party here with her dolls. Of course she never told her friends that she still played with dolls even though she was in third grade.

Today the cushions were all lined up and a man was sleeping on them. She moved closer, trying not to make a sound. It was a Japanese man. He was covered with flowers, bright red ones. They were all over him, except his head. He wore a red headband. His lips were drawn back and she could see his yellow teeth. But he wasn't smiling. He was making a terrible face, like a monster. He stared straight up, his eyes dull and unmoving. Flies swarmed around his face.

Slowly, Rosie backed away. Then she started to scream.

#

After Maelog left, Francesca sat on a rock and began weeding. The air felt cool but the sun warmed her back. Her mind wandered as she dug out the unwanted plants and placed them in her yellow bag. She thought about Doc's death and what Tom had told her that morning. Was Jack Banner capable of murder? She knew he had a temper, but could he kill an old man? The other question was why.

As she stretched briefly to ease her stiff back, movement caught her gaze. Melinda Jordan crossed the bridge leading to the Japanese islands, carrying a bag. Francesca thought of waving, but

Melinda had already disappeared. She settled back to work, digging around the deep roots of a particularly recalcitrant weed.

A horrific scream split the air, coming from the Japanese islands. Rosie had gone that way. Had she fallen? Francesca dashed down the hill, along the lake path and over the arched bridge. The scream had faded to eerie keening. She followed the path to the tea house entrance, marked by a mini labyrinth with high bushes on each side. The path opened up onto a clearing in front of the teahouse. Rosie was there, huddled on the ground, sobbing, her hands covering her face.

"Rosie, what is it?" Francesca hurried forward and gathered Rosie into her arms.

"Take me away. It's terrible." Rosie rubbed her tear-stained face into Francesca's sweatshirt. "I don't want to look." With one hand she gestured toward the tea house.

Francesca looked toward the wooden structure. She could see right through the small building out to the lake beyond. The partitions had been rolled back on both sides. There seemed to be a mass of flowers piled on the floor. Red ones. Francesca stood slowly, holding Rosie next to her.

"A man…in the flowers…he's dead…there's flies in his eyes." Rosie broke into fresh sobs.

Francesca pulled out her cell phone and called 911.

Chapter 19
Thursday morning

Tom Barnett stood with Edmund Hollister on the tatami-covered floor of the Japanese tea house. They were dressed from head to toe in white coveralls. Jones, the photographer was taking pictures from every angle while the crime scene crew collected evidence. Tom looked down at the Japanese man that lay covered with red chrysanthemums. His face was frozen in a tortured rictus.

"Looks like this fellow might have been poisoned," Hollister said. "Can we get the flowers off the body?"

"Have you finished with the pictures, Jones?" Tom asked the photographer.

"Yes, Chief."

"Send a couple of headshots to my iPhone."

"Right, will do."

Tom turned to a technician. "Samson, let's get rid of those flowers."

Samson and another technician began carefully removing and bagging the chrysanthemums. As they worked, the body underneath emerged. The man was dressed in a red-flowered, traditional Japanese silk robe. His arms had been arranged over his chest, with wrist stubs poking through the sleeves. Tom wanted to turn away. Hollister bent forward to look. The victim's hands had been severed. They lay on each side of the body.

"Hacked right off. The cut looks clean; probably with a sharp, heavy instrument, maybe an axe," Hollister said.

"Before or after death?" Tom asked.

"From the small amount of bleeding, he was already dead."

Tom watched as the technicians continued to remove the flowers. When they reached the victim's feet, they found the robe folded back, revealing two more stumps. The feet, in red silk slippers, had been hacked off and laid neatly on the mat.

Tom shook his head, perplexed. "Is this some kind of ritualistic murder? Maybe a Japanese symbolic death; maybe something we don't know about…or understand?"

"Could be. I've never seen anything like this, Chief. You'll have to do some research. But it could be some sick psychopath." Hollister bent down to better study the body and its state of rigor mortis.

Tom stepped back and looked around the miniature building. There were several alcoves, separated by sliding panels, all of which were open now. One alcove contained a scroll depicting a drooping tree with delicate, white flowers. The exterior panels were rolled back as well, offering a view across the lake that gave Tom a momentary sense of peace and relaxation. Quite a contrast with the state of the dead body…but maybe not. Maybe this death, with its carefully arranged and ritualized aspects, was in harmony with the feel of the building.

He eyed the low teak table in the middle of the tea house. On it were a cast iron tea pot and two small porcelain cups. One of them was full. The contents would need to be analyzed.

"Chief!" Tom looked up to see an officer beckoning to him. "Chief, the lady who runs the BBG wants to talk to you. She's on the other side of the bridge. We wouldn't let her come over, and she's ticked."

"Right, I'll come and talk to her." He turned to the ME, who was still bent over the body. "Hollister, give me a call when you've got something."

"Will do." He paused. "Like your momma said, keep your hands and feet to yourself…"

Tom shook his head but didn't reply. He stepped down onto the pebble walkway. To his left, water dripped into a stone basin from a bamboo pipe. A delicate ripple moved across the surface. Again he had a feeling of peace as though time stood still.

He followed the short labyrinth between tall hedges toward the carved wooden gate that marked the entrance to the tea house garden. He felt out of his depth. The cultural markers of the ancient Japanese customs escaped him. He turned right and took the path back to the arched bridge, the only access to the two Japanese islands.

As he approached the bridge, he heard a loud, commanding voice. "This is crazy. Give me one of those white coveralls so I can see what's going on."

Tom crossed the bridge. Yellow caution tape formed a barrier on the far side, where police officers were holding back an elegantly dressed woman in a black suit, with a yellow, white and black scarf at her neck. He recognized Taylor Emerson, socialite turned CEO. Definitely a force to be reckoned with.

She caught sight of him. "Chief Barnett, I need to go in there and see what happened. I'm responsible for everything that goes on in the Gardens." Although her attire was business-like, Tom picked up on a subtle undercurrent of sexuality. She was wearing four-inch heels that made her nearly as tall as he was.

"Ms. Emerson. For the next few hours, no one is allowed onto the islands. Our technicians are gathering evidence, which will take quite some time. This is a crime scene. It cannot be contaminated."

Taylor folded her arms across her chest. "I could put on one of those white coveralls, couldn't I?"

"Unfortunately not." He paused, then said more gently, "I wonder if I could have a word with you? Is there somewhere we could talk?"

She sighed. "Yes. Why don't you come up to my office?"

It was eerily quiet as they walked. Visitors and volunteers had been ushered out of the gardens. Police were guarding the entrances. They had the park to themselves.

"Today we're running a conference on the art of bonsai. We have people registered who came from all over the country. This is a disaster," Taylor said. "Can you tell me exactly what's happened? When I got the message to close the place down, I understood there had been an accident. But your officers are closemouthed." Her voice vibrated with anger.

"We didn't want to raise fears and cause a stampede. There's been a murder."

"A murder?" Taylor turned to look at him, clearly shocked. "Who? A visitor?" She halted and laid her hand on his arm.

"I'd prefer to discuss this in the privacy of your office," Tom said. In truth he wanted to watch her reactions as he talked with her. People often revealed themselves through inadvertent small movements and changes of expression. He moved away from her and kept walking.

They entered the administration building through glass doors that opened into a large enclosed courtyard. Displayed around the enclosure was a collection of bonsai trees on individual pedestals. There must have been fifty exquisite mini-trees. Some exhibits resembled tiny forests. Tom paused to look at several displays. He recognized a tiny pine, a birch and even sugar maples.

"These are amazing," he said. "I didn't know all these types of trees could be trained as bonsai."

"The classic trees are junipers, maples and pines. But just about any woody plant can be used. See over here, even flowering fruit trees." Taylor walked over to a simple yet elegant display. She waved Tom over to join her, looking at him over her shoulder. "This is our current show. Last night was the bonsai conference's opening dinner in the reception hall." She spoke with obvious pride.

Tom realized he'd been slow on the uptake. Bonsai cultivation was a big deal in Japanese culture. "Are there Japanese visitors at the conference?"

"Yes. We have a world-renowned bonsai specialist here for the week, Dr. Kaito Takahashi. He gave the keynote address last night. His talk was wonderful." She smiled as she looked around at the displays of miniature trees she had probably worked tirelessly to organize.

Tom pulled out his phone. He tapped on the photo icon and found the three pictures of the dead man Jones had forwarded. "Please take a look at these pictures and tell me if you recognize this person." He moved into the shade and beckoned Taylor over. She came so close; he could smell her musky scent. Her face was three inches from his, and her silky blonde hair swung across his cheek.

Tom tapped the first photo of their murder victim. "This is a picture of the body discovered this morning. Do you recognize this man?"

Taylor looked at the screen. She drew in a sharp breath, then turned and looked into his eyes. Her deep blue pupils were enormous. She licked her lips. "That's Dr. Takahashi. But what happened? And what about the flowers?" Her gaze shifted back to the cell phone screen. "It looks like he died in terrible pain." Stepping back, she shook herself as though waking up. "This can't happen at the BBG, not at my gardens. It will ruin our reputation." She raised her hands and ran her fingers through her hair. Anger flooded her face, and her full breasts rose and fell as she breathed. "Not on my watch. I'll kill whoever is responsible."

**Chapter 20
Thursday morning**

Detective Puchalski had studied the crime scene. In his protective gear he decided to walk around the small island and get a feel for the lay of the land. He had visited the BBG often with Bonnie and the kids, but he'd usually been distracted; chasing after one child or consoling another. He took the foot path that led into the sand garden. As he walked he examined the trees that had been carefully pruned to give the illusion of old age. Off to the right, a plot of vibrant purple iris grew. To his left, through the branches of a ginkgo tree, lay a vista of the lake and a weeping willow. Bonnie had taken courses at the BBG and told him that nature imitates nature in a Japanese garden. Every tree, plant and rock is carefully placed to give the illusion of nature without flaws. He was struck by the thought that the body of their murder victim had been displayed with equal care.

    He turned a corner and came upon the wooden gate into the sand garden. A path of stepping stones crossed the carefully raked sand. He walked slowly, examining the area, and then stopped. There in the middle of the perfectly raked swirls, someone had dug jagged lines into the sand. Puchalski moved closer and studied the vicious strokes. In ragged script, they read: *Avenge the Tree of Life.*

    Puchalski looked around the enclosure. Was someone watching him? A breeze rustled the branches of an overhanging plum tree. He turned quickly and looked behind him, but saw no one. He could hear the techies working at the tea house nearby. But here in this secluded glen he felt alone and vulnerable. He pulled out his gun and slowly turned in a circle, scrutinizing the trees and bushes surrounding him. After a careful study of the area he put his gun away, then started back toward the tea house. He needed to get Jones over to the sand garden to photograph the writing.

As he rounded a bend, he heard his name through his headset. "Puchalski, where are you?" It was Officer Romano. "I need assistance over on the little island. I've got a kid here that I just found hiding."

Puchalski turned and headed down to the zigzag bridge over to the smaller island. "Romano, where are you?"

"Behind the boulders at the top of the hill."

Puchalski walked around the perimeter of the little island looking for the path that led up to the large boulders at the top of the manmade hill. The rocks represented jagged mountains crowning the island. To his left he found a narrow path that snaked up the hill between bushes trimmed into perfect spheres. He could see Romano's stocky frame partially hidden by a boulder. As he came around the massive rock he found the officer standing next to a redheaded ten-year-old boy who was wiping his face. Puchalski immediately recognized the infamous Robbie Sumner. His own children talked about Robbie. The kid was aggressive and often in trouble. His mom had a laissez-faire attitude toward discipline. As far as Puchalski knew, Robbie's dad had flown the coop years ago.

Puchalski crouched down. "Hey, Robbie. What's the matter? Did you get lost?"

Robbie sniffled and wiped his nose on the hem of his oversized, orange tee shirt. "I'm scared I hurt Rosie," he mumbled. Tears welled up again and he looked down at the ground, rubbing his eyes with his fists. Beneath the tee shirt he wore baggy shorts and beat-up high-tops.

"Rosie's fine. Her dad came to pick her up."

He looked up at Puchalski. "I thought I'd hit her with that rock when I heard her start screaming. She's all right?"

"Yes, she's fine."

"Then why was she screaming? Why were there sirens and all the police?"

"Rosie saw something that frightened her."

"What'd she see?"

Puchalski weighed his options. He hadn't planned on telling this kid anything, but maybe Robbie had seen something. "She found a dead man in the tea house."

"Wow!" Robbie smiled. "A dead man? Cool!"

Ron looked up at Romano who was smiling and shaking his head.

"So tell me what happened? Why were you over here on this island?"

"I hit Rosie with a pebble and she chased me up over the hill to the waterfall garden, and then down to the bridge to the Japanese garden. I hid behind a bush in the maze by the tea house. Rosie ran past me, and then I threw a couple more pebbles over the hedge. Then Rosie started screaming like crazy. So I ran and hid over here. I saw the police and the paramedics come, and I thought…" He bit his lip and looked down at his shoes.

"Come on," Puchalski said. "Let's get you out of here. This is a restricted area while we're processing the scene."

As they headed down the narrow path Indian file, Robbie said, "I wasn't the only one watching."

Puchalski turned and looked at the boy, who was gazing off at the other island. "There was somebody hidden up in the big tall pine tree. They were watching all the action," Robbie said.

"A policeman?"

"No, somebody else. I couldn't see them real good."

"A man or a woman?"

"I don't know. After a few minutes, they kind of melted into the shadows."

Puchalski remembered his feeling of being watched, and shivered.

Chapter 21
Thursday morning

Francesca drove home after delivering Rosie Marshall to her dad. Martin had driven over as soon as she called. He arrived looking frightened behind his heavy black-framed glasses. Rosie ran to him and he picked her up. He was a tall gangly man with the distracted manner of an absent-minded professor. In fact he was a history professor at the college.

"What's the matter, sweetheart?"

"Daddy, I saw a terrible looking dead man. His eyes were open and there were flies and he was covered with flowers." Rosie began to sob again.

"It's all right, darling. You're safe now." He hugged her to his chest and kissed the top of her head. "I'm going to take you home." He looked over at Francesca, his eyes pleading with hers. They were both remembering when Rosie had been kidnapped by the lake monster and almost drowned. Luckily, Francesca had arrived and saved the little girl's life.

Martin walked to his car and Francesca followed. He put Rosie in the back in her booster seat. In one of the two car-seats next to her, baby Michael was asleep. The other was empty. Rosie's little brother Stevie must be in nursery school at the park district.

Francesca looked in at the sleeping baby, so sweet and innocent. She smiled at Martin. "Michael is adorable." He nodded. She couldn't pull her eyes away from the baby's sweet face.

Martin shut the car door and turned to Francesca. "God, what happened? I can't believe Rosie's been involved in another horrible incident." He pushed up his glasses and rubbed the bridge of his nose.

Martin was face-blind, meaning he couldn't recognize people by their facial features. A year ago he had received a pair of glasses that enabled him to distinguish familiar faces. The Department of Homeland Security had developed the technology. When he met someone new, the glasses took a picture of that person and Martin entered his or her name. The next time he ran into that individual, the eyeglasses transmitted an audible message with the person's name. Rosie called them his magic glasses.

"And where was Mrs. DeBeers?" he said gruffly. "Isn't she supposed to be watching these kids on the field trip?"

"Rosie ran away from the group, chasing Robbie Sumner who hit her with a pebble. They both came racing by me while I was working in the waterfall garden."

"Oh, Robbie is a rascal. He's always in trouble, I hear."

They both looked up at the sound of a helicopter overhead. It was hovering over the gardens. In the parking lot the media was setting up camp. Martin glanced back at Francesca. "So what about the dead man? Who is he?"

"I don't know. I only got a glimpse of the body and then I got Rosie out of there. It looked like an Asian man, probably Japanese. I don't know what happened or how he died. It was a macabre sight."

Rosie banged on the window. Clearly, she wanted to leave.

"I better go. She'll wake up the baby. Thanks for your help, Francesca. We'll keep in touch."

As Martin got in and shut the door, Rosie rolled down her window. "Bye Francesca. Thank you for saving me."

"You'll be all right, honey. Bye-bye." Francesca waved as they pulled away. *Saving her?* Francesca shuddered.

Chapter 22
Thursday morning

After Taylor Emerson calmed down, she told Tom that Dr. Takahashi had attended the dinner the previous evening with his daughter, Akiko. The girl had acted as translator for her father but had slipped out before dessert.

"Someone needs to tell her what happened. I can't be the one to do it." Taylor looked pale, perspiration beaded on her forehead.

"Where is she staying?"

"At the Deer Run Inn." Taylor pulled out a tissue and dabbed the sweat away. "I just can't tell her that her father is dead."

"We'll handle it." Tom took out a notebook, suppressing his frustration at Taylor's attitude. "We're going to need to interview the BBG employees who attended last night's reception."

Taylor thought for a moment. "There were seven staff members at the dinner. Everyone else left at closing time."

"Okay. If you could get them here, I'd like to interview them right away." He looked down at his notebook. "I'd also like a list of all the attendees."

"Okay, I can do that."

While she got on the phone, Tom went out into the hall and called Francesca. He wanted to see how she was doing and he had a big favor to ask.

A half hour later, Tom and Puchalski had set up shop in the library. Cindy Murray and Brendan O'Connor took the board room. They needed to interview the staff while the evening was still fresh in everyone's minds.

Tom sat at one end of a table, Puchalski adjacent to him on the side facing the door. The library was quiet and cool. A large selection of books surrounded them, some on open shelves, some in locked glass cabinets. LED spotlights beamed down on their table.

The first employee to enter the room was a tall, heavy-set man with an interesting face. He stood in the doorway looking uncertain, a hesitant smile slowly forming on his lips. He held a brown fedora and wore a scarf around his neck. Long wavy dark hair covered his ears.

"Maelog Gruffydd. You wanted to see me?" His speech was slow and ponderous, with a slight stutter.

Tom stood up and gestured to the chair across from Puchalski. "Yes. Please sit down. We just have a few questions. I'm Chief Barnett and this is Detective Puchalski."

Gruffydd walked over and settled himself in the chair. He put his fedora on the table in front of him and waited expectantly.

"You've heard Dr. Takahashi was killed last night?" Tom said.

"Yes, we all heard he was poisoned."

Tom wondered how they all knew that piece of information so quickly. There must be quite the grapevine at the Botanic Gardens.

"Can you tell us about the dinner and reception last evening?" Puchalski sat back.

"I got to the reception late." Gruffydd paused, looking down at his hands where they gripped the rim of his hat. Then he looked up at Puchalski. "I have some…difficulty speaking these days. I try to avoid events where I need to talk to strangers."

Puchalski nodded. "When did you get there?"

"The dinner was at seven. I got there at six-forty-five. Had a glass of wine and talked to Irma Hoffmann about the spring planting that was supposed to start today. Then we went in to dinner." Drool escaped from the corner of his mouth. He wiped it with the back of his hand.

"Did you talk to Dr. Takahashi or his daughter?"

"No, I did not. I am not a fan of the art of bonsai." He spoke without emotion but Tom noticed the cords in his neck tighten and he squeezed the brim of his hat. "I didn't want to come to the dinner but I didn't have a choice."

"How's that?" Puchalski asked.

"Lady Emerson ordered us to show."

"What about the bonsai trees?"

Gruffydd sighed. "I'm interested in trees in their natural habitat…not stunted and deformed ones."

"Did you speak to Dr. Takahashi at any time?"

"No, I did not." He smoothed his hat brim. "I was seated at a rear table with some minor donors. Taylor never wants me near the big-time benefactors. I'm not the ideal poster-child for the gardens." He smiled ruefully and his posture relaxed. He was a curious individual, Tom thought.

"What about at the conclusion of the dinner? Did you notice Dr. Takahashi talking to anyone?" Puchalski asked.

"I left early to avoid the after-dinner speeches. As I went down through the water gardens, I saw Takahashi's daughter. She seemed to be in a hurry to get out of there, too."

Tom scrawled a question mark beside Akiko Takahashi's name.

Puchalski continued with the interview. "Where did you go after the dinner?"

"Home. I live over Larson's Interiors in town." Gruffydd frowned and with difficulty asked, "Am I a suspect?"

Puchalski smiled. "No, Mr. Gruffydd. We're trying to understand everything that went on last night."

"Could you tell us a little about yourself? Did you grow up around here?" Tom asked.

"No, I'm from Maine originally."

"How did you get into the horticulture business?"

"My dad had a tree farm. After he died I sold it and went to work on Long Island on an organic farm. I've only been here for a couple of years." This time he spoke more smoothly and comfortably.

"Is there anything else you'd like to tell us? Anything you noticed out of the ordinary?"

"No...except I think Dr. Miyamoto might have been a little put out. He's been the big cheese for all the bonsai lovers. Last night they were all huddled around Takahashi. It looked to me like his nose was out of joint, if you know what I mean?" He looked from Puchalski to Tom.

"Who invited Dr. Takahashi here?" Puchalski asked.

"Taylor, but I'm not sure she consulted with Miyamoto."

Tom looked at his sergeant, and they both stood. "Thanks for your help, Mr. Gruffydd. If you think of anything, give me a call." Tom handed Gruffydd a card.

After the man left, Tom said, "What do you think?"

"I think he doesn't like bonsai specialists and he's not overly fond of Taylor Emerson."

"That's for sure. He got agitated about the bonsai trees."

"I wonder why he has trouble talking? It looked like his jaw and lips weren't in sync with his tongue," Puchalski said.

Tom studied his notes. "I wonder if there's anything to Miyamoto's supposed jealousy of Takahashi."

"We'll have a better idea when we interview Miyamoto."

The door opened and a tall woman entered, wearing a striped dress, dirty apron and rubber boots. She walked heavily across the room, smiled and sat down. She had a strong face with a rugged complexion. Friendly blue eyes were partially hidden behind a swath of grey-streaked hair falling from a messy bun. She stuck out her hand. "Irma Hoffmann. Pleased to meet you." Her hand was large and her grip powerful. Gardening must build muscles, Tom thought.

"What a terrible thing to happen right here at the BBG. We're all devastated." Irma shook her head. Another stray lock of hair escaped from her bun.

"Thanks for coming in to talk with us," Tom said. "We're trying to learn as much as possible about what went on here last night."

"You mean about the dinner?"

"Yes, anything that happened before, after or during," Tom said. "What can you tell us?"

"Well, Dr. Takahashi didn't get here until just before the reception. I saw him arrive with his daughter. I was parking my Subaru. I'd gone home to change."

"Had you met Dr. Takahashi previously?"

"Oh, no. I run the fruit and vegetable area." Irma smiled broadly. "I'm basically a glorified farm girl. I'm not involved with the bonsai exhibit." She paused and lowered her voice. "To tell you the truth, I'm not into anything Japanese. Those Japs killed my grandfather." She looked from Tom to Puchalski. "And maiming trees is not my thing."

A moment of silence fell. Then Puchalski spoke. "Tell us about the evening."

"Well, like I said, I got here about six. I went in to the reception, got a glass of wine and talked to some of the people who volunteer in my area. They had questions about planting tomatoes. We got into a discussion about the best varieties. I've got several heirloom varieties I really like. But you don't want to hear about that." She scratched her head. "Let's see, then I got introduced to Takahashi. His daughter did most of the translating, with Miyamoto adding a word or two. Then Maelog arrived. He's a buddy of mine. We talked about the planting." She frowned and placed her big hands flat on the table. "Hey, will we be able to get back to planting tomorrow? We've got hundreds of plants waiting in the greenhouses."

"I don't see why not. Only the Japanese islands will be closed off," Puchalski said.

"Did you notice any interaction between Dr. Takahashi and Dr. Miyamoto?" Tom asked, trying to get things back on track.

"Hmm…They were certainly cordial to each other. But you never know about Miyamoto. He's got a real poker face." She grinned. "Anyway, during the dinner I sat with a group of gardeners. We all had so much to talk about that no one was really listening to each other. It's a fun group, but everyone has their opinion about growing stuff." She crossed her legs and leaned her elbows on the table.

"What about afterwards? Anything unusual?" Puchalski asked.

"I was one of the last to leave. We were in the midst of our arguments when Taylor came over and told us to close it down." She giggled, then looked thoughtful. "On my way out, I saw Holmes going off towards his lab. He practically sleeps there."

"Holmes?" Puchalski asked.

"Yeah, Dr. Jared Holmes, our resident 'scientist.'" She made quotation marks with her raised fingers when uttering the final word. "He's a piece of work, not always easy to get along with."

"Where did you go after the dinner?"

"Me? I went home. I've got dogs and cats. I have to go home to my little family."

Tom leaned back. "Where did you grow up?"

Irma's carefree manner changed abruptly. She sat up. "I'm from the Eastern Shore… Maryland."

"How did you end up here?"

"A friend of mine started an organic farm and I worked with him for several years. That's where I learned the tricks of the trade. Then I was in California for a while and then I applied here…" She trailed off and stood up. "Is that it?"

They let her go with thanks. After she left, Puchalski looked at his notes. "That makes two of them who aren't bonsai lovers."

Chapter 23
Thursday morning

Francesca had just walked into the house when her cell phone rang. It was Tom.

"Hi, love. How are you doing?"

"I'm feeling a little shook up. Another dead body. What happened to the guy?" Francesca sat down on a kitchen chair.

"Hollister thinks initially he was poisoned but he'll have to run blood tests."

"Initially?"

Tom didn't respond.

"Who is he? He looked Japanese."

"He's a famous bonsai expert, Dr. Kaito Takahashi. He just arrived yesterday from Japan."

"For the conference?"

"Right. Last night they had the opening reception. Workshops and presentations were organized for today and tomorrow."

"Who could have wanted to kill him? It makes no sense if he just got here."

"It has to be someone familiar with the BBG. We've been interviewing staff members who were there last night."

Francesca stood and walked to the window. "I'm just thinking. Are you sure he didn't commit suicide?"

"Yes. There's additional evidence making that impossible."

She looked at the busy robins fluttering around the apple tree. "What evidence?"

"I'd rather not discuss that now."

"Okay." She knew not to push him. "Could this have anything to do with Doc Stoddard…two deaths within two days?"

"I don't think so. But at this point we can't rule anything out."

They fell silent. Then Tom said, "I've got a favor to ask. We're going to be busy here most of the day. I'm shorthanded with these two murders. I need someone to go over to the Deer Run Inn and talk to Takahashi's daughter, inform her of her father's death. By all rights, I should go over there, but I want to begin this investigation while the trail is hot. Could you go to the Inn and give her the bad news? If you don't want to do it, just tell me."

"What about Taylor Emerson or Miyamoto, the Japanese guy on staff?"

"Taylor refuses, and we want to interview Miyamoto as soon as possible."

"Well…"

Tom said nothing.

"Okay. I'll do it. What's the girl's name?"

"Akiko Takahashi." He spelled it out. "She's staying at the Deer Run and she speaks English. We haven't heard from her this morning so we're assuming she doesn't know what's happened. Sorry to dump this on you."

After they hung up, Francesca stared at the phone. Tom had handed her a difficult task. She didn't know this young woman, or how she would react. Normally, the police handled this job. Legally, they probably should. On the other hand, Francesca was curious. Talking to Akiko would be a way to learn more about Dr. Takahashi.

#

Half an hour later, Francesca went up the steps and into the Deer Run Inn. The Deer Run was a comfortable hotel that had existed in Banner Bluff for years and years. It had an Old World feel. She felt a little nervous. She'd dressed in black pants and a black and white Breton top, colors that seemed appropriate. She recognized Mark Riddell at the desk and went over.

"Hi, Mark." She looked down at the pink Post-it note where she'd written down the unfamiliar name. "I'm here to see Akiko Takahashi."

"You're in luck. She just went down to The Pub. It's right down those stairs." He pointed to an alcove across the lobby.

"Right. Thanks Mark." Francesca walked towards the stairway, righting her shoulders and standing a little straighter as if going into battle. You had to be strong to bring unhappiness. When she reached the foot of the stairs she turned right into The Pub, The Deer Run's less formal restaurant. At night it was a popular hot spot. Now, in the late morning, there was no one around except a young woman bent over her phone, her fingers texting a mile a minute.

Without thinking about it, Francesca had been prepared for a geisha girl dressed in a kimono. What she saw was a slim young woman in jeans and a pink long-sleeved tee-shirt. Francesca referred to her Post-it again. "Ms. Takahashi? Akiko Takahashi?"

The woman looked up. She had a perfect, oval face, framed by long, straight black hair and soft bangs. "Yes? Can I help you?" Her tone was cool; her English perfect.

Francesca stepped forward and held out her hand. "I'm Francesca Barnett. I wonder if I could sit down and talk to you." Her nervousness spiked.

"All right. Do I know you? Were you at the reception last night?"

"No, I wasn't there. I'm the police chief's wife." Francesca sat down across from Akiko. "Um…I'm here about your father."

"My father? I haven't seen him this morning. I knocked on his door but there was no answer. I thought maybe he'd gone over to the conference." Akiko glanced back down at her phone. She was obviously in the midst of a conversation. With bright red fingernails she texted a few more words, pressed *send* and turned off her phone. Then she picked up her coffee and took a sip, looking at Francesca from under the perfect bangs. "So? What about my father?"

Francesca leaned over and took the woman's other hand. "I'm not sure of the best way to do this. There is no best way." She took a breath. "I'm sorry to tell you, your father has died. He passed away sometime last night." She squeezed the slim hand. "I'm so, so sorry."

"What are you telling me?" Akiko yanked her hand away and looked at Francesca with disbelief. "This can't be true. Why are you here?"

"My husband asked me to come and talk to you. The police are tied up over at the Banner Botanic Gardens."

Akiko's mouth dropped open and she stared blindly at Francesca. Then she gave Francesca a suspicious look. "My father is dead. How?"

"He was poisoned sometime last night. A little girl on a school trip found him in the Japanese tea house at the gardens this morning. He was covered in flowers."

"Last night? Poisoned? Flowers? Father?" Akiko shook her head. "What is this crazy story you're telling me?"

"I know this is a terrible shock." Francesca felt hopelessly awkward. Maybe she'd told this girl more than she needed to know.

"I can't believe it." Tears streamed down Akiko's face.

Francesca reached out and took the girl's hand again. "When did you last see your dad?"

"I didn't see my father after the dinner. I came back here early. I was not feeling well. I drove back with the rental car. My father was being driven back later." Akiko spoke between sobs. "I can't believe this. He was fine yesterday. Wait, you said he was poisoned. Was there something wrong with the food? But I didn't get sick." Akiko's glance darted around the room. "Father is dead."

"I don't know all the details. They're investigating and interviewing people who were at the reception last night. Later on, you'll need to identify your father's body, if you're up to it."

"Why did I leave him there? I should have stuck around. 'She gazed blindly across the room then turned back to Francesca. "I lied." She averted her eyes. "I had to meet someone."

Francesca was curious. Who could Akiko possibly know in Banner Bluff? "Another bonsai expert?"

"No, no. It was stupid." Her voice dropped to a hoarse whisper. "I wanted to see a man I knew in Japan. I wanted to confront him and I did. But he could have cared less about what I had to say." She rubbed her temples, then looked up at Francesca. "Do you know him? Jack Banner?"

Chapter 24
Thursday, late morning

Tom and Puchalski continued their interviews in the library. Immediately after Irma Hoffmann left, the door swung open again and Dr. Miyamoto entered. He made a slight bow and walked across the room. "I am Hisao Miyamoto. I am happy to meet you." His voice was low and he articulated each word with care.

    Tom and Puchalski stood up. Tom introduced them both, and found himself bowing slightly as well. "Please be seated."

    "I must express my sadness that my esteemed colleague, Dr. Takahashi, has been killed. Who could possibly have done this?" Miyamoto's face remained unexpressive. He sat erect in the chair, legs straight and feet flat on the floor.

    "Did you know Dr. Takahashi?" Puchalski asked.

    "Yes, we have met before and we have communicated many times."

    "Would you say you had a close relationship?"

    "No. We were cordial when we met but we have argued many times in our writings. Dr. Takahashi had different views on proper pruning techniques, care and style of bonsai." He spoke softly, and Tom found it difficult to understand his accented English.

    "Did you argue yesterday?" Puchalski asked.

    "No, we barely talked. He was surrounded by many bonsai lovers. His English was very bad. His daughter translated for him." Miyamoto grimaced.

    "Did you talk to his daughter?"

"Only briefly, after the meal. She came to me and said she didn't feel well and needed to leave. I took her place as translator for her father during the speeches and questions." Again the poker face.

"When did you leave the reception?"

"I left with Dr. Takahashi and saw him safely to his limo."

"Did he say where he was going?"

"I assumed to the Deer Run Inn. That's where they're staying."

"Where did you go after you saw Dr. Takahashi off?" Puchalski asked.

"I went home. I was tired and I hadn't seen my wife all day."

"Where do you live?"

"On Elm Street, three-twenty-five, near downtown."

"Did you make plans to meet Dr. Takahashi today?"

"Not exactly. We both would have been on hand. Today, there were to be lectures and demonstrations beginning at ten o'clock, but that is when you closed the gardens. All the people that came from all over the country must be disappointed." He made a slight gesture with his hand.

"Do you know of anyone who would want to kill Dr. Takahashi?" Puchalski asked.

"No."

"You said you disagreed with him professionally."

Anger flared in Miyamoto's eyes. *Finally*, Tom thought, *a genuine emotion*. "Are you suggesting I would want to kill a man with whom I disagreed? I did oppose him on an intellectual level, but I would never kill anyone." He stood to leave. For him, the interview was over.

They let him go. After Miyamoto's departure, Puchalski turned to Tom. "Behind his poker face, that guy was really nervous."

"That's for sure." Mentally, Tom replayed the interview. "He mentioned escorting Takahashi to a limo. We need to find the limo driver."

"Right, I'll get Romano on that." Ron picked up his phone and sent a text.

#

A short while later, Dr. Holmes strode in and sat down. He was tall, thin, and grey: grey suit, grey-patterned tie, grey eyes, and grey hair. His skin was unusually pale and he wore round steel-rimmed glasses. "I'm Dr. Jared Holmes. I've got a lot to do today, so I hope we can get through this quickly. I've been out there waiting forever."

"Sorry about that," Tom said. "I'm Chief Barnett, and—"

"I know who you are. And the detective here. So what do you want to know? I had absolutely nothing to do with the dead man. I didn't even talk to him last night."

"So tell us what your role is here at the BBG," Puchalski said calmly.

A wave of pink rose from Holmes's skinny neck to his face. "Officer, are you patronizing me?"

Puchalski kept his tone neutral. "No, sir. Can you tell us what you do here?"

Holmes gave a sharp sigh. "I'm in charge of important research going on here at the Banner Botanic Gardens. I also teach at the college. I have nothing to do with the bonsai exhibit."

"What sort of research do you do?" Tom asked.

Holmes leaned forward. "What does that have to do with your investigation?"

"Dr. Holmes, right now we're just gathering information and learning about the gardens." This guy was itching for a fight, but Tom had no intention of giving him one. "The sooner you answer our questions, the sooner you'll be out of here."

"If I must. We're conducting studies concerning the suitability of plants and soil for rooftop gardening. The ecological use of rooftops in cities could provide residents with healthy, organic food. Another project involves the protection of Native American plants, sorting and freeze-drying the seeds for future generations. Students and volunteers provide the workforce for this labor-intensive process." He smiled with unabashed pride. "We're doing important work. The population at large has no appreciation of the power of plants."

Puchalski nodded. "Tell us about last night."

"What's to tell? I attended the reception with several members of my crew. We sat together during dinner and talked shop. Then we sat through the boring presentation and Q and A session. I was thrilled to get out of there. I went home for a stiff scotch."

"Did you talk with Dr. Takahashi?"

"His daughter introduced us. It took all of two minutes. I'd never met the man before. I'm not into the bonsai thing. It seems an unnecessary occupation, but some people are obsessed. They were crowding around the esteemed Dr. Taka-whatever."

A brief silence fell. Holmes looked from Puchalski to Tom. "Is that it? Can I leave?"

"Tell us a bit about yourself; where you trained; where you grew up," Puchalski said.

"Is this really necessary? All that's on file in the office."

Puchalski shrugged. "A little background wouldn't hurt."

Holmes heaved an exaggerated sigh. "I come from Spokane. Went to the University of Washington. Got my Ph.D. at the University of Wyoming. Taught there a while, then came to Banner College." His expression said *are you happy now?*

Tom spoke up. "Just one more question. I understand that after the dinner you headed over to the research building."

Holmes reddened again. "Right. I wanted to check on everything, make sure the doors were locked. Lately, I've found them unlocked several times. I don't like that." He shifted in his chair, as if preparing to stand and leave.

"And was everything in order?"

"No, not exactly. Someone had rearranged some Petri dishes in the lab. I'm worried it's this new kid they hired to do heavy work. I found him wandering in the lab the other day."

"What's his name?" Tom asked.

"I don't know. You'll have to ask Luis Gonzales. He manages those guys."

#

Taken aback, Francesca said, "Yes, I do know Jack Banner. But how do you know him?"

Akiko looked pale and drained as she leaned back against the padded leather seat. "It's a long story. After college in the States, I came home and was at loose ends. My father convinced me to work with him for a few years. He thought I owed him after the cost of the American University. But it was fine. We get along great." Tears filled her eyes. "My father traveled all over the world and I went with him." She stared into her empty cup, as if lost in memories.

The waiter appeared and asked Francesca if she wanted something. She said no. "What about Jack?" she prompted gently, after the waiter left.

"He was in the Marines, stationed on a base near my home. I met him by accident one day. He needed help locating an electronics store. I ended up taking him there."

She was so tense, there had to be more. Francesca waited.

"So we got to know each other. I guess I was excited by him. He's the opposite of me. I'm slow to make decisions. I don't jump into things. But Jack is fearless and impulsive…too impulsive." She shuddered. "One night a couple of months after I met him, we went back to his place. I should have known better." Akiko reddened and then looked at Francesca. "He raped me, just threw me on the floor and raped me . When I got home I was a mess. I told my father what happened. He had never met Jack but he soon learned all about him." She clasped her hands so tightly, her knuckles turned white.

Francesca briefly laid a hand over Akiko's clenched ones. "You don't have to tell me anymore. It's none of my business."

"No, I want to. Anyway, my father knew high-placed people in the government. They pulled some strings with the Marines. Within a couple of days, Jack was sent back to the States. I never saw him again." She sighed. "But I didn't forget about him. I've been going through therapy for over a year. When I knew we were coming here for the conference, I decided I needed to confront him. I thought I could banish my nightmares. So I contacted him. He agreed to meet me yesterday evening at nine-thirty, at a bar called the Gaslight."

"So you left the reception to go there?" Francesca prodded.

"Yes. He was at a table by the window. It didn't go like I planned. By the time I arrived, he had been drinking for a while. He was sarcastic and cruel. When I told him what I'd been through, he just laughed and said, 'You wanted me, I know you did.' Then he got angry. He said it was my fault he got kicked out of the Marines. He called me a little bitch. I realized I had made a big mistake in meeting him. I was so upset, I ran out of there and back here to the Inn. I didn't fall asleep until three in the morning."

Francesca thought through what Akiko had told her. "What time did you leave Jack?"

"I was only there a short time. Nine-forty-five, or ten o'clock, maybe."

Francesca wondered what Jack did after Akiko left. How angry was he? Angry enough to kill?

Chapter 25
Thursday afternoon

Tom and Puchalski finished their interviews about the same time as Cindy and Brendan. All four of them convened in the board room.

"We interviewed four people," Cindy said, seated on the edge of her chair. "We didn't nail the murderer, but we got an earful."

"Yeah, man oh man," Brendan said. "Lillian Roth, the lady who runs the education program, felt really guilty about the little girl who discovered the body. Neither she nor the teacher saw the two kids take off." He glanced at his notes. "Last night she didn't get a chance to talk to Dr. Takahashi. She was seated with some administrators from area schools and didn't notice anything out of the ordinary." He looked up. "It took her a long time to get that out."

"Poppy Jorgenson was next," Cindy said. "She runs the Welcome Program for volunteers. She's a senior citizen, just bursting with energy. By the time she finished talking, I was ready to sign up here."

"I know her. She's active on various committees in town," Puchalski said.

"She felt there was some tension last night. She witnessed an argument between Dr. Holmes and Irma Hoffmann." Cindy looked up. "You talked to them, right?"

"Yes, but neither of them mentioned any disagreement. When did it happen? How bad was it?" Tom asked.

Cindy consulted her notes. "Before the dinner, in the hallway. Poppy called it 'quite a shouting match.'"

"We'll have to look into that." Tom rubbed his forehead. "I'd like to interview several people again after we analyze what we've learned so far."

Brendan continued. "Ms. Halsey, the librarian, was worried about you disturbing the library books. You know, the Dewey decimal system and all that." He was grinning.

"She considers the library her private domain," Cindy said.

"Kidding aside, she was hoping to show Dr. Takahashi the bonsai collection in the library. Apparently, they have an exceptionally fine selection of books. She did talk to the daughter about it and they were going to stop by this afternoon." Brendan looked up, his eyes questioning. "What about the daughter? Who's taking care of her?"

"The daughter's name is Akiko. I asked Francesca to go over to the Deer Run and break the bad news. It's not proper protocol but she's good with people and I thought we needed to be here. Later, when Miss Takahashi is up to it, we'll need to bring her in to identify the body," Tom said.

They nodded, and Brendan went on. "Ms. Halsey is particular about her books and her patrons. She told us Dr. Holmes and his students come in to do research. She's okay with them as long as they don't talk. Let's see. Mr. Gruffydd comes in to read magazines. She thinks he might be mentally slow, but she admires the effort he makes to inform himself."

Puchalski laughed at this. "I don't think Gruffydd is mentally slow. He has some physical issues, but that guy is sharp. Don't you think, Chief?"

Tom nodded. "Yes, I do."

Chapter 26
Thursday afternoon

After talking about Jack Banner, Akiko looked exhausted and asked to be alone. Francesca told her a detective would probably come by later to ask her some questions, and gave the younger woman her cell phone number, "in case you need someone to talk to." Then she left.

At home, Francesca let the dogs out in the backyard. While they ran around, she texted Tom to call her when he got the chance. She wanted to tell him about Akiko and her meet-up with Jack. She peeked in the refrigerator, but there wasn't much to eat. She was starving and felt out of sorts. With the investigation into Doc Stoddard's killing and this new murder case, Tom would be M.I.A. for the next few weeks, if not the next few months. She needed some company.

She picked up her cell phone and called Susan, her college friend and former roommate. "I was just thinking about you," Susan said when she answered. "I heard about Doc's murder. How are you doing?" Susan's voice was warm and friendly, like a good bowl of warm soup. Francesca felt better just hearing it.

"I'm edgy and I'm starving. Are you free for a quick lunch?"

"Sure. How about coming out to the club? I just got here and I'm looking over some menu possibilities for the Oak Hills Invitational. You can help me pick the perfect menu."

"I'll be there in fifteen minutes. It would do me wonders to see you."

"See you soon." Susan rang off. She had been manager of the country club for a couple of years. Then she married Marcus

Reynolds, a well-known physician in town. After the birth of their baby, Susan had scaled back and now worked part-time as an event planner for the club.

Francesca settled the dogs with a chewy-bone and went out to the car. It was a quick drive over to the Oak Hills Golf and Tennis Club. The weather had turned warmer and the streets were dappled with sunshine under the new spring leaves. As she turned into the driveway leading up to the club house, she noticed the line of ancient live oaks. They marched up the hill like a magnificent army of giants. How old could they be, she wondered.

She pulled into a parking space between a massive Range Rover and a sleek Mercedes Cabriolet. She looked in the rearview mirror and applied some lipstick, then opened the door and stepped out of the car. Several men were loading their golfing gear into the trunk of their vehicle nearby. They looked up as Francesca passed and followed her with their eyes. She barely noticed them.

The club house steps led up to a large veranda where white-painted rocking chairs and porch swings with colorful striped cushions gave the feeling of a luxurious Southern plantation. Francesca had heard that the club house had been completely redecorated. She stepped into the entry hall. Before the renovation, the décor aimed for old-English-country-house, heavy in brown, burgundy and forest green. Now, the foyer had the elegance of a Japanese print. A modern Murano chandelier hung from the high ceiling. Tones of cool grey and muted green conveyed sleek comfort and simplicity.

Susan stepped into the foyer from a hallway. Her high heels clicked on the marble floor as she approached Francesca. Her royal blue side wrap dress brought out her startling blue eyes, and her blond hair was pulled into a low ponytail.

"You look fabulous," Francesca said.

"Well, I can get into all my pre-baby clothes, so I'm feeling pretty good. The last few pounds were killers." Susan reached over and hugged Francesca.

"How's Sophia?" Francesca asked.

"She's the best baby ever. She wakes up happy and barely ever cries. We're so lucky."

"Yes, you are," Francesca murmured.

Susan pulled out her cell phone and retrieved pictures of the baby. "Marcus says she looks like me. What do you think?"

"She's got your blue eyes," Francesca said, gazing at the image of the giggling baby with unabashed longing.

Susan put away her phone and led the way toward the dining room, which had been redone in apricot tones. Large windows looked out on the green fairways beyond. "Supposedly, salmon and apricot are the most relaxing colors for dining. Did you know that?" Susan said.

"No, I didn't but I love the feel of this room. Warm and airy…very *au courant*." They walked to an alcove in the back, where they could talk. As they sat down, the waiter came over with the menus.

"Good afternoon, *Mesdames*. Can I bring you a glass of wine? Maybe a nice Pouilly-Fumé?" He looked at Susan. She looked at Francesca, who drew in a breath to say no.

"Yes, we'll both have a glass," Susan said firmly. "And Pierre, we'll both have the Asian salmon on baby greens." Once Pierre had moved away she said, "My treat. I think you could do with a glass of wine. You look a wee bit stressed, my friend."

For no reason, Francesca felt tears spring to her eyes. What was wrong with her? She sighed. "Yes, I guess I am. You obviously don't know what happened this morning." She told Susan about Rosie Marshall and the dead body in the Japanese tea house at the Botanic Gardens. "I don't know anything more. I guess I'll go to the press conference and find out like everyone else." She played with her fork, turning it over in her hand. Then she looked up at Susan. "I don't want to be this close to death again." Then she told Susan about her encounter with Akiko.

Susan was sympathetic. "You've been through the wringer this morning."

Pierre delivered their wine. After he left Susan said, "What were you doing at the BBG?"

"I'm a volunteer. I'm trying to learn about gardening and I'm going to do a series of articles."

Susan gazed at her over the rim of her glass. "Why do you want to learn about gardening?"

"So I can turn our backyard into a horticultural masterpiece," Francesca said wryly.

"Is that really your thing? Or are you trying to be like Candy?" Susan said softly.

Tears welled in Francesca's eyes again. *Gosh, I'm a wreck.*

Susan reached over and touched her shoulder. "I think Doc's murder and this latest dead body is too much for you."

"You're right. I'm upset about that."

"And what else?" Susan always could read her like an open book.

Francesca took a Kleenex from her purse. "I want to have a baby. Tom doesn't. He can't forget that Candy died shortly after they learned she was pregnant." She wiped her eyes and took a sip of wine.

Susan gave her a sympathetic look. "You've only been married a couple of months. What's the rush?"

"I don't want a baby right away. But I'm thirty-five and I'm getting older every day. The thing is Tom doesn't want a baby ever."

"He's probably afraid of losing you. It's irrational but understandable."

"Upstairs, there's a baby's room with a crib and changing table. All decorated and set up for Candy and Tom's baby. Every day, I open the door and then he shuts it. It's like we're playing this game."

Pierre arrived with their salads. He avoided their eyes as he set the plates on the table. "Can I get you anything else?"

"This looks great. Thank you, Pierre." Susan turned to Francesca. "Come on, let's eat and talk about something else."

Francesca was only too happy to change the subject. Pretty soon they were reminiscing about college days and some of the crazy things they did as freshmen sorority sisters.

At the end of their meal, after Pierre brought coffee, Susan looked into Francesca's eyes and cleared her throat. "Here's what I think. Maybe you should move out of that house."

"But I love the house," Francesca said.

"Do you? Or is it a tremendous burden?"

Francesca didn't answer.

"You could start fresh in a house that's new to you both," Susan continued.

"I don't see that happening. I don't think Tom wants to move, and he's given me carte blanche to do what I want in terms of decorating."

Susan thought for a moment. Then she said, "You could empty the baby's room. Get rid of the furniture, repaint. Turn it into a sewing room, or your office. It doesn't have to be a shrine to Tom's memory of Candy's death."

Francesca thought about it as she stirred cream into her coffee.

"Francesca," Susan said.

Francesca looked up.

"Tom loves you. He'll come around. He wants you to be happy, and deep down I'll bet he wants a baby too. He's just afraid. Give him time."

Francesca's eyes filled again. She nodded and took out another Kleenex.

Chapter 27
Thursday afternoon

After sharing the results of their interviews, Tom and Puchalski drove back to the police station. Brendan and Cindy stayed on to go through the employment files at the BBG. When they arrived, Tom went in to talk to Coyote Blackfoot. He gave the forensic researcher a list of the people they'd interviewed that morning. Then he put in a call to the Japanese consulate to report the death of Dr. Kaito Takahashi.

He had a couple of hours to catch up on phone calls. The message from Mayor Criche was brief and to the point. He wanted these crimes solved. He told Tom to be in his office with a full report, the next morning at nine.

There were calls from TV and radio stations as well as the press. Undoubtedly they all wanted the gruesome details of the crime. Tom scheduled a press conference for late in the afternoon after the task force meeting. He didn't want certain details to leak to the media, but he needed to throw them a bone.

Although Taylor Emerson had identified Takahashi's body from the picture on Tom's phone, he needed to get the daughter out to the lab to make an official identification. He called Sanders and asked him to go over to the Deer Run and interview the daughter. Then he could accompany her to the lab to identify her father

At four o'clock the task force assembled in the lower level war room. "These next few days will be difficult for all of us," Tom said as he surveyed his team. "We'll be working 24/7. All scheduled leaves and vacation time are postponed. I'm getting pressure from the community and the village board. They want action. We're going to solve these murders, but it will take everyone's full commitment." Then he said quietly, "Even more important, we owe Doc Stoddard and Dr. Takahashi our best efforts to find and arrest their killers."

The room went silent as the detectives faced the monumental task before them. Tom nodded at Detective Ramirez.

Ramirez stood up. He went into a detailed description of the crime scene at the Japanese tea house using the displayed photographs. "We're surmising at this time that Dr. Takahashi was invited to drink tea laced with poison. After his death, he was dressed in traditional Japanese clothes and laid out on these cushions. Then the murderer or murderers chopped off his hands and feet with a heavy knife or cleaver."

Brendan O'Connor flinched at the description. He wasn't the only one. Even these seasoned detectives found it difficult to look at the crime scene photos. There was something diabolical in the careful planning and execution of this murder.

Ramirez continued, "ME Hollister puts the approximate time of death between midnight and two AM. The liquid in the teacups is being analyzed to see if it contains the poison administered to the victim. The forensic crew has gone over the teahouse and the immediate area. We'll have all the evidence processed and analyzed within the next few days."

Ricky Stiles raised his hand. "What about the flowers covering the body? Where did they come from? Are they significant?"

They all studied the blown-up photographs. The bright red blooms lay like a noxious blanket against the bloodless-looking Asian face. To Tom, their brilliant hue seemed a mockery.

"Those are from hundreds of chrysanthemum plants that were snipped off at the head. The plants are in the greenhouses at the Botanic Gardens."

"So anyone familiar with the gardens would have access," Puchalski said.

"Chrysanthemums…the flower of death," Cindy murmured.

"There's something else." Ramirez gestured to Puchalski. "Tell them what you saw."

Puchalski flipped a couple of pages in his notebook. "I walked the perimeter of the murder scene and looked into the sand garden." He stood and walked over to the picture gallery attached to the whiteboards. "Here's a picture of what I found. Someone wrote in the sand, 'Avenge the Tree of Life.' For the moment, let's assume this was written by the murderer, before or after the crime. He's sending us a message."

"'Avenge the Tree of Life.'" Cindy was thinking out loud. "Our perp cut off Takahashi's hands and feet just like Takahashi maimed the trees he clipped and pruned." She looked around the room. "Maybe it's about payback."

"It sounds like a cult to me," Puchalski said.

"Yes," Sanders chimed in. "In some parts of the world, people used to worship trees. They're symbolic of nature…life. Someone has a real hatred for the art of bonsai."

"Someone's a nut, if they'd kill over it," Brendan muttered.

"Okay, but why kill Takahashi? Why not kill Miyamoto? He's there on staff at the BBG," Puchalski said.

"When we get a full rundown on all the players, we might find the answer," Tom said.

Puchalski looked uncomfortable. "There was something else. When I was in the sand garden, I had this weird feeling of being watched. I looked around, but didn't see anyone. It was eerie." He swallowed. "Then, when Romano and I found Robbie Sumner, he told us someone was hiding up in the big pine tree and observing us as we investigated the crime scene. He didn't know if it was a man or a woman."

"In the tree?" Stiles said.

"Yeah. Then Robbie said the person just kind of…disappeared."

Tom turned to Deputy Chief Conroy. "Who was manning the entrance to the Japanese gardens?"

"Stevens. I make a point of remembering where my men are." Conroy was on the defensive.

"Good. Talk to him. Find out if anyone came off the island after we'd closed off the crime scene."

"I'll talk to him." Conroy got up and left the room.

After Puchalski and Ramirez resumed their seats, Tom addressed the rest of the task force. "I'd like to have your reports typed up and entered into the appropriate document-sharing site by eight o'clock tomorrow morning. I've got a meeting with the mayor and two members of the village board, so I'll need my ducks in a row before they bombard me with questions." He looked down the table at Blackfoot, who was intent on his laptop. His fingers raced across the keys. He hadn't looked up during the meeting but Tom was pretty sure he had followed everything. "Coyote, will you have something for me tomorrow?"

"Yes sir, things are coming together." He paused, took his hands off the keyboard and stretched. "I've got to tell you, there's some weird shit going on with all these dudes."

Chapter 28
Thursday afternoon

When Francesca left Oak Hills she felt renewed and revived. Susan accompanied her to her car and they hugged. "Thanks for being an awesome friend." Francesca said.

"You'd be there for me if I needed you. Go home and take the afternoon off," Susan said.

"No, I'm going to the office. I've got work to do and I'm happier when I'm busy."

They both looked up at the sound of screeching brakes. Jack Banner's car pulled into a parking space across the driveway.

"Here comes trouble," Susan said. "I wish we didn't have to put up with him. He rubs a lot of people the wrong way. But he's a lifetime member whether they like it or not. His great-grandfather was a founder of the club and the Banners have continually given large sums of money."

Jack got out of his car and slammed the door, then opened his trunk and got out his golf clubs. They watched him stroll over towards the caddy shack, shouting to a seasoned caddy, "Hey boy, over here."

Trouble is right, Francesca thought, remembering Akiko's story. Susan didn't know the half of it.

As she pulled out of the lot, Francesca's cell phone rang. It was Akiko. "Francesca? Detective Sanders has just been here interviewing me. They want me to go to the morgue to identify my father's body. Would you go with me?"

"Sure, I'll pick you up."

Ten minutes later, they were on their way to the Lake County morgue. Francesca tried to make conversation but Akiko was nonresponsive. Detective Sanders met them in the foyer. Francesca hated the place. The walls were painted a putrid green and the pervasive odor of chemicals made her feel sick. Sanders led them down some stairs and through a labyrinth of halls. They stopped outside a small glassed-in room. Inside was a gurney with a body covered by a white sheet.

Sanders and Akiko went in. Francesca waited outside, leaning against the wall. Sanders said something to Akiko, and she nodded. He uncovered the face of the dead man. Akiko stared at it, apparently transfixed. Sanders spoke again, and again Akiko nodded. Sanders carefully covered the white face.

Outside, Akiko followed Francesca to the car without speaking. Silent tears poured down her cheeks. Francesca bent over and hugged her thin shoulders. She helped Akiko into the car and came around to the driver's side. Once settled in her seat, she turned to face the younger woman. "Are you hungry? Would you like to go somewhere for a drink?"

"No. Please take me back to the hotel."

"I don't think you should be alone. Come over to my house."

"No. I want to be alone and think about my father." She sat motionless; her hands on her lap, staring ahead. "It's been just the two of us for many years. I can't believe he's gone." She swallowed a sob. "He died in pain. I could see it in his face. Who would want him to suffer?"

Francesca had no answer to that. She drove back to the Deer Run in silence. When they drew up to the front door, Akiko looked over at her. "I don't know why, but I keep thinking about the numbers."

"Numbers?"

Akiko's breath caught. "Oh, it's nothing. Just my mind reaching for a reason why someone would kill my gentle father." She got out of the car, her movements quick and agitated. "Thank you, Francesca. I'll be all right. Later, someone from the consulate is coming to help me."

Francesca stayed put until Akiko went inside the Deer Run. She drove away slowly, hoping the poor girl would be all right.

Chapter 29
Thursday evening

Tom arrived home at eight-thirty. He looked exhausted. Lines of tension pulled his face taut. His eyes were bloodshot and dull. Francesca figured she didn't look so great herself; two warriors home from battle. The press conference had been brutal, the media persistent and antagonistic. They wanted more details about Takahashi, and whether his murder was connected to Doc Stoddard's. When hounded with questions about possible suspects, Tom gave them the standard line: *Too early in the investigation, but we're following many leads.* Francesca had felt torn, watching him; she knew what it was like now on both sides of the fence.

Tom trudged upstairs to take a shower and change into shorts and a tee-shirt, while Francesca began cooking the stir fry she had prepared earlier. She quickly browned the beef strips in the wok, then tossed in the sliced vegetables. With the addition of garlic and ginger to the pungent sauce, dinner was ready to go. She divided steamed brown rice into deep white bowls. She was spooning the stir fry over the rice as Tom came into the kitchen.

"That smells great," he said, and kissed the nape of her neck. "Shall I pour us a glass of wine?"

"That would be lovely. There's an open bottle of pinot noir in the cupboard." Francesca placed the bowls on the kitchen table with a set of chopsticks for her and a fork for Tom. Meanwhile, Tom filled two stemless glasses. He handed one to her. Francesca raised her glass. "Here's to a speedy investigation."

He nodded as he took a forkful of Chinese peapods. "I don't know how you do it, but this tastes delicious."

"I figured you've been too busy to eat anything healthy these past few days."

By unspoken agreement they didn't discuss the murder during dinner, but it loomed over them like a dark, heavy cloud. Francesca talked about her luncheon with Susan. Tom mentioned the Criterium Bike Race that would be taking place in Banner Bluff in three weeks. It was a major event, with races all day and a village-wide block party in the evening complete with food and music. Eventually, they got back to the day's events.

"Tell me about Takahashi's daughter. How did she take the news?" Tom asked.

"At first she didn't believe me. Then she fell apart."

"Did she have any idea why her father was killed?"

"No. I avoided discussing that. It would have been too much." She pushed her food around in the bowl.

"Thanks for doing that. It's a hard job. I put you in a difficult position." Tom smiled ruefully. "Are you all right?"

She smiled up at him. "Yeah, I'm fine."

When they finished eating, Francesca placed the bowls in the sink and Tom poured them each another glass of wine. They carried them into the living room and sat close together on the sofa, their bare feet propped on the coffee table.

Tom laid his head back against the cushions and closed his eyes. "God, I'm beat. I hope I can sleep tonight. I've got so many ideas bouncing around in my head."

"Me too." Francesca turned to face him, pulling her legs up under her. "So let me tell you what I learned today."

He nodded, his eyes still closed.

"First of all, this morning when I left for the BBG, I said hello to the new family across the street."

"The family where the kids aren't allowed to eat cookies?"

"Right. This morning, the husband didn't want his wife talking to me. He hustled her into the car. I really don't like him. Anyway, after they left, I looked in their mailbox. The husband is George Raleigh. Frank Penfield told me the Raleighs were the family that sued Doc Stoddard forty years ago. After losing the lawsuit they, moved out East. And…"

Tom groaned. "And…"

"This afternoon, I researched George online. I'm pretty sure he's the brother of the baby that died."

"Hmm." Tom opened his eyes and sat up. "So this is someone who might have an actual grudge against Doc."

"Maybe. I thought you should know."

"I could send Cindy Murray over there for a chat. It wouldn't hurt." Tom rubbed his forehead. "So far, we're leaning toward Jack Banner for Doc's murder, but we have no proof."

"Here's something else I learned." Francesca told him about her meeting with Akiko and the young woman's connection with Jack Banner. "It was pretty awful. Her father had Jack discharged from the Marines, probably dishonourably."

"Wow, that guy gets around." Tom stood up and began to pace the room.

"Could Jack have been angry enough to kill Dr. Takahashi, too?"

Tom shook his head. "I don't see it, Francesca. Doc's murder looks like a crime of passion. It wasn't premeditated. It had to do with that phone call to the Banner estate and something Doc discovered the same night he died. Dr. Takahashi's murder was carefully planned and executed down to the cup of tea he drank."

"What about Takahashi's murder? You haven't told me the whole story yet. I just saw a dead man covered with flowers. And flies." She shivered.

Tom continued his pacing. "Are you sure you want to hear? It might give you nightmares."

"Why? Is it gruesome?"

He stopped and looked at her. "Yes."

"I better know everything if I'm going to help you out." She sat up straight, the better to accept the blow.

"Somebody invited Takahashi for a late-night cup of tea in the tea house. The tea was laced with poison. After he died, the killer dressed him in a kimono and a traditional Japanese headband, laid him out on cushions, and hacked off his feet and hands. We found them carefully placed beside him."

Francesca turned pale. Tom bent down and pulled her into his arms.

Chapter 30
Friday morning

Tom arrived at the station before six, after a restless night. He wasn't the only one there so early. Puchalski and Sanders were at their desks typing up their reports. He grabbed a cup of coffee in the break room they shared with the other village employees. The coffee smelled fresh. It would give him a kick.

In his office he logged on and entered the shared document site. Murray and O'Connor must have stayed late. They'd completed their reports on the interviews at the BBG. He read through the information to refresh his memory. Puchalski had already posted a play-by-play of the interviews they'd done. He read through those as well.

Hollister had sent the autopsy report. His email reiterated the information Tom already knew, and it also described the poison found in the dregs of the tea. It contained Atropa belladonna, commonly known as deadly nightshade. A concentrated dose had been added to the tea. The ME explained that the poison **paralyzes nerve endings in the involuntary muscles of the body, such as the blood vessels and gastrointestinal muscles. Where did one get belladonna, Tom wondered. Was it readily available? Maybe it was growing right there in the BBG. He'd get someone to check it out.

Conroy had sent an email as well. He'd talked to Officer Stevens, who was guarding the bridge into the Japanese islands. According to Stevens, after the police closed off the entrance to the crime scene, a couple of people had left the islands. Apparently, they were wandering around the Japanese gardens and were unaware of the police barricade. One woman was carrying a pad of paper and said she'd been sketching. Several minutes later a garden employee emerged, wearing garden gloves and carrying a rope. Stevens hadn't gotten their names.

Tom sat back and sipped his coffee. The artist could have been fully immersed in her sketching and missed what was going on around her. What about the garden employee with the rope? Could he have been the person up in a tree checking out their investigation? Many killers liked to revisit the scene of the crime. They got a thrill inspecting their handiwork and watching the police fumble around. Tom had learned that all BBG employees wore badges bearing their picture. Stevens could ID the employee he saw. They had the personnel files from the BBG.

Coyote Blackfoot had emailed at three AM, asking for more time and saying he'd be ready to report in the late morning. Coyote was getting help from some of his confidential sources. In the past when Tom had questioned him about his information-gathering, Coyote went silent and expressionless. He'd assured Tom that he was doing nothing illegal, and Tom chose not to pursue it.

He put down his coffee cup, picked up a paper clip, unwound it and stretched it out while he thought about what he'd learned from Francesca. They would need to interview Jack Banner concerning his whereabouts after his meeting with Akiko Takahashi. Later today, he would bring Banner in for a little talk. It might be good to have him in the police station instead of on his home turf, and Tom could record the interview.

His cell phone binged; a text from Romano. He was still working with the limo company. They would send Takahashi's driver to the station when they located him. Tom looked down at the paper clip that he'd twisted into a tight coil. For a moment, he just stared at it. So many details to nail down in these two cases…

Then there was the Raleigh connection. It didn't seem feasible to him, but better to leave no stone unturned. He wrote down the Raleighs' address on a slip of paper, then got up, went down the hall and took the stairs down to the war room. He was in luck. Cindy Murray was there; licking her fingers, a large cup of Dunkin' Donuts coffee in front of her and a half-eaten Oreo cream-filled doughnut on a napkin.

"You've caught me in the act." She giggled. "I know, no one should eat this thing, but it is so-o-o good."

Looking at Cindy's trim figure in her slim black jeans and close-fitting black shirt, Tom couldn't imagine where she put those calories. "Listen. I'd like you to go over to this address. It's across from my house." He handed her the slip of paper and explained what Francesca had told him. "It's probably a long shot, but talk to the family. See if you can find out where they were on Tuesday night when Doc was killed."

"Will do." Cindy took a big bite of her doughnut and smiled happily.

#

Mayor Criche was standing in the middle of his office when Tom entered. Beside him were Leonard Jansen and Joel Ford, two village board members. Tom felt like he was standing before a tribunal. Criche served as part-time mayor of the village of Banner Bluff but acted like he was running the city of New York. He'd made a lot of money as an ambulance chaser. His law firm was large and his ego even larger. Tom knew Criche wielded a certain amount of power in town. The man was of medium height, his body thick and heavy, his eyes small and calculating. He wore an Armani suit with a yellow patterned silk tie and matching pocket handkerchief.

Jansen and Ford spent a lot of time downing pints at the Village Brew that sold craft beer to hops connoisseurs. Jansen was jowly and jovial, Ford emaciated and taciturn. They made an odd couple.

Criche began talking. "Where do we stand, Barnett…two murders in three days? Look at the statistics. This makes Banner Bluff as dangerous as downtown Chicago. We're supposed to be a quiet village on the shores of Lake Michigan."

Not *Chief Barnett* or even *Tom*, just his last name. He'd planned to give them a brief outline of where things stood, but he didn't have a chance to open his mouth.

Jansen chimed in. "Yeah, we're in the running to be one of the top American coastal cities. This doesn't look good. The judges from the *Coastal Journal* will be here next week."

Now it was Ford's turn. "You know, we increased funding for the Police Department last fall. Shouldn't we be getting better service?"

Tom held up his hands. "Whoa. I'm here to make a report. Do you want to hear it?"

Criche kept up the barrage. "Banner Bluff hadn't had any murders for twenty years. Since you took over the department, we've lost two little girls to the Lake Monster, and two young people to the Russian mob. This week you added two more."

This was a kangaroo court, complete with the lion, the hippo and the depressed chimpanzee. Tom advanced into the room. "Gentlemen, we are doing everything possible to apprehend the murderer or murderers responsible for these deaths. We have several leads. Information is coming in and is being analyzed. The Lake County Homicide Task Force is actively involved in these cases."

"What leads?" Jansen, the hippo, asked. His cheeks wobbled as he talked.

"It would be unwise to share that information at this time." After the verbal ambush he'd just suffered, Tom had decided he wasn't telling these jokers anything.

"Is it one guy or a bunch?" Chimpanzee—Ford—asked. His scowl was a permanent fixture.

"At this time, the crimes appear unrelated. But it's too early to make that judgement official."

"Have you made any arrests?" Lion, the mayor, asked.

"No. We have insufficient evidence at the moment. We will be bringing in several persons of interest this afternoon."

"Who?" Hippo asked.

Tom had had enough of these clowns. He'd been hired by the village board, and he had planned to keep them abreast of the investigations, but they were irritating him no end. "Since these people are not under suspicion, it's none of your business who they are."

"Barnett, calm down," Criche growled.

"I'm perfectly calm. At this time, it would be unwise to share our investigation with everyone at the Village Brew." He nodded at Jansen and Ford.

"What about the magazine?" Jansen whined.

"Take them down to the beach. Buildings and Grounds just dumped a truckload of nice, white sand. It looks great!" Before any of the men could respond, Tom turned and left the room.

Chapter 31
Friday morning

Cindy finished her coffee and considered how she would proceed when she arrived at the Raleighs' house. In the hallway, she tossed the telltale Dunkin' Donuts cup and bag in the large orange receptacle. Then she made her way upstairs. The officer at the front desk slipped her a key to a patrol car under the bullet-proof glass partition. Lined up on the counter were several brochures for the public. She grabbed several and left the building. Outside, she inspected the car, walking around it slowly. Then she opened the driver's door and ascertained that all equipment was in place. Inside the car she typed the Raleighs' address into the computer and drove the short distance to their residence.

The house was grey clapboard with a wide front porch. The grass was trimmed with precision, as were the bushes along the front. There were no flowers. Cindy picked up the brochures and got out of the car. She walked quickly up the porch steps and rang the doorbell.

A fortyish woman in a pink housedress came to the door. Cindy had never seen anyone wear a housedress except her grandmother back in Iowa.

The woman eyed her with apprehension, then looked up and down the street. "Can I help you?"

"Hello. I'm Detective Murray." She flashed her badge. "Could I come in and talk with you for a moment?"

"Well, I don't know. I guess so. Okay." Indecision seemed to be this woman's middle name. She stepped back, and Cindy quickly went in before the woman changed her mind.

"Are you Rosemary Raleigh?"

"Yes, yes I am." She sounded tentative, her hands tightly clasped at her waist.

Cindy smiled broadly. "Welcome to Banner Bluff. I understand you moved here recently. I've got some brochures that I thought would be helpful to you."

Rosemary looked at Cindy and then shot a glance into the living room. Cindy followed her gaze. On the sofa a little boy was stretched out, his leg in a full cast. He looked skinny. His hair fell in his face and a dark blue shiner surrounded his right eye.

Cindy walked over to the boy. "Hey, what happened to you? Did you fall off your bike?" She bent down and looked at his face. His lip was a bit swollen. The kid didn't say anything. He looked down at the enormous book on his lap

From the hallway, Rosemary said, "He fell down the basement stairs. He was taking down a casserole dish to put in the freezer for me. He tripped and fell all the way down. It was a mess. I had to clean up the turkey divan. It was all over the floor."

Cindy didn't give a shit about the turkey divan. What about the boy? She looked down at the kid. "Did you go to the hospital?"

He nodded. He still didn't look up, and nervously fingered the corners of the heavy book.

More gently, she said, "What are you reading? That's a big book."

He looked at his mother as though asking permission to talk. "It's the encyclopedia. I'm in the G book. I'm reading about gorillas."

"Gorillas? What have you learned today?"

"Well, they don't eat meat. But they eat vegetation, you know, plants, and they eat all day long." He looked down at the page. "They like ants and grubs and snails."

"That sounds yucky," Cindy said. "I'd rather be a people."

The boy smiled.

"What's your name?"

"Peter." He looked over at his mother, who had edged into the room. It was a *did-I-say-too-much* look.

"Here, Peter." Cindy gave him the brochure on bicycle rules for kids. "You can study this. In the summer, a bicycle cop patrols the streets, making sure the kids stop at the Stop signs and stuff like that." She smiled at Rosemary.

"Can I get you a glass of apple juice?" Rosemary asked.

"Juice? Sure." She hadn't had a glass of apple juice since kindergarten.

"I was just getting one for Peter."

"That would be great." Cindy sat down in an armchair. "When did you fall down the stairs, Peter?"

"It was Monday, I think. Yes, Monday." He avoided her eyes, concentrating again on the book.

Rosemary returned with two small glasses of juice. She handed one to Cindy and one to Peter, then perched on the edge of another armchair. She reminded Cindy of a jaguar in a tree ready to spring.

Cindy took a sip. "Thank you. I haven't had apple juice in years." She turned to Peter. "So you fell down on Monday?"

Peter blanched. He looked down into his glass and nodded.

She felt for him, but pushed on. "What time Monday did you fall down?"

He mumbled, "After dinner."

From across the room Rosemary said, "In the afternoon, before your father came home, remember?"

"Yeah, that's right," Peter whispered.

After some more small talk, Cindy gave Rosemary the "Residential Security Guide" and the booklet about city services. Then she patted Peter's bony shoulder and headed for the door.

"Thanks so much for the juice. I hope you'll be very happy in Banner Bluff."

In the car, she sat looking out the window at the shady street. The Chief's wife was right; there was definitely something going on in that household, and she had a strong feeling Peter had not fallen down the stairs of his own accord. Cindy looked at her watch. She had forty-five minutes before the task force convened. She decided to drive over to the hospital and talk to someone in the emergency room.

Ten minutes later, she entered the ER, having left her car in the horseshoe drive. The waiting room was empty. At the desk she asked to speak to someone who was on staff Monday night. A few minutes later, a plump blond woman in light blue scrubs came through the swinging doors. Her light blue eyes matched her outfit. Her name tag said *Sandra Jean* and her smile was one hundred percent. "Hi, can I help you?"

"Yes, I have some questions about a patient who came in here Monday night with a broken leg and a black eye. His name is Peter Raleigh. He's about ten."

Sandra Jean's eyes narrowed. "I remember that kid. Why are you asking? Are you investigating what happened to him?"

"Should I be?"

Sandra Jean bit her lip. "I don't know if I'm allowed to tell you this…" The indecision in her face cleared, as if she'd made her choice. "The heck with it. I think he'd been beat up."

"Why do you say that?"

"Just a feeling I got. We brought in the social worker. She asked the dad and the boy a lot of questions. She was trying to trip them up, but she didn't get anything you could use in court."

"When did they come in here?"

"Oh, late. Maybe eleven. I can look that up for you. But you know what? I think whatever happened, happened a lot earlier. They probably didn't want to bring the boy in and be hassled. You know what I mean?"

"Have they been in before?"

"No, that's the thing. When a child is brought in more than once under suspicious circumstances, we call in the police.

"How long were they here?"

"Oh, it was busy. They were probably here until two in the morning."

Cindy left the ER thinking she'd closed one grisly door and opened another. George Raleigh hadn't killed Doc Stoddard. No, he'd beaten up his kid and pushed him down the stairs. Maybe he even threw the turkey divan casserole down after him.

Chapter 32
Friday morning

It was kind of like getting back on a horse. The next morning Francesca marched out of the house and drove over to the BBG. She'd received an email stating that the gardens were open except for the Japanese islands. Volunteers were greatly needed because there was a backlog of seedlings in the green houses that needed to be planted outdoors.

She pulled into the parking lot just as Colman arrived on his bike. She waited while he attached the chain and lock.

Colman grinned. "So who do you think did the dastardly deed?" He obviously didn't know all the horrific details of the murder.

"I don't know, but I understand there are several suspects. Tom didn't elaborate but there are candidates right here in the gardens as well as in town." She knew she couldn't share any information with Colman.

He picked up his lunchbox and they walked toward the volunteer center. "Let's see. There's Dr. Miyamoto. I hear he's pretty jealous of this other guy. Wouldn't he be the most likely to lure someone into the teahouse for a tea ceremony? Then there's Dr. Holmes. He'd make a gnarly suspect. I'm not sure why he would want Takahashi dead…but I've learned what he's up to." Colman lowered his voice. "I went back to the lab last night. I wanted to see what Holmes was being so secretive about. It was easy to get in. I've got this gadget that my roommate in college gave me."

"Colman that was not a good idea. Dr. Holmes is nasty. What if he'd walked in on you?"

"No one was around. I went into the inner lab and read some of the notations in the log. Then I looked on the computer and studied some of the test tubes. He's doing experiments with castor bean, English yew, snakeroot and Manchineel."

Francesca frowned. "So? What's the big deal?"

"They're all plants that are poisonous to human beings. I googled them last night. Either the flower, the root, the seed, the berries, or the entire plant is poisonous."

"So he's making poisons?"

"I don't know exactly. But here's the thing. Some Atropa belladonna was missing. There are carefully labeled vials in the fridge and two were gone."

"You've got to tell the police. That's something they need to hear about."

"I know, but I broke into the lab. How am I going to explain how I learned about the experiments?"

"Leave it to me. I'll call Tom and tell him. But you need to promise me you'll stop snooping around."

As they came around the corner, Colman touched her arm and whispered, "The thing is, if I could get in there easily, so could someone else. Wasn't the Japanese guy poisoned?"

"Yes, he was. So stay away from Holmes's lab."

#

Francesca entered the volunteer center and made a beeline to the coffee pot. She could really use another cup before work began. She hadn't slept all that great. Both she and Tom had done a lot of tossing and turning. A little more caffeine might give her a jolt.

Melinda Jordan was filling up a mug as she walked up. "Hi, Melinda. How are you?" Francesca asked.

"Oh, all right, I guess. I'm glad we're back at work today." She looked out the window at the volunteers who were gathering their tools. She seemed distracted.

"It looks like we're going to be really busy today," Francesca said.

"Yes, yes we are." She turned and looked directly at Francesca. "You were there to help the little girl who found the body yesterday."

"Yes. It was frightening."

The woman's eyes bored into hers. "Could you tell me exactly what you saw?"

Francesca swallowed. Why was this woman asking her that, and why did it matter to her? "I just saw the Japanese man's face. His body was covered with red flowers."

"Was there anything nearby? Anything on the ground? Anything that struck you as odd?"

"Listen. I've told you what I saw. I'd rather not say anymore. I've no desire to relive the moment." Without realizing it, Francesca had raised her voice enough to make people around them stop talking. She smiled apologetically and left the room without her coffee.

Outside, she took a deep breath to calm down. As she stood apart from the group, Maelog Gruffydd approached and asked if she wouldn't mind helping out with the planting in the fruit and vegetable area. "I'd be delighted," she said. The fruits and vegetable plantings were far away from the Japanese islands.

They walked together for a while. "How are you doing today?" he asked, his tone kind.

"I'm fine. But I've been thinking that crime can occur anywhere. Even in these beautiful gardens. I don't think I'll ever enjoy the Japanese islands again."

"Yes. Nature is the receptacle of mankind's cruelty."

What an odd thing to say, Francesca thought. Just then Emma Boucher called out to her.

"Hi, Emma," she said as the older woman reached them. "I've been promoted from lowly weed-puller to inexperienced planter."

"Great. I'm glad you've joined our group. How are you doing today? I heard about yesterday."

"To tell you the truth, I'd just like to forget it."

"I understand." Emma gave Francesca a brief hug.

When they arrived at the gardens, Irma Hoffmann greeted them with a big smile. She wore jeans and a purple shirt with the sleeves rolled up. Francesca was impressed by her lean, strong body and large biceps. She had her hair in a ponytail pulled through the back of a White Sox cap. She welcomed them and got down to business, explaining how they should plant the seedlings that had been hardened-off and were ready to face the elements.

Strings had been stretched along each furrow to guide the workers. They were given flats of potted tomatoes, peppers, eggplants and more. Porcelain markers indicated which vegetable was planted in each row. The name of each vegetable was written in calligraphy along with a miniature painting of the plant.

As Francesca worked, she listened to the people talking nearby. They were discussing the BBG honeybees that would soon be buzzing around. Francesca learned that eating locally produced honey could counteract allergies, since the bees feasted on local flowers. That would be something for Tom to try, since he usually started sneezing in August.

After a half-hour she stood and stretched. Her body wasn't used to this much hard work. Francesca looked across the gardens and over the bowed bodies of her fellow volunteers. At the far side she spotted Melinda Jordan on her knees. She'd removed her gloves and was texting, her thumbs moving madly over the keys.

Chapter 33
Friday morning

After the meeting with the mayor and his cronies, Tom had to get some air. He went outside and took a short walk over to Lilac Alley, an open area between two buildings that was paved with red bricks. Baskets of flowers hung on the walls over wrought-iron tables and chairs. Tom headed for the hole-in-the-wall coffee bar, a new favorite place of his since it opened up last year, and ordered a large double-shot latte. While waiting for his coffee, he said hello to several people he vaguely recognized, among them two young women in yoga outfits sitting at a table nearby, their toddlers asleep in aerodynamic strollers.

The blonde looked up, a worried smile on her lips. "We were just talking about the murders, Chief. Is there anything new?"

Her companion, a brunette, said, "Yeah, can we take our kids to the park this afternoon? Is it safe?"

God, it's starting already. His simmering frustration spiked, though he suppressed it before it could show. None of it was these women's fault. "I'm not at liberty to discuss the ongoing investigation," he said. "But these aren't random incidents, and you're not at risk. Go to the park, go for a run, do whatever you normally do. You're safe."

The blonde looked relieved. The brunette glanced down at her baby. "My husband is out of town. I couldn't sleep last night." She looked up at Tom. "I kept hearing things, you know what I mean?"

The barista set Tom's drink on the counter. He paid and took the cup. On his way out, a man he didn't recognize stopped him. The man was unshaven, in paint-spattered jeans and a dirty grey tee-shirt. "What you told those ladies is a pile of crap. This place isn't safe. Banner Bluff is attracting crazies because they've read about the Lake Monster and the mafia killings." He poked Tom in the chest. "I'm getting the hell out of here."

Tom grabbed the man's wrist and held it. "Sir, you're entitled to your opinion. But don't ever touch an officer of the law." He dropped the man's hand, turned and left the alley. As he headed back to the station, he thought about his overreaction. He knew he shouldn't have touched the guy. He should have just walked away. But after that morning's meeting, the adrenaline rush of pure anger ambushed his better judgement.

Back at the station he found Coyote waiting in the hallway, holding his laptop and a sheaf of papers. Out of uniform, in dark jeans and a ratty tee-shirt and with his hair falling over his eyes, he looked like he'd been working for the past twenty-four hours straight. "Chief, I've got some updates for you. It's not in report form yet…thought you'd want the latest."

"Right. Let's go down to the war room." Tom picked up the phone and called Arlyne. "Get the task force down to the war room. Now."

When they were assembled, Coyote began to speak. He sat at the conference table, hunched over his laptop. "I've been doing research and I dug up some info on several of the people you interviewed yesterday at the Banner Botanic Gardens. They all have gaps in their pasts. Let's start with Irma Hoffmann—aka Irwin Hoffman." He tossed his head enough to clear the hair away from his eyes.

Tom remembered Irma. A big woman, muscular. He glanced at Puchalski and raised his eyebrows.

"She grew up on the Eastern shore in Maryland, apparently male and treated like one, but ten years ago she moved out to

California. She held various jobs and then disappeared from view for several months. During that time she had a sex change operation. Irwin Hoffman became Irma. Afterwards, she worked in the Bay area for several years, at a large organic farm co-op. Then she took the position at the BBG." Coyote looked up. "Apart from her gender change, her life seems pretty straightforward."

"I remember she clammed up when we asked about her past." Puchalski looked at Tom. "All of a sudden she was in a big hurry to leave."

"Yes, and she also told us she didn't like the Japanese."

The door flew open. Cindy rushed into the room, plopped down in a chair and looked over at Tom. "Sorry I'm late. I was at the hospital. Tell you later."

Tom nodded. "What else have you got for us, Coyote?"

Coyote turned back to his computer. "Dr. Hisao Miyamoto grew up in Chicago. His grandparents ran a florist shop. It was easy to find stuff on him because his grandfather had been interned during World War Two. His name turned up in several news stories recently because the family has asked for reparations. The government took their land in California when they were shipped off to a concentration camp. After the war, they never got their farm back."

Coyote cleared his throat. "Okay, so Miyamoto grew up working in the family florist shop; went to college in Indiana, met his wife, Emily Crowder. Together they went to Japan for a year. He studied bonsai under a tutor of some renown. When they came back they opened the Floral Fantasy shop here in Banner Bluff, probably with help from Miyamoto's parents. When the BBG needed a bonsai specialist, Miyamoto was available right here in town." Coyote reached up and pushed back his hair again. 'Nowhere did I find a doctorate for him. He's only referred to as Dr. Miyamoto since he joined the BBG."

"Did he have motive to kill Takahashi? We've learned they'd fought about proper bonsai traditions. How deep did the rift go?" Detective Sanders asked.

Coyote shrugged. "Their relationship seems based on intellectual arguments in bonsai journals. Probably not a reason to kill, but who knows?"

"Let's get him in here for another chat," Tom said. "Who else?"

"I looked into Taylor Emerson. She's raised a lot of money for the BBG that's enabled the Gardens to flourish." He looked up and grinned. "No pun intended. So, Taylor grew up in Lake Woods in an affluent family, went to college in Madison, studied finance and management. She had a big-time job down in the city with Sandmark until one of the major donors for the BBG enticed her to come up here and run the Gardens. All well and good."

Tom nodded. "Go on."

"I'm not sure this has any bearing on our murder case. But since Taylor's been running the BBG, she's made a lot of money. Looking at her bank account, I see monthly automatic deposits from the BBG, probably her salary as CEO. I traced her investments, various bank accounts, earnings from real estate and so on. In addition to all those, there are periodic deposits from unidentified sources. I need more time to track it all down. But I wondered where these funds were coming from."

Tom thought about his conversations with Taylor. She took pride in her ability to raise money for the Gardens. Was she skimming a percentage off the top? If so, was it relevant to their investigation?

Sanders asked, "What sorts of expenditures does she have?"

"I haven't done an in-depth study, you understand. But she spends a shitload of money on clothes and jewelry. We're talking Cartier watches and Tiffany baubles."

"Do we know what car she drives?" Ricky Stiles asked.

"Some sort of Mercedes. I saw a bill paid to Zimmerman Motors. But like I said, this is all rudimentary. I'd need a lot more time to get to the bottom of it."

Tom sat forward and flattened his palms on the table. "Well, they say: follow the money."

"Yeah, but why would Ms. Emerson kill this famous bonsai specialist? Getting him to come here was a feather in her cap. She had people coming from all across the country to hear him speak and attend the workshops," Cindy said.

They all nodded in agreement.

Coyote looked back at the computer. "So then there's Dr. Holmes. Before he was invited here to Banner College, he was working at Sullivan College in Washington State. He was asked to leave there after a discovery of fraud."

"What sort of fraud?" Sanders asked.

"Again, I'm giving you the bare bones. But it looks as though he redirected grant funds targeted for a colleague's research project. At some point the fraud came to light and he was given the option to resign or have criminal charges brought against him. He resigned. Nine months later he got a job teaching botany and biology at Banner College."

Puchalski held up his pencil. He'd been taking notes as Coyote spoke. "What about the research he's doing at the BBG? How does he fund that?"

"I don't know. I didn't see any grants awarded to him at the college." Coyote yawned and stretched his arms over his head.

"We can certainly ask him or Taylor Emerson. Maybe the Gardens are funding the cost of his research." Puchalski tapped his pencil on his tablet of paper, then looked at Tom. "We'll need to talk to all these people again this afternoon."

Sanders had one more question. "Where was he for those nine months after he left the college?"

"I don't know. I'll have to do more research." Coyote scribbled on a note pad and then looked at Tom.

Tom nodded. "So what about Maelog Gruffydd?"

Coyote went back to his laptop, typed a phrase, and began reading. "Okay, Gruffydd…born in Maine…worked on the tree farm…then left for Long Island. He was there for six years." Coyote looked up. "I emailed the owner of the tree farm. He wrote me a long email back. He said Gruffydd was a nice guy but kind of gullible. He just quit one day and took off for Europe. He'd been chatting online with another Greenpeace activist and they made plans to travel together." Coyote smiled. "Here's a little useless piece of info. The Greenpeace guy's name was Rich. The farmer remembered that because his name is Rich, too. Rich Galbraith. Anyway, I followed Gruffydd's credit card for a couple of months and then it just stopped. He was in France, Italy and Greece, and then he disappeared. Maybe he had another source of money."

Coyote sat back and rubbed his eyes, then looked around the room. "This was just a skimmer. I need to deepen the research. There are still a lot of holes."

"I'm impressed by all the information you uncovered," Tom said. He chose not to think about what Coyote's "deeper research" might entail. "Go home and get some sleep. We'll take it from here."

Chapter 34
Late Friday morning

After her stint planting tomatoes and beans, Francesca walked up to the administrative building. She wanted to switch her volunteer schedule to two afternoons a week. She did her best writing in the morning. If she got to the office at one in the afternoon, she felt like she was behind the eight ball. Kathy, Taylor's secretary, was in charge of scheduling.

The main hall was light and airy. A pool of crystalline water ran the length of the gallery, bordered by luscious flowering plants. A skylight provided muted sunlight. Francesca walked all the way down the hall to the administrative offices, opened the door, and walked in. To the left was an empty meeting room. The receptionist's desk was straight ahead. Kathy, Taylor Emerson's secretary, wasn't there and the phone was blinking. To the right, the door to Taylor Emerson's large office stood open.

Francesca walked over and peered into the room. No one was there. At one end of the office was a dark rosewood desk. Behind it a window looked out on terraced gardens and a free-form lily pond. The other end of the room held a sleek seating arrangement in deep grey with turquoise accents. In front of the sofa was a low table displaying a variety of elegant bonsai trees

Francesca walked over to the window behind the desk and looked out. She could see Maelog trudging down the path between the terraces. He stopped to look at several plants and bent down to remove a leaf or pull a weed, then moved on. She smiled. He truly nurtured life, helping plants grow. She turned and looked at the gleaming desk. On the writing pad a file folder lay open. The top sheet of paper contained a list of names. Three had check marks beside them in green ink. She noticed the name of Roscoe Miller, a wealthy financier in town. This was definitely not her business, but she was curious. She bent down to read the other names.

From the foyer came the sound of the outer door whisking open. Francesca stepped around the desk and approached the low table just as Taylor strode in. She looked perfect, as usual, in a cream silk blouse and dark mauve pencil skirt. Francesca smiled at her. "These bonsai are lovely."

Taylor looked irritated. "Yes, they are. Why are you in here?"

"I wanted to talk to Kathy about my schedule. Sorry for trespassing. I just wanted to check these out." Francesca gestured to the mini-trees.

Taylor walked over to the desk and closed the file folder. She turned and leaned against the desk, crossing her arms. "I know who you are. We haven't been formally introduced, but you're the editor of the *Banner Bee*, right?"

"Yes. Francesca Antonelli. Barnett, now." Francesca came forward and held out her hand, only then recalling that she was dressed in her dirty sweatshirt and jeans.

Taylor's hand felt cool and smooth. Francesca looked down at her own hand; nails dirty from gardening, and pulled it away. "I've been working down at the fruit and vegetable area planting tomatoes."

"Weren't you the one who discovered Dr. Takahashi's body?"

"Yes." She didn't want to think about it.

"I'm sorry you had to experience that on your first day as a volunteer. I hope you aren't thinking of quitting?"

"Oh, no. I just wanted to change my time slot."

Taylor smiled. "Are you still planning on doing some articles about the Gardens? We can use all the PR we can get."

"Yes, next week when things have calmed down I'll be doing a series of articles highlighting different areas of the BBG."

"That sounds great. Now I need to get to work."

Francesca knew she'd been dismissed.

"And Ms. Antonelli, please don't enter my office again without an invitation." Taylor wasn't smiling when she turned to gaze out the picture window.

Chapter 35
Friday, noon

Tom slipped out the back door and walked around the tennis courts that backed up to the police station. He wanted to avoid the media maniacs stationed by the front door. He'd decided to walk over to Hero's and get something for lunch. He was hoping he could take it upstairs and talk to Francesca. He needed to decompress, and she gave him a sense of balance.

There were too many loose ends in this investigation—everything they'd learned about the BBG employees and Jack Banner's shady past. His analytical antennae, usually reliable, were leading him nowhere.

He chose to walk through the village green. The air felt cool under the canopy of trees. He noticed a village work crew bringing down a massive elm. *That tree must be a hundred years old*, he thought. *What a damn shame.*

As he walked, he hoped this time he wouldn't be approached by any worried or outright crazed people. He'd had enough from the two women and that scruffy guy at the coffee bar that morning. He turned his mind to the quantity of information they needed to work through. After the meeting, Cindy had told him about her visit with the Raleighs and the hospital. Though the police department needed to keep that family on their radar, he could scratch George Raleigh off the list of possible suspects in Doc Stoddard's murder. George had definitely been at the hospital that night.

There had also been a message from Conroy. It turned out Stevens had not seen the face of the BBG worker who had left the Japanese island after they'd put up the barrier. Stevens had been dealing with an angry foreign visitor and the employee had pushed past him. He'd been a big guy, Stevens said.

This afternoon they would be interviewing what he considered the major players in the BBG murder. Coyote's research had raised new questions for every staff member. Meanwhile, the department continued to receive bogus calls on the tip line. Nothing had popped up thus far. Deputy Chief Conroy had also organized a telephone marathon to all the guests at the BBG reception Monday night, but no one had any additional information. After the reception ended, the guests had all left the premises and gone home.

Tom had a gut feeling Jack Banner was responsible for Doc's murder, but they had no proof and no motive. Nor could they place him at the murder scene. Takahashi's murder had a completely different MO. It was precisely executed, almost beautifully in a macabre way, while Doc's killing reflected impulsive and unbridled anger.

Tom looked up at Francesca's office windows. He couldn't tell if the lights were on. He went up the short flight of stairs and entered the café.

"Chief Barnett." Hero came over to greet him. "Are you here for lunch? I just took a pizza out of the oven: mushroom and sausage."

"It smells great. Is Francesca upstairs?"

"Yes. She came in a few minutes ago. I think she'd been gardening."

Tom went up the stairs two steps at a time. He knocked on the door. "Hey, it's the police. Open up."

A minute later the door swung open. Francesca stood in the gap, beaming. She threw her arms around his neck. "I am *so* happy to see you."

He wrapped his arms around her and they held on to each other. "I wondered if you wanted to do lunch," he said into her ear.

"Do lunch? I'm feeling like doing something else right now." She scattered kisses across his face before landing on his mouth.

After a long moment, he said, "I feel like doing something else too, but I've only got thirty minutes to eat. How about I take a rain check for tonight?" Reluctantly they pulled apart. "Hero just took a pizza from the oven. I could get us both a couple of pieces."

"I've already got my lunch." She gestured to a Caprese salad on the oak table. "Go get a slice of pizza. At least we can talk for a few minutes."

When Tom came back upstairs with two slices and a Coke, they sat down together at the table. He smiled at Francesca. "You look cute with dirt on your face, very *paisana*."

"Dirt on my face?" Francesca got up, pulled a compact out of her purse, and flipped it open. "Oh, great. I've been walking around like this all day. Taylor Emerson must have thought I looked a mess."

"What are you talking about?" Tom took a bite of pizza.

"I stopped by her office before I left the Gardens." Francesca used a napkin to wipe the smudge off her cheek. "She's a bit forbidding."

"Forbidding? What do you mean?"

"She's so put together; clothes, hair, jewelry. She's a class act. But I don't know if she's so nice."

"I think she's a very smart woman, and kind of sexy."

"Sexy?" Francesca frowned. "So she turns you on?"

"Come on, Francesca. I'm just stating the obvious." He grinned.

Francesca picked at her salad. "I sort of checked out her office while she wasn't there. And..." She chewed thoughtfully.

"And?" Tom picked up his Coke.

"I went over to the window and looked outside. Then I happened to look down at her desk. There was an open file folder with a list of names. Three of them were checked."

"You just happened to look at this list?" Tom chuckled. "So who were they?"

"Roscoe Miller and somebody Talbot, I think. Maybe Leonard Talbot…" Francesca speared a *bocconcino* and chewed.

"Go on." Tom started on the second piece of pizza.

"I'm wondering what that list was about. When I heard her come into the outer office I scooted around the desk and was halfway to the display of bonsai trees on her coffee table before she came in. She was not happy to see me, and she made a beeline to her desk to close the file folder. I definitely felt like the intruder I was."

Tom thought this over. Could these names have something to do with the unknown source of deposits in Taylor's bank account? He took out his notebook and wrote down the two names. Here was more research for Coyote. For a brief moment he felt as though he was sinking in this miasma of names, facts and miscellaneous information.

Tom gave Francesca a brief rundown of what Coyote had reported. "What interests me is that all of these people have times in their recent pasts when they dropped out of view. Where were they and what were they doing?" He picked up his Coke can and sloshed the liquid around, deep in thought.

Francesca interrupted. "Oh, and I have something else to tell you. This morning when I arrived at the BBG, Colman came up to talk to me. He found out about the secret research Dr. Holmes is working on. He snuck into the lab there the other night."

"Secret research?"

"Apparently, volunteers in the lab are working on saving prairie seeds and freeze-drying them."

"Right, I heard about that."

"Well, according to Colman there's an inner sanctum where Holmes is studying poisonous plants."

Tom felt a jolt of alertness. "Poisonous plants?"

She nodded. "Poisonous to human beings. One of them is belladonna. Remember, the Romans killed their enemies with belladonna? Colman mentioned some other plants but I don't recall the names. Maybe this is where the poison that killed Dr. Takahashi came from."

Finally, something positive in this investigation. Dr. Holmes would have a lot to explain when he came in that afternoon. "How did Colman get in the lab? I thought it was locked up?"

Francesca sighed and looked away. "He jimmied the lock and went inside. I guess you could say he broke in."

"Oh, God. That kid could be in real trouble. I'm going to forget you told me that. But I am going to grill Holmes this afternoon and maybe we'll get some answers."

Tom told Francesca how the investigation was going and about his unpleasant meeting with Mayor Criche and his pals. "Something's got to give. I'm getting real pressure from multiple sources. People want these crimes solved." He looked over at the clock and stood up. "I better get going. We've got a long afternoon ahead. I don't know when I'll be home."

Francesca stood as well. "If you want I'll go over and talk to Emily at the Floral Fantasy shop. She advertises in the *Banner Bee*. Actually, I never knew she was married to Hisao Miyamoto. She goes by her maiden name."

"If you could find out what time her husband came home, that would be a big help."

Francesca reached out and touched Tom's arm. "I know you've got too many suspects. But I wanted to mention this woman I keep seeing at the BBG. She's a bit odd. I've seen her snooping around the place. She's supposed to be a volunteer like me, but I get the feeling she's got some ulterior motive. Maybe someone could check her out. Her name is Melinda Jordan."

Tom added the name to the list in his notebook. He gave Francesca a kiss and a pat on her rump. Then he was gone.

Chapter 36
Friday afternoon

After a couple of hours at the computer, Francesca was ready to do some detective work. Anytime Tom needed her help, she jumped in. Her natural curiosity was an asset, though it had also gotten her into trouble at various times in her life.

It was a short walk over to the Floral Fantasy shop. After a quick trip to the florist, she planned to visit Akiko, who must be feeling pretty lonely. That gave her an idea. She'd take some flowers to Akiko.

She pushed open the door to the floral shop. A bell tinkled at the back of the store.

"Hello, be there in a minute," Emily's voice sang out.

"Hi, Emily. It's Francesca. I'll just look around." She walked over to the cooler and looked at the dozens of roses of every possible color. They didn't seem quite right for giving to a bereaved young woman. Her gaze slid swiftly past the vases of red carnations. She shivered, remembering Takahashi's dead body, and kept looking. In one corner of the cooler was a small bouquet of cobalt blue irises and yellow tulips in a pretty porcelain vase.

"Hey, Francesca." Emily came into the main room. She was what Francesca's mother would call a "flower child" from the Sixties. Her long blond hair was parted in the middle, framing a perfect oval face and clear blue eyes. Today she wore a long jeans skirt and a pink tee-shirt with a Hershey bar on it and the words *Florists Need Chocolate*. On her feet were Doc Marten sandals. "Are you here about the ad?"

"No, actually, I came to buy some flowers and I've already picked out what I want." She frowned. "What about the ad?"

"I've got this friend who did some artwork for me. I thought I'd change the graphics on next month's ad."

"That'd be great. Have him send me the file."

"Okay. So what would you like to get?" Emily walked over to the cooler.

Francesca pointed out the iris and tulip bouquet. While Emily settled the vase in a box and wrapped it with green and purple cellophane, Francesca chatted with her about this and that. Then she said, "I didn't know your husband was **Hisao Miyamoto**. I've never seen him in here."

"That's because he's never here. The shop is in both our names but he's always at the BBG." Emily tied a bow and then looked up, her eyes clouded with worry. "This murder has really got him down. He's worried the police think he's involved. They asked him all sorts of questions."

Francesca reached out and touched Emily's shoulder. "Right now, they have to question everyone. Don't worry, they'll find the murderer."

Emily moved away, clasping her hands tightly together. "Wednesday night, I stayed late working on some centerpieces for a wedding. When I got home at ten, Hisao was into his second gin and tonic. Normally, he never drinks."

Francesca tried for a joke. "Gin and tonic doesn't sound very Japanese."

"Hisao was raised here, you know. He has an accent because he was home-schooled and spent the first twelve years of his life with his grandparents. But he went to public high school and Indiana University. I mean, he's really an American."

"Somehow, I thought he was a recent immigrant."

"When Taylor hired him, she told him to play up his Japanese roots…if he acted like he just got off the boat; it would make him more authentic. Gosh, one day she asked him to wear a kimono. He doesn't even own one."

Francesca looked down at the beautifully wrapped bouquet. "If he was home before ten, he has an alibi. Dr. Takahashi was killed after eleven, I think. There's nothing to worry about."

"After eleven? We were in bed by then." Emily handed Francesca her flowers with a tremulous smile. "These are on the house. Thank you for stopping by and making my day."

#

After leaving Floral Fantasy, Francesca sat in her car thinking. With no prompting, Emily had provided an alibi for her husband. Hisao Miyamoto had been home drinking gin and tonics. Francesca pulled out her phone and texted Tom, then drove over to the Deer Run Inn. In the lobby she asked the receptionist to call Ms. Takahashi and tell her Francesca Barnett was waiting in the lobby. A few minutes later Akiko came down the stairs. She looked wan and pale. Francesca handed her the flowers. "I hoped these would cheer you up."

They sat down in a corner of the lobby. Akiko unwrapped the flowers and set them on the low antique table. "Thank you, Francesca. They're lovely…such beautiful colors."

"Would you like to go out for a cup of tea? There's a place in town, the Green Tea Shop. They specialize in Japanese green tea. I thought it might be comforting for you."

Five minutes later they were on their way to the tea shop, a short walk away from the hotel. They had the place to themselves. Francesca chose a table by the window and they sat down. Francesca let Akiko select the tea blend. It was served with crispy almond cookies. Once she'd breathed in the perfume of the tea and taken a sip, Akiko seemed to relax. "This is wonderful. I'm glad you brought me here." She glanced around at the simple, elegant décor. "It's like a little piece of Japan."

"I'm glad I thought of it. I've never been in here before." Francesca took a sip of the delicately flavored tea. "So how are you?"

"I couldn't sleep last night. I kept trying to think of someone who would want to kill my father. I couldn't come up with a name or a reason. Father was a good and kind man. He did many good works in Japan to help others."

Francesca nodded.

"Maybe it's a crazy person that had some reason we can't imagine. Like an American who hates the Japanese." She looked uncomfortable. "You know, because of the war."

Seventy years later, Francesca thought that was unlikely, but chose not to say anything. "Considering the care that was taken to display your father's body, I think whoever killed him planned all this ahead of time. Why he committed this crime probably makes sense to him…or her. But why the chrysanthemums?"

Akiko's slim fingers gripped the delicate cup. "That's the flower of death…but usually white ones."

Francesca changed the subject. They discussed Akiko's plans for the future. When she got home, she planned to look for a job in public relations with an American firm. She wanted to leave the world of bonsai trees behind. Francesca told her a little about her own life, where she grew up, her divorce, the *Banner Bee* and of course Tom. Francesca pulled out her iPad and brought up the *Banner Bee* site, so Akiko could check it out. They laughed at some of the pictures people had sent in for the "Funniest Dog in Banner Bluff" contest. Akiko relaxed and color returned to her cheeks.

They finished their tea and walked back to the inn. "Jack Banner called me last night," Akiko said quietly as they drew near. "He asked to come over and apologize."

Francesca stopped dead in the street. "You've got to be kidding."

"No, he came to the hotel. We sat out in the back garden. He told me he was sorry for how he acted in Japan, and for his behavior at the Gaslight. He had tears in his eyes and spoke sincerely. I was surprised. He was like a different person."

Francesca shook her head. This did not sound like the Jack Banner she knew. What was he up to?

Chapter 37
Friday afternoon

Tom and Puchalski set up shop in one of the interview rooms. It contained a table and four chairs. The squad room was visible through a glass panel. A video camera hung from the ceiling in one corner. Before they got started, Tom went out to the squad room. Officer Romano was escorting Colman Canfield down the hall.

"Sir, Colman says he needs to talk to you. Do you have time?"

"Sure, we'll speak with him and then you can bring in Holmes." Tom nodded at Colman. "Go on into the interview room. I'll be there in a minute." He turned to Romano. "Any news on Dr. Takahashi's limo driver?"

"Yes, sir. He'll be here in an hour."

"Great, thanks."

Colman was dressed in dirty jeans and a sweaty grey tee-shirt. He started talking before they sat down. "Chief, I decided I better come over here. I'm on my break so I only have a few minutes. I talked to Francesca this morning. Anyway, I started feeling guilty, so here I am."

Puchalski looked mystified. Tom smiled and nodded at Colman. "Take a breath, Colman. Sit down and tell us what we need to know. Francesca already clued me in."

Puchalski reached over and shut the door. Then he and Tom sat down.

"Last night I broke into Dr. Holmes's lab." Colman's cheeks reddened. "I wanted to see what was so secret. I mean, this is a public garden…not some high-level classified laboratory." He looked from Tom to Puchalski. "Anyway, I found out he's doing research on plants that are poisonous to humans, like aconite and castor bean. You know how the Russians poisoned that guy in London with a metal pellet that contained ricin? That comes from castor beans." The words were tumbling out of his mouth.

Puchalski looked nonplussed. Tom nodded. "So what did you find?"

"Well, I checked out the test tubes and the notes lying around. Then I opened the refrigerator. Marked vials of various poisons are kept in there. I noticed two vials of Atropa belladonna were gone. That's deadly nightshade and it's very poisonous in concentrated levels."

Puchalski looked excited now. He caught Tom's eye. "Maybe we can nail Holmes when he comes in."

"Maybe," Tom said slowly. "How did you know these vials were missing?"

"There are plastic containers…kind of like drawers with the different vials. Two were missing from the Atropa belladonna drawer."

"Why didn't you tell us right away?"

"Well, because I broke in and…I guess I didn't think it was so important." He was looking at his hands, which were balled up in his lap.

"Thank you for coming in and being up front," Tom said pointedly. He thumbed through the pages of his notebook. Miyamoto, Holmes, Gruffydd, Emerson, Hoffmann, and then Jack Banner. He looked up at Colman. "Is there anything you can tell us about the other employees at the BBG?"

Colman cocked his head. "I don't really know much. I just started there this week." He thought for a minute. "I work for Luis Gonzales. He really keeps me busy, which is good. Dr. Holmes hates my guts but I guess that's my fault. Let's see…Irma Hoffmann is really nice but kind of bizarre. Then there's Maelog. I like him a lot, but he's kind of different too." Colman scratched a mosquito bite on his arm. "He's my neighbor. Did you know he lives in an apartment over Larson's Interiors? I've seen him around. He goes for late night walks." Colman pulled out his phone, looked at the time, and stood up. "Hey, listen, I've got to get back to work."

"Okay. Thanks again for coming in," Tom said.

Colman pulled open the door and bolted down the hall, almost running into Dr. Holmes and Officer Romano.

Holmes walked into the interview room with the same aggressive manner as the previous day. "I already talked to you," he growled.

"That was a preliminary discussion. We have a few more questions for you."

Holmes sat. "Make it snappy. I've got some specimens incubating and I need to get back to the lab."

"Do you mind if we tape this discussion?" Tom asked.

Homes looked up at the camera. "No, I've got nothing to hide."

Puchalski flipped the switch. Then he pulled out a yellow card and began to recite. "You have the right to remain silent…"

Holmes's eyes widened. "Wait a minute. Do you really think I'm guilty of this murder? Do I need a lawyer?"

"If you feel you need a lawyer, you can call one," Tom said.

Holmes seemed to be debating his options. "That would take forever. I want to get this over with." He gestured to the card. "Go on, keep reading."

Once the preliminaries were out of the way, Puchalski asked, "Why didn't you tell us about your research into poisonous plants?"

A deep flush rose up Holmes's face from neck to hairline. "I didn't think it had anything to do with the case."

"But you knew Dr. Takahashi had been poisoned."

"Well, yes, but I didn't think it could come from my lab." He sat up straighter in his chair.

"Yesterday morning you must have seen that someone had removed two vials of belladonna serum."

Holmes looked flustered. He glanced around the room as though seeking an escape hatch. "How did you know that?" Then understanding dawned. "It was that kid I caught sneaking around my lab, right? That's why he was here…to put the blame on me? You should be arresting him for breaking and entering."

"So the belladonna was gone," Puchalski continued.

"Yes, but luckily we have plenty more to continue our work."

"What is your work?" Tom asked.

Holmes lowered his voice and leaned forward. "We've come up with two drugs that might be the answer to pancreatic cancer. Perhaps you've heard of the work with English yew, *Taxus Baccata*. It's being used for its potent anti-tumor qualities. Today yew extract is used to formulate Taxol, which slows the growth of ovarian, breast and lung cancers."

"How are you funding this work?" Tom asked.

"The BBG. They've supported much of what we do."

"Does the board at the BBG know they're subsidizing your research?"

Holmes loosened his tie and ran a finger under his collar. "Listen, I'm only talking to you because of the theft. This is information that cannot be shared. We're in fierce competition with other labs across the country. You must promise you won't divulge the purpose of our work." He looked up, sweat beading his face.

"Does the board know what you're researching?" Tom repeated.

He regained his composure. "No, not really. But Taylor does. She's managing the funds."

Tom jotted down a note to talk to Taylor Emerson. Then he said, "Tell us about Sullivan College."

Holmes's face went wooden. "What's there to tell? I taught there for several years."

"Why were you dismissed?'

"I wasn't dismissed. There was a misunderstanding and I left."

Tom decided not to press the issue. Instead he said, "Where were you for nine months between jobs?"

"I borrowed my sister's RV and traveled around the Northwest. I was studying understory plants that grow under the forest canopy, primarily the wavelengths of light that are most effective for photosynthesis." Holmes's eyes brightened with excitement. "The BBG was interested in my research. I wowed them during my interview." He smiled with self-satisfaction. "Those studies are on the back burner right now, though."

"Have you ever been to Japan?" Puchalski asked.

"No, never."

"We understand you had an argument with Irma Hoffmann before the dinner. Can you tell us about that?"

"I don't believe this. Who told you that?"

"It doesn't matter. Just tell us what happened," Tom said.

"She and I had an argument earlier in the day. I've been interested in genetic engineering in plants. With my assistants, I've discussed growing some genetically modified vegetables at the BBG. Have you seen the green roofs at the south end of the gardens? We're studying which plants will grow well on rooftops in large metropolitan areas. Anyway, she freaked out. She's an organic fiend. She can't open her mind to the future."

"So you were continuing your argument from earlier in the day?" Tom said, somewhat lost in these horticultural disputes.

Holmes shot him a knowing glance. "She's transgender. Did you know that?"

Tom nodded.

"Well, I asked her what was wrong with a little genetic modification, when she's modified her sexual identity." His lips curled in a smug smile. "She did not take that well."

Tom and Puchalski shared a disgusted look.

"Tell us again what you did after the dinner," Puchalski said.

"I told you yesterday. I went to the lab for a while. I checked on some specimens and entered data into the computer. Then I got ready to leave. The gardens were quiet. The only person still there was Taylor. I saw the light on in her office."

"Does she often stay late?"

"I, uh, I don't know." His pale skin colored slightly.

"Where did you go when you left the BBG?" Puchalski asked.

'I went home. I told you that yesterday."

"Can anyone verify your story?"

"My story? There is no story. I live alone. I went home and went to bed."

Chapter 38
Friday afternoon

Ricky Stiles and Cindy Murray were set up in the second interview room. As Jack Banner walked in, the detectives both stood. Jack wore a red wife-beater shirt, dark blue cargo pants, and a red Cubs hat turned backwards. Snake tattoos slithered up his biceps.

"Well, look who's here, little Ricky Stiles." Jack laughed. "Ricky Stiles. I haven't seen you since high school. Shit, you haven't changed a bit." Still laughing, he turned to Cindy. "Didn't I meet you last winter? It was in a bar…maybe the Hog's Head?" He looked her up and down.

Cindy wanted to nail this asshole, if she could. She kept things polite with effort. "Sit down, Mr. Banner. Thanks for coming in. We've got a few questions to ask you."

Jack nodded, still smiling. "Sure, ask away." He sat down.

She gestured to the camera in the corner. "Do you mind if we tape this interview?"

"Go ahead." He crossed his legs and sat back in his chair. "You guys just won't give up."

Ricky switched on the video and Cindy went through the Miranda Rights. "You have the right to remain silent…"

When she finished, Jack nodded his agreement. She gave him a look. "Please speak up, Mr. Banner. Do you understand what I've just read?"

"I get it, and I don't need a lawyer. I've done nothing wrong. Even though you guys keep trying to pin this on me."

"Pin what on you?" Cindy asked.

"Old Doc Stoddard's murder. I didn't do it."

"Tell us again about that night." Cindy sat forward in her chair.

"Oh, come on, give me a break. I've already gone through this with Big Chief Barnett and Puchalski. I know for a fact they went out to the casino and watched hours of boring video, following my every move."

Cindy kept her face expressionless. "Humor us."

"God damn it. Okay." Jack sighed and launched into a description of Monday night. When he finished, they peppered him with questions until he turned red in the face. "That's enough. I came in here of my own free will, but this attack is overkill." He stood and made for the door.

"Please sit down, Mr. Banner," Stiles said, with a slight edge to his voice. "We'd also like to hear what you were doing Wednesday night."

Jack stopped, his hand on the doorknob. "Wednesday night?"

"Yes, Wednesday night. The night Dr. Takahashi was killed at the BBG. You've heard about it, right?"

Slowly Jack came back to the table and sat down. "Why would I have anything to do with that?"

Cindy leaned forward. "Because you allegedly raped Dr. Takahashi's daughter three years ago in Japan. Apparently, you received a dishonorable discharge afterward."

"Hey, missy. That was not rape. It was consensual. Her daddy just got the wrong idea."

Cindy stood, her hands flat on the table. "I'm not 'missy' to you. It's Detective Murray. Got it?" She jabbed her finger in his direction.

"Whoa…" Jack held up his hands and started laughing. "Pretty feisty."

Stiles stood up. He towered over Jack. Jack looked at the two of them and leaned back in his chair, crossing his arms. Slowly, Stiles sat down.

"Answer Detective Murray's questions," he said.

Jack sighed, took off his baseball cap and twirled it on his finger. "Ask away, De-*tec*-tive Murray."

"Where were you Wednesday night?"

"At the Gaslight. All night. I left at one o'clock when they closed."

"Who can verify your story?"

"About twenty people…James, the bartender…I talked to him for a long time. We were watching a Cubs game off and on. Then there was this girl from high school. You'd know her, Ricky. She was a babe back then, now she's butt-ugly…Sandy something-or-other." He continued to twirl his hat, studying it.

"What about Akiko Takahashi?" Cindy said quietly.

"Yeah, Akiko was there. She wanted me to apologize for our little hook-up. Like it was my fault and she hadn't come on to me. But you know what? I went to see her last night and we've made up. Everything's hunky-dory." He spun his hat across the room. It banged into the glass partition and fell to the floor.

#

After Jack Banner left, Ricky Stiles turned off the video camera. "I've got to tell you, I can't stand that guy." He rubbed his hand over his prickly buzz-cut.

"I hear you. Talk about arrogant. He's trying to needle us, get under our skin." Cindy stretched her arms over her head to release the tension in her shoulders.

"Well, he succeeded," Stiles said

"I'll go up front and get Irma Hoffmann. This shouldn't take long." Cindy went through the squad room and down the hall. She opened the security door. A tall woman wearing jeans and a purple shirt was chatting with the receptionist. She turned and smiled broadly.

"Irma Hoffmann?"

"That's me." The woman held out her hand.

Cindy smiled but didn't take it. It wasn't her policy to shake hands. Plus, Ms. Hoffmann outweighed her by about a hundred and fifty pounds and could probably toss her over her shoulder with no effort. "I'm Detective Murray. Will you please come this way?"

"I was glad to come in, but I really don't know anything about what happened on the Jap Island," Irma said. Her heavy boots clumped down the hall.

"We're just gathering all the information we can," Cindy said. "You might remember something that could help us."

They entered the interview room and Irma dropped into a chair. "Lordy, it's good to sit down. She beamed her toothy smile at Stiles. "I've been up since the crack of dawn. Planting is back-breaking work."

"We won't keep you long," Stiles said. "Could you just go over the other night again?"

"Right-oh!"

Cindy listened to Irma's recitation of the night of the bonsai reception and Takahashi's murder. Her language was punctuated by folksy expressions. Cindy wondered if they came naturally or if they were part of the down-home persona Irma wanted to project. It made Cindy wonder how much of this big, strong woman was for real.

"So you left to go home and attend to your animals?" Stiles concluded.

"Yes-sir-ee, I've got three dogs, two cats and some fuzzy lop rabbits. They need lots of attention."

"I'm sure they do." Cindy tapped her pencil on the underside of the table. "You didn't mention the argument you had with Dr. Holmes before the dinner Wednesday night."

Irma's eyes flashed anger and disgust. "Holmes is a pathetic individual. He's a mad scientist with a penchant for self-aggrandizement. I despise the man. Yes, we argued. I believe in natural, organic horticulture…using biological pesticides and natural fertilizers. He's on this kick to genetically transform plants."

"What about bonsai trees? Are they counter to nature?"

"You're damn right they are." Irma spat the words. "We're here to live on God's green earth within an ecological balance of flora and fauna. It's our job to maintain the natural order of things. But Holmes wants to play God. I despise the man."

"What about Dr. Takahashi?" Cindy shot back.

"I didn't know him. But he's Japanese and he maims trees. By definition I despise him, too." Her hands were clenched so hard, ropy sinews stood out along her arms.

Sweet down-home Irma had morphed into a railing maniac.

Chapter 39
Friday afternoon

The interview with Hisao Miyamoto produced nothing new. The man seemed frightened of his own shadow. Tom had received a text from Francesca confirming Miyamoto's alibi. After only a few minutes they told him he could leave.

"Go home and relax. If you think of anything that would help the investigation, please don't hesitate to contact us," Tom said.

Miyamoto smiled broadly. His eyes were moist. He shook their hands and bowed before leaving the interview room.

The last person on their list was Maelog Gruffydd. He walked in slowly, inspecting the walls. He stopped when he spotted the video camera. "Are you going to be recording this interview?" he asked, pronouncing the words carefully.

"We'd like to; if that's all right," Puchalski said. "We don't always remember everything in an interview because we're busy thinking about our questions. This way we can go back and review the information."

Gruffydd nodded and sat down heavily.

Ron took out the yellow card and went through the Miranda warning. Gruffydd didn't question the recitation and responded affirmatively at the end. As before, Puchalski shut the door and turned on the camera, and they began the interview. A couple of minutes in, someone knocked on the door. It was Officer Romano. Puchalski got up and turned off the video system, while Tom left the room to talk to Romano.

"What have you learned?" Tom asked once they were down the hall and out of earshot.

"The limo driver…" Romano checked his notes. "Kuznetsof, he's a Russian, came in a few minutes ago." The officer looked up. "I talked to him downstairs."

"Okay." Tom was having a hard time maintaining his cool today. He waited impatiently for Romano to get on with it.

Romano plodded on. "He said he picked up Dr. Takahashi at nine forty-five and dropped him off in front of the Deer Run Inn ten minutes later. Then he went down the street and parked. He was looking at his phone and figuring out where to go for his next pick-up. I think he said he was going to Lindenville and then to O'Hare. Or maybe all the way to Midway…"

Tom pounded a fist into his hand. "Okay. Is that all?"

Romano eyed him nervously. "No, sir. The driver glanced back and saw Takahashi still standing outside by the entrance to the hotel. A minute later a car drove up and Takahashi got in."

"Did he see the make of the car or the license plate?"

"No. He said he was blinded by the headlights."

"Did he see where it was going?"

"No, he took off and didn't look back."

Not much, but at least it was something. Tom managed a smile. "Thanks, Romano. Good work. Type it up, okay?"

"Yes, Chief. I'll get on it."

#

Back in the interview room, Puchalski and Gruffydd were shooting the breeze. Puchalski wanted to know what he could plant in his backyard, which was always in shade. Gruffydd suggested heuchera, ferns and hydrangea. By the time Tom reappeared, Puchalski had a short list of plants written down on the back of his notebook.

"Sorry. Let's get going," Tom said. He sat down and Puchalski turned the video camera back on. They talked about Wednesday night, and Gruffydd repeated his story.

"Someone at your table said you left the dinner a couple of times. Where did you go?" Puchalski asked.

"Let's see." Gruffydd frowned, as if thinking. "I went to the can once. I also stepped over to Irma's table. They were talking about blending soils. I wish I had been sitting there."

"What did you do after the dinner, again?"

"I went home."

"Did you go out for a walk?"

"A walk?" Gruffydd's eyes held a glint of curiosity.

"Yeah, we heard you like to go for walks at night. Where do you go?"

"I just walk around town. Sometimes it's hard to sleep."

Puchalski looked at Tom, who smoothly picked up the questioning. "We heard you spend time in the library. What do you read about?"

"Articles on global warming, *Nature* magazine, *Scientific American*, sometimes *TCI*." He ticked them off his fingers.

"TCI?"

"*Tree Care Industry* magazine. I try to keep abreast of what's going on."

"Oh, yes," Tom said. "You were raised on a tree farm."

Gruffydd nodded.

Puchalski cleared his throat. "Who did you go to Europe with three years ago?"

Gruffydd's eyes widened in surprise. "Three years ago? How did you find out about that?"

"Who did you travel with?"

"Umm…a guy I met online."

"What was his name?"

"I've got to tell you, I've forgotten. We traveled around France for a few days and then we split up. I didn't like the guy and the feeling was mutual."

"You were in France, Germany and Italy. Then where did you go?"

Gruffydd's speech slowed even more, the words coming with greater effort. "I was in Greece for several months. What does this have to do with Dr. Takahashi's death?"

"Just background information. So you had enough money to live abroad for over a year?" Puchalski leaned back in his chair and crossed his arms.

"Yes." Gruffydd's lips formed a firm line. An uncomfortable silence prevailed.

"What is your relationship with Dr. Holmes?" Tom asked.

Gruffydd shrugged. "He thinks I sneak around his lab. He's paranoid. I told him as much the other night." He wiped spittle from his chin with a handkerchief, then gave a lopsided smile. "I have zero interest in his 'secret experiments'. Maybe he'll invent a vegetable Frankenstein."

Chapter 40
Friday afternoon

Harry O'Connell was dusting Delia's car. She hadn't driven it for months. Once a week Harry took the BMW out for a spin and then cleaned it. As he ran the chamois over the gleaming surface, he wondered why Jack had the car towed to a garage out of state after the accident that injured Delia and killed her fiancé. Harry could have worked on the BMW right here. He knew this car intimately. But Jack claimed to know a hotshot mechanic who'd repair the car to perfection. *Some hotshot*, Harry thought. *Took him two months to fix this thing.*

    He was ready to put the BMW back in its place when he saw two men walking around the garage from the front circular driveway. From this distance he didn't recognize them, but his eyes weren't so great anymore. One was a big guy that looked like a body builder, in a red polo and slacks, the other a smaller man in a suit. They walked steadily past the ten locked garage doors as they approached Harry. He wondered how they got in. Jack must have left the main gate open again.

    The big guy had an intimidating presence, like a nightclub bouncer. Harry swallowed his nervousness and walked toward the visitors. "Can I help you?"

    "Yeah, we're here to see Mr. Banner." The big guy did the talking. His polo shirt bore the letters *VR* on the pocket. The short sleeves stretched tight over his biceps.

    "He's not here. Perhaps I can help you? Harry O'Connell." Harry stuck out his hand but neither man took it. He let it drop.

"This is the second time we've been here. The other night we waited around, but the guy never showed up. Mr. Venetucci doesn't like waiting." The big guy indicated the smaller man.

Apparently, Mr. Venetucci couldn't speak for himself. "What night was this?"

"Monday. We had an appointment at nine o'clock. Mr. Banner didn't show. We've been trying to reach him ever since." The big guy's muscles rippled under his shirt.

"I'm sorry. I don't know anything about it." Harry braced himself, ready to escort them back the way they came.

Mr. Venetucci studied Harry. Then he said in a low, rumbling voice, "Can you show us the car?"

"What car?" Harry felt out of his depth.

"The Bugatti."

"Mr. Venetucci has a deal with Banner to buy the Bugatti if he likes it," the big guy said.

"Listen. I don't know what Mr. Banner told you, but he can't sell that car."

Venetucci eyed Harry with annoyance. "Who are you to say what he can or can't sell? Aren't you the chauffeur?"

"His sister has to make the decision. And I won't let you see the car without her say-so." Harry crossed his arms and tried to look tough.

Venetucci glanced at the big guy and signaled with his left hand. "A long walk for nothing. Let's go." He looked at Harry. "Tell Mr. Banner we were here. We'll be back."

Harry heaved a sigh of relief as he watched them walk back along the line of garages. Only after they'd rounded the corner did he get into Delia's BMW and drive it into its usual place. He stayed in the driver's seat a moment, thinking over what he'd just learned. The two strangers were here Monday night but Jack wasn't. Or was he?

An hour later Jack drove up, pulling his Jaguar to a squealing halt. Pebbles flew in the air. Harry went down to meet him. He knew it would be wise to keep quiet but he couldn't do that, not now. Jack was parked in front of the main door, taking something out of the Jaguar's trunk.

"Jack, you had some visitors this afternoon," Harry said.

"Oh yeah, who was it?"

"A Mr. Venetucci and his bodyguard."

Jack came around from behind the car, his eyes spitting fire. He held a shovel in his hand. "What did you tell them?"

"I said you weren't home." Harry took a breath. "They said they'd been here before."

"Yeah?" Jack looked at Harry as though he were evaluating him.

"Monday night. They said they had an appointment with you at nine but you didn't show."

"Right. I was at the casino." He raised the shovel in a two-handed grip, like a baseball bat.

Startled, Harry stepped back. "They said you were selling the Bugatti."

Jack moved closer. "Don't mention Venetucci's visit to anyone…not to Delia…not to the police…not if you value your life." His steely gaze bored through Harry's skull. Then he threw the shovel across the courtyard. It smashed into the fountain and decapitated one of the stone figures dancing in the water.

Chapter 41
Friday, early evening

It was nearing five o'clock when Tom pulled into the parking lot at the Banner Botanic Gardens. Around him, visitors were chatting as they got into their cars. He caught phrases in Italian and French. The BBG had definitely become an international destination. Taylor Emerson must be proud.

He got out of the car and headed toward the administrative building. Hopefully, this trip would yield more information than the afternoon's repeat interviews of the BBG staff. Miyamoto's story had matched what his wife said, and the interviews with Maelog Gruffydd and Jack Banner had similarly turned up nothing new. It looked like Banner was free and clear for Wednesday night. Only Irma Hoffman had offered any surprises, but not enough to move her up the suspect list in Takahashi's death. "She's playing a role," Cindy Murray had said, during a brief consultation after the interviews were over. "Could be because she's transgender, and still figuring out how to be a woman. But she's also simmering with anger. She might be capable of killing someone, if her values and beliefs were at stake."

He reached the building and opened the door to the administrative offices. A pretty blond woman sat at the reception desk. He introduced himself and stated his business, and she put in a call to Taylor. "You can go right in. Ms. Emerson will see you now."

Taylor was standing behind her desk looking out at the gardens. She glanced over her shoulder as Tom and the receptionist entered. "Thanks, Kathy. Are you going now?"

"Yes, Ms. Emerson. I'll leave those papers to be signed on my desk."

"That's fine. See you tomorrow. Shut the door on your way out."

After Kathy departed, Taylor gestured to Tom. "Come look at this."

Tom walked over and joined her, gazing out at the terraced gardens. In the early evening light, the greens glimmered emerald and the flowers shimmered fuchsia, magenta and gold. It was an exquisite view. Taylor moved closer to him, held his arm and pointed to the swans swimming on the lily pond. "Intoxicating, isn't it?" She stood so close to him, he could feel her body heat, and he recognized her musky scent.

He stepped back. "Yes, you do have a great view."

"Why don't we sit over here?" She guided him to the sofa. He sat at one end, she sat at the other. She pulled up her smooth, tan legs and with one hand unbuttoned the top two buttons of her silky blouse, exposing more cleavage than was necessary for a police interview. He smiled inwardly at her attempt to vamp him. She was beyond sexy and definitely not worried about being interrogated by the police.

She reached out and touched his thigh. "What did you want to talk to me about?"

He removed her hand, pulled out his notepad, and leaned forward. "Just a few questions, Ms. Emerson."

"Please call me Taylor. I think we know each other well enough, don't you?" She leaned back against the cushions.

"Today we interviewed several of your staff members. I'd like to verify some information."

"Listen, can I get you a glass of champagne? I've got a nice bottle in the fridge." She got up and walked over to a small built-in refrigerator in a corner, bent over and took out a bottle, giving Tom a great view of her derriere. Then she took two flutes out of a cabinet and came back to the seating area. When she set the glasses and champagne bottle on the low coffee table, her full, round breasts swung in Tom's face.

"Could you open this for me?"

"Sure, but I won't have any. I'm on duty; got a long night ahead of me." He removed the foil and the wire from the bottle and pulled out the cork with a soft pop.

"Well done." Taylor poured herself a generous glass and sat back down. "Here's to the investigation. Let's hope you catch the bastard who ruined my bonsai show." She took a long sip and then licked her upper lip. Slowly she settled back against the pillows.

Tom cleared his throat. "Tell me a bit about how you finance the BBG."

Taylor was instantly alert. "Why? What does that have to do with the investigation?"

"We always try to get a broad picture of the environment in which a crime is committed. I assume you have a long list of donors."

"Yes, we do. I've worked long and hard to bring in money. But it's an ongoing battle. We've got big plans…a children's learning center, a butterfly pavilion, fountains in the English garden…" Taylor was sitting up now, her face intense as she described her plans. For a moment, Tom felt drawn to this passionate woman. There was something sensuous about her drive, her ambition.

He shook off the feeling. "How is Dr. Holmes's research funded?"

"Ah-ha. This is what you really want to know. I get it." She sipped champagne, her expression thoughtful. "It's not generally known, but the BBG is funding him. I'm not sure some of the horticultural aficionados would approve of our poison research but they don't get to pick and choose. If things turn out the way Jared is hoping, we should be patenting two new drugs in the next few months. He's a genius and I fully back his work." Her cheeks were flushed. She swallowed more champagne. "Who knows, maybe we can sell the patents to Aftat Labs, right here in Banner Bluff."

"That would bring in a lot of money, wouldn't it?"

"Yes, it would, yes indeed."

Tom looked at his notes, then back at her. "I never asked you about Wednesday night. Do you remember anything that occurred during or after the dinner that might have a bearing on Dr. Takahashi's murder?"

Taylor ran her fingers through her silky hair. "Not really. People seemed to enjoy the evening. They fawned over Dr. Takahashi and Miyamoto did a good job translating after the daughter left." She looked over at Tom. "Hey, how is the daughter?"

"Akiko seems to be taking it as well as can be expected. As soon as we've finished the postmortem, she'll accompany her father's body back to Japan."

"I suppose I should go over to the Deer Run Inn and give her my condolences…but I really don't like to be around sad people. It brings me down."

Tom had no answer for that. Passionate about her plans for the Botanic Gardens, yet callous toward a young woman in pain—Taylor Emerson had the emotional depth of an amoeba. "One more question. Where were you between eleven PM and one AM the night of the murder?"

She burst into laughter, and again placed her hand on Tom's thigh. "Come on. You think I murdered this world-renowned bonsai specialist? I spent a year wooing him here. His presence was a real coup. Why would I knock him off? That's nuts!"

Firmly, Tom removed her hand. "Ms. Emerson, where were you Wednesday night after the dinner?"

She looked annoyed and didn't answer.

Tom pressed the issue. "Someone said you were still here at eleven-thirty. The lights were on in this office."

"Who said that?" She smoothed her skirt and glanced up at Tom. "Do I need an alibi?"

"How late were you here?"

She sipped champagne. "I was entertaining a donor. We were having a nightcap."

"Who was it? I need the name."

A wave of anger washed over her face. Tom waited. After a moment, she sighed. "Okay. It was Roscoe Miller. But I don't want you bothering him. He's got big bucks."

"Roscoe Miller." Tom recognized the name. Francesca had given it to him earlier.

#

Back in his car, Tom called in to the station. "Arlyne, could you get me the address of a Roscoe Miller? He lives either in Banner Bluff or somewhere nearby."

A minute later she was back on the line. "I've got a Roscoe Miller at 223 Lake Avenue. It's that big house on Lake Michigan, north of the beach."

"Got it. I'm going over there now. Then I'll be back at the station. Contact the task force and tell them to be there at seven. Order a couple of pizzas and soft drinks. We'll make it a dinner meeting."

"Okay, Chief. Will do." She rang off.

It was a ten-minute drive to the Miller residence. The dinner hour wasn't an ideal time to barge in, but Tom wanted to nail down Taylor's alibi. He didn't really think Taylor murdered Takahashi, but he wanted to verify a hunch.

223 Lake was an impressive grey stone house perched on the bluff above Lake Michigan. An older woman opened the door. She

had curly grey hair and a pinched expression. Black pants and a baggy chartreuse sweater floated over her skinny frame. "Yes?" Her voice was low and scratchy, as if from years of smoking.

"Chief Barnett, Banner Bluff Police. I'm here to see Roscoe Miller."

The woman called over her shoulder, "Roscoe, you've got company." She turned back to Tom. "You might as well come in…but not for long. Dinner is almost ready." She stepped back to let him enter.

The entryway was large and clearly had once been impressive, but looked old and tired. The carpet was worn, the floors scuffed, the side table by the wall scratched. Dust motes floated through the air, illuminated by rays of late sunlight streaming through dusty windows.

"Come in here," the woman said, gesturing for Tom to follow her. "This is Roscoe's study."

Tom stepped into a dark and gloomy room. The odors of cigar smoke and wet dog permeated the air. Two golden retrievers lay sprawled on the floor. They wagged their tails but made no effort to get up. Roscoe was sitting in an armchair, a glass of bourbon or whiskey on the small table beside him. He pushed himself out of the chair with both arms. He was built like a fire hydrant—short, stubby and sturdy. He was mostly bald except for several strands of greying hair carefully combed over from one ear to ear. His small dark eyes appraised Tom.

"Good evening, Mr. Miller. Chief Barnett." Tom held out his hand.

"Right. I recognize you." He gripped Tom's hand and shook it. His own felt soft and moist. "Sit down. Do you want a drink?"

"No thanks. I'll just take a few minutes of your time." Tom sat opposite Roscoe on a cracked leather chair. One dog got up and came over to sniff Tom's shoes.

"So, is this about the murder investigations? I was just reading the *Tribune* on my iPad. Looks like you're getting nowhere."

Tom decided to hit him hard and fast. "I'm here to verify Taylor Emerson's alibi. She said she was with you until about twelve-thirty Wednesday night. Is that right?"

All color drained from Roscoe's face. He looked towards the door. "Oh, my God. She told you that? Oh, my God." He picked up his drink and shakily gulped it down.

Tom waited for the man to get ahold of himself. "Mr. Miller, were you with Ms. Emerson?"

The liquor had brought some of his color back. He bent forward and cradled his head in his hands "This will ruin me," he mumbled. "Oh, my God."

Tom gave him a moment and then asked again. "Yes or no? Were you with her in her office at the Banner Botanic Gardens Wednesday night?"

Roscoe looked up at Tom with a tortured expression. "Listen, I've got a wife and grown kids and grandchildren. No one can know about this."

Tom nodded. "No one needs to."

"You must understand. I just can't resist her. She's so damn sexy and she'll do anything I want. I just can't get enough of her." He eyes were glazed over. "That body, man."

"What do you pay her?"

Roscoe sank back in his chair and gazed blindly out the window. "Whatever she wants. I've spent thousands on her…I've given thousands to the BBG." His gaze came back into focus as he looked at Tom. "And you know what? It's all worth it…every penny."

Chapter 42
Friday, early evening

Francesca entered the empty house after her meeting with Akiko. The dogs came bounding to the door wagging their tails. Here comes dinner, they were thinking. She filled their bowls with kibble and replenished the water bowl. When they had finished eating, she let them outside and went upstairs to change into her running clothes. That morning she had skipped her usual run partly because she didn't feel so great and partly because she didn't want to arrive late at the BBG. Now she was feeling antsy. A run would get her back on track.

    The bedroom felt stuffy, so she opened the windows to let in some air. The day had turned abnormally warm. Back in the hall she paused in front of the baby's room. She opened the door and looked at the crib, the changing table and the yellow ducklings traipsing around the walls. What if she did what Susan had suggested and turned this room into something else…maybe an upstairs office or sitting room? Some of the furniture from her townhome was down in the basement. If Susan helped her, they could do the switch in a day…maybe even repaint?

    She pounded down the stairs, feeling excited about her plan. It would be a big surprise for Tom. When she let the dogs in, they recognized her attire and started jumping around, hoping to go along. She bribed them with a chewy stick, and while they were happily gnawing away, she snuck out of the house.

    Instead of going down towards Lake Michigan, she headed for the BBG. It was an easy fifteen-minute run if she took the bike path that ran along the train tracks. The long, straight path was not shaded and she'd worked up a sweat by the time she reached Beech Tree Road. She took the exit ramp down to the street and in another five minutes arrived at the entrance to the gardens. The gate to the entrance road was closed and no one was manning the booth, but the exit lane was still open.

Francesca ran through the open gate and jogged up the parking lot toward the natural prairie gardens. She would run around Prairie Lake, down to the lily pad garden and then back home. At the end of the lot, she halted. Tom's SUV was parked at the foot of the path that led to the administrative buildings. Was it really his car? She jogged around for a look in the windows and recognized his aviator sunglasses in the center console. The day he bought them, she'd caught him checking himself out in the mirror a dozen times. She'd teased him about looking like Tom Cruise.

What could Tom be doing here? Wasn't he conducting interviews at the station? She paused and looked up at the administrative building. Was he up there with Taylor Emerson? The windows were mirrors reflecting the cloudless sky. Hopefully her goofy behavior with Taylor earlier wouldn't cause any problems for Tom.

Francesca headed toward the prairie gardens. As she passed the volunteer center, she saw Melinda Jordan coming out.

"Hi! What are you doing here so late?" Francesca stopped and jogged in place.

Melinda seemed tense and in a hurry. In one hand she carried a clear plastic bag containing a green mug with the initials ATT on the side. In the other she carried a potted chrysanthemum. She was still wearing the dark track suit she'd worn that morning, along with a blue and grey checkered scarf. "I forgot something. I'm on my way home now." She glanced back toward the center and then toward the parking lot.

"Gosh, have you been here all day?"

Melinda shot her an intense glance. "Yes. I really enjoy working here." Again she glanced back at the volunteer center.

"We should have lunch someday. We never really got to know each other," Francesca said. She was babbling away like a teenager.

"Yeah, sure. That would be great."

Francesca heard the low buzz of a cell phone. Melinda wedged the plant under her elbow and pulled a phone from her pocket. She looked at the screen and then at Francesca with a brief, apologetic smile. "Sorry. I've got to take this." She started walking towards the parking lot, her phone glued to her ear.

Francesca turned to watch her go. The woman didn't seem like a ditz. She seemed purposeful and together, but stressed. Maybe Francesca shouldn't have mentioned Melinda to Tom. The truth was she didn't seem like a potential murderer.

Francesca took a long drink from her water bottle, then continued her run toward the prairie path. The asphalt reflected the absorbed heat of the day. Slanted rays of sunlight beat on her bare head. She continued another half mile. Sweat dripped down her face and she felt a little dizzy. Going all the way around Prairie Lake suddenly seemed like a bad idea. Up ahead on the left was the road to the Banner estate, a shady route through the woods. At the junction she turned left and was soon immersed in a world of deep green. Birds twittered softly, and up ahead she could hear the gurgling of Fishtail Creek.

The road dipped and turned and then she was on the bridge over the creek. She stopped for a moment to get her breath and wipe her forehead. The water was probably filthy but it looked cool and inviting. She felt a little dizzy again. What was that about? She sat down on a corner of the stone ledge and took another drink from her water bottle. Maybe she'd better walk for a while.

The forest canopy provided shade and quiet. The woods looked dark and impenetrable. She didn't know how big an area the forest covered but it must be several hundred acres. Far to the south, the woods bordered the Deer Way Golf Course. Since the woods were privately owned by the Banners, there were no public trails through the brush.

As she walked, she went over what Akiko had told her about Jack—that he'd showed remorse when he apologized for his past behavior. Could Jack be turning over a new leaf? It seemed impossible. She remembered the vicious way he'd spoken to Delia the day she was there for lunch, only four days ago. Undoubtedly he wanted to change his image with the murder investigation nipping at his heels.

Something caught her eye. Red and blue. Just off the road. She walked over for a closer look. Pebbles had been scraped away from the roadside, and two bushes had broken branches as if something had been dragged between them into the woods. Francesca looked up and down the road. No one was coming. She slipped in between the damaged branches and found herself in a small clearing, practically invisible from the road. Ahead lay a narrow path into the woods.

She looked slowly around, getting a feel for the spot. The leaf canopy whose shade she'd appreciated earlier seemed gloomy and oppressive here. To her right lay the object that had caught her eye—a weathered piece of wood, painted red and blue. From the disturbed ground cover, she could tell it had been dragged in there recently. She stepped around carefully and inspected her discovery. The wood was curved and partially charred. It looked like part of a boat, maybe part of the bow. Who dragged it in here? Weird.

Belatedly, she realized the forest had fallen silent. The birds had stopped chirping. She could hear her own heart beating. She looked quickly around. Except for the scraggy trail wandering off through the trees, it felt as if the forest had closed in on her. She could see nothing but dark green leaves, woody trunks and thick brush. And yet she could have sworn something—or someone—was watching her. She spun around. Nothing was there. On instinct she sprinted for the opening onto the road. She stumbled over the low branches and almost fell on the asphalt. Without looking back, she started running towards the BBG.

Chapter 43
Friday evening

At seven o'clock, Delia and Jack Banner sat down to dinner in the solarium. Luisa had set the table with a red and white checked table cloth with matching extra-large napkins. She brought in a platter of ribs slathered with whiskey-cola barbecue sauce. There were bowls of potato salad and coleslaw as well as a basket of Texas toast. In an ice bucket, Jorge had placed several bottles of beer. It was a feast for the two of them. Jack's favorite things, like Delia had promised.

She still didn't understand what had prompted her brother to drop by the library after breakfast, where she was working, and ask if she'd like to have dinner together. "I'll be around, and…well, I'd like to talk to you. Nothing important—it's just, you know, been awhile." He'd sounded so different from his usual self. No snide undercurrent to his words…he'd been subdued, even a little anxious, like when they were kids and he'd gotten her into some scrape, and wasn't sure if she'd forgive him.

Now, Delia surveyed the loaded dinner table and smiled. "Oh, my goodness! Thank you, Luisa. I hope there are plenty of ribs for you and Jorge?"

"Yes, thank you, Luisa," Jack said. "This looks great." Another marvel—Jack complimenting the help. Whatever was behind the change, Delia approved of it.

Luisa smiled and nodded. When she left, they dug in. Since the accident, Delia hadn't felt like eating much but tonight she was starving.

Jack picked up a rib. "I guess we can eat these with our fingers. Mother isn't here to tell us to use a knife and fork."

"Right." Delia giggled, remembering what a stickler Mother had been about proper etiquette. She took a forkful of the creamy potato salad. "We are so lucky. Luisa is a fabulous cook."

They ate and drank, talking about happier times when they were kids. Jack took a second helping of ribs, but Delia felt as though she couldn't eat another bite. She sipped her beer, chatting, while he continued to eat. It was so good to be together without unpleasantness. She hadn't realized how lonely she'd been these past few months.

When Jack had finished, Delia rang the silver bell, and Luisa and Jorge came to clear the table. Then Luisa brought in two large pieces of key lime pie and two cups of coffee. Jack smiled and looked over at Delia. "Key lime pie? All my favorites tonight." He glanced at Luisa. "Thank you, Luisa."

After the pie, Jack pushed back his chair. "Wow! What a meal! Tomorrow I'll have to detox with a kale and blueberry smoothie and a ten-mile swim."

"I guess we did overindulge." Delia felt relaxed after the good food and beer. Her meeting that morning with Robert Garfield, her financial advisor, had gone well too. They'd talked over several investment opportunities that he'd agreed looked promising. In the last year, with Robert's help, she'd gained an understanding of the family finances. She felt much more comfortable now in their discussions.

Jack leaned forward. "I'm glad we're together to talk." He looked down at his hands where they lay folded on the table. "I want to tell you, I know I've been a jerk. These last few months have been terrible for you and I haven't made things easier." He took a deep breath. "I want to make it up to you and try to be the brother I should." He took another breath and looked up at her. "I was always jealous of you. And when Dad died and left everything in your hands, I felt cheated and angry. I'm going to try and get over it." He took another big breath. "Will you give me a chance?"

At first Delia didn't know what to say. This wasn't the Jack she knew. Then she chastised herself. She should have an open mind. "Of course I'll give you a chance. You're my brother and the only family I have." She felt tears spilling down her cheek and wiped her eyes with a corner of her napkin. When she looked over at Jack, he was smiling.

"I've been thinking, Delia. Why don't we go up to Brevoort next weekend and open the cabin?"

"Just the two of us?"

"Yeah, it'll be fun. We can go for a long weekend. I'll drive the truck and we can bring up your kayak.

Brevoort Lake was up in the Upper Peninsula, in the middle of the Hiawatha National Forest. Every summer when they were kids, they spent a month in the family cabin. Usually, Jack complained that there was nothing to do. As a teenager he'd drive over to Lake Michigan and escape to Mackinac Island on the ferry. But Delia had loved the quiet. On the estate in Banner Bluff there were always people around, and her parents were often out at social events or entertaining guests. In Brevoort, Delia had her parents to herself. They went sailing, canoeing and hiking. She spent hours reading, cuddled up in the over-stuffed sofa in the cabin's cozy living room.

Delia frowned, puzzled. "I thought you hated to go up to the cabin."

"When I was younger, sure. But I think it'll be good for the two of us to get away. You know, reconnect and all that. What do you think?"

"Okay, I'm game. When do you want to go?"

"How about next weekend? We can leave Friday morning."

She looked at him, her eyes alight. He smiled at her. Briefly she saw something, a glimmer at the back of his eyes. It must have been her imagination. She gave herself a shake. "All right, Jack, next Friday it is."

Chapter 44
Friday night

Tom turned into the driveway. Francesca's blue Mini was in the garage. He pulled in next to her car and switched off the engine. For a minute he just sat there thinking about his visit to Roscoe Miller's house. Did sex make the world go round? Yeah, it did…along with power and money. His job repeatedly taught him that truth. But when he got home he wanted to forget the tawdry world out there.

He got out of the car and slammed the door, then went in by the side door. "Hey, anybody home?"

"Hi! I'm out here in the back."

Tom put his gun away in the safe and then walked through the living room to the screened-in porch. Francesca was curled up in a padded garden chair, a glass of ice water with lemon beside her. She was wearing her old jeans shorts and a rosy V-necked tee-shirt. Her hair was damp and hung down her back. She looked up at him and smiled. Her face was clean and free of make-up. She was beautiful, much more beautiful than Taylor Emerson and eminently more sexy. Her perfect oval face and high cheek bones were worthy of a top model. He bent down and brushed her lips with his, then kissed her deeply.

"I'm so glad to be home," he murmured when the kiss ended. "What a day." He straightened up and rolled his shoulders to work out the kinks.

Francesca unwound her legs and stood up. She came around behind him and massaged his shoulders, digging her thumbs into the muscles.

"Hmm. That feels so good." He closed his eyes and relaxed. "Have you been home long?"

"No." She paused. "I have lots to tell you. I've been busy this afternoon."

"So have I." He groaned like a big, old bear.

"Why don't you go up for a shower and I'll get our dinner on the table. I wasn't sure if or when you'd be home, so we're just having chicken breasts and a salad."

Ten minutes later, Tom came downstairs. The table was set in the dining room complete with candles and a bottle of sauvignon blanc. A platter of grilled chicken breasts with an apricot mustard glaze sat next to a large white bowl of tossed salad with heirloom tomatoes, cucumbers, avocados and parmesan shavings. A basket of warm focaccia rounded out the meal. Tom poured them each a glass of wine and they toasted each other.

"Here's to an end of the violence in Banner Bluff," Francesca said.

"And the speedy apprehension of the murderer or murderers."

They were silent for a few minutes while they both ate as if starved. Then Francesca told Tom about her meeting with Emily Crowder. They agreed that Hisao Miyamoto was not a suspect.

"Then I went to see Akiko at the hotel. I brought her some flowers and took her out to the Green Tea Shop. It's mostly Japanese tea and she knew what to order."

"Did she have any more ideas about her father's murder?" Tom took a sip of wine.

"No. She told me she was up all night trying to figure out who would hate her dad enough to kill him. All she could think of was someone who's still angry about Japanese atrocities during World War II. As unlikely as that sounds."

"Yeah, we thought about that angle too, after talking to Irma Hoffmann again. She doesn't like the Japanese much. She actually called them 'Japs.' Like it's still 1945."

"Irma?" Francesca chewed thoughtfully on a piece of focaccia. "Is she a suspect?"

"She said she was home with her menagerie when Takahashi died. But get this. Irma was *Irwin* Hoffmann up until a few years ago. She moved to California and had a transgender operation."

Francesca sat back. "I knew there was something different about her. Today, I was noticing how big and strong she is. It makes perfect sense now." A cloud came over her eyes. "You don't think she's the killer, do you?"

He jabbed his fork into his salad. "Right now, it could be almost anyone over there except Miyamoto. And of course there's Jack Banner, but he has an alibi for both murders."

"Oh, I didn't tell you the strange thing Akiko told me. She said Jack came over to the hotel and apologized for taking advantage of her, and also for being a jerk the other night. She said he was completely sincere."

Tom nearly choked. "Give me a break. I can't believe that."

"Me either. He must have an angle."

He sipped more wine, with a thoughtful look. "I wonder what."

When they had finished eating, Tom cleared the table while Francesca scooped vanilla ice cream into two martini glasses. On top she spooned a compote of raspberries and strawberries that had been macerated in *crème de cassis*. They took their dessert dishes and their wine glasses out to the screened-in porch, and talked quietly as they finished their dessert. Tom felt himself finally unwinding.

Later, upstairs, they lay entwined in bed after making frantic and exquisite love. Tom had used their intimacy to banish the day's anxieties. He'd wanted love to conquer the anger, violence and greed he'd witnessed. Francesca embodied everything that was pure and beautiful and wonderful in the world.

"Tom?"

"Yes," he said lazily, stroking her thigh.

"I forgot to tell you about my run. Or maybe I was avoiding it."

He was instantly alert. "What happened?"

She told him about running to the BBG, about the heat and her decision to go through the woods. "I saw something in the underbrush, something red and blue. There were broken branches, like someone had dragged a big heavy object into the woods. I went in to investigate."

"What was it?" Tom propped his head on his hand.

"A piece of wreckage, curved wood, like the bow of a boat."

Tom's mind was racing. "You said this must have been dragged there recently?"

"Yes. I saw the marks in the gravel beside the road and the twigs were freshly broken."

"Where exactly was this?" He switched on the light.

Francesca shaded her eyes. "Ouch. I don't know exactly. I was running from the BBG. I stopped at the bridge over the creek for a drink. Then I walked for a bit. I don't know…maybe a quarter of a mile after the creek."

"What side of the road?" Tom got out of bed and pulled on his underwear.

"On the right. The south side." She turned over, away from the light. "Why are you getting dressed? It's late. Come back to bed."

He finished buttoning his uniform shirt, then bent over and gave her a kiss. "Go to sleep. We're going to retrieve that wreckage you found. It might be the clue we've been looking for."

After Tom left the room, Francesca lay back and sighed. In a way she wished she'd kept her mouth shut. They could just as well have looked for that piece of junk in the morning. She should have known Tom would want to be on top of it. She reached over to turn off the light and then changed her mind. She remembered the feeling she had in the woods…that someone was watching her. She shivered and pulled up the sheet, leaving the soft light to drive away shadows.

Chapter 45
Saturday morning

In the morning, Francesca slipped out of bed. Tom was fast asleep, his breathing deep and regular. Downstairs she let out the dogs and made herself a cup of coffee. From the open window she could smell the lilacs from next door. The robins had stopped their frantic nest-building. She thought she could see the top of a little, round head sticking out of the nest.

She took her coffee and laptop out to the porch and sat down at the glass table. This morning would be a busy one. She wanted to write a post about the planting yesterday. The series of articles about the BBG was titled "Gardening 101". Irma had given her a multitude of tips that she would pass on to her readers, and she'd taken several pictures with her phone.

At nine o'clock she planned to head over to the fire station where the Boy Scouts were having a pancake breakfast to raise money for the Jamboree in Colorado. David, her photographer, was meeting her there. Her readers loved pictures of themselves and their children. David was outstanding at catching the perfect candid shot. She was in the middle of her article when Tom came out to the porch, already dressed for work. He sat down heavily with his coffee and a bowl of cereal. His blue eyes were smudged with dark circles.

She looked up. "What time did you get home?"

"It must have been after two."

"So did you find the wreckage?"

He looked irritated. "No, we didn't. Are you sure it was there?"

Francesca frowned. "Of course, I'm sure. Would I make that up?"

"We found the spot, the broken twigs and the crushed ferns, but there was no bow of a boat. There wasn't anything."

"You're kidding. I saw it for sure, Tom."

"We had the Max Million spotlights and our heavy duty flashlights. It was the right spot. But we saw no evidence that anything had been dragged away, either. It just…disappeared."

"Did you go down that little path into the woods?"

"Yeah. Stiles and Romano followed it quite a ways. They ended up in a clearing. Nothing got dragged down that path. They'd have seen broken branches or skid marks along the ground."

"Maybe whoever put it there decided to move it."

Tom ate his cereal mechanically. "And that person lives right down the road."

"You think Jack hid the wreckage?"

"What I'm thinking is, Doc found this chunk of wood on the beach. Jack killed him to keep him quiet. Then he hid it in the woods, thinking no one would come by." Tom thunked his bowl on the table. "I would love to search the Banner estate, but no judge would write me a warrant with the evidence we currently have on Jack…which is zip, zero, nada."

"You're thinking what I'm thinking," Francesca said. "Jack and Delia's parents disappeared last fall when they were out sailing."

"And their boat was never found."

"We need to find out if this *is* part of that boat." Francesca reached over and covered Tom's hand with her own. "Later today, I'll drive over and see Delia. As I remember, there are pictures of her parents in their sailboat in the gallery on the second floor. I'll think up a reason to go up there and check out the photos."

"Be careful," he said, concern in his eyes. He turned her hand over and kissed the palm. Then he got up and reached for her coffee cup. "Want another?"

"No thanks, it doesn't taste right today." Francesca sat back, thinking about the Banners.

From the kitchen she heard Tom say, "Not another one." He came back onto the porch with his phone in hand. "Check this out."

It was another of those odd text messages. It read:
E006.2E965.0E849.4

"Are these the same numbers, or different?" Francesca asked.

"I don't know. I forgot all about the last one. I never showed it to Coyote."

"Wait a minute; I wrote that one down." Francesca went into the kitchen and came back with the blue kitchen scratch pad. Together they compared the series of numbers and letters Tom had received previously to the one he'd just gotten.

Tom shook his head. "They're not the same."

"Let me write this one down, too." She took his phone and copied the letters and numbers, then handed it back. "You should text this to Coyote."

An alert text flashed across the screen. Tom looked up at Francesca. "I've got to go. Something's up." Two minutes later he was out the door.

Chapter 46
Saturday morning

Zoë had not wanted to play golf at six-thirty AM. It was totally lame. And Grandma was totally crazy. Her mother said Grandma's best friend Helen fell and broke her hip. Now Grandma had no one to play with on Saturday morning.

"Mom, I'm not even awake at eight o'clock. I'm like, dead to the world. Can't you play with her?"

"Come on, Zoë. You can do it this once. You better go to bed early tonight."

"On a Friday? No way, I'm going over to Jenny's house to watch a movie."

"Well, just be home at ten."

That was yesterday. Now, Zoë made a lengthy par putt and was ready to move on. Grandma was lining up her shot. Her washed-out yellow golf-skirt showed her knobby knees and spotty legs. On her feet were black and white golf shoes that were at least a hundred years old. Zoë loved her grandma, but really—some things were just too much.

They were coming up to the thirteenth hole. Zoë felt fidgety. "Grandma, I'm going to get a drink."

"All right, dear." Grandma looked up. Her white hair stuck up out of her pink sun visor. Her smile made her eyes all crinkly. Zoë smiled back, feeling warm and kind of guilty at the same time.

She walked across the asphalt path towards the tee for the thirteenth hole. Next to the steps up to the tee was a red water tank. Zoë took a little paper cone and stuck it under the spigot. She drank that first cup down fast and stuck the cone under the spigot again. The water tasted a little weird but at least it was cold.

To the right, behind some bushes she spotted a wooden shelter, an overhang with a wooden bench underneath. Zoë thought she'd sit down and check her Instagram account. When she came around the bushes, she saw a lady already sitting there. The woman was leaning back with her head resting against the wooden wall. Her dark hair was plastered on her head. She had a track suit on. Her feet were crossed at the ankles and her arms were wrapped around a little pot of red flowers. Her eyes were fixed on Zoë.

"Hi." Zoë said, feeling uncomfortable under the unwavering stare.

The woman didn't answer. She didn't move. She didn't blink. Zoë stepped closer. Then she saw the bullet hole and the gun lying on the bench. She spun on her toes just as Grandma came around the bushes.

"Ready to go Zoë. I just got a par three on that hole."

Speechless, Zoë pointed at the woman on the bench. Grandma walked over and inspected the body. Holding her hand to her chest, she said, "I think she killed herself. See the gun? Have you got your phone?"

Zoë nodded.

"Call 911. Tell them there's a suicide at the thirteenth hole."

Chapter 47
Saturday morning

As Francesca got out of the shower, she heard sirens wailing in the distance. Probably an accident out on the North-South Highway. That would account for so many emergency vehicles.

She put on red capris with a black sleeveless knit shirt, and tied a silky black and red scarf loosely around her neck. She pulled her hair into a high ponytail and added some small gold earrings. Now she looked like a professional editor on the job.

It was a short walk over to the village green. On the streets surrounding the park, the media circus was still going on. Francesca said hello to a journalist from the *Sun Times* that she recognized. The woman looked tired and frazzled. She was waiting for that morning's press conference, she said, and then she was going home.

The fire department building was on the green next to the police station. The firemen had moved the trucks out into the parking lot so the Boy Scouts could set up tables for the breakfast in the large open hangar. Francesca saw several people she knew. She spent time talking with the scout leaders and then interviewed some of the boys. Dave trailed along behind her and snapped pictures. She was invited to sit down with several groups, but she declined.

In a corner, she stopped to talk to the Marshalls. Martin, wearing his high-tech glasses, rose from the bench. "Hi, Francesca. How are you doing?" There was concern in his voice.

"I'm fine." She looked over at Rosie, who was giggling with two other little girls. "It looks as though Rosie is doing all right."

He nodded. "Kids are amazingly resilient. She hasn't had any nightmares, but who knows what's going on in her head."

Martin's wife Kate was seated with baby Michael on her lap, feeding him bits of pancake. He was licking her fingers like a puppy. Next to her sat Stevie, the Marshalls' three-year-old son. He had a sausage in each hand and was alternately taking mini bites out of each one.

Kate looked up at Francesca. "Actually, Rosie is enjoying her notoriety. The kids think she's ultra-cool because she actually saw a dead body." Kate shook her head. "What a world."

An older boy came barreling over, nearly knocking Francesca down. His scout uniform bulged at the waist. His dark hair was gelled into a point on his head. "Hey, you guys," he yelled to some of his buddies at the other end of the table. His loud voice got everyone's attention. "They found another dead body."

"Where?" a big kid asked, his mouth full of food.

"Over at the golf course. I just got a text." The boy was bursting with excitement.

"Do you know who it is?" another kid asked.

"A woman this time," said a girl as she studied her phone.

The little kids stopped giggling and looked around at the big kids. Kate stood up and grabbed Stevie's hand. "Martin, will you please get Rosie? We're out of here." In less than a minute they were gone.

The atmosphere changed quickly. The air felt charged. Everyone started talking at once and looking at their phones. Francesca heard a girl behind her say, "Hey, here's a picture of the dead body. It's from Jenna, who got it from Zoë. Zoë's the one who found the body."

Another girl said, "Ooo, look at her forehead. There's, like, a big hole."

"Zoë said it was suicide. See, there's a gun right there."

Francesca whirled around. Two girls, a blonde and a brunette, were standing together looking at an iPhone. They must have been fourteen or fifteen, and wore off-the-shoulder shirts over camisoles and teeny shorts. Their long hair hung down their backs.

"May I look at your phone?" Francesca asked, keeping her tone bland.

The two girls looked at her, glowing with excitement. "Sure, like, isn't this amazing?" the brunette said. She held out the phone. Francesca took it and stared at the picture. She swallowed and felt a wave of nausea flow over her.

"Is that your friend or something? You look, like, really upset," the blonde girl said.

"No, not a friend, but it's someone I know." Francesca felt dizzy and reached for the edge of the table. She recognized Melinda Jordan in spite of the bloody forehead, the slack-jawed expression and the empty eyes.

"Oh my God, someone you *know*?" The girls stared at her, wide-eyed.

Francesca handed the phone back. "Have a lot of kids seen that picture?"

"Yeah, like, it's gone viral. Jenna is the Instagram queen. I mean, everyone in the world has seen this picture by now."

"Thanks." Francesca walked unsteadily between the tables and out to the street. The Boy Scout picnic had been taken over by media hounds. They must have found out these kids had the picture that would make the front page. As she approached the street, someone grabbed her arm.

"Hey, lady. Those girls say you know the victim. Could you tell me who it is?"

Francesca turned and found herself facing a skinny guy with slicked-back hair and a sharp angular face.

"No, sorry, I can't help you. I don't know who it is. I've only seen her around." She shook off his grip. She could tell he didn't believe her.

He kept yelling as she crossed the road towards the gazebo: "You could be on the news if you told me." She didn't turn around, but kept walking across the green.

Chapter 48
Saturday morning

It was déjà vu with all the same players, ME Hollister, Ramirez and his crime scene technicians as well as the task force investigators. Deputy Chief Conroy was first on the scene after the squad car. He contacted Tom and told him to drive around to the back of the Deer Way Golf Course. The body had been found on the thirteenth hole, on the north end of the course. A bike path running east–west separated the course from the Banner Woods. There was a wide opening into the golf course from the bike path.

When Tom arrived, Jones the photographer was taking pictures of the crime scene. Under a tree several yards away, a teenage girl and an older woman were seated on a bench. Cindy Murray was standing beside them, taking their statement. Behind them the lush green fairways rolled into the distance. Tom used to play golf, but he'd stopped. He never had enough time to work on his game.

Conroy came up as he walked on to the course. "Chief, that's the girl who found the body. She and her grandmother were the first ones out on the course today. They don't seem too shook up."

"Okay, I'll see what they have to say."

He stepped onto the green of the thirteenth hole, circled a sand trap and approached the women. As he walked he listened to a frantic call from Arlyne on his headset. "Pictures of the murder scene are on cell phones all around town," she said. "Damned Internet…"

He broke the connection as he neared the woman and her granddaughter. Anger pulsed through his body. He curbed it, not wanting to show his feelings while talking to civilians.

Cindy nodded a greeting as he reached them. "Chief Barnett, this is Zoë Richter and her grandmother Nancy Wright."

Tom shook hands with both of them. "Can you tell me what happened this morning?"

"Zoë got there first. I was still on the putting green." Mrs. Wright patted the girl's arm. "Tell them, Zoë."

"Well, I got a drink of water and I saw the lady sitting under the shelter. See, I was going to sit there. But then I realized she was staring at me, you know, not moving or saying anything. I got closer and that's when I saw it." The girl blanched and then swallowed. "I saw the blood on her forehead and the bullet hole. That's when Grandma came over."

"Yes, I told Zoë to call 911. I could tell it was suicide with the gun right there."

Zoë shook her head. "Grandma, she's got that flower pot in her hands. She couldn't shoot herself, put down the gun and pick up the flowers. That totally couldn't happen."

"You mean it's another murder?" Mrs. Wright's voice quivered. "Oh, dear God." Her hand went to her chest.

"Looks like it." Tom breathed deeply to keep control of himself. "What did you do then?"

"We just waited here. They told us to." Zoë glanced up at him.

"Is that all you did?"

Zoë looked at the ground. Her cheeks were pink under her freckles. Tom waited.

"Well…" She twisted her fingers together. "I took a few pictures. You know, so my friends could see."

Mrs. Wright looked shocked. "Zoë, you had no right to do that. My God! You should respect the dead." The old woman looked up at Tom. "I'm sorry, Chief. I don't know what to say."

Seething, Tom turned to Cindy. "Get their statement and then escort them off the course." He walked away and didn't look back.

At the crime scene, Hollister was finishing up his preliminary examination of the body. He looked up as Tom approached. "Do you play golf?"

"Nah. I used to."

"Me too. So do you know what Babe Ruth said?"

"I bet I don't." He wasn't in the mood for Hollister's jokes.

"'It took me seventeen years to get 3,000 hits in baseball. But I did it in one afternoon on the golf course.'" He chuckled. "That could have been about me."

Tom's smile was brief. "So what can you tell me?"

"What's got you riled up, Tom? And by the way, you look like hell."

"Ultimately, it's probably nothing. But that little girl over there took pictures of the victim and posted them on Instagram. Now they've gone viral. This means more media attention and more pressure on the task force and more calls from Criche and his cronies."

"And they want answers yesterday."

"Right. So let's get down to business." He gestured to the crime scene.

"I would say this woman died between midnight and two AM. She was killed somewhere else and brought here afterward."

Tom gazed across the golf course trying to concentrate. "Right."

"She was shot at close range. There's an abrasion ring around the wound, and the imprint of the weapon's barrel. Then she was brought here and arranged on that bench." He gestured at the shelter.

"Complete with a pot of red chrysanthemums in her hands. I'm thinking this must be the same person who killed Takahashi, but what could be the connection?" Tom said. "We need to find out who she is. I'm told there was no ID on her."

"With her picture all over the media, someone is bound to come forward."

"Yeah, I suppose." Tom's phone vibrated in his pocket. He pulled it out. Francesca had sent him a text. He read it and looked at Hollister. "The victim is Melinda Jordan, a volunteer at the BBG. Francesca just identified her."

Chapter 49
Saturday morning

Francesca walked across the village green as if in a trance. Someone had killed Melinda Jordan. Shot her in the head. Why? Why would someone want her dead? Francesca had talked to her just yesterday. She remembered Melinda carrying the red flowered plant and a plastic bag. What was in the bag? She tried to remember. Something green. Oh, right, it was a mug, a green mug with some initials on it.

Still in a fog, she realized she'd reached Hero's Market. She started up the steps. Inside, the Saturday morning crowd was all buzzed up on caffeine. Even here, some people were looking at their cell phones. It made her think of the crowds who rushed to the guillotine during the French Revolution to see the heads roll.

She made for the alcove and the stairs up to her office. Several people called out her name. She waved, smiled and kept on walking. At the foot of the stairs, Vicki caught up with her. "Can I come upstairs and show you a piece I wrote? It's about a cancer patient. I wanted you to check it out."

"Sure, just give me a few minutes." Francesca raced up the stairs, opened her office door and shut it quickly. Then she leaned back against the smooth wood, her eyes closed against a wave of nausea. Another murder. Tom must be going nuts. She'd better text him and tell him who the murder victim was. She pushed away from the door and walked over to the oak table. Her phone had disappeared in the depths of her bag. She dug around unsuccessfully, then dumped the contents onto the table. There was her phone, in between her house keys and the slip of blue paper from the kitchen pad. She'd stuffed it into her purse and forgotten about it.

She sat at her desk and texted Tom. Then she gazed out the window at the waving branches of the trees. They were lucky not to be part of the human race. They soaked up rain and inhaled the sun's rays. Life was simple for a tree. Her mind went back to the picture of Melinda sitting dead on a bench. In the corpse's hands was the red flowered plant she'd been carrying yesterday. Red flowers, just like those covering Dr. Takahashi's body. Another wave of nausea built, and Francesca closed her eyes again.

A timid knock on the door sounded. "Francesca, can I come in?" Vicki said.

"Sure, just a sec." Francesca went over and unlocked the door.

Vicki stood there in khaki shorts and a dark green polo shirt, the summer uniform at Hero's Café and Market. She must be helping her grandfather today. In her hand was an iPad, on her face a hesitant smile.

"Come on in. I was just going to make a cup of tea," Francesca said. "Do you want one?"

"Sure. Thank you. I could have brought a cup from downstairs.

"No, I'll make a pot of Earl Grey and we can share. I've got some almond biscotti."

As they waited for the tea to brew, they discussed the third murder. Francesca didn't reveal that the dead woman was Melinda Jordan, figuring the police didn't want to share the information yet. "It's all anybody's talking about downstairs," Vicki said. "People are frightened, Francesca. They don't think the police are doing enough."

"Well, I can tell you the police are working night and day to find the killer. Or killers. Don't forget, most of the detectives and officers live right here in town. They want to find the murderer as much as anyone else does."

When they were settled with their tea, Vicki scrolled down her iPad and found her story, then handed the tablet to Francesca. Francesca took another bite of the dry biscotto and a sip of tea. The combination seemed to have settled her stomach.

Vicki was looking shy and hopeful at the same time. "I'll be quiet and you can read."

Vicki had written about a ten-year-old girl, Mallory Upton, who'd been fighting a losing battle with leukemia for the last four years. Her prognosis was not good and she was growing weaker by the day. Vicki depicted the strength of the girl and her positive outlook on life. Apparently, Vicki had been visiting Mallory regularly after her shift was over. They played *Sequence* and *Scrabble* together. It was a poignant, heartfelt depiction of a young girl's struggle against a devastating illness.

She heard Vicki get up and walk around the room, probably out of nervousness, and then sit back down. "This is a wonderful piece, Vicki," she said as she read the final paragraph. "Your writing was good before…but this is superb."

"Second semester I took a writing class. The instructor was great. The first few weeks she slashed my papers to bits, but she also helped me see what I did wrong. By the end of the term, I'd really improved."

Francesca tapped the iPad. "I'd like to publish this in the *Banner Bee* but since we're talking about a child, I think we need to get permission from her parents first." She looked up and saw Vicki holding the blue slip of paper.

"What are these letters and numbers supposed to be?" Vicki asked.

Francesca shook her head. "I don't know. Tom got them in two texts this week. I copied them down, thought I'd do a little research online. Tom meant to send them to Detective Blackfoot—he's in digital forensics—but things have been so crazy."

Vicki hesitated, then said, "They look like medical coding, but they're all smooshed together."

"What are you talking about?"

"During lunch at the hospital this week, I sat with some women in the billing department. There's this woman, Kelly, who's a champion coder. Really, she's been in competitions. Anyway, I went up to the offices where they do the billing and coding, and she showed me these massive volumes of codes for every illness and every part of the body. It's called ICD-9 or 10, I think. I can't explain it all, but there's a series of numbers and letters that indicate the patient's illness and the procedure followed to treat them. There are even codes that tell when and where an accident occurred. It gets really detailed and complicated."

Francesca had heard vaguely about medical coding. She knew physicians and hospitals used codes to communicate with Medicare and insurance companies, but she didn't know much else. "Like, how complicated?"

"Here's the example Kelly gave me. Let's pretend you're pregnant, and you go to a hockey game and get hit by a puck. When the doctor or hospital contacts the insurance company to get reimbursed, they need to spell out what happened. So there's a code for a hockey rink, and a code for getting hit with a puck in the eye, and another one if you get hit in the arm. Then there's a code for riding in an ambulance and a code for the X-ray they take in the ER. There's a code if the patient has a background condition like pregnancy that doesn't have anything to do with the accident. There are E codes and V codes with all sorts of numbers and decimal points." Vicki pointed at the letters and numbers on the blue paper. "Like those."

"Do you really think these are medical codes?"

"I don't know. I could call the hospital and see if Kelly's around."

"Why not?" Francesca took the slip of paper and went over to the copier, made a copy and handed it to Vicki. Five minutes later Vicki was out the door and on her way to the hospital.

Chapter 50
Saturday morning

Tom got back to the police station later than he'd wanted. He'd emailed Melinda Jordan's name to Coyote Blackfoot from the golf course. Criche had scheduled a press conference for noon and wanted to see Tom before it started. Great.

Tom went downstairs to the war room. Coyote was crouched over his computer in a corner. In camo cargo shorts and a washed out brown tee-shirt, with rubber flip-flops on his feet, he looked like he'd thrown on his clothes. He was oblivious to the detectives talking around him. Tom walked over and said his name, but got no response. He put his hand on Coyote's shoulder and the young man looked up at him with glazed eyes. "Hey, Chief."

"Melinda Jordan. What did you get? We're having a press conference in half an hour."

Coyote shook his head. His hair fell over his eyes and he brushed it off. "Nothing. She doesn't exist. There are plenty of Melinda Jordans, but none in Banner Bluff."

"Did you check the information she gave to the BBG when she signed up to volunteer?"

"Yeah, Romano found the copy for me. We checked the address. It doesn't exist. The phone number she gave goes to voicemail with a generic message. Her listing of previous jobs doesn't check out. I tried everything. I'll keep on looking if you want, but right now it's a dead end." Coyote drummed his fingers in frustration.

"What about vehicle registration? Driver's license?"

"Nothing."

"Okay. At the morgue we'll get her fingerprints and DNA. For now she's the mysterious Madame X." Tom headed for the door. The mayor was not going to like this latest piece of information.

At the mayor's office, the receptionist was watching the media scrum through a front window. Police officers were outside, keeping people off the streets so traffic could get through. "Good morning, Chief," Gloria said as Tom entered and approached her desk. "The mayor is waiting for you. Go on in."

The office was in semi-darkness, shades were closed and no lights on. Criche was walking up and down the room, and didn't stop when Tom came in. "So what in the hell is going on, Barnett? Three murders now—Banner Bluff is becoming the nation's most dangerous city." He stopped and shook his finger at Tom as though scolding a kindergartener. "You're supposed to be preventing crime."

Tom stifled the impulse to swat the mayor's hand away. Or better yet, slug him. "Mayor Criche. A woman of about thirty-five was shot to death last night between midnight and two AM. We believe she was killed somewhere else and brought to the bench of the storm shelter at the thirteenth hole of the Deer Way Golf Course. At this time, we do not know her identity."

Criche stabbed his finger at Tom again. "No one knows who she is? How can that be?"

"It looks as though she was pretending to be someone she wasn't."

"Well, find out who she is." He went back to stomping up and down the room. "Are you going to tell the press?"

"We'll say we don't know her identity at this time. We'll ask for the public's help to identify her."

Criche threw himself into his office chair and lowered his head into his hands, his elbows resting on the desk. "Do we have a serial killer? Will this go on and on?"

"I think the murder of this woman is somehow related to Dr. Takahashi's murder, but we don't know enough yet."

Criche groaned and covered his face with his hands. "I'm not coming to the press conference. I can't handle it."

Tom left the room, closing the door quietly.

#

The parents of Mallory Upton approved publication of Vicki's article. Mrs. Upton told Francesca, her voice cracking with emotion, that Vicki's visits meant so much to their daughter.

At noon, Francesca went to the press conference with all the national media hounds. Between photographers, TV cameramen and journalists, she figured more than a hundred people. Tom struck just the right tone, she thought, in presenting what they were up against. Though it surprised her when he said they didn't know the identity of the murder victim. Why was Melinda Jordan's name being held from the public?

"Many of you have seen a picture of the woman who was killed today. I know the inappropriate and insensitive photo is circulating on the Internet. If anyone knows the name of this woman, I ask you to please come forward."

"Who took that picture?" someone shouted.

"A misguided young lady."

"What about the red flowers? Are they connected to the Japanese guy's murder?"

"It's too early to comment."

After a few more questions, he closed the conference down. Francesca went back to the office and typed up a short article to go into the *Banner Bee*. She didn't mention Melinda's name.

With that out of the way, she called Delia and suggested a short visit. Delia sounded unusually upbeat when she agreed. It was good to hear her happy voice after these long months of depression.

When Francesca arrived at the Banner estate, Harry came out to say hello. She saw a tightness around his eyes, and he wasn't his usual jovial self. He and Doc Stoddard had been such great friends, he probably still felt awful about Doc's murder.

"You know you can always talk to me if you feel like it." Francesca patted his arm.

"I'm feeling old. Maybe I should quit this job, but I don't know where I'd go. I've been here over fifty years."

She searched his face. "What's this talk about?"

"It's nothing." He turned away, limping across the courtyard. Francesca watched him go. When she turned toward the front steps, she noticed one of the dancing girls in the fountain had been beheaded. How had that happened?

She went up the stone steps and rang the bell. Minutes later, Jorge opened the door. "Good afternoon, Ms. Francesca. Please come in. I'll call Ms. Delia. She's upstairs in her sitting room."

"Don't bother, Jorge. I'll go on up there myself. I know the way, and Delia is expecting me." She smiled and headed for the stairs before he could stop her.

The stairs were wide and curved. A thick Persian carpet runner ran up the middle. At the top of the stairway, a wide gallery ran around three sides of the upstairs hallway. Delia's room was to the right, but Francesca turned left towards the framed family photographs. They began with the wedding of Jack and Delia's parents. Then came a bunch of pictures of Jack as a baby, then three-year-old Jack with baby Delia. There were pictures of family outings and birthdays. Francesca was so immersed in her study that she didn't hear Delia come out in the hall.

"Francesca, I'm sorry, I didn't know you were here."

"I told Jorge not to bother calling you. I was on my way up when all these pictures caught my eye."

"Yes, sometimes I come out here and take the tour. I like to remember happy times with Mom and Dad." Delia hobbled over to join Francesca. She had comments to make about each picture.

Francesca was looking for a photo of the Banners' sailboat. The pictures on this wall depicted birthday parties and school events. She spied one with Jack in a black rubber diving suit. "What's this?"

"Didn't you know? Jack's a fabulous swimmer. When he came back from the Marines, he swam in the lake just about every day. He was on a mission to increase his strength and stamina."

"I had no idea."

On the last wall were several photos of the sailboat. Delia walked by them without looking. "I've been thinking about taking these down." She gestured toward the photos. "I can't stand to look at Mom and Dad on that boat."

Francesca stopped by a family picture of Delia and Jack seated beside their parents in the sailboat, the *Banner Blue Ray*. Jack was scowling, Delia smiling. Francesca eyed the red and blue stripes encircling the hull, then compared them to her memory of the curved hunk of wood she'd seen in the forest. It could very well have come from this sleek wooden sailboat after spending nine months in the lake.

Delia walked on slowly in silence. Francesca followed her around and down the corridor that led to the south wing, her mind flitting like a bird through all the ramifications of her discovery.

They went down the hall and into Delia's study. Francesca had been here often last winter after the car accident, bringing magazines, books and homemade cookies. Delia had spent weeks on her chaise lounge staring out at the lake.

Delia gave her a bright smile. "Please, sit down. How about a glass of prosecco? I know we have a bottle or two in the bar downstairs."

"That would be lovely." Francesca walked to the window and looked out at the gardens and Lake Michigan beyond. Today the lake was a Mediterranean turquoise. She could almost believe she was on a bluff above Antibes.

Delia called down, and a few minutes later Jorge appeared with two delicate flutes full of chilled bubbling wine.

"Let's toast to sibling friendship," Delia said.

Francesca felt disconcerted. "Why sibling friendship?"

Delia laughed. "Because Jack and I have reconnected. We're starting to become friends."

Francesca watched the bubbles rising to the surface of her glass. "That's great. Tell me about it."

Delia sat up straighter, her face animated. "Yesterday, Jack came and apologized for his behavior this past year. He told me he'd always been jealous of me, and when Dad left me in charge of the finances, it made him feel worthless. He wants to work at being friends and sharing the responsibilities."

This was the second time in the last forty-eight hours that Francesca had heard of Jack's transformation. Could Jack actually be turning over a new leaf? It was hard to believe. She had to say something, but what? "That's great, Delia."

"We're going up to Brevoort to the family cabin next weekend. Just the two of us. We're going to bring my kayak and we'll visit Mackinac Island and go fishing. It'll almost be like old times." Her voice bubbled with happiness.

Francesca gripped her glass. Cold seeped through her fingers as she thought of Delia, far away and alone with Jack.

Chapter 51
Saturday evening

At nine, the Homicide Task Force convened in the war room. Pictures of Melinda Jordan were tacked up on the white boards along with photos of the other two murders that week. Three murders in the quiet village of Banner Bluff. Tom couldn't get his mind around it. Things were spinning out of control and the team was getting nowhere.

The low murmur of voices died away when he entered the room. The weight of the investigations was heavy on everyone's shoulders. He could sense their feelings of frustration and insufficiency, feelings that plagued him as well. Tired eyes looked up at him.

"Good evening. I hope to make this brief. We need to hear the latest evidence and put our minds together. The mayor, the village board and the community are breathing down our necks…with just cause. They're frightened and they expect us to solve these murders."

"In an hour, just like on TV," Romano said. They all nodded, their faces grim.

"We need to ramp it up. I think we're missing something in our investigation of Doc's murder. Stiles and Sanders, tomorrow morning go down to the beach. Take a look around at the crime scene. Go over to the Banner estate. Talk to everyone again. See if you can get a fresh look at Jack and Delia Banner. Talk to the cook, the butler, and Harry O'Connell. Ask him to show you the cars. Look around. That piece of wrecked boat, or whatever it is, could be somewhere on the estate property."

"Are we sure this wreckage…this piece of a boat exists?" Brendan O'Connor looked skeptical. Others nodded in agreement. "I mean, how did it disappear into thin air? It wasn't dragged out of the woods. We would have seen drag marks through the ground cover."

"Maybe a few guys picked it up and put it in a truck?" Puchalski suggested.

Brendan rolled his eyes. "Right, and this happened between six PM and ten-thirty when we got there?"

Tom's irritation mounted. They were questioning Francesca's story, and he instinctively wanted to leap to her defense. He gripped the back of the chair, but kept his cool and spoke evenly. "Let's move on. Ramirez, give us an update on our latest murder, Jane Doe, alias Melinda Jordan."

Ramirez went to the white board where the photos were displayed. "We're one hundred percent sure Jane Doe was not killed at the thirteenth hole. She was carried there and arranged after her death. The bullet entered from the front and went straight through. We found no blood at the scene, except around the hole in her forehead." He used a pointer to indicate the blood residue around the entrance wound. "There's no gun casing, or bullet hole in the wood behind her. The gun, probably the murder weapon, had been wiped clean. Only the victim's fingerprints were on the plastic flower pot. We assume the killer was wearing gloves."

"So where was she killed? Do we have any clues?" Cindy asked.

Ramirez continued. "The victim was dressed in a track suit. We've found evidence of ground cover on it…leaves, pine needles and dirt, particularly on the woman's back and knees. There are scratches on her hands and dirt under her nails. They're ragged and broken, like she was scratching the ground." Ramirez looked up. "It looks like she fought for her life."

Tom's gaze was drawn to the map of Banner Bluff. The thirteenth hole of the Deer Way Golf Course was twenty feet from the Banner family's private woods. *Is that where Jane Doe was killed?*

"In addition, we found residue of duct tape on the victim's wrists, face and ankles. She was likely bound and gagged before being shot."

"So while we were busy looking for the fantasy piece of wreckage on the north side of the Banner Woods, our chrysanthemum-killer was busy on the south side." Brendan slapped his notebook on the edge of the table.

Everyone looked down at the table. The tension was palpable. Then Sanders said with aplomb. "The BBG is west and north of the Banner Woods. To the east is the Banner estate. To the south is the golf course. Our murderer is playing hide and seek in this general area."

Tom nodded. "Early tomorrow morning, Conroy will lead a team to comb the Banner Woods, looking for evidence of Jane Doe's murder.

Chapter 52
Saturday night

Francesca rolled over when Tom slipped into bed. He reached for her and she moved into his embrace.

"Anything new?" she whispered into his neck.

"Nothing." His voice was gruff with fatigue. "Nothing." Two minutes later, he was asleep. She lay in his arms and dozed off. An hour later there was a loud knock downstairs. Bleary-eyed, Francesca looked at the clock. Twelve-thirty. The knock came again. She sensed Tom awake beside her. "You stay here," he whispered. He got out of bed, pulled on shorts and a tee-shirt, and went down the hall.

Francesca got up and wrapped herself in her red silk kimono, then followed Tom down the hall. She stopped at the top of the stairs and looked down.

Tom stood at the open front door, his gun held by his side. He was talking to two men dressed in dark suits and ties as they showed him identification. She heard the words *FBI*. Tom ushered them in and showed them into the living room.

She tiptoed down the stairs and into the kitchen. From the doorway into the den she could hear the conversation in the living room. She leaned against the wall and listened.

One man spoke in a deep voice, with authority. "We picked up on the picture circulated on the Internet, but we were already on alert for Karen."

"Karen?" Tom said. "I understood her name was Melinda Jordan."

"Your 'unidentified' body is Karen Grimes, a seasoned FBI agent. She contacted us late yesterday afternoon and told us she'd tracked down Richard Barnes."

"Richard Barnes?" Tom asked.

"Karen Grimes had been tracing Barnes for the past two years," the second man said. He spoke with a strong Southern drawl. "She's been with the agency for twelve years. She was an excellent detective and strategist. About a month ago, she went undercover. We were pretty sure Barnes was living in or near Banner Bluff. We think he discovered who she was and shot her."

Tom spoke again. "I'm lost here. But the name Barnes is familiar." There was a pause, and Francesca could almost see him thinking. "Wait a minute. Isn't that the guy who lived up in a tree for a year?"

"That's him," the deep-voiced man said. "Barnes lived for two years in a California redwood. The tree was supposed to be fifteen hundred years old. The Pacific Lumber Company was going to cut it down."

"Two fucking years, up there living on a six-by-six foot platform," said Southern Accent.

"I remember now," Tom said. "There was a resolution with Pacific Lumber and the tree wasn't cut down."

"Right. But Barnes didn't stop there," Deep Voice said. "The experience unhinged the guy. He became a vigilante and joined a group called Avenge the Trees, or ATT. He's responsible for the bombing of several loggers who were clear-cutting in another western forest. That landed him on the America's Most Wanted list."

"Yes, I remember now." Tom said.

"We also believe he killed several poachers that were removing burls from ancient redwood trees," Southern Accent said.

"Burls? What are those?" Tom sounded out of his depth.

"They're big bumps, big growths on the trunk of the tree. Poachers cut them out and sell the wood through the black market. Unfortunately, it damages the trees and allows insect infestations and disease to get under the bark," Deep Voice said.

"Isn't that illegal?"

"It's a felony," Southern Accent said. "Poachers are fined or even jailed, but we don't fucking shoot them, and that's what Barnes did."

"Do you have a picture of him?" Tom asked.

Francesca heard someone get up from a chair. Then she heard the clicking of a laptop keyboard.

"Here's a close-up of Barnes wearing a baseball cap. This is the best we've got, taken a while ago. He's always avoided the camera, and we don't have any clear frontal pictures of him."

"He doesn't look like anyone we've been investigating," Tom said slowly. "He looks tall. Am I right?"

"Yeah, he's maybe six-foot two. Light brown hair. Weighs maybe one-fifty. Fucking skinny fella," Southern Accent said.

"He could have gained weight or changed his hair color…but his features don't resemble anyone we've interviewed." Tom sounded puzzled and a little irritated.

"You mean the employees at the Banner Botanic Gardens," Deep Voice said.

"Yes. We've interviewed the staff a couple of times."

"Karen was convinced Barnes murdered the Jap doctor. She said it was about the trees, the fucking bonsai trees," Southern Accent said.

Francesca groaned softly. Fucking bonsai trees…the guy had only one adjective in his repertoire.

"So what's the name she gave you for Barnes?"

"It was a weird one." More clicking of the laptop keys. "Maelog Gruffydd." Deep Voice said carefully, pronouncing the unfamiliar name.

"Maelog Gruffydd?" Francesca heard tension in Tom's voice. "But he looks nothing like Barnes. He's got different coloring, a hefty build, and some kind of handicap. A speech impediment. I can't believe it."

Francesca couldn't believe it, either. Maelog was such a kind man. She had seen how lovingly he treated plants. And his handicap—Barnes didn't have one, or the FBI agents would've mentioned it. They had to be wrong.

Deep Voice continued unperturbed. "Karen was convinced he was the guy. She was going to follow him last night, finally run him down. Then we didn't hear anything from her. Her phone went to voicemail. We checked out the motel room she was using south of Banner Bluff. All her stuff was there, but her car wasn't. And she'd disappeared. Then we saw the picture."

"What make is the car? Have you got the license number? I'll get some officers to track it down."

More clicking. "She was driving a black 20__ Ford Fiesta. License plate XRT 5649."

Rapid footsteps approached Francesca, and before she knew it Tom came barreling around the corner and practically ran into her. She shrieked. He swore, then said. "What are you doing down here?"

The two FBI officers came charging around the corner, their guns raised. Francesca stood holding the edges of her kimono across her breasts. She wanted to disappear.

"Gentlemen, this is my wife, who was supposed to be upstairs asleep," Tom growled.

The two men put their guns in their holsters. Their gazes were hostile.

"Hello." Francesca tried to add a friendly lilt to her voice. She beamed at Tom and the men. "How about a cup of coffee?"

After a minute, Deep Voice stuck out his hand. Francesca took it tentatively, still holding her kimono together with her left hand. "Agent Bob Smith. This is Agent Larry Brown. I'm sorry we woke you. Coffee sounds great."

Smith and Brown. Francesca doubted those were their real names. Larry nodded to her. He probably thought she had a *fucking* nerve to listen in on their conversation.

"Let me brew a pot," Francesca said in her chirpiest voice.

The agents returned to the living room. Tom came further into the kitchen. "I told you to stay upstairs."

His scolding tone irritated her. "Sorry, boss. I'm just too curious for my own good."

"You can say that again." He reached for his phone and called the station to send out an alert for Karen Grimes' Ford Fiesta. Before going back in the living room, he whispered, "And go get some clothes on."

While the pot of coffee was brewing, Francesca ran upstairs and put on jeans and a tee-shirt. She swept her hair up into a ponytail, then headed back down.

The coffee was ready. She set the pot on a tray along with mugs, cream and sugar. In the living room, she served the coffee and then sat on a chair near the window. Why hide in the den? She wanted to know everything.

"We're going to get Barnes in the next hour," Agent Smith said. "I've got a team on the way. We'll need your help. We know where he lives, and we've got someone watching the front and back of the building. But we need more manpower."

Tom nodded. "I can call in twenty officers."

"The SWAT team will be going in, but we need your guys to encircle the apartment block, to form a net, in case Barnes escapes."

Agent Smith looked at his laptop. "Who lives in the other apartments?"

"Above Churchill's Café is a kid, Colman Canfield. The other apartments should be empty at night. There's a hairdresser and the offices of an architect and a construction firm," Tom said.

"Someone needs to get Canfield out of there before we move in."

"I know his phone number. I could call him," Francesca said.

They all turned to look at her, as if they'd forgotten she was there.

"Good. Do it," Smith said.

"Barnes is extremely dangerous. He will not hesitate to kill. Tell the kid to be careful," Brown said in his Southern twang.

Francesca went into the kitchen and unplugged her phone from the charger. She turned it on, found Colman's number, and connected. The phone rang and rang. Colman didn't pick up.

Chapter 53
Saturday night

Tom met the task force at the station. He'd asked the dispatcher to send out an urgent request to return to the station immediately without specifying what was going down. The radio wasn't necessarily secure, and they needed to take precautions. He'd also sent Ricky Stiles, who looked relatively young and harmless, over to the apartment building where Barnes was holed up. If Maelog Gruffydd *was* Barnes, which Tom still had trouble believing. Stiles' job was to get Colman Canfield out of the building before the raid, without tipping Barnes off. He hadn't gotten back by the time the task force assembled in the war room, dressed for action but clearly exhausted.

Tom cleared his throat. "I've asked you to come in because we're going to assist the FBI with a raid in one hour."

"What the hell is going on?" Brendan O'Connor asked. He sounded tired and belligerent, the confusion on his face clearly shared by his fellow officers.

"Melinda Jordan was an undercover agent for the FBI," Tom said. "Her real name is Karen Grimes. She was on an assignment to find Richard Barnes."

Some of the detectives had heard of Barnes and nodded in understanding. Coyote immediately began typing on his laptop.

"Richard Barnes spent two years in a redwood tree several years ago and then became an active member of ATT, Avenge the Trees, a radical group that uses violence to protect trees and save forests. Barnes disappeared for several years and, according to the FBI, reappeared in Banner Bluff two years ago with a different name and a changed appearance. He calls himself Maelog Gruffydd and has been hiding out as a gardener for the BBG."

Startled faces met this announcement. Tom kept going before anyone could ask a question. "Yesterday afternoon, Agent Karen Grimes contacted her superior and told him she'd found Gruffydd alias Barnes and was going to bring him in. That was the last they heard from her. She was killed last night sometime after midnight."

"That's why he cut off Takahashi's feet and hands," Cindy said.

Brendan scowled. "How's that?"

"He killed Takahashi, and pruned him just like Takahashi pruned bonsai trees and prevented them from growing naturally."

"And Barnes wrote those words in the sand garden: *Avenge the Tree of Life*," Puchalski murmured.

"So what are we here for?" Brendan asked.

He was totally out of line, but there was no time to discipline him now. Tom looked at his watch. "In thirty minutes, we're going to assist the FBI in Barnes' arrest." He walked over to a map of Banner Bluff. "This is Barnes' apartment, over Larson's Interiors. An FBI SWAT team will be entering here. We're going to encircle the area." He'd placed an X at key points on the map when he first arrived, and he used a pointer to indicate each location as he told each officer where to be. "Our goal is to keep any stray individual from entering this downtown area and to be on the lookout for Barnes if he escapes the FBI raid."

The door flew open. "Chief, he wasn't there," said Ricky Stiles as he charged into the room, out of breath. He wore shorts and a tee-shirt rather than a uniform. "I went in and up the stairs. I saw a light under Canfield's door. I knocked several times. No answer. Then I tried the doorknob and the door swung open. No one was in there."

Unease crept up Tom's spine. He'd feel better if he knew where Colman was. Still, the minutes were ticking by. "If Colman isn't there, then we don't have to worry about him." Tom turned to the group. "Any questions?" He surveyed the room. "Okay, everyone to their post. Remember, Barnes is a murderer. He's killed before and he'll kill again."

As the officers left the room, Tom radioed Agent Smith. "We'll be at our posts in ten minutes, ready to go. Good luck."

Chapter 54
Sunday, early morning

Against Tom's orders, Francesca left the house shortly after he and the FBI agents had gone. The streets were quiet and she walked the few blocks to the village's downtown area. Once there, she made a wide circle, walking around the village green and coming up behind Hero's Market. When she looked down the street, she saw no one and heard nothing. But she knew there were FBI agents hiding nearby.

She unlocked the side door to the market and quietly made her way up the stairs to her office. Once the door was shut and locked, she turned on the low light over the copier, which couldn't be seen from the outside. Then she went to the shelves along the side wall and took out the Nikon camera with the long-range scope. From the high window facing east she had a good view of the street in front of Larson's Interiors and the apartment above. Through the camera lens, it looked as though lights were on in Maelog's apartment. She sat on the floor and settled in for the wait.

She still couldn't get over the fact that Maelog was a vicious murderer. She'd liked him and felt sympathy for him. The agents hadn't said anything about a handicap or difficulty speaking. Maybe he'd been in an accident while he was hiding out from the police.

She looked at her phone. Twenty-five minutes to go. She went over to the desk and fetched her laptop, then sat back down on the floor and googled Richard Barnes. She got hundreds of hits, including a picture of him up in the massive redwood tree. He was wearing a hat with a brim and she couldn't make out his features. There were newspaper accounts of his radical criminal activity, but none of them contained a clear photo of his face. From the stories, she learned that he was indeed a vicious criminal. Three years ago he'd disappeared, and his activities stopped. There were no recent articles about him. Could he really be Maelog Gruffydd?

Francesca looked at her phone. Only ten minutes to go. She stood up and aimed her camera down the street. A minute before three o'clock, a truck came down the road. Suddenly, bright lights illuminated the area from the roof across the way. FBI agents in riot gear poured out of the truck. They stormed the entrance to the second floor apartments between Churchill's Café and Larson's Interiors. Francesca snapped pictures. The same thing was happening in the alley on the other side of the building. It was like a movie set: lights flashing, guns gleaming, men dressed in black.

Five minutes later, all was silent. She saw the agents slowly pour out of the building. They stood together in groups on the sidewalk and street. She zeroed in on their faces. From her perch, she could feel their dejection. Clearly, the raid was a fiasco. What had happened? Maelog must have escaped. How?

Francesca texted Tom. Miraculously, he texted back. Barnes had flown the coop and they didn't know where he'd gone. Francesca took the camera and her laptop back to her desk. For the next forty minutes she wrote furiously. When the citizens of Banner Bluff woke up in the morning they would have the story of Karen Grimes's murder and the failed apprehension of Richard Barnes, complete with pictures.

#

Agent Smith stood at the door to Tom's office. He was livid. "You've got a squealer."

"What do you mean?"

"We know Barnes was in there. We saw him. Someone tipped him off."

"No one on my team squealed. I'd stake my life on it," Tom said.

"Well then, you're pretty much dead meat," Smith countered. "We don't know where he's gone. He could be hiding in Chicago or halfway to New York. I'm telling you, this guy is an escape artist. Here today, gone tomorrow." Smith threw himself into the visitors' chair.

"I'm wondering if there's another way out of that building," Tom said slowly. He stood up and called down the hall to the dead-shift dispatcher. "Bernie, can you get me Mark Larson's number?"

He sat back down, and he and Smith eyed each other like two tomcats. A minute later, the phone rang. It was Bernie. "I'll put you through, Chief."

"Mark? Sorry to bother you at this hour. A question about your building. We've just raided Maelog Gruffydd's apartment." Pause. "Yes... a great guy." Pause. "The FBI wants to question him." Pause. "Here's my question. Is there another exit to your building? Some way in or out besides the door next to your shop and the alley entrance." A long pause as Mark explained. "Right, behind the chest." Another long pause. "Used back in the day by Al Capone." "Yes, we think Gruffydd escaped through there…. Okay, sure. Go back to sleep." Tom set the phone down and raised his eyebrows. "Guess what? In the basement, behind an old chest, is a passageway under Lilac Alley that leads into the basement of the Paris Boutique. Get this; the basement was used by Al Capone in the thirties when he was shipping booze down from Canada. It's well known that he used the cove down at the beach."

Smith looked incredulous.

"Anyway the hole in the wall is only four feet high, and no one knows about it except Suzie, owner of the Paris Boutique, and Mark."

"And Richard Barnes. We were down there. That basement is jam-packed with old furniture. We missed the hole in the wall." Smith leaned over, elbows on his knees, holding his head. "The truth is we went into that raid half-assed. But there wasn't any time to do a proper reconnoitering of the premises."

They were quiet for a moment. Smith stirred in his chair. "Tell me more about Barnes," Tom said. "How did Agent Grimes track him down?"

Smith studied his hands, which were clenched on his lap. "It was ingenious, really. Barnes had a pal who was part of Avenge the Trees. Guy named Clive Siemens. Clive kept in touch with Barnes through *TCI* magazine. TCI stands for Tree Care Industry. Each month one of them would put a small ad at the back of the magazine. Siemens worked for a printing company that printed various magazines for the 'green' industry. You know: plants, trees, nature, that sort of stuff. Karen did a careful analysis of the magazines and figured out their code. She had Siemens under surveillance, and his phone was bugged. A month ago, Barnes called. He was only on the phone a minute. He bragged that he was still an activist and a revolutionary for the cause, and he said to watch the BBG." Smith looked up. "See, he needed to tell someone. That was his first and only slip-up." Smith gestured with his hands. "Karen figured he'd be involved with plants and trees: thus the Banner Botanic Gardens."

Tom sighed and rubbed his eyes. They felt tired and itchy. "So where do you think Barnes was, the year he disappeared? We know he's been at the BBG for the last two years. Where was he before that?"

Smith sat up and leaned forward. "Karen tracked him to Europe three years ago. He met someone and traveled with them for a while. In France, I think, and Italy. Then he went to Greece and disappeared."

Tom remembered what Coyote had told them. Maelog had been in France and Italy, traveling with someone. He wondered if Coyote was still hunched over his laptop downstairs. He knew the officer was a night-owl.

He stood up. "Follow me. I've got an idea."

Tom and Smith went down the hall and took the stairs to the war room. Just as Tom thought, Coyote Blackfoot was in the corner typing, even though it was nearly four AM.

"Coyote!" Tom called. "Find the info on Maelog you pulled up. I want to check something."

Without questioning, Coyote typed and then opened a screen. He looked up. "Got it. What do you want to know?"

"What was the name of the guy Maelog was going to meet in Europe? You said the owner of the truck farm on Long Island gave you a name."

Coyote typed some more and scrolled down. "Here it is. The man said he thought Maelog planned to travel with a Greenpeace activist named Rich. He didn't have a last name for the guy."

Tom looked at Agent Smith. "Rich."

Smith nodded.

"The real Maelog Gruffydd is excited to travel to Europe with another Greenpeace activist named Rich…" Tom said. "AKA Richard Barnes. Somewhere in Greece, Barnes kills Gruffydd and assumes his identity."

Smith frowned. "What about his appearance? You said the man you call Gruffydd that works at the gardens doesn't look anything like the picture of Barnes I showed you."

Tom eyed the white board covered with pictures. He could see Takahashi's lower limbs and the bloody stumps where his feet should've been. In the fluorescent lighting, the body seemed to float in a glowing miasma. Tom turned back to Coyote. "Do your magic.

Go back to Long Island and Maine. See if you can find a picture of the real Maelog Gruffydd."

Chapter 55
Sunday morning

Francesca pulled herself out of bed at nine o'clock. Her head felt heavy and her mouth dry. As she sat up, she felt slightly woozy. She'd returned home at four AM and fallen into bed. Later on, Tom had come home. She'd woken just enough to be aware of his presence, but now he was gone again. How could he manage to keep going with practically no sleep?

Downstairs she found a note. *The dogs have been out and fed. Don't know when I'll be home. Text me. Press conference at 10 AM. Love always, Tom*

If she was going to make the press conference, she'd better hurry. She could get a triple shot latte at Hero's. The weather had turned warm and muggy. After a shower, she donned a yellow sleeveless cotton dress and a pair of white wedge sandals. By nine-thirty, she was out the door.

Rosemary, in a drab housedress and leaning on a cane, was standing in the driveway across the street, looking up and down the empty road. Francesca waved and said hello. Instead of responding, Rosemary turned tail like a scared jackrabbit and limped away. Worry curdled in Francesca's stomach, but there was no time now. As soon as she could, maybe this afternoon, Francesca would go over and see if Rosemary needed some help.

It was pointless to take the car, because parking had become a real problem with all the media vehicles. Francesca walked toward the Village Hall at a fast clip and arrived as Tom stepped up to the podium outside the building. He was accompanied by Agent Smith. The media throng had grown and she was pushed to the back of the crowd. From there it was practically impossible to hear. The crowd was like a vicious animal, ready to pounce. Reporters and others repeatedly interrupted Tom, with harsh questions, catcalls and strident whistles. What would she learn here? Nothing she didn't already know. She turned away and headed toward Hero's Market.

The store was nearly empty. Everyone was across the green at the press conference except for Vicki, who was wiping down the counter, and one old guy sitting at a table nursing a mug of coffee and reading the newspaper.

"Hi Francesca. Did you get my email? I showed Kelly your numbers and letters. She told me they could be medical codes. Then this morning she sent me an email with some of the codes that might match. I forwarded it to you. It's kind of freaky considering what's been going on."

"What do you mean?"

"Well…" Nervously, Vicki looked around the empty room. "Maybe we should go upstairs." She went into the back room and called out to her grandfather. "Pappou, I'm going upstairs with Francesca. I'll be back in a few minutes."

Once they had entered Francesca's office and closed the door, they sat at the round oak table, where Francesca opened her laptop and found the forwarded email. She clicked on it and they looked at the message together.

> *Hi Vicki,*
> *These are not in the normal sequence of code. I analyzed the digits and letters. These are E codes that denote the external causes of an injury or poisoning. There are no codes to denote diagnosis or treatment. Am I right that these have to do with the murders? Someone has a very sick mind.*
> *Code 1:*
> *E849.4 Place for recreation and sport*

> *E016.1 Gardening*
> *988.2 Toxic effect of noxious substances eaten as food or drink—berries and   other plants*
> *E962.9 Homicide and injury purposely inflicted by other persons: unspecified.   Assault by poisoning.*
> *E966 Assault by cutting and piercing instrument. Homicidal: cut any part of body.*
> *Code 2:*
> *E006.2 Activity, golf*
> *E965.0 Intentional homicide—handgun*
> *E849.4 Place for recreation and sport*

Francesca read through the message twice. Then she looked at Vicki, whose eyes were wide and questioning.

"I told Kelly not to tell anyone. She said she'd keep it secret. I mean, I thought it was probably police business, right?"

Francesca nodded. "Chief Barnett received this code in a text. I'm trying to remember…the first one came before Dr. Takahashi was murdered…a couple of days before, in fact. The second one came after the woman was killed on the golf course."

Vicki chewed her lip. "The murderer wants to broadcast what he's doing."

"Yeah. He wants bragging rights. With the first one he wanted to give the police a heads-up. I think he hadn't planned on killing the FBI agent."

"FBI agent?"

Francesca realized Vicki didn't know anything about what had happened overnight. "The woman killed on the golf course was an FBI agent tracking a guy named Richard Barnes, who was hiding out at the BBG. Barnes is allegedly the one who killed the Japanese bonsai specialist…and probably the agent, too."

"And the one who sent the codes." Vicki frowned. "But what about Doc Stoddard? There's nothing about the beach here."

"Right. That must be someone else…another murderer."

Vicki shivered. "Gosh, do you think we're safe? Last night I was afraid to take the trash out back. Pappou and I did it together."

"I'm sure you're safe. Barnes is all about protecting nature. His perceived enemy is someone who cuts and destroys trees." She sighed. "As for Doc's murder…I think it must be personal."

Vicki still looked upset. "Francesca, there's something else. I'm worried about Colman. He hasn't answered my texts since last night. I don't know where he is."

**Chapter 56
Sunday morning**

It was a media circus; wild animals and a bunch of clowns. The crowd at the press conference had grown, not only members of the press but a pulsating mass of townspeople. They were like a school of sharks, not wanting to listen, only to attack. One man wearing a White Sox hat was shouting obscenities. The hat was pulled low on his forehead and Tom couldn't see the man's face.

By the time the conference ended, Tom was shaking and drenched with sweat. He ducked his head and turned away from the flash and clicks of cameras, and headed into the building and the safety of his office. Inside, he leaned against the door, breathing hard. Was he losing it? These murder investigations were spinning out of control. Smith had explained that the FBI was leading the search for Richard Barnes, suspected of hiding in Banner Bluff for the past two years. But the crowd wanted answers from *him*, from Chief Barnett. And he didn't have any.

Someone knocked at the door. "It's Coyote, sir."

Tom grabbed a handful of Kleenex from the box on his desk and wiped his face and hands. Then he opened the door. "What's up, detective?" His voice was rough with stress and fatigue.

"I've got some pictures of the real Maelog Gruffydd." Coyote's face was taut with exhaustion. He handed Tom a print-out. Together they looked at the picture. The man somewhat resembled the fake Maelog from the BBG, but not quite the same. Tom studied the man's face. The real Maelog stared out of the photo with a kind of innocence, a kind of purity, in his eyes. He could imagine how the poor man had fallen for Barnes's invitation to tour Europe with a

Greenpeace activist. In comparison, the Maelog Gruffydd Tom knew had eyes that were dark, calculating and watchful.

"Thanks for your excellent work." There was something else he wanted Coyote to check out, but he couldn't remember what it was. He paused, hoping it would come to him. Then he said, "Why don't you get some sleep? You've been at it for twenty-four hours."

After the forensic detective left, Tom called Conroy to hear how the hunt was going in the Banner Woods. Nothing so far, Conroy said. It was a nightmare to get through the underbrush. There were few pathways and they all terminated in dead ends. The team had found several clearings, but no evidence yet of a shooting or a body being dragged through the brush. They would continue their tedious systematic search, but Conroy didn't hold out much hope.

Tom sat down at his desk and logged on to his computer, to look at his email and check the reports the detectives had posted. For a moment he just sat there, struggling to concentrate. He closed his eyes and shook his head trying to clear the cobwebs. He needed to get a grip. The crowd at the press conference flashed through his mind. The voice of the jerk with the Sox hat rang in his ears. He remembered how annoyed he'd been that he couldn't see the guy's face, and then it hit him. He opened his eyes, took out his phone and called Puchalski.

The phone rang several times before the sergeant picked up. "Meet me at the casino," Tom said, without even a "hello" first.

"Now? I'm filthy, just walked through a bog. The mosquitos are something fierce in here."

"No time to explain. Get in your car and meet me at the casino."

Five minutes later, Tom was out the door and on his way to Wilder's River Casino. As he drove, he went over their previous visit. He knew what they had to do.

Twenty minutes later, he pulled up at the casino. It wasn't yet noon and things were quiet. As before, several tour buses were parked outside. Tom walked up the gangplank and entered the casino. Jessica was there, in a long purple dress that showed significant cleavage. Her dangling diamond earrings sparkled in the light of the chandelier. Her smile was less genuine this time. "What can I do for you, officer? Slots, poker?"

"I'd like to speak to Mr. Wilder."

"I'm not sure if he's available." Jessica's gaze darted from Tom to the doorway.

"Tell him to be available. Now!"

Jessica stared past him at the open door. Tom turned around. Puchalski was coming up the ramp in filthy camouflage pants, muddy boots and a sweat-stained tee-shirt. He looked miserable.

Despite his tension, Tom couldn't help grinning. He knew how finicky Puchalski was about his appearance. "Thanks for coming, Detective."

Jessica eyed Puchalski with distaste. "He shouldn't come in here looking like that."

Tom turned back to her. "Get Wilder. Tell him I want to look at the security footage again."

She turned and went to the security door at the back. Puchalski pointed to the restrooms. "I'm going to wipe myself down."

"Hurry up. There's no time to lose."

Puchalski looked annoyed. "What are we doing here again? We already looked at the footage."

"You'll see. Hurry up," Tom snapped. They were all on edge, running on empty.

Five minutes later, Puchalski was back but Wilder hadn't arrived. Tom paced the lobby and checked the time on his phone every thirty seconds. Puchalski stepped outside and took off his boots, bent over the balcony, and banged them together several times to dislodge the mud. By the time Wilder arrived, he'd laced his boots back up.

"What's the problem this time?" Wilder asked. His shirt was misbuttoned and his hair stood on end, as if he'd just pulled on his clothes. He looked down at Tom with flat eyes.

"Sorry to inconvenience you. But we've got three murders in Banner Bluff and they take precedence over your morning nap."

The big man's hands balled into fists. "What do you want?"

Tom could feel Wilder's animosity. "Just another look at the footage from last Monday night…the same stuff we looked at last time."

Wilder turned and pointed a finger at a security guard who was hovering in the background. "Take them upstairs. Tell Guido to get them what they want." He pointed at Jessica. "Don't bother me again for anything. Got it?"

"Yes, boss, got it."

Tom and Puchalski followed the security guard to the back of the lobby and the security door. Upstairs Guido let them in and soon they were sitting in front of the computer screens. When he stepped away, Tom turned to Ron. "We're going to go through the footage again from seven to eleven. Look to see if Banner's face is ever visible. I don't mean the Cubs hat or the white shirt. I mean his actual face. Okay?"

"Okay, Chief." Puchalski shook his head and started rolling through the footage from the entrance security camera. Soon he saw Jack Banner coming into the casino. His face was visible beneath the Cubs hat as he smiled up at the camera. On his way out, the man's face was visible as well. Just like they'd seen before. Puchalski sighed in exasperation.

Tom worked his way through the footage from the cameras in the slot machine gallery. Then he moved on to the camera aimed at one of the craps tables. Puchalski was working quickly as well. He probably wanted to get this over with, figuring it was a giant waste of time. As before, Tom recognized Jack Banner by the Cubs cap. But the more he watched, the clearer it became that Jack's face was barely visible from any angle. He was obviously avoiding the cameras and keeping his head down.

After Tom finished, he rolled his chair over to Puchalski's monitor. The detective sergeant was zipping through his last video, from a camera aimed at an angle on a blackjack table. Tom watched as the images flashed by. Jack Banner had been sitting there from about nine to nine-thirty, according to the counter on the video. He was hunched over a stack of chips and seemed to be doing pretty well.

Puchalski finished scanning the footage and looked up at Tom. "So what's the deal? We saw the same stuff four days ago. I don't get it."

Tom leaned toward him. "Don't you see? That wasn't Jack Banner. He hired someone to wear that hat and spend three hours at the casino. It was no accident his face was visible when he entered and when he left, but not while he gambled."

Slowly, Puchalski nodded. "Right, I get it. You think he snuck out and murdered Doc. But it still doesn't follow." He stretched his arms over his head and stifled a yawn. "We think Doc was killed after placing a call to the Banner estate's garage. Doc was calling Harry, and we think Jack happened to pick up. Then he went to the beach and killed Doc. But Jack couldn't have known ahead of time that Doc was going to call. Why would he set up this ruse and hire someone to impersonate him?"

"I don't know, but I'm sure he wasn't here during the window of time when Doc was killed. Let's check the screens the security guys are monitoring. Maybe we'll find one of the dealers from that night."

They stood and walked over to the screens that Guido and Rog were scrutinizing. On the last monitor in the row, they both spotted the blackjack dealer they'd just seen in the Monday night videos—a bald man with a pudgy nose and thick arms.

"Who's that guy?" Tom asked Rog.

"Bellini. He's here a lot. Doesn't need much sleep." Rog chuckled.

"Can you get him up here? I want him to look at some footage," Tom said.

"Sure, we'll get someone to fill in down on the floor."

He called downstairs. They waited. Five minutes later a security guard and a buxom blond in a tight-fitting black dress arrived and stood behind Bellini. After a few minutes he stood up and she took his place. The security guard led Bellini away. Before long they were at the door to the control room. Bellini looked a little worried. Tom went over and shook hands.

"Hello, Mr. Bellini. I'm Tom Barnett, Chief of Police in Banner Bluff. I need your help."

"I'm not in trouble, am I?" He looked from Tom to Puchalski.

"No. I just want you to look at some footage from last Monday night." Tom beckoned him over to the computer monitor Puchalski had been using. "Sit down, please.

Once Bellini did so, Tom asked, "Do you know Jack Banner?"

Bellini reddened. "Yeah, I know him."

"So you'd recognize him if he sat at your table?"

"Yeah."

Tom bent over and scrolled through the footage, fast-forwarding until it displayed Bellini dealing cards and Jack Banner in his white polo shirt and Cubs hat. Tom slowed the video down. "Can you remember what was going on here?"

The footage continued to roll. Bellini watched it, concentrating. "It's funny, I do. There was that old guy there…" he pointed to a man next to Jack. "He was losing in a big way. I got the feeling he didn't know what he was doing. Like maybe he had Alzheimer's."

Tom pointed to the Cubs hat. "Do you recognize that guy? We can't see his face from this angle."

Bellini answered right away. "No, I'd never seen him before. He was new that night and he was a good player…won a nice chunk of change. I remember."

Tom looked at Puchalski, his eyes alight. "So the man with the Cubs hat is not Jack Banner?"

Bellini turned around and looked up at Tom. "Jack Banner? No way. This guy was all bent over his chips, like he was hoarding them. Jack's all out there when he plays, sprawled in his chair, taking up space so everybody'll notice him." He grinned, and Tom saw he was missing two teeth. "And Jack is a massive loser when it comes to cards."

Chapter 57
Sunday morning

After Vicki left, Francesca went online and googled Richard Barnes again. She found him on Wikipedia. Barnes grew up in an Oregon commune. His parents were full-fledged hippies. At about age ten, he was removed from his parents by the state after the commune was deemed an abusive environment. He lived in a foster home near Tillamook State Forest. As a teenager, he often disappeared for days in the woods and learned to live off the land. In spite of this dismal childhood, he managed to get an Associate's Certificate in accounting at the Yakima Valley Community College. Later, he completed a billing and medical coding certificate and worked in a local hospital.

Ah-ha. Francesca felt confident Barnes was the one who'd sent those strange texts to Tom. Medical codes had become a way of communicating.

Francesca continued reading. With a seemingly normal life and a job in a hospital, hiking and camping in the forest continued to be a big part of Barnes's life. At some point, he was drawn into the environmental movement. In one of the few interviews he gave, Barnes said he had a spiritual awakening. He knew he was on earth to protect nature from the evils of mankind. That was why he'd volunteered to live up in the redwood tree as a protest.

Francesca leaned back in her chair and looked out the window at the green tops of the trees reaching into the blue sky. They were magnificent; solid friends, enriching people's lives. She could see how someone could go nuts over trees…but not to the point of killing another human being. Though it sounded like Barnes's childhood could have put him over the edge.

Francesca had emailed Tom the explanations of the codes, but he still hadn't responded. She looked at her watch. Susan would arrive at Francesca's house at noon. She closed the office and went downstairs, waved to Hero and Vicki, and left the building. She needed something quick for lunch. Next door to Sorrel's restaurant was The Other Door, a Mexican-inspired organic fast food joint. Francesca joined the short line inside and ordered two vegetarian bowls with lettuce, tomatoes, beans, rice, guacamole and a spicy salsa. By the time she got home Susan was already there, sitting on the porch feeding her baby.

"Hi, sorry to be late," Francesca said.

"No problem. I'll put Sophia down for her nap after she's done eating and we can get to work."

"I'm excited. I hope this settles the unspoken disagreement Tom and I have been having." She held up the brown bag. "I got us two bowls from The Other Door."

"Yum! I'll be with you in five minutes."

Inside, Francesca let the dogs out and went upstairs to change into some old jeans shorts and a tee-shirt. When she came down, Susan had tucked Sophia into her infant seat and put her in the living room. The baby was already asleep. Francesca shut the glass French doors so the dogs wouldn't bother the little girl.

They sat down at the kitchen table and ate their lunch, talking quietly. Francesca told Susan all about Richard Barnes and last night's activities. "The FBI is taking over the hunt for Barnes," Francesca said as she speared a chunk of tomato.

"Is Tom off the hook, then? Wouldn't that be a relief?" Susan said.

"I don't think so. I'm sure Tom considers these murders his affair. I doubt he wants to give up hunting Barnes down. He'd rather finish what he started. You know what I mean?"

"Yes, but he still has Doc's murder to solve. People in Banner Bluff are more concerned about one of their own."

Francesca nodded. Susan was right. Dr. Takahashi and Karen Grimes weren't part of the fabric of the village.

After lunch they went upstairs and got to work. Dismantling the baby furniture was quickly accomplished. Susan had recently put a similar crib together with her husband Marcus. Together they carried the various parts downstairs to the basement. They packed up the baby clothes in a box, then removed the drawers from the bureau and carried it down to the basement as well.

Susan had brought over a can of light grey paint and some tarps. They pulled the decorative ducky strips off the wall and began painting. After a first coat, they went downstairs to the kitchen for a glass of iced tea. Then they went back up and did a second coat. By then, Sophia was awake and hungry. While Susan warmed a bottle, Francesca cuddled the baby. Sophia grabbed onto her pinkie and smiled up at her. It took her heart away.

While Susan fed the baby, Francesca went down to the basement and looked at the glass-topped modern desk she was planning to move up to the bedroom. It weighed a ton. How would the two of them get it up the stairs? She went out to the garage and looked for Tom's metal trolley, but it was nowhere to be seen. As she came back out onto the driveway, she noticed a Jaguar slowly passing by. Jack Banner was driving by with the top down.

"Hey, Francesca. Want to go for a ride?"

"Thanks, Jack, but I'm busy moving furniture." No way did she want to drive around with him. Then she had a thought and went over to the car. "Listen, do you have a minute? I need some help."

She must be crazy, asking a favor from Jack—but she'd heard he was a changed man, and besides, Susan was in the house.

He pulled into the driveway and got out of the car. "What's the problem?"

Lingering misgivings made her hesitate, but they really needed the help if they hoped to get the makeover project completed that afternoon. She wanted everything to be in place when Tom got home.

Susan came out the side door, followed by the dogs. She had Sophia in her arms. She looked from Francesca to Jack, clearly not thrilled to see him. Benji and Bailey growled and Sophia started to cry. Susan went back inside.

Jack stepped back and held up his hands. "Whoa, sorry, didn't mean to cause trouble." He bent down to pat Benji, but the dog bared his teeth.

"I don't know what's got into them. Let me put the dogs in the backyard." Francesca grabbed both dogs' collars and pulled them through the gate and into the yard. Then she led Jack into the house. "We've got a heavy desk to get up the stairs from the basement to the second floor. Can you help us?"

"Sure. No problem. Show me the way."

Chapter 58
Sunday afternoon

Puchalski, Stiles and Sanders sat around the table in the war room, chowing down on a pepperoni pizza. Tom paced the room, too tense to eat, as they talked about that morning's discovery at the casino.

"We knew Jack Banner wasn't continuously at the casino from seven till eleven. We didn't know exactly when he left, but we figured out he was back at twenty minutes after ten. That's when he left the men's washroom," Tom said.

"Once Bellini told us the guy in the Cubs hat wasn't Banner, we ran through the footage from the camera aimed at the washroom door again. Five minutes after Banner left, his impersonator came out. He'd changed his shirt and was bare-headed. Bellini recognized him immediately," Puchalski said. He carefully cut a piece of pizza using a fork and knife.

Tom picked up the narrative. "We've got his picture now. Arlyne is making copies upstairs. We'll canvas the local bars, Jack Banner's favorite haunts. Hopefully he recruited this guy from around here."

Ricky Stiles finished his can of Coke. He'd devoured three pieces of pizza in about as many minutes. He looked over at Detective Sanders. "We didn't learn anything new over at the Banner estate. Jack wasn't there. We talked to Cordelia Banner. She was real nice and told us we could look around if we wanted to."

Sanders nodded. "We didn't learn or see anything that wasn't already in the reports. Harry O'Connell showed us around the garages." He raised his eyebrows and cocked his head at Tom. "And we didn't see any hidden boat wreckage."

"Man, I loved those cars," Stiles said. "Think of the fortune in that garage." His eyes glowed.

Sanders looked pensive as he studied his water bottle, twirling it in his hands. "I did feel some vibes from O'Connell. There was something there." He looked at Stiles. "Did you feel it?"

Remorse flitted across the younger detective's face "No. I guess I was too interested in the cars."

Sanders smiled. "It's okay. But I think that guy's hiding something."

"Let's bring him in," Tom said. "We're on the cusp here. Before we bring in Banner, we have to nail down our case."

Sanders stood up. "Come on, Stiles, let's go get O'Connell."

While they were gone, Tom went upstairs to his office. He logged on to his computer and opened his emails. There seemed to be hundreds. Just looking at them exhausted him. He scrolled down, then spotted Francesca's address. He opened her email and read it, his heart beating faster as the words sank in.

Tom –Here's the possible meaning of the codes you've been getting in those texts. They're medical codes that were run together. Kelly at the hospital figured them out. It looks like Barnes was alerting you to what he was going to do. I guess they're useless now. XXXOOO

Code 1:
E849.4 Place for recreation and sport
E016.1 Gardening
988.2 Toxic effect of noxious substances eaten as food—berries and other plants
E962.9 Homicide and injury purposely inflicted by other persons: unspecified. Assault by poisoning.

> *E966 Assault by cutting and piercing instrument. Homicidal: cut any part of body.*
> *Code 2:*
> *E006.2 Activity: golf*
> *E965.0 Intentional homicide handgun*
> *E849.4 Place for recreation and sport*

Tom sat back and rubbed his forehead in frustration. He should have emailed those weird texts to Coyote Blackfoot. He'd dropped the ball. With prior knowledge of the codes, could he have foreseen Takahashi's murder? Probably not. He needed to talk to Agent Smith and find out if the FBI knew of Barnes's subtle form of communication. Smith's number was on his phone. He was about to call when Harry O'Connell appeared at his door, flanked by Sanders and Stiles.

"Hi, Harry. Come on in." He gestured to the elderly man, then addressed the two detectives. "Just leave Harry with me. Stiles, could you please shut the door."

After the officers left, Tom gestured to a chair beside the round conference table. "Please sit down, Harry. I think we need to have a talk." He got up and moved from behind his desk to a chair by the table.

Harry looked uncomfortable and frightened. Definitely frightened.

"Would you like some coffee or a soda?"

"No. No sir, I'm good."

Tom studied his hands for a minute. The silence filled the room like a heavy damp blanket. Good—it would put Harry on edge.

"What do you want to talk about?" Harry finally said, his voice rough.

Tom took a while to answer. "We think you know something about Doc Stoddard's murder that you haven't told us." He looked into Harry's eyes. "You need to come clean."

Harry's gaze darted around the room and came to rest somewhere over Tom's head. More silence. Then the words tumbled out. "I can't really talk about it…I don't know where I'd go…It isn't safe."

Tom leaned forward. "Why don't you explain it all to me? Tell me what you're scared of. We'll figure it out together."

More silence stretched between them. Then Harry hunched his shoulders and kneaded his hands together. "A couple of days ago these two guys came by. They were looking for Mr. Jack. A Mr. Venetucci and his bodyguard. They were tough characters."

"What did they want?"

"They said they had an appointment to check out the Bugatti…that Jack was selling it to them." Harry rubbed his forearms.

"So?"

"Well, they said they'd been there before."

"And?"

"They said they'd been at the estate Monday night. They had an appointment with Jack, but he didn't show. That's why they came back." He looked up at Tom. "Monday night."

"Ah." Tom's mind was doing cartwheels. "So Jack might have been there Monday night to answer the phone when Doc called?"

Harry swallowed and nodded.

The puzzle pieces of the case were beginning to form a picture in Tom's head. "Doc calls you at the estate garage and says he's found something incriminating on the beach. Jack answers the phone. He forgets his appointment and rushes down to the marina." Tom could see it now. The ruse at the casino wasn't intended to alibi a murder; he just got lucky. Jack set it up because he didn't want Delia to know about the possible sale of the car.

"I told Jack those men came, and what they said about Monday night, and he said he'd kill me if I told anyone." Harry's eyes were wide with apprehension. "And you know what? I think he would."

Chapter 59
Sunday evening

Francesca was curled up on the sofa with her cell phone. Bailey and Benji were sprawled on the floor, drowsing. She envied them as she yawned for the hundredth time. She hoped Tom would be home soon. It was nine o'clock and she was having a hard time staying awake.

She checked her Facebook account. Most days she was too busy to look at the news feed. Tonight there was a picture of her niece and nephew at Disneyland. They were cute kids. Her sister posted pictures of them daily. Whenever Sandra called, she wanted to know what Francesca thought of the kids…at the beach…on their bikes…at McDonald's. Many times Francesca lied. She gushed about how special and adorable they were without having seen the picture. Tonight she was "liking" indiscriminately every news item and picture she saw.

Benji jumped up and scrambled to the door. Tom must be home. Francesca got up, went to the side door as Tom got out of the car and approached the house. When he came inside, the dogs ran circles around him. He looked up and grinned. "Nothing like a welcoming committee." There were dark circles under his eyes. He'd been running on empty for days now. "I'm glad you're still up, I've got lots to tell you." He gave her a quick hug.

She nestled her face in his neck. "Welcome home, soldier."

He kissed her on the forehead and pulled away. "Let me run upstairs and change, and then we can have a glass of wine and talk."

"Did you get dinner?"

"Yeah. Hot pastrami on rye. Not exactly healthy." He removed his gun and placed it in the safe, then headed for the stairs.

Francesca watched him go. The lights were on upstairs. Hopefully, he would look in at the newly decorated room and be amazed at what she and Susan had accomplished in one afternoon. She decided to follow him up and see his reaction.

At the top of the stairs, she looked down the hall. Tom stood in front of the second bedroom, his posture rigid. When he turned and looked at her, his eyes were cold. "What in the hell have you done to the baby's room?"

Her stomach felt hollow. "I…we…made it into an office or sitting room…" She trailed off.

"What right did you have to touch that room?" He was yelling now. "That was Candy and my baby's room. We planned it together."

Francesca felt tears welling in her eyes. "I thought you didn't want to see it anymore. I thought it was painful for you. That's why you shut the door every day."

"You have no right to change things in my house without asking me."

"*Your* house?"

"Yes. The house I bought with Candy."

"Candy? I thought *we* were married." She wanted to hurt him as badly as he'd hurt her. "Candy is dead. I live here now."

He slammed a fist into his palm. "Yeah? That's why you want to obliterate the past?"

She took a breath. "I'm sorry, Tom. We can put all the baby furniture back if you want." She should have stopped there, but she continued, "And keep the door shut as some kind of monument…a monument to you and Candy."

He jabbed a finger at her. "Nothing should be done in this house without consulting me. *Nothing*."

"Whatever." She crossed her arms and leaned against the wall.

"How in the hell did you get all this stuff up here by yourself, anyway?"

"I got help," she snapped.

He came down the hall towards her. "Whose help?"

"Susan." She knew she shouldn't mention Jack, but she was feeling bitchy. "And Jack Banner. He helped get the desk up here. I couldn't have done it without him."

"Jack Banner?" Angry red crept up Tom's neck and face. "You let him in my house? Jack Banner, who's a murderer and a rapist? You invited him in here?" He took a step towards her, fists clenched at his sides. They glared at each other. Francesca could feel the adrenaline pumping through her veins. She had made a major miscalculation, but he was treating her like a recalcitrant child.

The air vibrated like a taut violin string. Then Tom seemed to regain control. Without a word he turned and headed for their bedroom. A moment later she heard the bathroom door slam and the shower come on.

She sagged against the wall. She wanted out. Out of this house. Away from Tom and his memories of his dead wife. He didn't care about her. Maybe he'd never really loved her. Maybe this marriage was a sham. She stamped down the hall to the bedroom, opened the closet and took out the duffle bag she used for yoga. She put in a dark blue track suit and her running shoes. What else did she need? She had toiletries at the office, even a toothbrush. She put in some underwear and a pair of socks.

Downstairs she grabbed her purse and her laptop. Her phone was in the living room on the sofa. She put it in her purse and got out the car keys. The dogs were following her around, questioning what she was up to. She gave them a treat and headed for the side door.

She would come back tomorrow and get them after she figured out what to do next.

Outside, Francesca threw the duffle bag into the back of the car. Tonight she'd check into a motel and try and get some sleep. Tomorrow she'd decide what to do—live at her office for a while, or maybe look for something more permanent. She could still feel the adrenaline rush, a searing red-hot anger. Tom had some nerve telling her what she should and shouldn't do in *his* house. What a control freak.

She backed down the driveway and drove towards the highway. It was very dark. The heavy leaves on the trees blocked out the light from the street lamps. She turned on to Lakeland and drove through town, under the tracks and past Zimmerman Motors, then continued over the highway. About a mile down the road, she pulled into a motel lot. From the car she could see a couple watching TV in the lobby. Hopefully, they didn't know who she was.

As she entered the reception area, the screen door banged behind her. Two grey heads swiveled around to look at her.

"Hi, I wonder if I could get a room?" Francesca said.

"Sure, honey." A thin man with a long face and a beaked nose came to the counter, smiling. He wore suspenders and a short-sleeved checked cotton shirt. He peered through the front window at her car, probably wondering if she was alone. "How long will you be staying?"

"Oh, just one night." She gave him a flat smile.

He pushed a form across the desk. "Please fill this out. It'll be eighty-nine dollars plus tax." His gnarled hands were spotted and shaky.

"Right." Francesca took out her Visa card and handed it to him. She kept her head down. She didn't want to invite conversation.

"So where are you off to? Taking a road trip?" His breath reeked like sour milk.

"No." She scribbled her name and address on the form and slid it over to him.

He looked at what she'd written. "You live right over in Banner Bluff. What are you doing here?"

She didn't want to discuss her marital problems with this nosy grandpa. "Listen, can I just have the key to the room and I'll be out of your hair?"

He stepped back as though she'd hit him. "Calm down. Just trying to be friendly." He turned, grabbed a keycard and handed it to her.

Francesca tried to smile. "I'm sorry. That was rude. I'm just exhausted."

From across the room, the woman said, "You'll feel better in the morning, honey. A good night's sleep will make everything rosy."

"I'm sure you're right." Anything to get out of here and be by herself.

Outside, she got in her car and drove around back. She pulled her little Mini in between two big SUVs. The spot was right in front of the door to her room. She got out and grabbed the duffle bag. At the door she slipped the keycard into the slit. Nothing happened. After a couple of tries, the green light blinked and she pushed open the door. The room held a queen-sized bed with a green, orange and yellow patterned bedspread. A stale odor permeated the air. She checked out the bathroom, which was clean but tired. Thin towels and a small bar of soap were the extent of the amenities provided.

She made sure the door was locked and slid the chain in place. The room felt chilly. She took out the track suit and changed into it from her shorts and tee-shirt. Then she pulled on the socks. After removing the worn bedspread, she collapsed onto the bed, feeling the weight of what she had done. Her head was pounding and she felt nauseated. She closed her eyes and rubbed her forehead.

How had everything escalated to this point? She had left Tom, the love of her life. In her mind, the specter of Candy expanded like a balloon. Candy's ghost had taken over and pushed her out of the house. Unwanted tears sprang to her eyes. What would happen now? Could she go back, patch things up? If not, what future did she have? Could she face being alone again? She turned on her side and pulled her knees to her chest.

Her cell phone dinged, the notification sound for a text. Probably from Tom. She didn't want to see it. Her feelings were too raw. Another *ding*. She sighed. It wouldn't hurt to just look. She sat up, swung her legs over the side, and reached for her phone.

It wasn't Tom. The message was from Colman. Why would he be texting her this late? Then she remembered Vicki; worried about Colman that morning; saying he hadn't answered his phone or responded to texts; that she didn't know where he was. Quickly, Francesca clicked on the text message. She read it, her heart pounding:

Help! Come alone to the spot where you found the boat wreck. You have 1 hour. If you contact anyone, I will be killed.

Chapter 60
Sunday night

Tom stayed in the shower for a long time, letting the hot water run down his body. He had to get ahold of himself. He was still seething with anger. What had Francesca been thinking? Why hadn't she consulted him before ripping the baby's room apart? He'd agreed she could set up the kitchen the way she wanted. Together they had worked on the den and living room. As for the dining room, it was empty when she moved in. He and Candy had always eaten in the kitchen. He'd been happy to make a place for Francesca's maple table and chairs and matching glass breakfront. It wasn't as if he wasn't open to changes. But couldn't she have left the baby's room alone?

He stepped out of the shower and toweled off. In the bedroom he put on some shorts and a tee-shirt. He hesitated before going downstairs. The light was still on in the baby's room. Francesca had placed a floor lamp in the corner that gave the room a soft glow. He stood there looking in. Admittedly the cool grey color was attractive, and matched the heavy glass-topped desk and muted patterned club chair that stood in the corner. On the wall were four black and white California seascapes he recognized from Francesca's townhome.

In his mind's eye, he could see Candy painting the room yellow. Together they had measured and applied the duck trim around the walls. They'd been so happy that day. The following Monday, they'd received the diagnosis that Candy was dying, and their baby along with her.

Tom went in and sat down in the club chair. He closed his eyes and thought about what Francesca had said to him about the room being a monument. She was right in a way. It represented the end of a dream; of his first marriage that had begun when he and Candy were both eighteen, young and impetuous. Back then, the world was their oyster.

Had he kept this room a monument to their youthful hopes and dreams? Maybe so. He sighed. Maybe he needed to let it go. The past was gone. The realization hurt, as though Francesca had dumped a pail of ice water over his head.

He looked around the room again. It was attractive in a sleek way. But it didn't feel like something Francesca would have designed. If he went downstairs and explained how he felt, they could talk about it. He got up and went to the door, switching off the light as he left the room. Then he headed downstairs.

He went into the kitchen, but Francesca wasn't there. The dogs were in their baskets, settled down for the night. They didn't even look up. She wasn't in the den or the living room, either. He looked out at the screened-in porch, but she wasn't there. He went back to the hall and opened the side door. Francesca's Mini was gone.

Tom stood there, feeling hollow, wondering what to do. He could call or text her, but they needed to talk face to face. He closed the door and headed for the den. He'd leave her to herself for a while. They both needed time to cool off. They could talk when she came home.

He opened the liquor cabinet and took out his prized bottle of Glenmorangie, poured himself a healthy portion, and sat down in the leather chair. He rarely drank hard liquor. Usually he had a nip when he'd closed a case and all was right in the world, or when things seemed desperate and he needed to relax. Tonight was definitely option two.

A knock at the front door disrupted his mental meanderings. He placed the glass on the side table, retrieved his gun and went to the front hallway. Through the peephole in the door, he saw his visitor was Harry O'Connell. What in the world was he doing here?

"Chief, sorry to bother you," Harry said when Tom opened up. He held his cap in his hands. "I've just been thinking…"

"Come in, Harry. No problem. I'm still up."

Harry smiled uncertainly. "I want to tell you what I learned this afternoon."

"All right." He led Harry into the den. "Can I pour you some Glenmorangie?"

"Well, maybe a wee one. It's a treat, all right."

"That it is." Tom poured a half inch into another tumbler.

"Is Francesca out? I didn't see her car." Harry stood in the middle of the room, still holding his cap.

"Yeah. She should be back soon." Tom glanced at his watch, then handed Harry the whiskey. "Here, sit down. So what did you learn?"

Harry sat on the edge of his chair and took a sip of the dark, golden liquid. "That's exceedingly good. Thank you." He took another sip and said, "I'm going to tell you what I think, even if I lose my job."

Tom sipped his own scotch, his questioning gaze on Harry's face.

Harry swallowed. "Okay, so I think Mr. Jack killed his parents when they went out sailing." He locked eyes with Tom. "I don't know how he killed them, but I think Doc found a piece of that sailboat that disclosed something, and Jack had to get rid of him and the evidence. You and I both know Jack was at Doc's place Monday night even though we can't prove it." He gulped scotch. "Then I think he tried to kill Miss Delia."

Tom put down his glass and leaned forward. "What?"

Harry swallowed the last of the Glenmorangie. Tom held out the bottle. Harry shook his head and held his hand over his glass. "You've got to understand, I've been taking care of Miss Delia's car since she bought it. I know every inch of that BMW, and it was running just fine before the accident. After the accident, Jack had her car whisked away to some body shop in Iowa. He didn't want me to deal with it, or a body shop here in Banner Bluff. I think he wanted to hide that it'd been tampered with."

Tom raised his eyebrows and nodded, encouraging Harry to continue.

"I forgot about the sticker at the front of the engine. I saw it there after the car got back, but it didn't register with me. You know what I mean?"

"Sure. Go on."

"So I went back and looked at the sticker this afternoon, after I got back from the police station. Jack probably didn't know it was there. Anyway, I called the garage in Iowa and talked to a couple of people." Harry pulled a piece of paper out of his pocket. "Monroe Garage in Hildeport. I talked to Mike Monroe. He said he still couldn't figure why a car from Banner Bluff was brought to his garage. The transport must have cost a fortune. `We discussed the repairs…I said I admired his work, and then we came around to the brakes. He admitted he thought there was something fishy, like maybe the lines had been cut, but he never said anything to Mr. Banner." Harry's face reflected disgust. "Apparently he was very well paid and didn't want to rock the boat."

"Wow." Tom sank back in his chair as his mind shifted into high gear. They had a mountain of circumstantial evidence in Doc Stoddard's murder, but nothing to nail Jack Banner. If Harry was right, Jack had not only killed Doc, but his parents as well, plus an attempt on his sister. They needed direct evidence to prove it beyond doubt. Was there something he was missing?

Chapter 61
Sunday night

Francesca pulled out of the motel parking lot and drove back toward Banner Bluff. There weren't many cars on the road. She went over the highway and soon found herself in the village. The gazebo on the village green was lit up and looked pristine. Laughing children were chasing fireflies under the trees. Across the park, people were sitting outside the Village Brewery, chatting and enjoying the night air. There still was a dinner crowd at Sorrel's seated at the outside tables. Even Yari's Mexican restaurant was still lively with customers. Normally, Francesca felt blessed to be living in this special town. Tonight, though, the scene failed to work its usual magic.

    She paused at the stop sign. She would be safe here among the crowd. Maybe she should park and go get a glass of wine someplace, forget about Colman and his strange text. Maybe it was a prank. Or it wasn't, and she should tell Tom. But if she did that, and the text was real, Colman might die. She shivered with fear and indecision. A car honked behind her and she accelerated as she turned right towards the BBG.

    There was a stop sign at Linden. If she turned there, she'd be home in minutes. But Tom didn't want to talk to her tonight. In her mind's eye she saw him in the hallway, his eyes burning with anger. No, she couldn't go home. And the text had said to come alone, or….

    She reached over and turned on the radio. Bryan Williams, singing *Please Forgive Me*. "Please forgive me; I can't stop loving you…" She felt tears coming on. That song got right to her heart, delved into her soul. She sang along as the tears streamed down her cheeks. Somehow, she had to talk to Tom. She had to ask him to forgive her. She knew she couldn't stop loving him.

Traffic picked up as she neared the BBG. Tonight's sunset concert on the terraced gardens was letting out, and people were streaming out of the park. Frank Penfield had told her he would cover the event. It had completely slipped her mind. The entrance gate was open and she drove in. She wound her way down the access road and through the parking lot. At the far end, she parked and checked the time. She had twenty minutes. She set off, jogging at a steady pace.

She passed the *Do Not Enter* sign at the turn-off onto the Banners' private road. There was no turning back now. Under the trees, the dark closed in. The air felt thick with an earthy smell. She took out her cell phone and switched on the flashlight app to guide her way. Insects darted into the bright light. Ten minutes later she arrived at the Fishtail Creek bridge. She stopped to get her breath. Below her the water gushed over the rocks.

Francesca continued, walking now. Her heart was beating rapidly as she approached the entrance into the woods where she'd seen the wreckage. It was only a couple of hundred feet further. She slowed down and used the flashlight to illuminate the woods on her right. Here was the spot. When the police were there, they'd broken more branches and trampled the ground cover. She stood on the road, breathing heavily. Her mouth felt dry and she was perspiring. What was she doing? This was crazy. Should she turn around and run for help? But if she contacted Tom and the police, Colman would be dead. She reached out, pulled back the branches, and stepped into the clearing where the bow of the boat had lain.

It was eerily quiet and very dark. She flashed her phone around the perimeter of the glade. Nothing; nobody. She stepped forward into the middle of the clearing and circled the area again with her phone light. Her sixth sense told her she wasn't alone, but she could see no one. What should she do? Maybe this was someone's sick joke.

She was turning back toward the road when something whooshed overhead. She looked up and in that split second saw a nest of snakes hurtling towards her. Something thumped on the ground and she heard the singing of a moving rope. Abruptly, she was whisked off her feet and thrown backward. Her phone went sailing as she was yanked up into a rough net. She cried out from fear and pain, her right foot caught as the net was cinched tight.

The ropes swayed with her weight as the net was ratcheted up into the branches of the trees. She fought to get loose but the netting surrounded her. A hammock—someone had rigged a hammock as a trap.

"Help. My foot. It's caught," she screamed. "Is anyone there?"

A voice came from somewhere above. "Stop fighting. Gently loosen the rope around your foot. Then pull your foot in toward your body." She recognized Maelog Gruffydd's thick, slow speech.

She reached down. The hammock swayed back and forth. She could feel a nylon rope cinched around her ankle. Too tight—no way she could loosen it. She managed to get her fingers through the netting and pulled at the laces of her running shoe. Then she pushed at the heel. The shoe fell off and landed on the ground. She pulled her stockinged foot inside the netting. The hammock swayed as it rose.

She lay back, breathing heavily. Tears of anger stung her eyes. "Maelog? Why are you doing this?"

"Hello, Francesca. Thank you for coming. Did you contact the police or the FBI?"

"I didn't contact anyone. But they'll come looking for me sooner or later."

"They won't find you. No one will find you where we'll be going." Maelog gave a brittle laugh.

"Where's Colman? Is he all right?"

"He's still alive, but not for long. He's a nice kid, but too nosy. He's been following me. I had to stop him."

"I know who you are. The FBI came to our house. You're Richard Barnes."

"My name doesn't matter. My actions speak for me. I am a force of nature."

Francesca felt helpless, afraid even to shift her weight because the hammock swayed at the least movement. "What do you want with me?"

She heard a click and the blinding beam of a flashlight pinned her from above. She flinched and looked away.

"You…are…beautiful. I want to look at you." Maelog's voice was a caress. It made Francesca's skin crawl. How had she ever thought he was kind? "You will be useful for the cause."

"Please turn off that light."

"I want to look at you."

"What cause?" Francesca covered her face with her hands.

"The ATT. You wrote those beautiful stories about the trees." He paused, and when he spoke again his voice was hazy with emotion. "I cried when I read them. I could tell you understand. You're one of us."

Desperation overwhelmed her. How could she escape from this mad man? She needed to keep him talking as long as possible, until Tom came.

"Tell me about the ATT. What does it stand for?"

"Avenge the Trees. We believe in the sanctity of Nature. For centuries mankind lived in harmony with Nature. But in modern times we have broken the ties that bind us. Our materialism is endangering the air and water that sustains life. Plants and trees are suffering. Someone must be their advocate." The long speech was clearly enunciated, as if Maelog—Barnes—had often repeated it. A true believer. She shivered.

The clearing below her was lit up like a stage production. She could see her running shoe and her phone. If he would only let her down, maybe she could get to it. "What could I do for the ATT?"

"You could be our voice, writing articles to sway the public. We need to be heard."

"Killing people won't sway anyone to your point of view. If you want change, you need to work with local and state governments. Commit murder and you're only making enemies."

He sounded angry when he answered, his words taking more effort. "Those people don't care about trees. They cut them down to build houses, roads, malls. Mankind is decimating the very plants we need to help us breathe."

"But killing isn't the answer."

"I had to kill Takahashi. I needed to make a statement. He wounded all those little trees, stunting their growth. Bonsai is a criminal act." He was tripping over his words now.

"Please turn off the light."

The brightness vanished.

Francesca opened her eyes. After a few seconds, she could make out the trunks of the trees around her. "What about Melinda Jordan? Why did she deserve to die?"

"The FBI bitch was following my every move. I lured her here, right to this spot. Then I caught her in my net and shot her dead."

Chapter 62
Sunday night

Jack had seen the cops pick up Harry that afternoon. Why? What had they wanted to know? Did he squeal about Venetucci and the Bugatti? Jack should have shut him up yesterday. Harry could have died in his sleep from an overdose. After all, his best friend had been killed on the beach. Suicide was certainly plausible.

Jack couldn't sleep. Nervous tension was making him stir-crazy. He dropped to the floor of the library and did fifty push-ups. Then he stood and paced the room, going over his plans.

As far as Doc went, he was sure he was safe. Wally was back in New York, and the police would never know about him. He'd played his role beautifully, hanging out at the casino in Jack's hat and shirt. The police thought Jack had been at the casino all night. No way could they pin Doc's murder on him.

Monday night when Doc's call came, he was waiting for Venetucci in the garage. He'd picked up the phone immediately in case Harry was still awake. Who knew if the old coot had grabbed his nightly beer bottle that Jack had doctored with sleeping pills? But Doc figured it was Harry who picked up and just started talking, about the wreckage he'd found on the beach. "Scorch marks, Harry," he'd said. "Like from a fire, or an explosion. It's proof of what I've long believed that Mr. and Mrs. Banner didn't die in a boat accident. They were murdered. You have to come and see."

Jack had quietly replaced the receiver, then gotten into his truck and driven around the back way, past the south wing, so he wouldn't run into Venetucci. In ten minutes he was on the bluff and through the gate, using a key he'd stolen during the fall regatta.

Luckily, when he got to the beach, Doc was still there. The old man didn't know what hit him when Jack shoved his way into the shack and let rip with the oar.

God, it had felt good smashing the old geezer's skull to smithereens. Jack had wanted to kill that bastard ever since he was a teenager. Doc had acted so self-righteous over that girl, reading Jack the riot act and calling his parents. Telling them he'd raped the little bitch. Doc had made Jack's life hell. Well, now Doc was gone and his parents were gone. He'd made sure they couldn't swim back to shore after the explosion. They'd been weighted down and were sleeping at the bottom of Lake Michigan. He still felt a little bad about his mother—she'd mostly been an inconvenience, but he couldn't get rid of dear old Dad without her going along, so he'd been forced to kill her, too.

He dropped again and did one hundred sit-ups with military precision. Then he walked to the desk and looked down at Delia's laptop and papers. Now only she was left. Little Miss Perfect, little Miss Goody Two-Shoes, the apple of their father's eye. He couldn't stand her cloying sweetness, her quiet sense of superiority. Well, he would get the last laugh. Miraculously, Delia had survived last winter's car wreck. Not this time, though. Up in Brevoort she'd fall asleep in her kayak and tragically drown. Then he'd be in control of the Banner estate, the cars…and the money.

Nervously, he paced the room again. Then he made a decision. He raced up the stairs two at a time. At the top he turned right toward Delia's suite. There was still light under the door. He knocked on the door to her sitting room. "Come in," Delia said.

Jack strode into the fluffy feminine room. He managed a friendly smile. "Listen, I've been thinking. Why don't we drive up to Brevoort tonight?"

"Tonight? It's ten o'clock. We wouldn't get there until six AM." She was stretched out on her chaise lounge in a pale blue dressing gown, her straight blond hair fanned around her, the book she'd been reading propped on her chest.

"We'd be there for the sunrise." He was hopping from foot to foot like a little kid.

"The sunrise?" She started to laugh.

He made himself join in. "I just don't want to wait until next weekend. Let's go now. We can each pack a small bag in a few minutes. We don't need much. We won't be seeing anyone."

Delia shook her head. "I don't know Jack." She sat up and swung her legs to the floor.

"Haven't you ever done anything on a whim?"

She cocked her head. "No, I don't think I have." Then she laughed again. "Are you for real?"

"Yes, come on. Get up and get dressed." His laughter was genuine now. He had her.

"Okay. This is totally crazy, but kind of fun." She grabbed her cane and managed to stand up.

"I'll go down and load the kayak into the truck. We'll leave a note for Jorge and Luisa. You write it. I'll be back up to get your bag in a few minutes." He bent over and gave her a hug, then left the room. *Like a piece of cake.* She'd stepped right into his trap.

Chapter 63
Sunday night

Mosquitos buzzed around Francesca in the dark. She slapped at her cheek. The rope hammock swung in the humid air. She could hear Maelog's breathing nearer to her. Her vision had improved and she could make out the shapes of branches in the dark. "Where were you when the homicide team was in here looking for you?"

"In a willow tree over by the pond. People never look up. They are unaware of the upper ecosphere."

"Ecosphere?"

"The bio-bubble that contains life on ground, in water and in the air." His tone was condescending. "I have a platform in that tree. I slept most of the day while those morons stumbled around in the woods."

"What about the wreckage?" She wanted to keep him talking.

"I saw the guy drag it in here. He almost saw me. Then on Friday I followed you on your run. I realized the boat could be a problem. You'd tell the cops. So I swept it up into the branches…just like you. When Barnett and his minions came here that night it was hanging right over their heads." Maelog chuckled. She could hear him moving around above her.

"So what about it, will you help the cause? I can get us both out of here to a safe place. I have friends who will hide us."

"Where would we go?"

"Out West."

"My husband will be looking for me. He'll find me."

"We'll disguise you. You'll hide deep in the forest." His voice had taken on a wild note, like a prophet proclaiming the end times.

This man was a lunatic. She had to get back to the ground. Then she would run. "I can't go anywhere with you. My life is here. Please let me go. You can take off for the Western forests, but I'm staying here."

There was a long silence.

Then Maelog screamed, "You're a lying bitch like all the rest of them. You don't care about the future of the planet. You only care about your own personal comfort."

The ropes jerked, and she felt herself being lowered toward the ground in abrupt lurches and drops. She clung to the netting as the hammock swung wildly back and forth. As she approached the forest floor she curled into a ball to protect herself from a sudden plunge to the ground. "What are you doing with me now?"

He didn't answer. With a final jerk she hit the ground.

In the dark, Francesca could just make out Maelog descending the trunk of a massive oak, rappelling down it with swift, easy moves. He reached the lowest branch and paused, to wind the rope and fix it to a bough. Then he jumped the last several feet to the ground.

Francesca lay in a fetal position amid the netting. Maelog walked over, bent down, and loosened the nylon rope that ran through heavy canvas tubing. A ripe earthy smell of sweat and mold filled her nostrils. She leaned away from him as best she could. He wore night-vision goggles that made her think of a giant praying mantis. Finally he loosened the rope enough to push it over her feet. "Stand up."

She stood, holding her breath against the moldy smell as he pulled the heavy netting over her. She thought of running the moment she was free, but Maelog spoke. "Stay there. Don't move. I have my hunting knife." He began an elaborate folding of the netting.

"Can I put on my shoe?"

"Where is it?"

"Right there in those bushes."

"Okay. But don't take off on me. You'll regret it." He pulled on a rope line and the netting rose into the air.

Francesca hobbled over to her shoe. She could see her phone partially hidden under the bush. She looked back. Maelog was busy raising the net. She got down on all fours and then on her stomach, slid under the bush and reached the phone. She looked back. He was still busy. Holding the phone close to her body, she punched the home button, swept the screen and punched in her passcode. She looked around again. Maelog still had his back to her. She tapped the message box. Tom's name came up and she typed 911.

Undergrowth rustled as he approached. "Hey, what are you doing?"

"I thought my shoe was right here." Francesca shoved the phone under some leaves and inched back onto all fours. He kicked her in the buttocks. She fell to her side. When she groaned he bent down, grabbed her by her pony tail, and yanked her to her feet. She whimpered from the pain.

"It's over there. Pick it up and put it on. We've got to get moving."

"Where are we going?"

"Underground, where no one will ever find you."

Chapter 64
Sunday night

After Harry left, Tom sat down in his leather chair and picked up his glass of scotch. He took a drink and leaned back, closing his eyes. Even though he was exhausted, he knew sleep would not come easily. He was worried. Where had Francesca gone? He didn't like to think of her out there and Jack Banner on the loose. Right now, Banner Bluff wasn't a safe place. Frustrated, he put his glass down on the side table and stood up. He would go out and find her. Maybe now that they'd both cooled off, they could talk rationally.

Tom went back upstairs, where he put on a fresh uniform and his Kevlar vest. Downstairs he slipped his Glock into his holster and attached his headset. He was arming for battle. In five minutes he was outside and walking to the car, dizzy with fatigue but also charged with adrenaline.

He drove down the street and turned on Green Bay. As he approached the village green he slowed to a crawl and studied the people walking through the park. The sidewalks outside the local restaurants were still busy. He drove slowly around the green looking for Francesca's car. She could be anywhere. He passed Hero's Market, turned the corner and parked across the street beside the post office, then got out and looked up. The lights weren't on in Francesca's office. Nonetheless he walked over to Hero's. Through the window he saw the Greek grocer closing down the shop. Tom walked up the front steps and knocked on the glass.

Hero looked up, then came over and opened the door, with an apologetic smile. "Chief, I am sorry, I am closed."

"I don't want anything, but…" Tom glanced around the shop and then met Hero's eyes. "Have you seen Francesca?"

Hero frowned. "Francesca was here earlier today…but not tonight." He studied Tom's face. "Is she lost?"

"No…she left and I don't know where she went…oh, well…thanks," Tom mumbled. Unable to take Hero's questioning gaze, he turned abruptly and walked back to the car. He sat for a minute in the driver's seat and then decided to go to the station. If he wasn't going to sleep, he might as well get some work done.

Things were buzzing in the squad room when he walked in. Arlyne, the dispatcher, was on duty. She looked up. "Chief…didn't expect to see you. Did you hear the racket across the street from your house?"

"No. What's going on?"

"There's a domestic at 224 Linden. Isn't that right across from your house?"

"Yeah, that's the Raleighs'." Tom thought fast. "Who's working tonight?"

"Murray, Romano, Stevens and Lister."

"Send Murray and Romano over there. Cindy knows the family." Tom recalled the report Officer Murray had made about her suspicions of domestic battery and child abuse in the Raleigh household. It sounded like her assessment was right on.

"Okay, and Chief…"

"Yeah."

"Coyote's downstairs. I think he has some good news for you."

About time. Tom headed down to the war room, where he found Coyote bent over his laptop, typing madly. For once he wore his uniform and his hair was neatly combed.

Tom rounded the table, pulled out a chair and sat down across from him. "Detective Blackfoot. I hear you've got good news for me."

Coyote glanced up and nodded. "I isolated a still from the casino's security footage and sent it in to the NGI database. You know, the new FBI biometric system that can recognize and match faces? I got a hit." He angled the laptop so Tom could see it. "It turns out this guy's name is Walter Frey. From what I've learned, he was in the Marines and did a stint in Iraq about the same time as Banner. Since then he's led a life of petty crime in New York City. Did a short stretch in prison, but he got out last year."

"We need to get someone to interview him."

"I contacted the precinct where Frey resides. He's on parole, which means he shouldn't have left the state of New York."

"If they bring him in and exert a little pressure, he'll give us Banner's head on a platter." Tom grinned. "Good work, Detective Blackfoot!"

His phone vibrated in his pocket, and he heard the ding that indicated a text. He pulled the phone out and eyed the screen.

The text was from Francesca: *911.*

Chapter 65
Sunday night

Francesca staggered to her feet. How could she escape from this man? He exuded violence and a deep-seated anger. He was so different from the person she'd first met at the BBG.

Maelog prodded her from behind with a heavy flashlight. "Move it."

She moved toward the path that led into the forest. The bouncing flashlight beam illuminated the way. In her fear, she imagined leaping monsters and poisonous snakes scuttling across the path. "Where are we going? There's nothing in these woods."

"We're on our way to my safe house." He prodded her again from behind.

Francesca stumbled, but managed not to fall. "Is that where Colman is?"

"Shut up and walk faster."

Francesca laughed bitterly. "If you're worried about being seen, I can tell you no one is wandering around in these woods."

"Move it!" Maelog slammed the flashlight into her back. She fell forward, breaking her fall with her hands. A sharp pain lanced through her right palm as it struck a jagged stone. She tried to sit up and look at the wound, but Maelog grabbed her pony tail again and pulled her to her feet. They continued walking. Francesca felt blood running down her fingers. She applied pressure with her left hand, trying not to panic. How could she escape? This madman was a giant with quick reactions. She needed to choose her moment. Behind her Maelog made a noise under his breath that sounded like a gurgled whistle.

She heard rustling in the undergrowth. A small animal scurried across the path. Startled, she stepped back and Maelog crashed into her. The flashlight fell to the ground. Francesca kicked it into the brush. Maelog swore as he bent down to pick it up. She took her chance and ran, feeling her way in the dark. She crashed through the underbrush, hands in front of her, praying she'd miss the tree trunks. Her fingers brushed the tops of some bushes. She curled into a ball and plunged under them just as the flashlight beam caught her pink running shoes. Maelog grabbed her foot, wrenching her ankle, and pulled her out as though she were a rag doll. He lifted her again by her ponytail. "Don't try and run. You can't hide from me in these woods. I'll hunt you down."

They continued walking. Francesca was limping and blood dripped from her hand. Eventually they came to an opening in the trees. A half-moon bathed the glade in an eerie light. Maelog pushed Francesca aside and strode to the middle of the clearing where an enormous oak tree spread its branches. He placed his flashlight on a log, reached down, and grabbed a root. He yanked the root backward with both hands. After several powerful pulls, a grass-covered trapdoor opened up.

He gestured to the hole in the ground. "Come on. You're going down here."

Francesca felt like running again but she knew it was futile. She walked over and looked down. A ladder led down into the pitch-black abyss. She hesitated, her legs shaking.

"Turn around and climb down facing the ladder. It's sturdy. You won't fall." Maelog grabbed her arm and pushed her toward the dark hole.

She hung back. "Can't you just let me go home? What good am I to you?"

"Absolutely none. I thought you were one of us. But you're not. Start climbing or I'll kick you down." He moved one foot in its heavy boot.

Francesca started down the ladder, feeling her way with her feet from rung to rung, into the void.

Chapter 66
Sunday night

"What's up?" Coyote searched Tom's face.

"A text from my wife. 911." Tom's voice quavered. "God, what does this mean?"

Coyote stood and held out a hand. "Give me your phone. I'll go notify the CID. With their coordinates we can locate her phone in a few minutes. If it's on and there's power, they can use triangulation software to estimate the phone's position." Tom handed his phone over, and Coyote left the room.

Of course, CID. They could find her. Tom knew all that, but fear kept him from thinking clearly. He felt adrift, like a leaf on a flood-swollen river. He listened to Coyote's feet pounding up the stairs as he scanned the white boards covered with crime scene photos of Doc Stoddard, Dr. Takahashi and Karen Grimes. He shivered at where his thoughts feared to go. He needed solid ground under his feet where he could take back some measure of control.

"Chief, get up here," Coyote yelled down. "We've got the location of the cell phone."

Adrenaline hit Tom like a flash of lightning. He raced for the stairs. Coyote met him on the landing. "It's in the Banner Woods…near where you looked for the boat wreckage a few nights ago."

Tom's heart beat rapidly. Had Jack Banner dragged Francesca into the woods, maybe in retaliation? He walked briskly down the hall, shouting to Arlyne, "Call in the troops. We'll set up a search." As he walked into his office, his phone buzzed. He felt a jolt of irrational hope. It would be Francesca. Everything would be all right. Looking at the screen, he saw it was Harry O'Connell. What did the guy want now? Maybe Harry knew something about Francesca. He answered the call. "Barnett. What's up, Harry?"

"Chief, I'm worried." Harry's voice shook. "I looked down at the driveway a few minutes ago and saw Jack loading Miss Delia's kayak onto his truck. Then he backed up and drove around to the front of the house. Miss Delia was with him. They took off down the drive. It's eleven o'clock. Something's not right."

"Are you sure it's Delia in the truck with him?"

"I couldn't see for sure, but I think so. Listen, you need to stop them. I swear he's up to no good."

Tom felt a rush of fear. Was it Delia in the truck with Jack? Or was it Francesca? Maybe he'd grabbed her in the woods and had her manacled in the truck? "Thanks, Harry. We'll get right on this." He loped back down the hallway. "Arlyne, are Murray and Romano back?"

"Romano's downstairs. He's booking George Raleigh."

"What about Murray?"

"She went to the hospital with Mrs. Raleigh."

"Okay, contact Stevens and Lister. Tell them to search the roads from the Banner estate, look for Jack Banner's black Ram Charger. He's usually doing twenty miles over the limit. Tell them to pull him over for speeding, or any traffic violation they can dream up, and bring him and his passenger into the station."

"Yes, sir. Got it."

Chapter 67
Sunday night

Francesca inched down the ladder, deeper into the dark hole. The wood was rough and she felt a splinter jab the soft pad of her left middle finger. Her other hand had stopped bleeding, thank God. As she felt her way down rung by rung, she looked up expecting to see the trapdoor bang into place, imprisoning her underground to die.

One foot hit a solid floor. From above, Maelog targeted his flashlight on her. She raised an arm against the blinding light and saw him coming down after her. Could she dislodge the ladder enough to make him come crashing down? Probably not, he weighed too much. He hadn't shut the trapdoor, though. Maybe she could still escape.

Maelog reached the floor of his lair and aimed his flashlight onto a flat surface across from the ladder. He walked over, bent down and switched on a camp lantern, then another one on a shelf. Francesca looked around. They were in a small underground cave, with a desk and some shelving along one wall. To the left, clothing hung on nails. Beneath the ladder a pipe extended from the wall. It ended in a rough-hewn faucet. Drops of water pinged into a bucket underneath it.

She heard a loud groan and spun around. To her right, thick tree roots formed a sort of enclosure. Someone—Maelog—had augmented the roots with steel bars and cemented them in place. Within this makeshift pen, Colman lay on a pallet, eyes shut tight against the sudden brightness.

Francesca rushed toward him and fell to her knees, clutching the roots that formed prison cell bars. "Colman, it's Francesca. What's wrong? Are you hurt?"

He groaned again. He lay in a fetal position on the thin mattress, one leg pulled under him and the other sticking out at an unnatural angle. His arms were wrapped around his torso. There was dried blood on his face and neck. Francesca stood and turned toward Maelog. "He needs help. We've got to get him to a hospital."

"Shut the fuck up." Maelog pushed her aside. He reached up to a large steel padlock and punched in a code with his thumbs, then removed the shackle from around two steel bars and pulled open a gate in the side of the pen. Then he pushed Francesca into the enclosure and slammed the makeshift door shut. She stumbled over the threshold and braced herself against the wall over Colman's inert body.

Maelog snapped the padlock back in place. He was drooling from his misshapen mouth. With a dirty hand he swiped the saliva across his cheek. The gesture revolted Francesca and she looked away. She pushed herself off the wall and crouched down beside Colman, her hand resting on his shoulder. "I'm here, Colman. Everything's going to be all right." He groaned again, clearly in pain.

Maelog walked over to the shelving and picked up a canvas bag, gathered together various items and put them inside it. Then he moved to the hung-up clothes and grabbed a dress shirt and a pair of dark pants.

"I'll be back." He headed to the ladder; bag and clothing in one hand, and began his ascent to the clearing. Seconds later she heard a thump as the trapdoor banged shut.

She choked down a fresh jolt of fear and eyed her right hand. The wound was minor, but crusted with dirt. Colman didn't look any better. The blood on his face came from a gash on the side of his head, as if he'd been hit with something. "Colman? Can you hear me? We have to get out of here."

He gave another low moan, then whispered, "I hurt all over. I think my leg is broken." Tears seeped from under his eyelids and trickled down his blood-spattered cheeks.

Francesca crouched beside him, stroking his hair. "We'll figure it out. We've been through bad times before." He didn't respond. She stood up and looked more closely at the small room. It looked like a bomb shelter. The walls were paneled but the floor was hard dirt. In the area under the ladder were shelves bearing cans of vegetables and packages of dried food. Maelog could hide them down here for quite a while…or leave them here to die.

She grabbed the roots that formed their prison and tried to shake them loose. They didn't budge. She pulled and pushed on the bars next, but they didn't move. Staving off panic, she looked around for something she could use to dig their way out. The enclosure was empty except for the pallet and a cotton blanket. In the far corner, she spotted a balled-up piece of fabric. She leaned over Colman and picked it up, holding it out from her body in case something gruesome fell out. When it unfurled, she recognized it as the blue and grey checkered scarf Melinda Jordan had worn the afternoon Francesca had last seen her. She dropped the scarf and shuddered. Maelog had killed before and he would kill again.

She looked over at the rough-hewn desk. On the corner nearest their cage was a key ring with several keys, a wallet and a passport. A jar next to them contained pens, pencils and a pair of scissors. She tried reaching through the bars to grasp the jar, but it was too far away. What could she use to reach the scissors? Colman moaned again and in a scratchy voice asked for water. He was shivering from cold or shock. They had to get out of here. "We'll ask for water when Maelog comes back. I see a spigot over there."

She bent down and picked up the scarf. An idea struck. She dug in her pocket for her car keys—Maelog hadn't bothered to confiscate them. She rolled the scarf into a long, thin tube, threaded one end through the key ring, and tied a knot. Then she thrust the weighted end through the bars. She swung it back and forth, getting a feel for it and gaining momentum. Then, pressing close to the bars, she swooped the scarf over to the desk. The keys clinked against the jar, but it didn't budge. She pulled the scarf back and tried again, swinging harder. This time, she managed to sweep the jar and the passport onto the floor. The jar shattered, scattering its contents, and the passport landed beside a thick root. She tried to grasp the scissors but they were beyond her reach. She swung the scarf toward the scissors. Her keys caught in the handles, and she dragged her prize close to the enclosure along with bits of broken glass. With a feeling of triumph, she reached for the scissors, brushed off the glass shards, and slipped the scissors into her pocket.

Next, she reached for the passport. Sitting cross-legged on the packed dirt, she flipped through the pages. It bore the name Samuel Robbins. The passport picture looked vaguely like Maelog, obviously counterfeit. There were stamps from France, Italy, Greece and Turkey. Looking at the entry and exit dates, she saw Maelog had been in Turkey for nearly a year. What had he been doing there for so long?

From above, she heard the trapdoor opening. Maelog's legs appeared on the ladder. She slid her uninjured hand into her pocket and gripped the scissors, ready for her chance to strike.

Chapter 68
Sunday night

Tom sat at his desk, listening to the search convoy's sirens recede in the distance. Members of the search and rescue task force had convened downstairs for a brief meeting, then headed out to the Banner Woods. Coyote had assured them the phone was there and giving a strong signal. They'd narrowed the location down to within a couple of feet. The team would look for the phone and sweep the surrounding area for Francesca, or signs of where she might have gone. He'd give anything to be out there with them, but he also wanted to be here when Stevens and Lister brought in Jack Banner. If the searchers in the woods found the phone but no Francesca, he figured she'd be in the truck with Banner when it got pulled over. Tom was thirsty for blood, Jack Banner's blood. He could almost taste it. If the man had touched one hair of Francesca's precious head, Tom would kill him.

    He smacked a fist into his palm, again and again. He needed to cool down. Abruptly, he stood and went down the hall. "Any news?" he asked when he reached Arlyne's desk.

    She was on a call and shook her head "no." He turned away and pounded downstairs, then turned right toward the security door that led into the holding cells. He entered the code and stepped into the processing room. Romano was filling out arrest forms for George Raleigh.

    Raleigh himself was in a cell, ranting about his treatment and banging on the bars. "A man's home is his kingdom. He's free to maintain discipline in his own home. This is a free country. You have no right to incarcerate me. I demand to be released." Romano seemed oblivious to the racket as he completed the entry forms.

Tom walked over to him. "What did you find?"

Romano lowered his voice. "He beat his wife to a pulp. The paramedics came and took her to the hospital. A neighbor offered to take care of the children. They're next door for now. The mother was frantic, didn't want them sent to Children and Family Services." He glanced over his shoulder and shook his head. "This guy is a piece of work. Those kids were scared to death."

As they talked, Tom heard the door to the underground security garage roll open and a squad car drive in. The engine cut out, and they heard loud voices and swearing. Romano went over and entered the code to open the entrance to the holding cell area. Stevens and Lister were there, dragging Jack Banner toward the door.

"What the fuck are you doing? I ran a light. That's not a major crime." His hands were cuffed behind his back, but he was fighting the officers all the way. They hauled him up the steps and into the booking room.

Tom stood there watching. Banner didn't notice him at first. Then he glanced up, scowling. "You're the one who sicced them on me, right? You needed a reason to bring me in. I'm going to sue your ass for this. Goddamn fucking police." He spat in Tom's direction. The saliva landed on the grey cement floor.

Tom knew they had very little on Jack Banner, all of it circumstantial. What they knew now about last Monday night might do the trick: that Jack wasn't in the casino all night, that ex-con Walter Frey had impersonated him, and that Jack hadn't met Venetucci as planned. If they could interrogate him before he lawyered up, they might just get him to slip-up.

Right now, though, Tom only wanted to know one thing. He stepped back as Lister and Stevens shoved Jack into a holding cell and then walked over to join them. Lister was chuckling. His white teeth flashed against his dark brown skin. "Man, that guy's a tiger. We had a terrible time getting him out of that truck and into the squad car. He put up a royal fight."

Stevens, a smaller man with a sinewy build and thin blond hair, pulled up his pants leg to inspect his shin bone. "I'm going to be black and blue tomorrow." He grinned at Tom, who looked from one man to the other. He was almost afraid to ask the question.

He licked his lips. "What about the passenger? Wasn't there a woman in the car?"

Lister wiped his sweaty forehead with the back of his hand. "Cordelia Banner. She's driving the truck over and should be here soon." He gestured with his thumb toward the holding cell. "Hard to believe a nice lady like her has that jerk for a brother."

Tom felt his heart plummet.

Chapter 69
Sunday night

Maelog jumped the last few feet off the ladder and landed on the dirt floor. He had changed into the clothes she'd seen him carry away: a white shirt, dark blue pants and shiny loafers. His hair was wet and she could smell Ivory soap. He looked like an entirely different person.

She fingered the scissors in her pocket. "Where did you go?"

"I took a dip in the pond and washed up." He didn't deign to look at her. He set down his bag, dug his old clothes out of it and folded them, then took down a sports coat and inspected it.

"Are you going somewhere now?" She had to keep him talking. Tom would be looking for her. She needed to stall for time, keep Barnes here. If he left them in this underground prison, she and Colman would never be found.

He didn't answer. She tried again. "Where are you going? Will you come back to get us?"

"Shut up." He walked over to the desk and took down a heavy spiral-bound book from the shelf above. Francesca couldn't see what the title was. He reached for a pencil and realized that the jar was gone. He looked down and saw the shards of glass, the pens and pencils scattered on the ground. Finally he looked at her, his hard dark eyes reminding her of a hungry shark circling its prey. Then he smiled his crooked smile. "You are resourceful, but you're never getting out of that cage." Saliva dribbled down his chin. "Never." Spittle shot in her direction.

Francesca turned away. She needed to distract Maelog so he wouldn't think about the scissors. Colman groaned and she looked down at his crumpled body. "Could you give me a bottle of water? Colman's thirsty."

"I don't use bottled water." He went to the opposite corner, lifted a metal cup from a hook, turned on the water and filled the cup.

"Is that clean?" Francesca asked.

"I've been drinking it for a year and haven't died yet." He brought the cup over and passed it through the bars. Then he went back to the desk, sat down and began writing on a notecard.

Francesca set the cup on the floor. She knelt down and raised Colman's head in the crook of her arm. "Colman, here's water. Take a drink." She picked up the cup and held it to his lips. He could only take baby sips. He coughed and gagged, then sipped some more.

Francesca was frightened and angry. "You've got to take Colman to the hospital. He's in terrible pain."

Maelog didn't respond. He kept writing, referring to the heavy book. Francesca cradled Colman's head in her arm and smoothed his hair. With her free hand, she picked up the passport and waved it in the air. "What did you do in Turkey for a whole year, Sam Robbins? Did you have an accident? Is that why your face is misshapen and you talk like a freak?"

"Shut up, bitch."

"You can't talk right, and you look pretty weird." If she goaded him enough, maybe he'd do something stupid—or let something slip that she could tell Tom later. She refused to acknowledge that there might not be a *later*. "What happened? Did you walk into a telephone pole?"

"You know nothing," he mumbled.

"So tell me. An accident? What?"

With difficulty, he said, "I had a full face transplant."

Stunned, Francesca sat back. She'd never heard of such a thing. She studied his face. "It must have hurt terribly."

"I was drugged up for weeks. Now I take anti-rejection medicine that someone gets for me in Canada." He turned sideways and pulled back his hair so she could see the scar that ran down his hairline and into his neck. "It takes a long time to heal…and a long time for the nerves to connect to the new face."

"So that's why it's difficult for you to talk normally."

He nodded.

"What happened to the real Maelog Gruffydd? Did you kill him so you could steal his face?"

"He died for the cause," Maelog—Barnes—snapped. "He gave me his face. I was supposed to look like him, but it didn't work…"

"Was it worth it? You're still being hunted. The FBI knows who you are." She was beginning to feel desperate. Would the FBI ever be able to capture him? Time and again he'd magically escaped like Houdini from a straitjacket.

"No one will find me where I'm going."

"What about us? Are you going to poison us, or shoot us? What's the plan?"

He looked over at them. "You'll stay right here when I leave."

"So we'll suffocate. Slowly."

"Not exactly."

"The FBI will find you."

"Not in the forests I know well."

"What do you mean? Where are you going?"

"Back to Oregon where I have friends."

"Why won't you let us go? We're no threat to your plans."

He shut the book and put it on the shelf. Then he stood up, took a cell phone from his pocket, and set it atop the notecard.

"Whose phone is that?"

"Colman's. I'm going to send a last message to your husband."

"My husband is looking for me right now. I sent him a text back in the woods and you didn't even notice. The woods will be crawling with cops. They'll find you and us." Her voice belied the fear she felt.

"They've already combed these woods and they never found a thing." From a shelf he took a striped tie and knotted it around his neck. Next, he removed the sports coat from its hanger and slipped it on. He looked like a well-heeled businessman. He tugged something from beneath the desk—a black leather computer bag—and checked its contents.

"I have to leave. I've got a plane to catch." His face was devoid of expression. He stepped over to the spigot and turned on the water. It gushed out into the bucket. Then he started up the ladder. Francesca heard the trapdoor open and then bang shut. A minute later there was another thud. She looked over at the bucket. The water had spilled over the edge and was pooling on the floor.

Chapter 70
Sunday night

Tom called Puchalski. The sergeant answered after several rings. He sounded groggy. "Puchalski here."

"Ron, sorry to disturb your sleep. I've got Jack Banner in custody. A lot has happened in the last couple of hours." Quickly, he summarized what he'd learned from Harry O'Connell. "Things are coming to a head. I need you to interrogate Jack. We need to break him."

"Right! Give me ten. I'll be there."

"And Ron…" Tom stopped, worried his voice would break. He took a breath and said, "Francesca has disappeared. She sent a 911 text from the Banner Woods. The task force is out there searching for her."

Silence on the line. Gently, Puchalski said, "Keep it together. They'll find her."

"Right. I'll see you in ten."

He'd barely hung up when a call came in from Conroy, who was leading the hunt for Francesca's cell phone. Tom punched the answer button and noticed his hand was shaking. "Barnett."

"Chief, we found the phone. It was under a bush, right near where we looked for the vanished boat wreckage. We've done a preliminary search of the area." He paused. "But we haven't found Francesca, I mean, Mrs. Barnett."

Tom's heart dropped into his gut.

Conroy continued. "There's evidence of a scuffle, but we don't know which direction she might have gone." He paused again. "Sir, I don't know how we'll find her before daylight."

"Keep looking. You can't give up." Tom's voice betrayed his fear.

Conroy sounded hesitant. "Okay. We'll keep looking. Oh, and sir—along with the phone, we found a tan leather driving glove. Officer Porter says he thinks there's dried blood on it."

"A tan leather driving glove?" Francesca didn't own a pair like that. Tom thought a moment. "A woman's glove or a man's?"

"Looks like a man's glove, from the size."

Tom remembered the boat wreckage that had disappeared from the same spot. The glove could be Jack Banner's. With luck they would find Doc Stoddard's blood on the outside and Banner's DNA on the inside. "Listen, Conroy. Could you send someone back here with the glove? Make sure it's safe in an evidence bag."

"Will do."

Tom could hear someone talking to Conroy. Then the deputy came back on the line. "Chief, we need to contact the SAR for some search and rescue dogs."

"Yeah. Good idea." Drops of perspiration beaded his forehead. His mouth felt dry. Where was Francesca? She'd vanished, just like the chunk of boat. Could Jack Banner have hidden her somewhere? But Detective Stevens had said Delia was in the car with Jack. Not Francesca. He rubbed his temples, trying to think. How could he find Francesca? Then it came to him. *Home. Benji and Bailey.* Waiting for SAR would take too long.

As he stood to leave, his phone dinged. He picked it up and saw a text message from an unknown phone. Another series of letters and numbers, like the previous ones: *E913.2E964E849.8.*

Tom clutched the phone tight. Oh God, what did this mean? He flew out of the office. What was the girl's name at the hospital? Francesca had mentioned it in her email about the other texts, the medical codes. He couldn't remember. He shouted to Arlyne as he pounded down the hall. From behind the glass enclosure she looked up in alarm.

"Find Hero Papadopoulos's number. I need to talk to his granddaughter. Vicki." He paced the hall. Everything was happening at once, spinning out of control.

Arlyne raised a finger. "I've got her on the line."

"Ask her the name of the woman at the hospital who specializes in medical coding."

Arlyne nodded and spoke into the phone, then to Tom. "Kelly Webster."

"Does she have Kelly's phone number?"

Arlyne relayed the question, then shook her head at the reply. "No, she doesn't."

He drew a deep breath. "Okay. Call the hospital and get Kelly Webster's number. Tell them it's a matter of life and death."

A message pad lay on Arlyne's desk near the pass-through. He reached in and grabbed it, then opened his phone and found the code. Carefully, he copied it down. Then he passed the code to Arlyne and started pacing again. She made another call, her voice muffled by the protective glass. He stopped pacing and watched her. She gave him a thumbs-up, and he approached the pass-through. "After you've talked to her, get her email. Send her that medical code I just gave you. Ask her if she can decipher it from home. Otherwise, we can pick her up and drive her to the hospital."

As he turned away, he saw Delia Banner hobbling through the outer double doors into the police station. He hurried over and opened the inner set of doors for her. She reminded him of a wounded animal. Her pale cheeks were tear-stained and her lips trembled with emotion.

"Delia, let me help you. Sorry about this." He took her arm.

She shook it off. "Why did your officers arrest Jack? I can't believe they took him in on a speeding ticket."

"We needed to talk to him. I'm sorry if we inconvenienced you."

"We were going away to Brevoort…to the cabin. Now I don't know…I don't know why I believed him." She turned to Tom, her eyes deep pools of pain.

Tom helped her sit down on the polished wooden bench under the department display case. "What do you mean…believed him?"

"Like I said, we were going to Brevoort to spend a few days together. He said we'd reconnect and be friends. He put on this whole dog and pony show, pretending he'd turned over a new leaf." Her eyes brimmed. "But when your officers arrested him, he turned into his old self. I wanted to help, to explain. Jack screamed at me to shut up. He swore and then said it was my fault we got stopped." She shook her head. "I believed him, but now I think…" She clutched her hands in her lap. "I think he was luring me up to Brevoort to kill me." She started to sob.

Tom reached out and laid his hands over hers.

Delia took a breath. "I've been sitting out in that truck, thinking things over. I think my brother is a murderer. I think he killed our parents. I think he tried to kill me, in the car wreck when Lincoln died." She looked into Tom's eyes, horror and pain in her face. "I think he killed Doc Stoddard, too."

**Chapter 71
Sunday night**

Francesca watched the widening pool inch its way towards them. In a couple of minutes the water would reach the enclosure. The water's force had pushed the makeshift bamboo pipe out of the wall. Now a mini-waterfall was gushing into the cellar. Where was it coming from?

The water had no odor and looked crystal clear in the metal cup she'd shared with Colman. It was probably from a spring Maelog had tapped. She looked around their narrow prison. They were going to drown unless she got them out of their cage and up the ladder.

She pulled the scissors out of her pocket and studied the roots and bars. The largest root narrowed at the corner of the cage. She started sawing on it. If she could cut through at the bottom, she could force it outward and they could slide underneath.

Colman groaned and briefly opened his eyes. He was out of it, alternately gaining and losing consciousness. Not good signs with a head injury. She spoke to him. "Colman, I'm going to get us out of here. Just rest. It's going to be all right."

He made no response.

#

Puchalski had come in several minutes ago. They'd gone down to Tom's office, where he'd filled the detective sergeant in on the latest developments with Jack Banner. "Let him stew for an hour or so," Tom had said. "He's more likely to slip up when he's ticked off. If we're lucky, the bloodstained glove Conroy found in the woods will put Jack Banner away for a long time."

Now, Tom sat on the bench with Delia. He told her about Francesca's disappearance and the sequence of medical codes that Richard Barnes had texted to him before the murders of Takahashi and the FBI agent. "I just received another code sequence. It could be a key to where we can find Francesca. I'm waiting for someone at the hospital to decipher it."

"Oh, my God. What a nightmare."

Arlyne's shout brought Tom to his feet. "Chief, I've got it." He muttered an *excuse me* and dashed to the dispatcher's station. Arlyne handed him a slip of paper. He stood in the middle of the lobby, reading out loud: "E913.2. Suffocation in air-tight enclosed place. E964. Assault by drowning. E849.8. Accident occurring in a forest." He crumpled the paper. "It's got to be the Banner Woods. That's where we found her phone. She has to be somewhere nearby. But where?"

Delia dragged herself upright and hobbled over. "Let me look." She spread out the paper and read the three lines. "Chief, I've got an idea. Years ago my brother and I used to play in the woods. We found the remains of an old farmhouse with a vegetable cellar. One day we opened up the trapdoor to the cellar and went down inside. It was pretty scary. The worst was when Jack slammed the door on me and I was stuck in there for a couple of hours. He was a mean kid, even back then." Her eyes flashed. "Maybe that's where whoever took her is keeping her. But I don't get the business about drowning."

"Could you find that spot, do you think?"

"Maybe in the daylight. I don't know about at night."

"We can't wait until daylight. We've got to look for her now." He was frantic. "Where was this ruined farmhouse located?"

"Not too far from the gate to the estate. I remember we walked into the woods, down a path, and came to a clearing. The ruins of the house were right in the middle. But it all could be overgrown by now. We're talking about twenty years ago."

"It might be the only chance we have." Tom rubbed his chin. "Could you come with me now?"

"Sure. I want to help."

"I'm going to go home and get Francesca's dogs. I'm hoping they can pick up her scent and lead us to this clearing you're talking about."

"Okay, let's go."

Tom called to Arlyne, "We're going to get Francesca's dogs and join the search team in the woods. Notify Conroy we're coming."

#

Richard Barnes set down the computer bag and dropped the trapdoor into place. Then he picked up the heavy stone by the tree and placed it on top. Francesca and the kid would never get out of there alive. But he had to make sure.

Using Colman's phone and the note card, he typed in the E-codes and sent the text. He loved torturing that cop. He opened the phone, took out the battery and slipped it into his pocket, then took another phone from his bag—one of several prepaid phones he'd acquired recently. He never used a phone more than once, in case someone was tracking him. He dialed a number from memory. The phone rang once. Then a gruff voice answered, "About time."

"I should be there in twenty," he said.

"I'm right outside the Botanic Gardens. There's a lot of traffic in and out of the place. What's up?"

"The police are tracking me. I'm ready to go. I'll meet you across the street from the entrance to the gardens. Wait for me on the east side."

"All this action around here makes me nervous."

"You have nothing to worry about. Just sit in your car and play Candy Crush until I get there." He hung up. This agent was useful, but Barnes didn't like him. He'd never trusted the guy. If someone interrogated him, he'd cave before they asked the first question.

Barnes started walking through the woods, taking hidden paths that only he knew. Luckily, it hadn't rained for the past few days so his shoes wouldn't get muddy. He wanted to look like a clean-cut young executive at the airport. As long as he didn't open his mouth, he'd be able to get on that plane. No one would recognize him. He'd soon be far from Banner Bluff.

Too bad about the kid. Colman had followed him last night, down into the basement and through the hidden passageway. He'd led the kid across town and into the woods before turning on him. The kid put up a good fight, but Barnes had trained in jungle warfare. He knew how to fight dirty. Then he'd dragged Colman's inert body to the safe house. He'd had to shove the kid down the ladder, breaking his leg when he landed. It hadn't been too difficult to drag him into the cage. Lucky for Colman he'd still been passed out. Lucky for Barnes, too. Someone might have heard the kid screaming.

He'd built the cage just in case anyone ever came after him, tracked him to his secret place. He liked the feeling of the roots and the bars. He sometimes slept in the cage, the roots forming a cocoon around him.

Where had he gotten the crazy idea that Francesca Barnett would want to join the cause? She didn't have the drive or the motivation for the crusade. She was grounded to the earth and didn't appreciate the upper realms. He'd thought she understood the glory and superiority of trees…of nature…of the goddesses' green earth. But her mind was too small to see the destruction modern-day life had wrought. Like everyone else, she was blind and deaf to Nature's plea for help.

He walked fast, deep in thought. He needed no light—his eyes were used to the forest's glow. Up ahead he heard voices and saw the flickering beams of flashlights. It sounded like they were heading in his direction. He walked a little further, thinking rapidly. There was movement in the underbrush up ahead. Could he get through the line of police to meet his driver? He turned quickly and ran toward a white oak off to the right.

He pushed through the brush and lunged over to the tree. He removed his shoes and socks, tucked them in the side pouch of his bag, and slung the bag over his shoulder. Then he reached up and pulled himself onto a low branch. He felt around the trunk for a loop of rope. Cautiously, he stood and used the rope to shinny up the tree, hand over hand, his callused bare feet clinging to the rough trunk. Higher and higher he went, until he was hidden in the upper branches. A few more feet and he arrived at the platform he'd built last spring. He pulled himself up and over, sliding onto the rough surface on his stomach. His breath came in short gasps. He looked down and saw the flashlights, bobbing around where he'd been. He'd gotten up here just in time. But now he was screwed. He'd never make it to the plane, and didn't dare take out his phone and call the driver.

Chapter 72
Early Monday morning

The water had risen to about two inches. Francesca eased the pallet partway out from under Colman's body, folded the thin mattress several times, then settled Colman back on it with his head above the encroaching water. His clothes were wet and he was shivering as he groaned in pain.

The pants of her track suit were sopping and her shoes felt like sponges. She kept sawing back and forth with the scissors, ignoring twinges from the cut on her right hand and blisters developing on her finger and thumb. Periodically, she switched the scissor blades to get another angle. It was slow going. She was about a fourth of the way through the tough root. As she worked, she thought about Maelog. He would be horrified that she was cutting the life blood of a tree. That gave her pause. Could this root still be a functioning root for a tree? She didn't know.

With her back against the wood-paneled wall, she kicked the root with both feet. But she wasn't strong enough or heavy enough and the root didn't give. She went back to sawing. Only a few inches more. She couldn't give up.

#

Tom parked behind the other squad cars lined up along the road. He got out of the car and opened the back door to let Benji and Bailey out. They shook themselves and ran up and down the road, overcome with joy at going on an adventure. Tom heard voices and saw lights among the trees. Delia opened the passenger door and got out on the other side.

Tom called Conroy on his headset. "We're here with the dogs, out on the road. Can you come and show us where you found the phone? We'll start the dogs hunting from there." Next, he reached into the car and got out two flashlights. He handed one to Delia. She started walking along the road, eyeing the woods as if trying to remember where she used to play.

Ahead, Conroy appeared in the roadway and hailed Tom. "Come down here."

Tom called the dogs and they trotted obediently by his side as he made his way down to where Conroy stood. The deputy chief looked skeptically at Tom. "Are these dogs trained for search and rescue?"

"No. But they're wild about Francesca. They might be able to find her. We don't have time to wait for the SAR dogs." Tom pulled out the piece of paper with the transcribed medical codes. "Here's what we're looking for."

Conroy studied the paper. "Suffocation and assault by drowning, taking place in the forest? I don't get it."

Tom gestured to Delia. "This is Cordelia Banner. She remembers playing in a cellar in a clearing around here when she was a kid. I'm hoping the dogs will lead us to that spot."

Delia smiled. Conroy barely acknowledged her presence, scowling as if he thought including a member of the Banner family was a bad idea. "Follow me." He led them between some trees into a small clearing and pointed with his flashlight. "The phone was over there under the bushes."

"Okay," Tom said. "Let's see what the dogs do." Bailey and Benji were sniffing around excitedly. Tom ordered them to sit, then said, "Find Francesca."

Bailey looked around as though Francesca might be right behind her. Tom repeated the command: "Find Francesca." They knew *find the ball* and *find the toy*. He was gambling that they'd figure it out.

Benji sat with his head cocked, as if trying to understand. Tom pointed and repeated the command a third time. The dogs began to sniff, running in circles in the middle of the clearing. Benji whined and looked around. Then he ran to the bushes Conroy had pointed out, scratching at the leaves and barking. Tom pulled him out by the collar. Meanwhile, Bailey was sniffing the ground, her tail wagging. Abruptly, she made a beeline for a break in the clearing and took off down the narrow path.

"She's on to something." Tom looked back at Delia. "You better get back in the car. This terrain will be too difficult for you."

"No. I want to come. You go ahead. I'll manage." With determination, she headed toward the path, dragging her injured leg, cane in one hand and the flashlight in the other.

Tom nodded and headed after the dogs. He heard Conroy sigh heavily and start after him. Up ahead, the dogs ran back and forth, sniffing excitedly. "Find Francesca," Tom called to them, his heart pounding hard in his chest.

#

Francesca was losing hope. Her fingers were raw and bleeding from holding the scissor blades. She had tried repeatedly to dislodge the root with her feet, but it wouldn't give. Three inches or more of cold water filled the cellar that would soon become their crypt. They would probably die from hypothermia before drowning.

Colman was more lucid now. She'd badgered him to sit up, and he was propped against the wall. Francesca kept talking to him, figuring it would help him stay awake. "I've almost got it…another half inch and I'll be able to split this baby." She tried switching hands, but she wasn't a lefty and it was harder to apply enough pressure, so she switched back. The cut on her right hand from earlier throbbed, but she ignored it.

"Why did I get us into this mess?" Colman muttered. "We're going to die."

"Colman. You didn't lure me here. Maelog did…and I should have notified Tom when I got that text from your phone. But I was being bullheaded." She stopped to flex her fingers. "You of all people have to have hope. Think what you've been through and you've never given up." She stopped to wrap Melinda Jordan's sopping scarf around her hand and sawed with more vehemence.

"How will I get up that ladder? My leg is useless."

"You'll pull with your arms and I'll push. We'll make it."

She lowered the scissors and eyed her handiwork. Then she backed against the wall and started kicking the root, slamming her heels into it again and again. At last, the root broke. She got on all fours, grabbed the piece sticking up from the ground, and forced it down with all her weight. Now there was a small opening they could squiggle through. She slid through the gap, scratching her abdomen on the protruding root. Her body shook from the cold. She looked over at the water gushing from the wall. They didn't have much time.

"Colman, this is going to hurt, but you've got to get down on your stomach and reach through the opening I've made. I'll grab your hands and pull while you wriggle your way through. It'll be easy with the water. Like swimming."

Colman was young and strong. Deep inside, his will to live was indomitable. She was counting on that. Moaning with pain, he slithered on his stomach into the water. He kept his head up like a turtle and reached out to Francesca. She grabbed his hands and pulled. It was difficult slogging through the freezing water. Several times their hands slipped. She reached down and took Colman's wrists, wrapping her fingers around the cuffs of his wet sweatshirt. "Come on, you can do it. I've got you."

Colman kept trying, his face contorted. At last he was through the opening. Francesca was breathing hard from the effort. "Let's see if we can get you up on the desk, out of the water. You're shivering like crazy."

He dragged himself over to the heavy wooden desk chair. "No, don't worry about me. You need to go up the ladder and open the trapdoor."

Francesca nodded and sloshed towards the ladder, then started up. Her wet running shoes slipped on the wooden rungs. She kept climbing. When she was right beneath the trapdoor, she braced herself, holding on to a rung with one hand. With the other, she pushed at the hatch. It didn't budge. She felt around for the hinges behind her and pushed on the opposite side. Was the trapdoor that heavy? She tried again. No deal. She hunched up closer to the top of the ladder, braced her shoulders against the hatch, and heaved.

The trapdoor stayed shut. Tears welled up and ran down her cheeks.

Chapter 73
Early Monday morning

They'd been walking for ten minutes. Benji had disappeared into the brush. Tom figured he was distracted by the scent of a rabbit or a deer. Bailey seemed on task but several times she turned around and headed back the way they'd come. Once, she stopped and sniffed for a full minute at a rock in the middle of the path. Who knew if the dogs were really hunting for Francesca or just out for a frolic?

"Come on Bailey, move." He nudged the Lab with his knee. "Find Francesca." The dog was sniffing some bushes now, her tail wagging frantically. Abruptly, she darted forward and disappeared around a bend in the path.

Tom ran after her. Benji came up behind him, and Tom panted, "Find Francesca." The dog danced in a circle and then ran after Bailey.

Behind Tom, Conroy was trotting along. "This is a wild goose chase. I don't think these dogs have a clue what they're looking for."

Tom didn't respond. In the distance he could hear the other members of the team. Their flashlights reflected off the trees like enormous fireflies. It looked as though some of the crew were coming in from the south near the golf course.

He went around a bend and spied a large opening in the trees. Bailey and Benji were barking loudly and racing back and forth across the moonlit clearing.

Hope shot through Tom. "Find Francesca."

In the middle of the clearing, a large oak tree spread its branches. The dogs were barking and whining at a spot several feet from the oak. Tom zeroed in with his flashlight. The beam illuminated a large rock and several tree roots protruding from the ground.

Conroy came up beside him. "They must smell a raccoon or an opossum."

"I'm not so sure." Tom moved away, walking the perimeter of the clearing, looking for any sign of footprints.

The dogs kept racing back and forth by the rock. Tom went over to it and looked closely. He didn't see what they were so interested in. What were they smelling—some trace of Francesca, or just wild animal scat?

Conroy cleared his throat. "Chief, I don't think your dogs know what they're up to. We better go back with the crew. Maybe they'll have better luck."

Tom didn't want to give up. But maybe Conroy was right. The idea of bringing the dogs had been a mistake. What had he been thinking? He should have joined the search crew. Maybe they would have found Francesca by now. He directed his flashlight around the glade one more time. "Okay. Let's go."

Delia appeared at the edge of the clearing. She walked slowly forward, stopped, and looked around. "This is it. You've found the spot." Her voice was full of wonder. "I remember that big oak tree, and the dilapidated house was right there." She pointed. "But it's gone. There's nothing left." She hobbled forward. "Somewhere near here is the trapdoor to the cellar. It must still exist." She eyed the enormous tree again and walked toward the rock. "It should be about here." She stood looking down.

Tom came over. Delia studied the patch of ground illuminated by her flashlight. "Can you move this rock? I want to see what's underneath."

"Okay." Leveraging with his legs, he picked up the stone and hauled it up, then dropped it several feet away. The dogs sniffed and whined with renewed frenzy at the spot where the rock had been.

Tom bent down and searched the ground closely. The grass looked uneven in spots and formed a rough square. Near one side was a thick, curved root.

Delia drew a sharp breath. "Francesca's here. I know it." She poked around the spot with her cane. "We've got to dig her out. Or maybe…" She stared at the protruding root. "Tom, pull on the root. Pull it up."

Tom braced his feet, grabbed the root, and pulled. The root was like a handle. He pulled harder and the earth began to move. The squared-off patch of grass was the trapdoor to the old farmhouse cellar. He looked over at Delia with wonder. Then he picked up his flashlight and pointed it down the hole. The beam revealed a makeshift ladder, with water lapping at the bottom rungs. *Assault by drowning in the woods.*

Hesitantly, fearing the worst, Tom called down. "Francesca? Are you down there?"

"Tom?" Francesca spoke through a veil of tears. "Tom? We're here. We're all right. Hurry, though, or we're going to drown."

Chapter 74
Early Monday morning

It took the paramedic's precious time to come through the woods with their stretchers and medical equipment. After Tom called for help, he climbed down the ladder and found Francesca and Colman huddled on top of a desk, freezing and sopping wet. To reach them, Tom sloshed through two feet of water. He clutched Francesca to his breast, his heart nearly breaking in two.

"Oh baby, I'm so glad you're alive and safe." He could feel her shivering uncontrollably against him like a fragile baby bird. "Help's coming. You'll be all right." He tried to lift her into his arms, but she held back.

"I need to stay here with Colman. I can't leave him alone. His leg is broken and he was beaten up pretty bad."

"No, darling. We need to get you out first so the paramedics can climb down here to help Colman."

She turned to Colman. "They'll get you out soon, okay?"

Colman barely nodded. He was deathly pale, his lips blue with cold.

Tom picked Francesca up and sloshed through the water to the ladder.

"I'll climb up myself. I can do it." Francesca reached for the side rail. He eased his grip on her as she grabbed onto the ladder. Slowly she started the climb, rung by rung. Tom was right behind her in case she slipped.

When they reached the surface, she turned to him and held on tight. Bailey and Benji were jumping around, glad to see their mistress. Delia stood back, watching Tom and Francesca with tears in her eyes. In the distance, they could hear ambulance sirens.

Tom gazed down at his wife. "Francesca, how long ago did Barnes leave?"

"I don't know. Time stopped while we were down there."

"Do you know where he was going?" He held her tighter, trying to warm her with his body heat.

Francesca shuddered with cold and fright. "He said he was taking a plane. He left here dressed in a business suit."

"I'm wondering if he's still around. When I got your 911 text, the task force was working their way through the woods. If he didn't escape their net, he'll still be here."

Francesca pulled back and met Tom's eyes. "Look up. He'll be in the trees."

#

Barnes secured his computer bag in a nylon mesh sack that hung from a branch. He believed in being prepared…just like a Boy Scout. Throughout the forest he had several trees that could serve as short-term hideouts. In the sack was a pocket that contained a bottle of water, some freeze-dried food and a folded poncho. He could stay up here for a day or two if necessary.

He lay on his back and thought through his options. Beyond the leaf cover he could see the waning moon high in the sky. From afar he heard dogs barking and muffled voices. Daybreak wasn't far off. Should he stay up here for a day or two until the search was called off, or climb back down and use his knowledge of the area to pass safely through the woods? He knew how and where to hide, but dogs could be a problem.

The last twenty-four hours had thrown a monkey wrench into his plans. First, he'd had to get rid of the FBI operative. Then he'd thought he had more time to prepare his exit from Banner Bluff, but the FBI had moved quickly. He'd spotted their lookout by his apartment, hunched behind a chimney on the roof across the street. He'd left right away, but attracted Colman Canfield's attention. He knew the kid was following him, and he had to get rid of him.

But his major error was luring Francesca. What a fool he'd been, thinking she'd join the cause because she'd written a couple of articles expressing the beauty and necessity of trees. He'd imagined she would follow him. There were hundreds of them working surreptitiously throughout the country. They would have welcomed her with open arms.

He closed his eyes and listened to the forest. In the distance he heard sirens, but the sound didn't worry him. He felt safe up here. It was like his year in the redwood tree. He was one with Nature. The wind blew through the branches and rustled the leaves. He hadn't realized how exhausted he was. The woodland lullaby worked like a sleeping potion. He dozed off.

#

The paramedics sent three men and a stretcher down into the cellar to extract Colman, while two other medics worked on Francesca. They stripped off her sodden clothes and wrapped her in blankets, placed hot packs around her body, and laid her in a Stokes basket positioned in their ATV. There was no room for Tom on the vehicle, but he knew she was in good hands. Before the paramedics drove away, he bent down, stroked her cheek and kissed her. "I love you."

Still shivering, she smiled up at him. "Love you too," she whispered.

After they left, he felt elated. Francesca was safe. At the same time, an unquenchable anger burned in his gut. Nothing would keep him from catching Barnes. The guy was a murderous lunatic, he had to be stopped, and Tom wanted to be the man to do it. It wasn't only his job, his reputation, his honor…no, now it was personal.

He strode into the middle of the clearing where Conroy was talking to two officers. "I think Richard Barnes might still be here in these woods. Francesca said we should look up. She said Barnes would be hidden in the trees."

Conroy gazed up into the trees surrounding them.

Tom continued, "Remember the presentation on the PrecisionHawk drone last month? We learned how it could be used for search and rescue missions? The guy told us the drone could stream live video of an area it flew over, if we were looking for a lost child, for example."

Conroy nodded. "Uh-huh."

"He also talked about thermal sensor capabilities…that at night the drone can detect the heat signature of a body below."

"Right, I remember. His name was Reed Donaldson. He lives in Lake Woods."

"Let's give him a call."

Chapter 75
Early Monday morning

Richard Barnes came instantly awake. How long had he slept? He needed to be more vigilant. He reached into the mesh sack and felt around for the reusable water bottle. He opened the cap and took a long drink, then placed it back in its pouch.

Above, he heard a gentle whoosh. He looked up. Something flew overhead. He couldn't see what it was…a large bird, he guessed, like a hawk on the hunt.

He lay back down on his stomach. Something wasn't right. It was too quiet. He didn't hear normal woodland sounds. He took a chance, scooted to the edge of the platform and looked down through the branches and leaves. With the back of his hand, he wiped off drool that had dripped down his chin. He hated the lack of control of his mouth and jaw. Sometimes, he wished he hadn't gone through with the operation. They'd told him it was successful, but he felt like a fucking Frankenstein. All that suffering, and now the government knew who he was and where he was anyway. They were hunting him down like a wild animal.

He heard something rustle, spotted movement below. He couldn't see without his night goggles. Suddenly the tree was bathed in light, strong beams shooting up at him like spotlights.

"Richard Barnes, you are under arrest. Climb down now. You are surrounded. We are armed and ready to shoot if you make a false move. Come down now."

How could they see him? He knew he was well hidden by the platform and the tree branches. How did they know he was there? Maybe he could wait them out.

"We know you're there. I repeat, come down now."

He was sweating; his thoughts thick and slow like sludge. How to escape? There was no large tree nearby to swing to. They'd caught him in their web. No one cared about his beautiful trees. They would probably mow down this small forest that had become his home.

"Richard Barnes, we know you're there." The booming voice sounded angry. "Come down now!"

The sky had started to lighten. Off to the east the dark grey clouds were etched with pink.

"You have no choice. You are surrounded. Climb down now."

Overhead he heard the *pft pft pft* of a helicopter approaching. Soon it would be on top of him. He crouched and slid over to the tree trunk, and reached for the rope he had pulled up earlier. At the end was a thick loop.

The helicopter hovered overhead. He held on to the trunk against the power of the downdraft. A dazzling beam of light swept the platform, then moved off. They wanted him to give himself up. But he never would.

"It's over, Barnes. You can't escape this time. I repeat: Come…down…now."

There was only one thing left to do. He crouched on his hands and knees and shinnied out along the largest branch. He looped the rope around the branch several times. Then he put his head through the loop, let go of the branch, and fell.

Epilogue
Three months later

Darkness had fallen. The sweet smell of roses perfumed the air. Francesca and Tom lay close together on a chaise lounge in the garden of their new home. Upstairs, Francesca's niece and nephew were asleep in one bedroom. Tom's sister, her husband and their son were in another. Francesca's sister, her husband and Francesca's parents had opted to stay at the Deer Run Inn.

It had been a marathon day. In the morning Francesca's parents had hosted a family brunch at the Inn. Then in the late afternoon, friends and acquaintances had arrived for the long-overdue wedding reception. Francesca wore a soft pink dress. Her hair was piled on top of her head with pink roses nestled in the curls. Tom wore a blue dress shirt and black slacks.

The caterers had provided an elegant selection of hors-d'oeuvres including sushi, bruschetta and mini crab cakes. The cocktail hour was marked by champagne toasts and stories galore told by family and friends. After that came a Texas-themed dinner of barbequed brisket, with all the fixings. Bonnie's Bakery had provided a tiered white wedding cake with raspberry filling, beautiful and delicious.

Now Francesca and Tom were finally alone. Francesca kicked off her shoes and snuggled closer to Tom. She kissed his cheek. "Love you. Thanks for a superb day."

"I love you, too. Now that we've finally had our reception, are we officially married?"

She giggled. "I guess we're no longer living in sin."

Above them the stars twinkled and the moon was coming up in the east. Tom pulled Francesca closer. "What was the best thing about the day?"

She thought for a minute. "Well…that my parents really like you. My mom is always so critical of everyone. But you won her over. She thinks you're the cat's pajamas."

"I like your family. We should take a vacation out to California and visit them in the winter."

They fell silent, listening to the breeze rustling the leaves of the maple tree.

"Tom?"

"Huh?"

"I've been thinking about Maelog Gruffydd."

"Why?" His voice took on a hard edge. They'd barely discussed what happened in the Banner Woods two months ago.

"All the wildfires out West…Maelog would be miserable. All those thousands of acres of his tree-friends going up in smoke."

"Call him by his name, Richard Barnes." His tone was flat.

"In a way society needs people like him. Who else would protect the trees?"

Tom stirred, restless. "Come on, Francesca. You're not going to defend the guy. He wanted to kill you."

"I know he was crazy and a murderer, but he killed because he believed in something. Compare that to what Jack Banner did. Jack killed out of greed, selfishness and jealousy. It was all about him. Somehow, Barnes's crimes seem more…I don't know. Honorable?"

"*Honorable?* We're talking philosophically here, right?"

"Yes. They were both killers, but what Jack did seems more insidious."

Jack Banner had been indicted for Doc Stoddard's murder, and was currently being held without bail in the Lake County jail.

They'd found Doc's blood on the outside of the brown leather driving glove found in the woods, and Jack's DNA on the inside. In addition, Delia had come forward and said she heard Jack's truck roll under her window the night of the murder, in the early evening when he'd claimed not to be home.

In New York City, the ex-con Walter Frey had caved as soon as the New York detectives applied a little pressure. He admitted he'd been paid a thousand bucks plus airfare to fly to Chicago. Jack had picked him up at O'Hare and driven him to the casino. Frey had hidden in the bathroom until Jack appeared. They'd switched shirts and Frey had donned the Cubs cap. Jack had also given him gambling money and his credit card to buy dinner. They'd pulled the same switch in reverse awhile later, after Jack called to say he was ready. As to Frey's motive, apparently Jack had helped him with some nefarious deal when they were stationed in Iraq. Frey said he owed Jack big-time.

Tom was sure Jack Banner had killed his parents. They'd found the piece of boat wreckage hanging in a net high in a tree. The blackened wood showed evidence of an explosion, but there was no way to pin the crime on Jack, even though Delia had talked about the hours Jack spent swimming in Lake Michigan prior to her parents' disappearance. She suspected he'd carefully planned their murder. Then after killing them he had swum to shore. As for Delia's car accident last winter, the garage owner in Hildeport, Iowa refused to confirm his suspicions of foul play with Delia's BMW. When Puchalski called and questioned him, he acted like he didn't know what the detective was talking about.

Tom knew he had to be satisfied with nailing Jack for Doc's murder. The task force had worked carefully to make certain their case would hold up in court, and Tom felt sure of a conviction. Hopefully they'd put Jack Banner away for a long, long time.

As for Richard Barnes, they would never know the full story. They never found Dr. Takahashi's phone, and it remained a mystery how Barnes had lured him back to the BBG so late in the evening. Even Akiko Takahashi couldn't illuminate what happened, though she did talk about her father receiving a strange coded message before they left Japan. Tom guessed it was the same code he'd received announcing Takahashi's imminent death.

The water in Barnes's underground lair ceased gushing when it hit the level of the spigot. Most of the possessions he'd kept there were damaged, but they found the 2010 ICD-9 volumes of medical code he'd used to warn Tom of Takahashi's death, Karen Grimes's murder and Francesca's near death. There were books on tree classification and identification. One book entitled *Dendroclimatic Studies: Tree Growth and Climate Change in Northern Forests* would undoubtedly have ramped up Barnes's anger toward mankind and their destructive civilization. Delia had told Tom she planned on filling in the cellar once the investigation was complete.

Tom pulled Francesca closer. Thoughts of Richard Barnes filled him with unease. Francesca reached up and touched his cheek. "I'm here. I'm safe. We're together." It amazed him, how swiftly she responded to his feelings of anxiety. Often in the last few months, he found their bodies and minds were in sync. He'd sense what Francesca was thinking and vice versa.

She took his hand and placed it on her stomach. "Feel it? He's doing the fandango in there." Her laugh was low and tremulous. Tom felt the slight quiver of a kick. Francesca placed her hand over his.

Upstairs in the fourth bedroom was a white crib, an antique rocker, and a cuddly teddy bear.

CPSIA information can be obtained
at www.ICGtesting.com
Printed in the USA
LVHW112214111118
596764LV00001B/131/P

9 781519 392572